COLD SANCTUARY

BOOK TWO of The Nessemiah

Andrew Beardmore

ryelands

This novel is entirely a work of fiction. The characters and incidents portrayed in it are the work of the author's imagination. However, a number of character names are anagrams of real, historic people, long-since deceased. Examples include the 7th century monk Ebde (based on the Venerable Bede), Jake Oscom (based on the 18th century explorer and naval captain, James Cook), and one of the most recent, David Grey-Doogell (based on the early 20th century British Prime Minister, David Lloyd-George), while the 18th century ruling dynasty in Glennad are the Havreno family (an anagram of Hanover, the monarchical dynasty of Great Britain and Ireland in the 18th century). Other character names can be portmanteaus – a blending of two names such as Calidius (Caligula + Claudius), or combinations, such as the corpse smugglers Williams and Hauberker (based on William Burke and William Hare). Occasionally (as with Grey-Doogell), I have loosely aligned the character's past career to be similar to their historical alter ego as well. Elsewhere, real (but deceased) horses are referenced, too, such as Horsed Credit (Desert Orchid), Rum Dearg (Red Rum), Broriece (Corbiere) and The Snail (L'Escargot).

First published in Great Britain in 2025

Copyright © Andrew Beardmore

All rights reserved. No part of this publication may be reproduced, stored in a retrieval system, or transmitted in any form or by any means without the prior permission of the copyright holder.

British Library Cataloguing-in-Publication Data
A CIP record for this title is available from the British Library

ISBN 978 1 906551 56 8

Ryelands
Halsgrove House,
Ryelands Business Park,
Bagley Road, Wellington, Somerset TA21 9PZ
Tel: 01823 653777 Fax: 01823 216796
email: sales@halsgrove.com

Part of the Halsgrove group of companies
Information on all Halsgrove titles is available at: www.halsgrove.com
Printed and bound in India by Nutech Print Services

Cold Sanctuary is a major departure for Andrew Beardmore. A professional copywriter in the IT industry, Andrew is also the author of many non-fiction books, including the nationally popular "Unusual & Quirky" series of county history books, also published by Halsgrove Publishing. However, Andrew's greatest literary love is epic fantasy and he has finally joined the fray with this four-book historical fantasy series, known as *The Nessemiah*. It was David Eddings who captured his fantasy heart in the early 1980s – the same time that a seventeen-year-old Andrew was playing guitar in his father's dance band, supporting bandleader giants like Victor Silvester and Joe Loss!

Praise for Andrew Beardmore:

Cold Sanctary: These books continue to remind me of *A Song of Ice and Fire*, with a deadly looming threat overshadowing peril and conflict in the lives of our characters. Bearmore knows when to finish a book leaving you asking questions and keen to discover more. *LoveReading*

The Strains of Malice: Andrew Beardmore is a fantastic storyteller with a penchant for meticulous details. He crafts a world so humanistically flawed and tremendously intriguing. I am bouncing in anticipation of the second book, and would give an arm and a leg to have this book directed into a movie series. *onlinebookclub.org*

Up The Ramblings: "This is an incredibly clever story...and which also showed a huge amount of wit on the part of the author." *Stephen Booth*

Back From The Dead: This was an extraordinarily well-told and economically written tale about a gangland killing with a real twist at the end." *Don Shaw*

Derbyshire Unusual & Quirky is delivered in a lateral and humorous format that promises to engage readers. If you think you know Derbyshire – think again! *The Buxton Advertiser*

Nottinghamshire Unusual & Quirky is a real gem. With beautiful photographs, maps and well-researched information, this book is written in a charmingly conversational style. If you buy it as a gift, I promise you will find yourself reading it before you hand it over! *The Bookcase*

Quirky facts abound, but there is much more to *Leicestershire and Rutland Unusual & Quirky*, as the entire history of both counties is also covered in detail from the Stone Age to the 21st century. *The Stamford Mercury*

Theran Maps: Western Thera: 1789

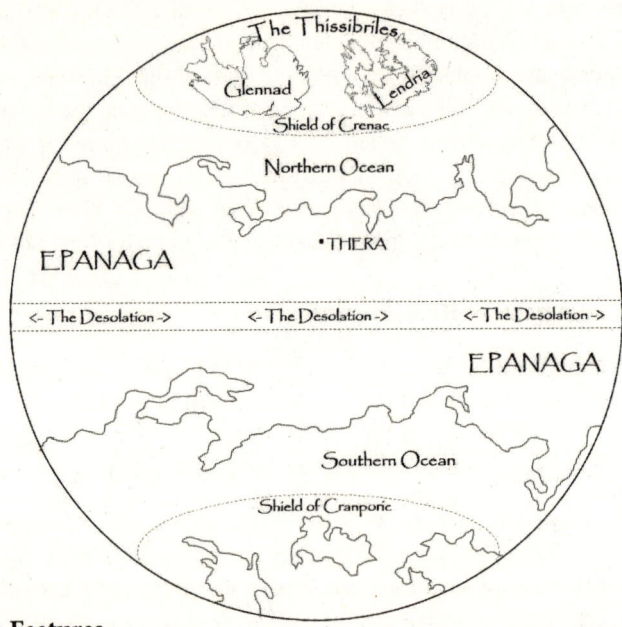

Theran Features

- The super-continent known as Epanaga circumnavigates the Theran globe. Boats cannot therefore sail from the Northern to the Southern ocean and vice-versa.

- The arid central Epanagan area known as *The Desolation* also circumnavigates the Theran globe, and is uncrossable, due to day-time temperatures of up to 165 degrees above zero.

- In 1789, with the power of flight yet to be invented, folk cannot by any means get from one hemisphere to the other.

- Indeed, no one in the northern hemisphere has ever *been* to the southern hemisphere in post-prehistoric times, or knows what it looks like – and vice-versa.

- Hence northern hemisphere globes look like that shown above, while globes in the southern hemisphere only map the south, with the north an uncharted empty space.

Theran Maps: The Thissibriles: 1789

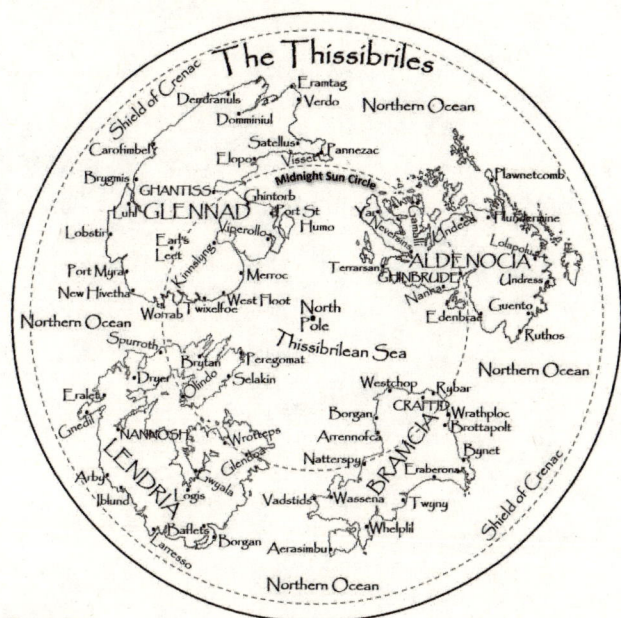

Theran Features

- The Thissibriles are comprised of four major islands ranged around the North Pole. They are heavily populated as the polar regions on Thera are temperate.

- The "Shields" appeared in the year 410 AT.

- They are enormous magnetic fields that form two lethal, unbroken belts around Thera at c.55 degrees north and south.

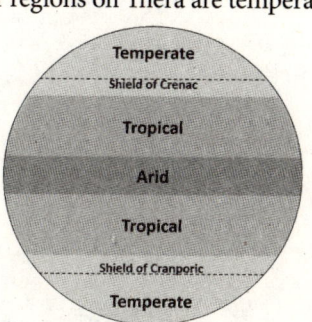

- The sea eddies around them, forming chains of whirlpools, and the air above fizzes with an electro-magnetic current.

- Crossing them is fatal:
  - It scrambles the brain on approach.
  - Those who cross suffer "The Madness", before their bodies begin to shut down.
  - Death follows within three days.

- The Shields thus become a punishment for criminals, and are also used as a dangerous sport by others.

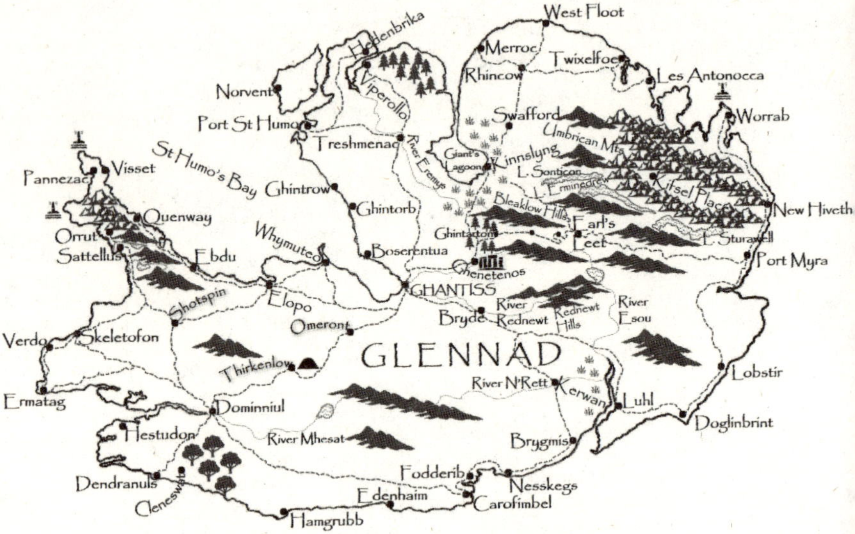
West Floot
Merroc
Twixelfoe
Les Antonocca
Rhincow
Norvent
Port St Humo
Viperollo
Treshmenac
Swafford
Worrab
Umbrican Mts
Giant's Lagoon
Kinnslyng
L. Sonticon
L. Erminedrew
Kitsel Place
River Eremys
St Humo's Bay
Ghintrow
Pannezac
Visset
Quenway
Orrut
Sattellus
Ebdu
Ghintorb
Bleaklow Hills
Earl's Leet
New Hiveth
Ghintarton
Whymuteo
Boserentua
Ghenetenos
Port Myra
GHANTISS
Elopo
Shotspin
River Rednewt
Rednewt Hills
River Esou
Bryde
Omeront
Verdo
Skeletofon
GLENNAD
Thirkenlow
Lobstir
River N'Rett
Kerwan
Luhl
Ermatag
Dominniul
Doglinbrint
Hestudon
River Mhesat
Brygmis
Fodderib
Nesskegs
Dendranuls
Edenhaim
Carofimbel
Hamgrubb

Peregomat
Bluekingcolemill
Selakin
Mekaren
Glendoa
Goulden
Brytan
Rembatlio
Wrotteps
Calleyblast
Omerun Mts
Tygal Mts
Olindo
Spurroth
Gwyala
Borgan
Lake Hegan
Baflets
Logis
Unbild
Ekilek
Borgan Riser
Black Suet Mts
Dryer
LENDRIA
R. Nannosh
Hoggbraeg Mts
NANNOSH
Eville Bosom Mts
Erelat
Larresso
Lake Reen
Iblund
Gnedil
Wraklo
Arby

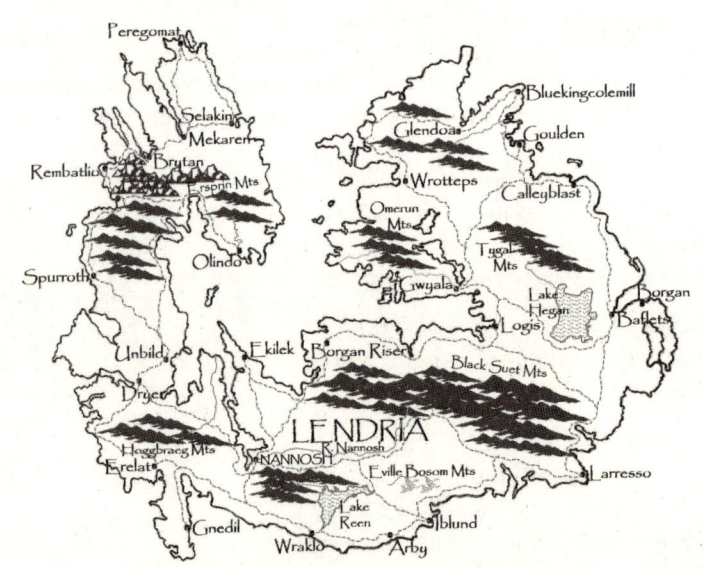

Theran Maps: Western Epanaga (North)

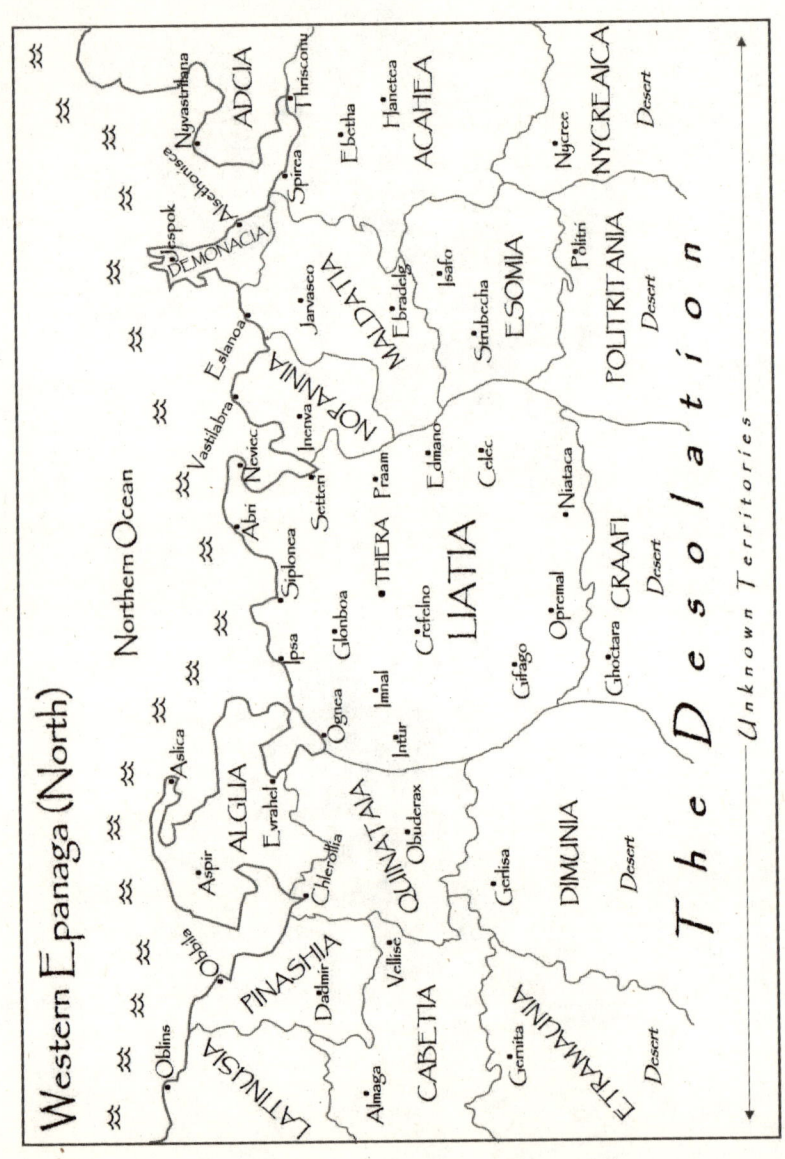

Layout of Kifsel Place Monastery

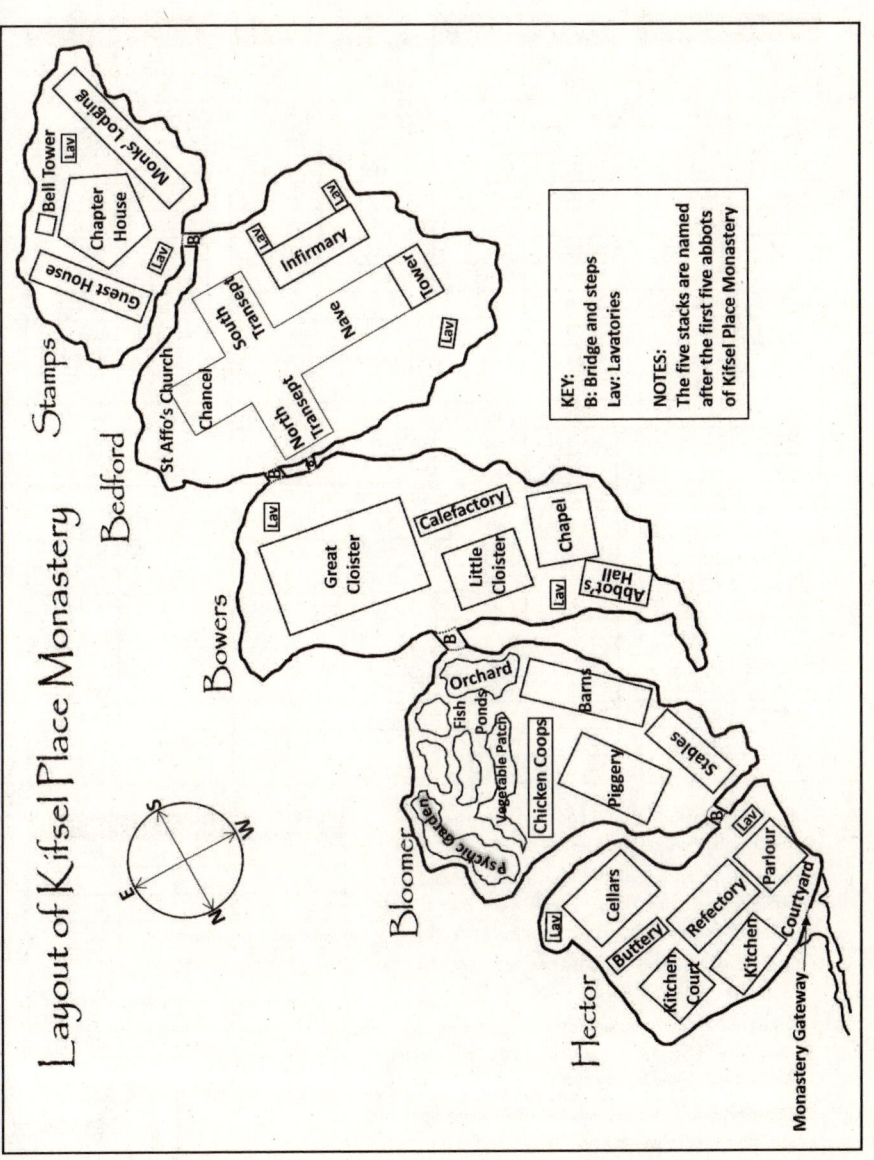

Theran Daily and Monthly Cycles

The following table lists daylight hours in Ghantiss at each equinox and solstice:

Vernal Equinox		Summer Solstice		Autumn Equinox		Winter Solstice	
Theran Hour	Light/Dark	Theran Hour	Light/Dark	Theran Hour	Light/Dark	Theran Hour	Light/Dark
01:00	Dark	01:00	Twilight	01:00	Dark	01:00	Dark
02:00	Dark	02:00	Twilight	02:00	Dark	02:00	Dark
03:00	Dark	03:00	Light	03:00	Dark	03:00	Dark
04:00	Dark	04:00	Light	04:00	Dark	04:00	Dark
05:00	Dark	05:00	Light	05:00	Dark	05:00	Dark
06:00	Twilight	06:00	Light	06:00	Twilight	06:00	Dark
07:00	Twilight	07:00	Light	07:00	Twilight	07:00	Dark
08:00	Light	08:00	Light	08:00	Light	08:00	Dark
09:00	Light	09:00	Light	09:00	Light	09:00	Dark
10:00	Light	10:00	Light	10:00	Light	10:00	Dark
11:00	Light	11:00	Light	11:00	Light	11:00	Dark
12:00	Light	12:00	Light	12:00	Light	12:00	Twilight
13:00	Light	13:00	Light	13:00	Light	13:00	Twilight
14:00	Light	14:00	Light	14:00	Light	14:00	Twilight
15:00	Light	15:00	Light	15:00	Light	15:00	Twilight
16:00	Light	16:00	Light	16:00	Light	16:00	Dark
17:00	Light	17:00	Light	17:00	Light	17:00	Dark
18:00	Light	18:00	Light	18:00	Light	18:00	Dark
19:00	Twilight	19:00	Light	19:00	Twilight	19:00	Dark
20:00	Twilight	20:00	Light	20:00	Twilight	20:00	Dark
21:00	Dark	21:00	Light	21:00	Dark	21:00	Dark
22:00	Dark	22:00	Light	22:00	Dark	22:00	Dark
23:00	Dark	23:00	Light	23:00	Dark	23:00	Dark
24:00	Dark	24:00	Light	24:00	Dark	24:00	Dark
25:00	Dark	25:00	Twilight	25:00	Dark	25:00	Dark
26:00	Dark	26:00	Twilight	26:00	Dark	26:00	Dark

- The Theran year lasts for 365.256 days – the time it takes Thera to orbit the sun.
- Every 4 years, Primar has 46 days to make up for the surplus .256 of a day it takes to orbit the sun. This re-synchronises the Theran calendar with Thera's orbit.
- The Theran year is also subdivided into 52 weeks of 7 days apiece.
- Day numbers are also accumulated throughout the year – hence the last day of the year is Day 365 (every fourth year accumulates up to Day 366).
- The two equinoxes and two solstices occur on the 1st day of the 2nd month of the season: Winter Solstice: (1st Primar); Vernal Equinox (1st Tertiar); Summer Solstice (1st Quinar); Autumnal Equinox (1st Septenar).

Theran Month	Season	No. Days
Primar	Winter	45
Secondar	Spring	46
Tertiar	Spring	45
Quarternar	Summer	46
Quinar	Summer	46
Senar	Autumn	46
Septenar	Autumn	45
Octonar	Winter	46

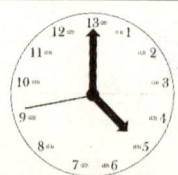

Thera and the Inner Solar System

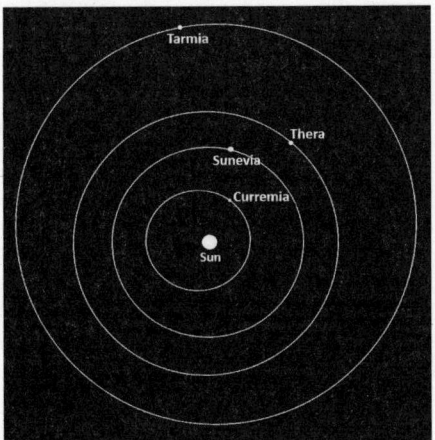

Thera and the inner solar system (not to scale).

Planet	Tilt (degrees)	Diameter (miles)	Circum. (miles)	RotSpeed at Equator (m/hr)	Rotation (hours)	Length of Day (hrs)	Rotation Direction
Curremia	0.03	3,032	9,525	6.7	1,407.60	4,222.6	AntiClock
Sunevia	177.36	7,521	23,628	4.1	5,831.50	2,802.0	Clock
Thera	22.74[1]	3,963	12,451	498.2	25.98	26.0	AntiClock
Tarmia	25.19	4,220	13,263	539.4	24.62	24.7	AntiClock

Planet	Mass (% Thera)	Orbital Speed (m/sec)	Orbit (days)	Density (kg/m^3)	Mag Field (x Thera)	Gravity (% Thera)	Mean Temp (C)
Curremia	11.0	29.5	87.97	5,427	0.0006	37.8	332
Sunevia	163.0	21.7	224.70	5,243	0.00	90.5	867
Thera	100.0	18.5	365.26	2,757	1.00[2]	100.0	85[3]
Tarmia	21.4	14.9	686.98	3,340	0.00	37.9	-149

Key Points

[1] Thera's tilt brings about the four seasons of winter, spring, summer and autumn.

[2] Thera has an unusually strong magnetic field for such a relatively small planet. The other inner planets either don't have a magnetic field at all (Sunevia and Tarmia) or the magnetic field is negligible (Curremia). NOTE: That the outer gas giants have much larger magnetic fields than Thera.

[3] Thera has a high mean temperature as it doesn't have any icy polar temperatures which would counter-balance the hot equatorial and the blistering desert temperatures.

CHAPTER 70 — WILL

12th Tertiar, 1789 Day 103, 17:30

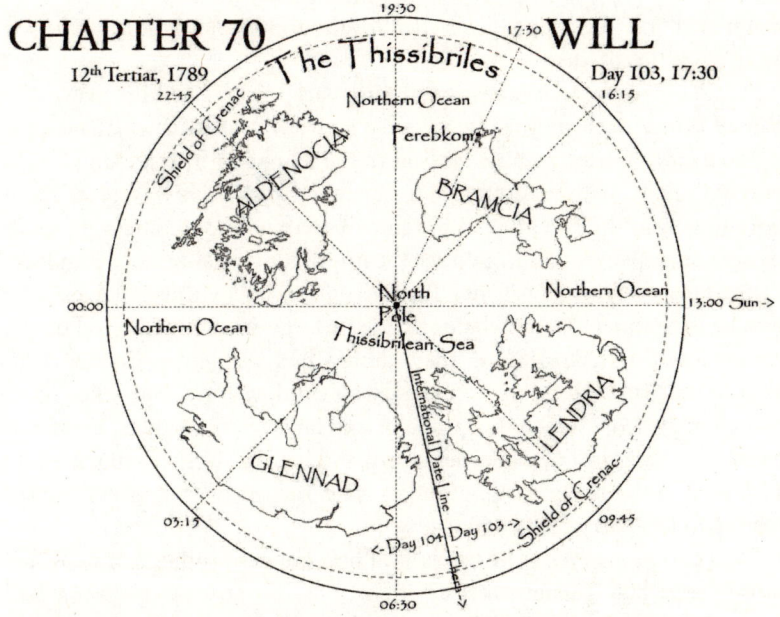

It had been approaching three days since they had taken to the Northern Ocean at Wrathploc in the middle of the night. As the first day had dawned, Will had realised that not only could he see again, but there had been no lasting impairment to his vision. He had been sat on the back seat of the rowing boat that Nate Turner had stolen from Wrathploc the previous evening, the vessel bobbing up and down on the waves around a quarter of a league from the east coast of Bramcia.

The first thing he had focused on had been the wooden boards beneath his feet. He had studied their texture, the differing grains, the different colours, imagining how they had been cut in some Bramcian sawmill. He then studied a length of rope and could see the fibres which bound it together, noticing for the first time how each segment was twisted diagonally into the next, but how the rope *threads* ran horizontally throughout the structure; his restored sight was enabling him to see things he had not noticed before.

Presently, it was late afternoon and the weather was fine – and Will found himself studying the oars, as Nate Turner drew them back and forth with powerful strokes. Will then stared, mesmerised, at the droplets of the displaced seawater as they briefly glittered in the late afternoon sunshine before plopping back into this tiny speck of the vast Northern Ocean –

which Turner had explained stretched for thousands of leagues, all the way around Northern Thera.

Suddenly aware that focusing on one place might give him away, Will feigned blindness again, using the ruse to study Nate Turner as his eyes passed over him from right to left, left to right, apparently searching for his returning sight. Without doubt, Nate Turner looked ill. He was thinner and more drawn in the face than Will remembered, with dark circles beneath his now-sunken eyes. Will could see the line of his cheekbones, too; indeed, it wasn't too difficult to visualise Turner's entire skull. He also had less hair than he remembered, and what remained was greyer and plastered down, wet, against his scalp. But as they approached Perebkom Estuary, Will decided that Turner's eyes were the most alarming feature. He looked like a man condemned – which was probably not far from the truth if Davy had found his secret trail of penknife, gloves and hat. Strangely, Will felt guilty at his part in the likely condemning of Nate Turner. Even stranger, he was starting to feel sorry for the man.

Will closed his eyes as he thought of his younger brother and he willed himself to re-hate Turner. Once again, he mused over what it was that had made Dylan so scared? Whatever it was, it certainly hadn't happened to Will. He also knew that Davy and Robbie had veiled their opinions about Turner in front of him; he didn't like to think on why.

Thoughts of Robbie filled Will's heart with a familiar sorrow. *"I can't move, Will. I'm burnt to a crisp."* The thoughts prompted Will to question Turner once again about the likely fates of Robbie and Dylan, given Turner was one of the most experienced coal miners in Bramcia. "Mr Turner," he said, looking in the vague direction of his companion.

"Yes, Will," said Turner, his tired eyes focusing on Will's face, even as he leaned forward to push the oars, and then leaned backwards to drag them back again.

"You said yesterday that around half of the miners in blasts like ours, survive – but are left with horrible burns."

"I did," confirmed Turner.

"And you also said that even though they may have these horrible burns, they can still live long and healthy lives."

"Aye, lad, that's the truth."

"So, you didn't say that to make me feel better – about Robbie?"

"I said it because it's the truth, lad."

"But when you first reached me in the tunnels – after the explosion – you said very different things."

"I can't remember what I said, Will. I was likely in as much shock as you were."

"You said something like: *We're the only two survivors. I've walked past at least fifty dead or dying.*"

Nate Turner stopped rowing, a look of pain creasing his features. He bowed his head and said nothing.

"Mr Turner?" said Will, still feigning sightlessness.

"I said those things…because I'm…flawed, Will."

Will didn't know what to say to that, so remained quiet. After a few more seconds, Turner took up the oars again and began rowing them around the headland. Ten strokes, eleven strokes, twelve strokes…and then he stopped again and rested the oars across his legs, allowing them to bob and drift a little. Eventually, he spoke. "I couldn't have helped them, Will. I was suffering from severe carbon-monoxide poisoning and I had to get us to the surface as fast as possible."

"So, we weren't the only two alive then?"

"No, lad. There were others alive. Badly burned – like your Robbie. And because there weren't any more explosions, the chances are that the rescue party got a lot of them out. Some will live, some will die. I can't be any blunter than that, Will. The trick is to keep low and breathe shallow – until the rescuers arrive. As for Robbie and Dylan, they would have been in one of the worst-hit areas so, being brutally frank, their chances of getting out alive weren't good. What Robbie Russell did for you was heroic and selfless." Turner paused, looking bitter. "He was a far better man than I will ever will be."

"Was?"

"'Is', then. He *is* a far better man. And there is a chance – albeit a small chance, Will."

"Why did you say it then?"

"Say what?"

"What you said in Level Z. That we were the only two survivors."

Nate Turner just stared at Will. Eventually, he spoke. "You certainly know how to twist the knife, son."

"I don't understand."

"I said what I said because I was thinking only of myself and the likely ramifications for me if it really was Dylan that caused the explosion. I guess I was hoping that there weren't any witnesses and – God strike me down for saying this – but maybe I thought that if I said it out loud…"

Will stared down at the wooden floor of the boat, but he could still see

Turner peripherally. He knew well enough that Dylan had caused the explosion. He was a prime witness. Will decided to keep quiet about that for now. "I wish I could see me Mam," he said, instead.

The impact on Turner was fascinating. Will could see agony all over his face and tears in his eyes, but he was also striving not to make any sounds that would give his grief away to a poor blind lad. Instead, he clammed up, picked up the oars again, and started rowing them towards the mouth of the estuary.

It took another three hours to reach Perebkom on the eastern side of the estuary, around two-thirds of the way up. Turner rowed the boat into a sizeable harbour full of fishing vessels of all shapes and sizes. Will looked up in the direction of Turner, still feigning blindness. "Please could you describe what Perebkom looks like, Mr Turner."

"You still not got any vision at all, lad? Not even a pinpoint of light?"

"Nothing," responded Will, moving his head from left to right.

"Well, I must confess, you're starting to worry me now."

"You once told me it had taken 'several days' for one miner. Well, several can mean five days, can't it?"

"Let's hope so, young Will," he said, gravely. "Anyway," he began, as he rowed them into the harbour, his speech pausing each time he drew on the oars. "The harbour walls are – made of limestone. The harbour is – slightly angled – on both sides – but the shore end – is still quite wide – which is where – the main town begins – and then stretches – backwards – inland. So – as you head out to sea – the harbour gets – gradually wider. And through the middle – of the harbour – there's a long stone – jetty – which divides it – into two. We're making for – the right-hand half."

"How far does the jetty come out?"

"More than halfway. It's long."

"And how many boats are in and what type?"

"Mostly fishing vessels – all different shapes – and sizes. Perhaps sixty or seventy – on each side."

"And are there houses."

"Lots of houses – on all three sides. All mainly – built of stone."

"Are any of the houses painted?"

"A few. I can see – a pale-yellow house – another painted – a mid-blue – and another – a pale-green."

Will closed his eyes and feigned visualising Turner's description. "I can see it all," he said, a smile playing across his face. When he opened his 'blind' eyes, he could see that Turner was smiling, too. Something about the conversation they had just held had warmed the man.

"Would you like to be -," Turner paused for breath and another draw on the oars, "a fisherman, Will? A fisherman's son?"

"I think I would, yes," agreed Will.

"It's still a risky – occupation. The waters – south of here – can be treacherous. But it's probably – a healthier occupation – than mining."

Five minutes later, Turner was helping 'blind Will' to disembark. "I've moored us to the central stone jetty," he said. "Let me guide you, as the jetty is only a few feet wide.

Will let Turner put his arm around him and help propel him forward so he could step out of the boat and onto the jetty – just an everyday father and son coming back from an afternoon's row out into the estuary. They arrived on Perebkom's busy promenade, shortly after, Turner gently steering Will.

"Right," said Turner, looking around. "I'm going to look around for fishing job vacancies. And I also need to buy some supplies, too."

Despite all that had happened, and Nate Turner's likely role in that, a part of Will was excited at the prospect of being a fisherman's lad. He was in the process of imagining a trawler in rough weather when Turner began leading him to the market square, just beyond the harbour frontage, Will playing the dutiful son, not looking to escape or call out to anyone. He wasn't sure why he was being so compliant. It would be so easy to suddenly run off and beg for help. But there was something about the way that Turner was looking after him which prevented him from doing so. Something… but which Will couldn't quite put his finger on…or maybe didn't want to, or was too afraid to.

As they reached the market place, it was clear that most traders were folding up their awnings and tables following the end of a day's trading, but Turner was able to spend around twenty minutes getting end-of-day supplies at a very good price; certainly, enough to feed them for another five or six days. His next plan was to collar one of the fishing boats as it came in with its daily catch. They were just making their way back to the harbour when Turner froze. Will turned his 'blind' eyes in a few directions as if trying to get his bearings – whereas what he was really focusing on was that which had made Turner pull up sharply. It was a poster. At the top it said: "HAVE YOU SEEN THIS BOY?" Underneath was a fairly accurate drawing of himself – and underneath his face, information stated that the boy was missing, and would likely be with a middle-aged man. The description of Nate Turner was very accurate. Finally, anyone noticing such a man and boy that they couldn't vouch for, was being asked to report it to their local JP's office.

"There's been a change of plan," said Turner.

"What do you mean?" asked Will, innocently.

"I've decided fishing isn't for us, Will. At least not here. I'll think of something else. I don't like it here. I'm taking you back to our boat."

For a couple of seconds, Will stood his ground. This was his opportunity. He could run straight to the nearest JP's office and hand himself in. *I'm the boy that you're looking for.*

But he didn't. He allowed Turner to guide him down the central jetty and back to their boat. Turner loaded the food and water flasks onboard and wasted no time in casting off. It was too late to run – but Will was already wondering where they would go next. Despite the tragic circumstances that had precipitated this voyage, and the potential danger he was putting himself into, this was the kind of adventure that most twelve-year-old boys only dreamt of. Particularly those poor souls who would spend the rest of their lives underground. Furthermore, if he didn't go home, if he didn't see the truth, first-hand, then Robbie and Dylan would remain alive – at least in his mind and memory. Even at twelve, Will recognised that he was probably running away from reality. But if he couldn't see it, it wasn't necessarily true. Was it?

The now-familiar whoosh of oars sounded strangely comforting, even though the potential sanctuary of Perebkom was now slowly receding into the distance.

CHAPTER 71 — ALICYA

13th Tertiar, 1789
Day 104, 07:00

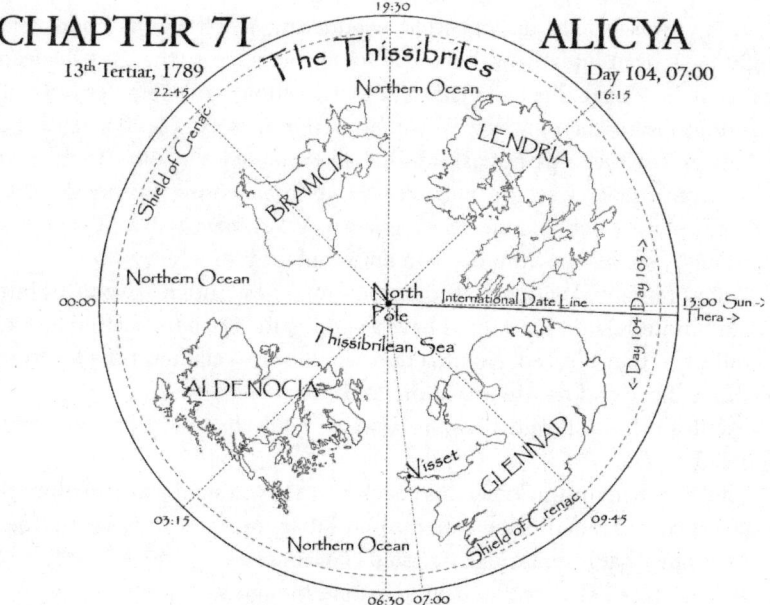

Alicya's cheek was resting on Gawain's chest, enjoying the sensation of her upper body moving slowly up and down in time with his breathing. She was blissfully happy. Sure, she had been happy one week ago, riding her horses, teasing Maddox and laughing with her ladies-in-waiting. But that had felt nothing like this.

Alicya smiled. If she could go back in time by one week and tell her younger self that she was about to lie with a man for the first time, 'innocent Alicya' would have scoffed derisively, with events in between, derided as far-fetched fantasy. And yet, here she was; Gawain's breathing was real, as was the sensation of her skin against his.

They had slept together that first night after the kiss, now three days ago. It had felt like the most natural thing in the world. There had been concern about consequences, initially. But there was a point of no return — and they had crossed it in double figures since. What was done was done. The way that she felt, Alicya would happily give birth to Gawain's child, and however many more children they decided they wanted. To be married to a doctor, and to have their own country house as Gawain had promised, with several children, pets and horses, offered far-greater contentment than she could ever have had as a princess — where she would have been married off to an older member of another Thissibrilean royal family and forced to live away from Glennad.

Alicya was briefly disconcerted, wondering if a Magnus equivalent might have been lying in wait for her somewhere across the Thissibrilean Sea. Well, no longer. She had made all the right choices on Cemetery Island, including the rescue of Vixey, who they were now seeing less of. This did pull at her heart-strings, but as Gawain had explained, the forest to the rear of his apartments was the perfect habitat for a young fox to develop naturally. And when she did briefly return, Vixey wasn't so wild that she didn't enjoy some fuss from her human friend for life.

Alicya remained with her head on Gawain's chest until he awoke, twenty blissful minutes later. He did not have a surgery today, so they could lie like this all day if they pleased. Not that they would spend all their time inactive, of course. Love and nature would dictate otherwise.

"Hello, Princess," said Gawain, a warm smile brushing his now-fair-stubbled cheeks.

She stretched up and kissed his cheek, just above a small, dark birthmark that she loved as much as the man himself. "Rise and shine, husband-mine."

"Ah, now that is tempting fate," said Gawain.

Alicya's face fell. "Are you having second thoughts."

Gawain shifted slightly so he could look Alicya full in the face. He cupped her face gently with his left hand. "I've never been more certain of anything in my life...Al."

"Alicya smiled – both at his words and the nickname that had stuck. She made a silly contented sound and then cuddled up to him so that her body melded with his. She could feel his passion, instantly, and was glad."

Fifteen minutes later, she was lying in his arms again, both bathed in a sheen of sweat. The sensation had been no-less heavenly than the previous dozen or so.

"I meant to tell you something last night," said Gawain, suddenly remembering. Alicya loved the vibrations from his voice through his chest. "But, of course, you distracted me as soon as I came through the door," he added, kissing her on top of her head.

Alicya smiled at the memory. "I am naughty, aren't I?"

"Perfectly naughty," agreed Gawain, kissing her again in the same spot.

"So, what were you going to tell me?" asked Alicya, now curious.

"We've been invited to a ball being held by Lord and Lady Visset at Summer Hall."

Alicya sat up at that and looked down at Gawain. "But what will you say? I mean, about me?"

"I will tell them what I've told Mrs Baker. That you are my cousin from Ghantiss."

Alicya's face fell. "Can we not -," Alicya paused, thinking. "Can I not be the lady whom you are courting?"

"Not given you're staying under my roof, darling," he said, touching her cheek again.

Alicya screwed up her face. "Silly rules."

"These are the ethics of a gentile society, Princess," he said, smiling. "I would have thought you of all people would -."

"Huh," interrupted Alicya, now turning her back on Gawain. "I'd rather not go at all, then."

"Oh, come on, Al," said Gawain, wrapping his arms around her from behind. "Don't you want to wear a beautiful ball gown and a tiara and dance all night? I will buy you whichever gown you desire."

"I'll be expected to dance with other men," she said. "And I only want to dance with you."

"I'll not allow it," said Gawain.

Alicya turned around to face him again. "And what about when we become engaged – and then married? How will you explain that away to the *gentile* folk of Visset?"

"Because, my love, as I have mentioned before, I have plans to return to my hometown of Sattellus, and practise there. My old mentor, Charles Green, runs the town practice, and he always said he would pass it to me when he retires. He is nearing retirement and he reiterated his wishes to me in a letter sent last week. So, we would marry in Sattellus and 'Aunt Sally's bloomers' to anyone who objects."

"But who would we say I was? For the marriage, I mean? There is no such person as Alyona Piran, and in any case, even if there was, she would be your cousin!"

"All taken care of, Alicya," responded Gawain, dropping his eyes, somewhat guiltily. "I, erm, sign death certificates for those patients in the parish who pass away. I then post them on to the Births, Deaths and Marriages Registration Office in Ghantiss on a quarterly basis. The next post is due next week – except it will be missing the certificate for poor eighteen-year-old Mabel Holmes."

Alicya looked at Gawain, open-mouthed. Should she be berating him for contemplating such an action? And yet, it would enable her dream incognito life to come true. "I don't know what to say," was all she could manage.

"No one will be hurt or disadvantaged by my actions," said Gawain, gently. "And then, if all goes to plan with the practice, I would soon be expanding it into the Glennadian hinterland. Unless you'd rather I resurrect my plans for becoming the Royal Physician, that is?"

Alicya smiled at that. "With me as your good lady wife, Mabel? Can you imagine the look on my brother's face? He'd fear he was going insane. Although he's not the type to feel guilty."

"Well, I'll not have you going anywhere near him. Ever."

"My hero," she said, as she cuddled up to him again, more-than content with Gawain's proposal.

"My parents still live in Sattellus, too," continued Gawain. "So, it would be good to be near them as they grow older. But I would buy a house on the outskirts of the town, where we could keep horses – just as you wanted. It will be perfect for our children, too." Gawain put his hand on Alicya's tummy as he said that.

Alicya responded by putting her hand over his. She was being silly about the ball. She had everything she could ever want, right now, and Gawain had just offered her an extension of that for the rest of her life. "All right," she agreed. "We shall go to the ball then." Her words briefly evoked a memory of issuing similar words a dozen days ago – to her horse Sebastian. The memory triggered a pang of loss, but she was then reassured at the thought of her stablemaster; Maddox would be caring for her horses, and he was the best stablemaster in the kingdom. Poor Maddox would be missing her, though.

"Good girl," said Gawain, cutting through her thoughts.

"Oh, I'm a *good* girl now, am I?" she asked, looking up at Gawain, coquettishly. "I thought you liked me 'perfectly naughty'?"

"Oh, I do," agreed Gawain, who then proceeded to kiss her again.

CHAPTER 72 — MADELEINA

13th Tertiar, 1789   Day 104, 15:45

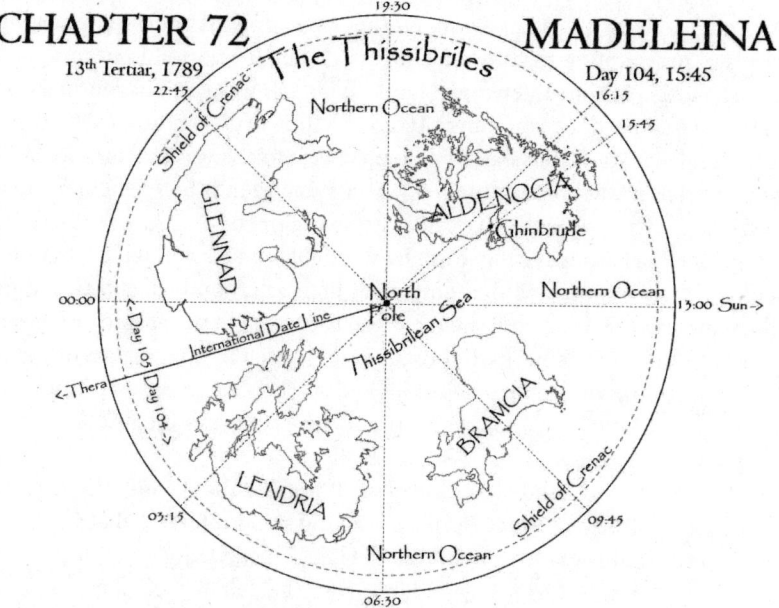

Madeleina was furious with her mother and father. The King and Queen of Aldenocia had just excused themselves, taking Madeleina's younger sister and brother with them and leaving her alone in the palace rose garden with Prince Bernard.

She looked at him to find Bernard already looking back at her. Madeleina immediately glanced away. "The bees are very active, don't you think?" It was the first thing that came into her head.

Prince Bernard of Lendria looked about the walled garden, which contained hundreds of vibrant flowers and plants including myriad rows of roses. "They particularly love fuchsias, my dear," he said in his gentle, lilting voice. "Of which you have many."

Madeleina could sense that he was studying her again. From the corner of her eye, he seemed at least to be looking at her face, this time; she had lost count of the number of times she had caught him looking at her chest that afternoon. What was even more annoying, was that she knew that her mother had noticed as well – but her mother had just continued to smile, politely.

Prince Bernard, for his part, was the epitome of geniality. His attire could not be smarter, either, with expensive linen and silks in burgundy and emerald. Nevertheless, despite being of the utmost quality, his clothing was unable to hide the large paunch that overhung his short legs, nor the beads of perspiration that permanently occupied his florid forehead.

Bernard's baritone interrupted her thought. "It was good of your parents to leave us alone, don't you think? To give us time to get to know each other."

Madeleina knew that she had to look at him to answer that question and pretend that it was a good thing. She somehow found the strength to turn and smile. "They were most considerate," she agreed.

Prince Bernard was sat across the wrought iron garden table from her, and which still contained the remains of their afternoon tea and two large glass pitchers of water. Both the table and the wrought iron chairs had been painted white. Prince Bernard took it upon himself to pour a glass of water for them both, whilst Madeleina looked at the crumb-strewn crockery, willing one of the maids to come out and collect it, imminently. Anything to provide a distraction.

Prince Bernard handed her the glass of water. "Thank you," she said.

"I see also," began Prince Bernard, looking at her intently, "that you have many birds in this garden. As well as the bees," he added.

Madeleina was furious with herself as she felt herself flush. Prince Bernard, meanwhile, was laughing gently at his own apparent cleverness. "I'm sorry, my dear," he said. "But I am a man of the world."

Madeleina didn't know how to respond to that, so she kept quiet.

Prince Bernard sighed, and Madeleina noted his chins wobble at the action. She briefly thought that things couldn't get any worse when Bernard rose creakily to his feet and moved to the seat alongside her. "My dear," he said, holding out his hand. She felt she had no choice but to take it. His touch was clammy. "As we're to be married, we really must learn more about each other, don't you think?"

"I suppose we should," she replied, flicking a glance to his eyes, and then immediately flicking away again.

"You're nervous, I understand that," said Bernard. "And you are so young."

Although she was still looking away, Madeleina could sense that Prince Bernard was craning to look down the front of her dress.

"And you must feel disappointed in being betrothed to an old crock like me," he continued.

"Oh no," Madeleina said, automatically, forcing herself to look at him. "I'm not -. I mean, you're not *old*, Prince Bernard."

"Well, that's very sweet of you to say," said Bernard, now gently massaging her hand with his. "But I am old enough to be your grandfather.

I realise this is probably not what you wanted from life."

"I -." Madeleina clammed up. She had no words, so she let Bernard do the talking.

"Of course it isn't," continued Bernard. "But I promise that I will be as devoted to you as any other man in the Four Kingdoms could possibly be. You are beautiful even to your contemporaries, sweet Madeleina, so imagine how much more beautiful you are to an old man like me. To a very lucky old man like me."

Madeleina managed to give him a shy smile. "Thank you, Prince Bernard," she said.

"Please, Madeleina. Call me Bernard. Or Bernie if you prefer."

"Bernie?" she said, unable to stop herself from smiling.

"There you go," said Bernard. "That wasn't so bad, was it?"

"I suppose not. You are very…kind…and understanding…Bernard."

"Lucky is what I am," responded Bernard. "For not only are you beautiful, but you are also the most talented musician in the Four Kingdoms. I attended your recital, last night, along with several of my household. We all agreed that you have written a piece of music which will live forever, and were honoured that you paid such fine justice to fair Lendria. The intertwining of the pipes and fiddle was inspirational."

"Thank you," was all Madeleina could say.

"Forgive me for asking," said Bernard, changing the subject. "But have you had any previous gentlemen courting you?"

Madeleina was shocked. "Am I a maiden, is that what you're asking?"

"Is that so callous a question to ask of your fiancée?"

"I am only eighteen years of age, Prince Bernard," Madeleina replied, quite shocked. "I don't even know what it is like to be kissed."

As soon as she'd said the words, she knew they were ill-fated.

"I will shower you with kisses, my dear, he said, squeezing her hand again. He then placed his other hand on her thigh.

Madeleina was unable to suppress a shudder. Bernard noticed, and for the first time, she saw something other than geniality in his manner. He withdrew his hand, though, and apologised. "I am sorry, my dear," he began, his genial smile already reinstated. "But we will be wed on 1st Quinar – on Midsummer's Day. I thought that perhaps we should build up to that day slowly." His eyes were now twinkling again, although there was a hunger there as well. "Rather than everything being experienced in one go. I'm only thinking of you, my dear."

Madeleina looked hard at Bernard now, remembering the advice that

Charlotte had given her. "And are you comfortable yourself, Bernie?" she asked. "Comfortable marrying a girl who is thirty-seven years younger than you and – as you say yourself – old enough to be your granddaughter?"

Madeleina saw a brief flicker of doubt in Bernard's eyes – but then they fixed onto her chest again – before they rose to meet her face. "I will have no discomfort in being married to you, my dear. Why ever would I? I shall be the luckiest man in the Four Kingdoms."

This time, Madeleina held Prince Bernard's gaze. He had made his position perfectly clear. He could clearly see what this meant to her and yet he quite blatantly had only one thing on his mind. That was the moment when Madeleina knew that she wasn't going to allow this to happen to her. The thought gave her strength, so much so that she gave Bernie her first natural smile. "And I shall learn to become the luckiest woman in the Four Kingdoms."

Prince Bernard's eyes became even hungrier at that response, but Madeleina used the moment to stand, offering her arm to her prince. "Would you walk me back to the drawing room please, husband-to-be. I need to begin preparations for this evening's concert"

Prince Bernard stood and did as she bid – but was clearly disappointed that she had destroyed his carefully built-up moment. He offered another of his myriad smiles, while Madeleina tried her darndest not to look at the awful bulge in his white breeches – although the thought would haunt her for many nights to come.

"Of course," he said. "It will be my pleasure."

And with that, they sauntered steadily back to the palace.

CHAPTER 73 — EMILYA

14th Tertiar, 1789   Day 105, 12:00

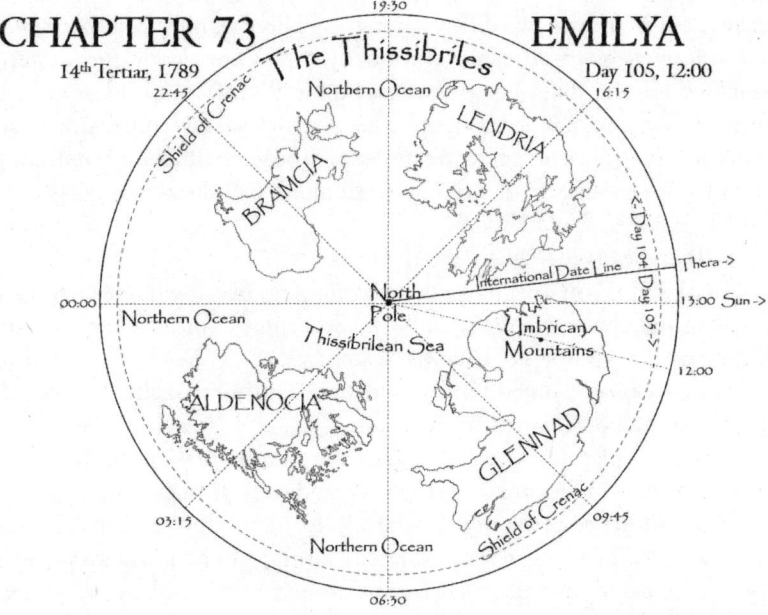

Emilya, Elyse and Jared, were taking a break from their incessant climbing in the Umbrican Mountains. They had shrugged off their backpacks and were viewing the scenery – which was unlike anything Emilya had seen before, with nothing but snow-clad peaks ahead of their climb to the north-east, and the sparkling lakes of Erminedrew and Sturawell in the valley over three thousand feet below. The Bleaklow Plateau had been invigorating, and the highest elevation to which Emilya had ever climbed. But as she looked back west, the plateau was now over one thousand feet *beneath* their current position.

Elyse was smiling at Emilya's look of awe. "You've seen nothing yet, Emilya."

"But we're so high up! And you can see so far," she added, breathlessly, looking out at the vista. The sun was behind her to her left, and the skies to the west were totally clear. Better still, there was no haze, and so even the features on the horizon were starkly clear. "I can see the sea," said Emilya, pointing into the distance and slightly to her right. "Where is that?"

"Kinnslyng," responded Jared. "And the 'sea' behind it is the Giant's Lagoon. But if you look over there," he said, pointing some way to the left, "can you see the two rivers that gradually converge?"

Emilya looked, and sure enough, two thin silver snakes converged, each heading out west from two different ranges of hills that must have been over twenty leagues apart. The more northerly hills were clearly the western Bleaklows, so she followed what must be the River Yew on its westward journey to where it merged with the other river – and suddenly realised that on that far-flung horizon, there was more sea to be seen with the sun reflecting brightly from its surface. "Is that Port St Humo's Bay?" she asked, aghast.

"It certainly is," said Jared.

"So that means that where the rivers merge…"

"That's right. You can't make out the buildings because of the curvature of Thera, but that's where Ghantiss is. Sometimes you can see the sun glinting off the windows of Ghantiss Cathedral."

"Wow-wee!" exclaimed Emilya, suddenly a little girl again. "So, we can actually see half of Glennad from up here?"

"You'll see that and the east coast from the top of Keplif Scale," said Elyse. "The views there are three hundred and sixty degrees.

Emilya didn't respond to that. She was looking into the near-distance, trying to trace their journey from Jared's farm, just north of Earl's Leet – when Elyse came up and put her arms around her from behind. Emilya smiled and crossed over her hands to hold Elyse's arms closer. "I'm trying to spot Jared's farm."

Jared pointed again. "Do you see Earl's Leet there?"

Emilya followed his pointing finger to the shelf on which Earl's Leet had been built. Because there were hills all around it, the town was in total shadow, but as her eyes became accustomed to the light, she saw it – row upon row of tiny brick-built buildings. "Got it."

"Right, so now do you see the two roads that converge from the north?" he said, moving his pointing finger slightly to the right.

"That's close to where Edwyn caught up with us." Her heart flipped at the thought of Elyse's nephew. He was never far from her thoughts.

"That's right," Elyse was saying. "And if you follow the lower road, you will see it disappear behind those hills – but if you keep your head moving to the north for this much," she said, holding up forefinger and thumb slightly apart, "that's where Jared's farm is. So, in that valley, I'll bet little Theo is being fussed over by Mitzy, Rollo and Luther."

The thought of the little terrier brought unbidden moisture to her eyes. Elyse noticed, hugged Emilya even tighter and kissed her on the cheek. "You saved his life, darling. He's a very lucky, happy boy now."

Emilya smiled a watery smile; not just for Theo's wonderful new life, but also at being called 'darling'. They had only been travelling companions for ten days, but she knew that Elyse already loved her as if she were her own. Emilya was certain their paths crossing was meant to be. She hoped and prayed the same applied to Edwyn as well.

In the meantime, Jared had taken up the instruction. "You can't see any of the paths that we took to head north and then east of Earl's Leet, as they're hidden by the foothills below. But if you look down there," said Jared, pointing and squinting towards the south-west, "you can see the pass that we came through where we stopped two nights ago."

Emilya followed his finger and saw the pass. "Oh yes! And after that, our path is pretty clear; horseshoes to the left and then the right."

"And over there," said Elyse, "pointing back at the Bleaklow Hills, "if you track the River Yew back towards the hills, then just before you start climbing is Ghenetenos – although you can't see it from here."

"I hope Jake is all right," said Emilya, Ghenetenos having reminded her of how Jake had spotted the stones first, on their approach from the west.

Elyse didn't respond. They had both given up so much to find sanctuary in these mountains. When Elyse remained quiet, Emilya turned around and gave her a big hug. Eventually, she pulled back and plucked up the courage to ask something that had been on her mind for the last four days. "Do you love him, Elyse?"

Elyse's face broke out into a big smile. But still she remained silent. Eventually she said: "I don't know."

"But you *must* know," said Emilya, confused, like it was a totally black and white issue. "I know beyond any doubt that I love Edwyn."

"It's not quite so straightforward when you get older, Emilya."

"But why?" Emilya was now troubled as well as confused.

Elyse considered before answering. "If you're very lucky, the first person you fall in love with will be the *only* person you ever fall in love with. And," she paused, looking up at the blue skies, "even if that happens when you are very young, Emilya, you must *never* let them go."

"But why would you let them go – if you love them and they love you?"

"Oh, Emilya!" said Elyse, placing the palm of her hand against Emilya's cheek. "You are such a darling."

"But I don't get it," said Emilya, all frowns. "Did you love someone and let them go?"

Elyse closed her eyes and Emilya saw her chin briefly wobble.

"But why?" asked Emilya again, still confused. "Did he stop loving you? No sane man would stop loving you, Elyse. Jake will never stop loving you." Emilya stopped talking, seeing that she was upsetting Elyse more and more.

Elyse took out a tissue, and gently wiped her eyes. All this time, poor Jared was keeping a safe, silent and respectful distance, but Emilya could tell he was feeling very awkward. Nevertheless, she had to know what had gone so wrong. "Did he die?" she asked gently.

"No, thank the Goddess," replied Elyse. "He's still alive now – but with someone else."

"Well, if he left you for someone else, he isn't right in the head."

Elyse cracked up laughing at that and gave Emilya another hug. "It wasn't Raich who wasn't right in the head, Emilya. It was me."

"You?"

"I ended it."

"But why?"

"I honestly don't know. Because I was young and stupid and possibly thought I could do better. It took about three or four years to realise that no one else compared. But how could I have known that when we were together? We were only seventeen; each other's first loves. By the time I knew the truth, it was too late. He had married someone else."

"Oh Elyse!" said Emilya, now understanding the sorrow that she sometimes saw in Elyse's eyes. "But maybe Jake does compare."

"That's what frightens me," said Elyse, beginning to fill up again.

"But that's *good,* isn't it?"

"Yes, of course. But I've loved and lost once, Emilya. I couldn't bear it if it happened again. And it's been so long…"

Suddenly, despite her mere fifteen years, Emilya understood everything – and she felt dreadful for the peril that Jake had put himself in on her behalf. "What have I done?" she whispered.

"Come here," said Elyse. And there, in that stunning place, they embraced again, and cried together – for loves both past and present.

CHAPTER 74   MAGNUS

14th Tertiar, 1789   Day 105, 13:00

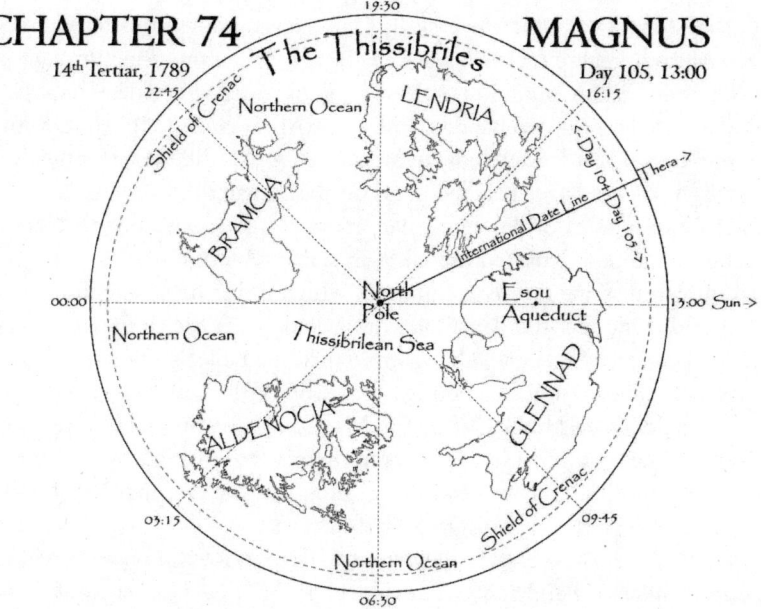

Prince Magnus was resting in the shade of a row of poplars whilst the wind brushed the tops of the tall trees back and forth. He felt a peculiar serenity that was at odds with events of the last three days. Of course, it helped his mood that Oscom and Black hadn't made much of an effort to conceal their passage – although Magnus was certain there was chivalry behind their carelessness, essentially leading he and his men away from wherever Emilya Luca and Elyse Dolmen were heading.

Well, Jake Oscom, I'm afraid it is you that I really want.

Of course, Oscom was completely unaware that his dead body would absolve Magnus of any involvement in Alicya's disappearance. Emilya Luca would have been a bonus, but looking at the wider picture, she was of relatively little value or concern, now.

Magnus closed his eyes and forced himself to re-live the serial humiliations of the last three days. The fact that Oscom would even deign to think he could ambush a royal prince and turn the tables on him, had never entered into Magnus' head. Even though his escort had been reduced to seven, Magnus had considered that ample protection. And as far as he had known, Oscom was travelling with a woman and a girl! Of course, he'd heard the rumours about Harry Black being in the neighbourhood, but again, the two of them teaming up had never crossed his mind, either.

The lessons were therefore clear. One: Never underestimate your foe. Two: Always prepare for the worst-case. Three: When travelling throughout the kingdom, take a minimum of twenty guards which would deter anywhere between two and a dozen bandits. And Four: Always look for enemies with a common cause. Under different circumstances, with a different enemy, any of those factors could have resulted in his death. He had been very lucky.

The first victim of his wrath had arrived around an hour or so after Oscom & Co had departed the ambush scene. The unfortunate Gage still had the whiff of ale on his breath, too, which didn't help Magnus' mood. Neither did the fact that Gage hadn't tracked down their quarries, in the first place, which had enabled Oscom to turn the tables on them.

Needless to say, once he had cut their bonds, the gaunt Gage had been forced to donate his filthy clothing to Magnus – meaning that, once again, Magnus had borrowed a smaller person's apparel to cover his own modesty! It was beyond ludicrous! Even more galling was the fact that Jake Oscom had been a major protagonist in *both incidents!*

Once attired in Gage's grubby, odour-stained clothes, Magnus had re-mounted his horse and cantered on ahead to Earl's Leet, on his own – thus avoiding association with six naked men in a carriage being ridden into Earl's Leet by a naked, one-eyed coachman! Hell's teeth, had he been part of that pantomime, they would have been singing about it in the music halls for decades!

As for his own men, three of them had died in the attack, including Hoskyns who had been shot dead by one of Black's lackeys when the fool had tried to draw his own pistol. *Stupid to the last.* Also dead was young Munton – killed after having raced back to warn them that he and Gage had been unable to locate Oscom and his party in Earl's Leet. In his new and more-ordered frame-of-mind, Magnus decided that he would posthumously decorate young Munton for his efforts.

Magnus forced himself to move onto his next humiliation. Again, a bit of forethought and less arrogance might have prevented that, too. He had assumed that all he needed to do was to waltz up to Earl's Leet's council house and requisition as many JP's and local militia as he needed to help flush out Oscom and Black. The last place he'd expected to end up was in the town's pound – alongside three petty crooks.

"What's 'e done then guv?" the smallest of the three men had asked – he who looked like a rat and smelt worse.

"Ah, the daft twat's telling everyone he's the Prince Magnus!" the cocky official had replied.

The three crooks had belly-laughed at that, with not a single white tooth to be seen amongst them.

Magnus had at least had the good sense not to attack them. He'd banked on the fact that the 'naked carriage' would soon pass along this route, past the market square with its pound for local ne'er-do-wells and its proud statue of Albion Gurch, the town's founder. He'd been right. Although even the most creative of music hall artists couldn't have envisioned a more bizarre tableau than several motley-clothed men – plus two of whom were still naked – trying to convince the local militia that their prince was locked up in a pound, but who was looking very much like the three grubby low-life's that he'd been incarcerated with! Thank heavens one of his own soldiers heralded from the town and knew one of the attendant Earl's Leet militiamen. That militiaman had then run back to the council house and brought everyone of importance back with him, including the mayor – who had promptly soiled his small-clothes when he realised whom his men had imprisoned!

Magnus actually found himself quietly smirking at the whole episode, now. The look on the mayor's face had been priceless – as, no doubt, would have been the look on his laundryman's face, too! In the end, Magnus had had to tell the mayor that if he apologised one more time, he would be locking the man up in his own pound! Naked!

Things had gradually improved from that point – the absolute nadir of his life, to date, for sure. The mayor had seen to all of their needs – clothes, bath, refreshment, stables for the horses, beds for the night – and, most importantly – men. Hence why he was now sitting in the shade of these poplars, dressed in a beautifully tailored black coat, waistcoat and breeches and the best riding boots Earl's Leet could offer – alongside a force of twenty men made up of the last two uninjured palace soldiers, Marler and Gage, and sixteen of Earl's Leet's finest militia. The mayor had also agreed to attend to the bodies of Hoskyns, Munton and the other palace soldier. "I expect them to be buried in respectable coffins and graves," Magnus had demanded.

A couple of days later they had got the tip-off they were looking for. "He's heading for the Upper Esou," their informant had said.

"Ah," had responded a now-calm prince. "Very clever – a highwayman not taking the highway."

Confident that Oscom and Black would be making their way down the length of the River Esou to the estuary port of Luhl, and having found plenty of signs of their passage, Magnus and his men were currently encamped around the upper eastern end of the collapsed Esou Aqueduct, about fifty yards from the surviving masonry. Magnus was just taking a swig from his water flask when he heard a commotion over by the edge of the gorge. "They're over there," he heard one militiaman say.

Magnus' heart sank, but he still sprang to his feet and hurried over to the surviving sheared and wrecked canal trunking on the east side of the Esou Gorge. It was another bitter pill to swallow. Sure enough, there on the opposite side of the collapsed aqueduct, was Oscom, Black and his two lackeys. Oh, and how the lackeys were enjoying themselves – shouting and taunting and gesturing with their fingers. Then, as Magnus watched, Harry Black's two lackeys dropped their trousers and began shaking their bare backsides at them.

Still ice-cool, Magnus unslung and then shouldered his specially-adapted musket, took aim and fired. An instant later, one of the two lackeys wasn't laughing any more. The other three then dragged their buttock-impaired colleague and themselves out of harms' way and back into the trees.

"Great shot, Sir," said Captain Gotch of the Earl's Leet militia. "What's the range on that?"

"A hundred-and-twenty yards, Gotch. I had it specially made."

"Well, I think you might have just turned the tables, Sir. I mean, it's a long way down into the gorge and up the other side – but they've got a passenger now."

"If I were them, he wouldn't be a passenger," said Magnus, grimly.

"No Sir, you're right, Sir. They'll likely leave him behind. No pun intended, Sir."

Magnus looked at Gotch. He was as strait-laced as they came, and clearly hadn't meant it in jest. Nevertheless, it tickled Magnus. Once he'd started laughing, everyone else joined in, some literally roaring with mirth.

When the laughter had subsided, Magnus rallied them. "Come on, men, let's get packed up and back down the track. We can be over where they were in less than an hour and a half, I reckon. Then we shall see what they've done with their foolish colleague."

CHAPTER 75   JAKE

14th Tertiar, 1789   Day 105, 13:20

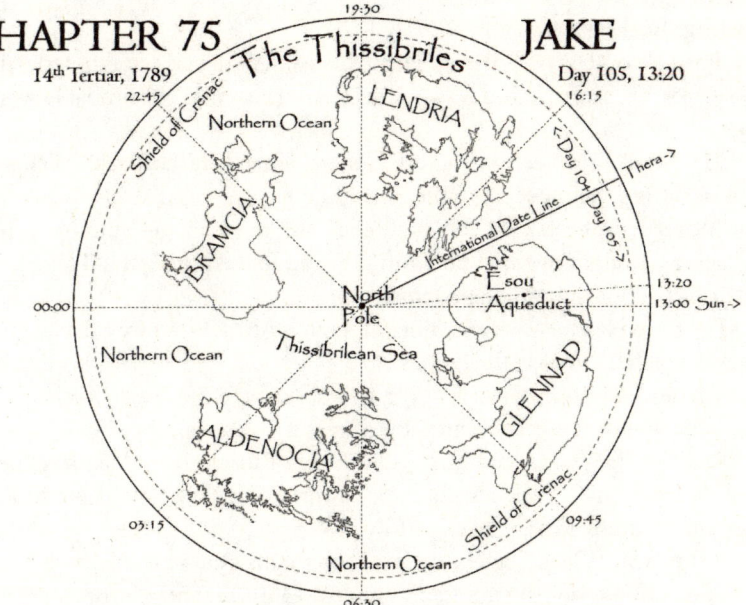

"You daft bloody idiot," scolded Jake, as he and Harry Black hauled Turnip into the cover of the trees.

"How the hell did he have the range?" cried Swede, aghast.

"It doesn't matter how," said Black. "The fact is, he did."

"You're not gonna leave me are you, boys," gasped Turnip, his hand clasping his ruined buttock whilst blood continued to seep through the cloth of his breached breeches.

"We need to get that bullet out, sharpish," said Jake, ignoring him.

"We need to get out of here sharpish, too," reminded Black.

"If we leave him, they'll execute him."

"I'm open to ideas," said Harry Black, spreading his hands. He hadn't stayed alive and one step ahead of the law by being overly sympathetic.

"How long have we got before they get here?" asked Swede.

"An hour and a half, maybe," said Jake.

"What are our options?"

"Still Plan A," said Black. "We leave Turnip here and head for the Rednewt Hills as a trio and make them think we're heading for Bryde."

"You're all heart, boss," responded Turnip, with a grimace.

"Except they'll torture Turnip to reveal our true plans," said Jake.

"Well, we could always, you know," said Swede, nodding at Turnip, his earrings jiggling away.

For a second or two, Turnip forgot his pain. "Are you actually serious -." He broke off as he saw Swede's wide grin. "You bastard! You probably would as well, though."

"Looks like Plan A is a dead duck, then," agreed Harry Black. "Seems I'll not be letting them peel my little Turnip here."

"Agreed," said Jake. "Which means we need to get him to safety, somehow. Roth's Cave isn't far from here, on foot. Although it'll be a good hour or two for him, in that condition."

"I've used Roth's Cave as a hideout, many-a-time – but we can't all go, as there's nowhere to hide the horses."

"True. And Roth's Cave is not exactly a secret, either," worried Jake.

"It might be to a prince, and townsfolk of Ghantiss…"

"Except they had more men," said Jake. "Those others must have been militia from Earl's Leet. This is their country. They'll know where to look and they'll know Roth's Cave."

"They will indeed," agreed Black, rubbing his chin in thought.

"So, I think we have to assume that they'll split their forces and send men to Roth's Cave," responded Jake. "Even if we cover our tracks."

"Yes, but then again, Magnus isn't likely to leave himself under-protected again, is he?"

"Which means he's likely to send a smaller group up to Roth's Cave," said Jake. "And if he does, that group won't include him. So, if I can get that bullet out of Turnip's backside sharpish, we can hide in the cave and pick off the smaller party as they approach."

"And announce your presence to Magnus with a bang?" queried Black, eyebrows raised.

"Ah, yes! I'll just have to make a judgement call – if it comes to that."

"Well, there is one thing about Roth's Cave," said Black. "Towards the back, there's a narrow fissure in the rock. It looks like it's just a crease in the wall, but if a thin man squeezes into the space and then crouches down, there's an opening. You have to crawl through it, but after about ten yards, it opens up into a sub-cavern. The chance of those Earl's Leet militiamen knowing that is much less likely."

"That's our fallback plan then," said Jake.

"And if by chance they *do* know about the sub-cavern," said Swede, "they'll only be able to enter one at a time. Easy targets."

"Except," began Jake, "the second-in-line would just pull back and then they'd likely block up the tunnel and leave us to starve."

"Well," said Black. "Thanks to numbskull here, it's our only option short of leaving him to the wolves."

"Agreed," said Jake. "It's a gamble, but there are other strategies we can use up there. In the meantime," he said, pulling out his gutting knife, "I need to perform some rapid surgery."

Turnip's eyes expanded to twice their normal size, transfixed by Jake's knife.

"Give him the flask of wine, Harry."

Black did as he was asked, and Turnip quaffed pretty much all of it, although a few rivulets ran down his chin and onto his already-stained tunic.

"Now then, old chap. If you wouldn't mind bending over," said Jake. "And please bite on this," he added, handing Turnip a flat piece of wood he'd picked up.

Turnip meekly took the wood. "You done this before?" he asked, clearly terrified.

"I've removed bullets from legs, arms and shoulders, yes. But never from a hairy arse," he joked. "But look on the bright side, mate. With a fleshy rump, I might not need to go down to the bone."

At that point, Turnip's eyes rolled up into his head, but both Jake and Black were alert enough to see it happening and catch him. "Now's your chance, Jake," said Black.

Jake didn't need a second invitation. As soon as Black draped Turnip over his knee, Jake began digging. It took about thirty seconds to eke out the musket ball, which came out with a wet sucking sound and much blood – just as Turnip was beginning to come around. Harry immediately picked up the dropped piece of wood and jammed it back into Turnip's mouth to silence him.

Jake pocketed the bullet. "Best not leave that to be found, eh?"

Meanwhile, poor Turnip had begun to whimper in pain before spitting out the piece of wood. "It feels like you've removed half of my bleedin' arse-cheek," he moaned.

Jake ignored him. "Right, we'd better be off," he said, turning to Black. "What's your plan, Harry?"

"I'll not desert you, sir," said Black, gravely. "We'll take the horses down to the Rednewt Hills; make Magnus think all four of us are heading for Bryde and then Brygmis or Luhl. Instead, we'll double back into the Rednewts. I'll probably use the River Rednewt to throw them off our trail – and then head back upstream towards the source. From there, we'll make our way back to Roth's Cave. I reckon we'll be back with you in five or six days. Assuming you're both still here, that is."

"If we're not, and we have to cut and run, shall we arrange to meet at Clyve's farm at dusk on, say, 24th Tertiar – Day 115?"

"Oh, he'll thank you for that," said Black, drolly.

"He owes me. As for Magnus, he'll not expect us to double back, as there are no immediate escape routes from Glennad if we do that."

"This does worry me slightly," admitted Black.

"I think it will totally throw him, Harry. We've then got a pick of ports to the north and the east – admittedly distant – but perhaps where they'll least expect us." Jake nodded his head, convinced himself. "For now, the beauty of this chase is that Magnus hasn't got enough men. Once you throw him off your trail, he can't cover every angle. And the further away you get from him, the greater the number of angles he has to cover."

Black nodded once. "I agree with this plan."

"Good man. Although once you're finished leading Magnus a merry dance, you might want to get changed out of that gear," said Jake, nodding at Harry Black's notorious flamboyant attire."

"Yes, a wise precaution."

"Right, let's get Turnip bandaged up. We don't want to leave a blood trail, do we?"

Black held out his hand to Jake. "You're a fine man, Jake Oscom."

Jake looked Black in the eye, a vague smile on his face. "You're not so bad yourself, Harry Black." Their handshake was firm and warm.

Black chuckled before nodding at Turnip. "Right, let me help you get this clot's wound dressed and then you can hobble off to your cave."

"You might as well give me your silk shirt then, matey – seeing as you only really need the red coat."

"Oh Lord," said Harry Black, his face falling. "My favourite shirt, ripped into strips and rubbing against Turnip's hairy rear?"

"Oi, I am here, you know," complained Turnip, who was now just about managing to cope with his pain.

Ten minutes later, they had gone their separate ways, and Jake was helping Turnip hobble uphill. Like the western Bleaklows, their path was surrounded by aspen, pine and fir trees which provided total cover from the path below. Another minute further on, and Jake let Turnip rest on a chair-shaped boulder, with the injured rogue somehow managing to keep his wounded buttock off the stone. "Give me twenty minutes," said Jake. "I need to cover our tracks." And with that, Jake jogged back down the needle-strewn path, pausing to break off first a hefty branch of leaf-laden aspen, and then another branch of needle-laden pine. He soon reached the path that headed south into the valley, with the short path due east heading for the ruined aqueduct. Jake studied the ground, and was satisfied to see four sets of fresh hoof-prints heading south. He then set to work with his branches on the two sets of human footprints that led up through the trees, a current dead giveaway of recent passage.

Swishing both branches backwards and forwards, eradicating the footprints and also shedding leaves and pine needles aplenty, it took Jake another fifteen minutes to reverse up the hill back to the waiting Turnip.

"How long do you think it will be before they get to our side of the aqueduct?" asked Turnip.

"Another forty-five minutes, I reckon," said Jake, casting aside his two branches. "By which stage, we might be high enough to watch them arrive and see what they do."

"How far to Roth's Cave?"

"With you like that? Another hour and a half, matey."

"We'll be jiggered if they start walking up here then."

"Calculated gamble," said Jake.

The wiry Turnip just looked up at Jake. He then opened his mouth, half-smiling, revealing his missing front tooth. "And if they do?"

Jake patted Turnip on the shoulder, Elyse foremost in his mind. "It's nothing personal, old chap."

Turnip rolled his eyes, but then offered Jake his hand. "We'd better get a move on then."

Jake hauled Turnip back onto his feet and put his left arm around his waist, whilst Turnip draped his right arm over Jake's shoulder. "I'm only joking, matey," said Jake. "I'll think of something."

As they continued upwards, Jake had to smirk, as poor Turnip was now hopping considerably faster than he had earlier.

After another forty minutes of uphill hopping, and constant complaining from Turnip, their path through the trees took a turn to the right. After another two hundred yards, the path began to double back to the left – but at the corner, a view into the valley below opened up before them. And there, around six hundred feet below them, they could see the jagged ruins of the western end of the Esou Aqueduct.

"Two choices," said Jake to Turnip. "Number one: we wait here and see what they do. Number two: we carry on to get a better lead, but we'll not know if they're following us."

"My arse is killing me," moaned Turnip. "So, it's number one or number one for me."

"Fair enough. But we need to get down low," said Jake approaching their lookout pragmatically.

"I'll just go and sit down in the trees, matey," said Turnip. "On one cheek! I'll trust you to do the looking."

"Makes sense," said Jake. Already he was sliding on his backside down towards some hardy thorn bushes that were growing out of the side of the hill. They weren't huge, and they weren't particularly thick, but if he lay on his side and kept still, he would remain unobserved.

He settled barely a moment too soon – as Magnus and his posse cantered up the steep slope alongside the western end of the aqueduct. Jake counted the mounted men: one, two, three…nineteen, twenty, twenty-one. Whilst he was counting, Magnus and Marler dismounted along with one of Magnus' soldiers and one of the Earl's Leet militiamen. The four of them were scanning the ground on the approach to the aqueduct – and spotted the trail of Turnip's blood. They soon found an end to the trail too – round about where the hoof prints headed off in a southerly direction. Magnus then pointed, perhaps at the gap in the trees where the 'path' led upwards. The soldier moved towards it, disappearing from Jake's view. Jake held his breath. Magnus and Marler continued to converse – and then the soldier returned, shaking his head. Jake slowly let out his breath. Magnus then addressed all of his men, pointing in a southerly direction. Shortly afterwards, the four re-mounted, and the posse trotted off to Jake's right, soon disappearing from view. Jake waited a full sixty seconds before vacating his hiding place. He rushed back up to the path. "I'll be back in five minutes," he said to Turnip. "Need to count twenty-one horses," he gasped. He then ran back *down* the path, knowing there was another viewpoint break in the trees two hundred yards to the south-west.

It took another minute or so after his arrival at the viewpoint for Magnus' posse to appear – now further south down into the valley. One, two three…sixteen, seventeen, eighteen…

Jake's heart went cold. Where were the other three?

He kept watching for another three minutes, torn between going or staying. When the other three still didn't appear, Jake sprinted back up to Turnip. "We've got company," he said, breathing hard.

"How many?"

"Three. I think."

"You're sure?"

"I'm not sure of anything. But I counted twenty-one mounted men up that side," he said, pointing to their left, "and only eighteen mounted men went down into the valley that side."

"You sure you got there in time? The other three might have been well ahead."

"Do we take that chance?"

"How long do we have?"

"I can't see them bringing their horses up here – it's too encumbered by trees. So, anything from five to twenty minutes, depending how quickly they're moving.

"We best start praying they give up looking after a few minutes then."

"Yes," agreed Jake, simply.

"And if they don't?"

"Then this is what we'll do…"

Jake heard them coming. They'd not last long in a war. Then again, they were probably expecting one able-bodied man and one cripple.

From his position behind thick foliage on the lower bend where he'd seen the eighteen horses heading southwards, Jake kept totally still. Then he saw them. He'd been right. Three of the Earl's Leet militiamen, unmounted. Jake felt a surge of guilt for the lives they were going to have to take, and the manner in which they would have to take them. Harry had been right. Magnus may have been gone for some time now, but sound carried long distances in these valleys and they couldn't afford to take the chance of using pistols.

Jake thought of Emilya and Elyse, and gripped his gutting knife more firmly. The men came nearer and nearer. And then they were taking the corner, their boots less than five yards from Jake's hidden face. The trap was then sprung.

"He's here, John," said one of them.

"Ah, I told you they'd leave him for dead," said another.

The third laughed. "Look at the state of his bloody arse."

"Yeah, he's probably passed out with blood loss, and whoever was with him thinks he can hide out in Roth's Cave," said the first man.

"You can see the other bloke's tracks heading up the slope, look," said the second.

"Sweet," said the third.

"Turn the rogue over then," commanded the first, who appeared to be their leader.

It was the second who had that unfortunate task – only to find Turnip's dagger plunged into his heart. Before the other two could react, Jake had hurled his throwing knife which embedded itself into the back of the third man.

Two and Three were down, and Jake was already running at One with his gutting knife drawn. The leader of the trio had recovered though, and rapidly levelled his musket – only for a rock thrown by Turnip to crash against his temple. He dropped the gun, and Jake was on him. They went down in a tangle of arms and legs, crashing through foliage. The man was strong, though, and was managing to hold Jake off, but Jake was still the stronger of the two and his knife was very slowly being forced towards the man's throat. The poor bloke saw it coming and his eyes widened in terror. "Mercy," he pleaded.

Jake closed his eyes, but relentlessly kept up the pressure. All he had to do was increase that pressure and it was all over. Except the poor man didn't deserve this.

Then, inexplicably, the man's throat opened up. He gurgled for a few seconds, and then died.

Jake raised his eyes to meet those of Turnip. "Thought you were going soft there for a minute, Oscom," said Turnip.

Jake closed his eyes and said a silent prayer for the three poor militiamen, who had probably left behind wives and children. And for himself. If he hadn't been damned before, he certainly was now. He looked back at Turnip. "I'm no cold-blooded killer."

Turnip flashed his gap-toothed grin. "Just as well I am then, innit?"

Jake just looked at him, wondering how he'd got himself into this mess. "We need to bury them," he said.

That wiped the smile from Turnip's face.

CHAPTER 76 — MADELEINA

14th Tertiar, 1789 — Day 105, 18:30

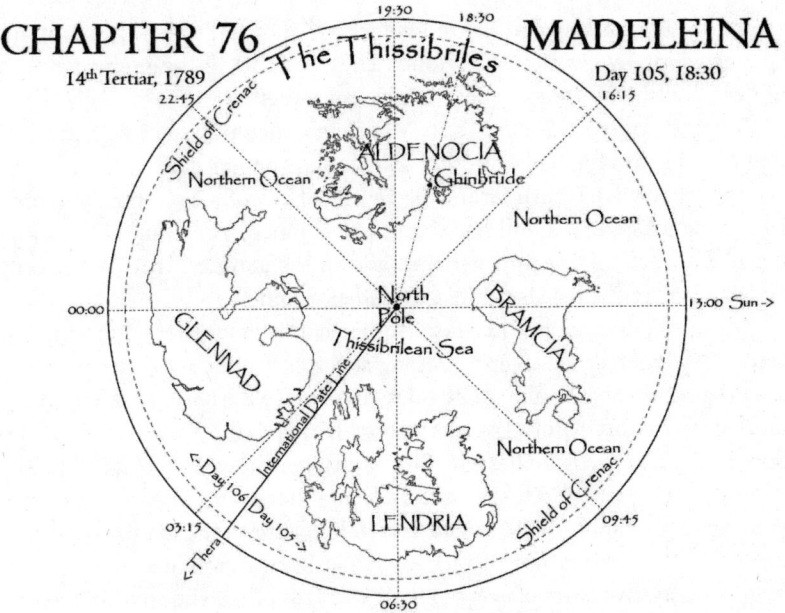

"Would you like me to escort Prince Bernard to his seat?" asked Charlotte.

"Yes please," responded Madelina. "I need to meditate for a few minutes. I want to make my final performance in Ghinbrude my best."

As Prince Bernard switched his attention back to Charlotte, Madeleina gave her a quick nod of thanks.

"Would you care to take my arm, Prince Bernard," asked Charlotte, offering it to the Lendrian prince.

"I should be delighted, young lady," gushed Bernard, taking her arm with a smile. Madeleina rolled her eyes. It would be nice if, just once, the man managed to look at Charlotte's face for more than one second. Hopefully, the difference in their respective endowments would make the Prince think twice about marrying her – although she still found herself strangely annoyed that Bernard's goggle-eyes favoured Charlotte's ample bosom to her own modest offering.

"And I should be delighted if I should have your other arm," said Aggie, skipping up to Bernard's right arm and offering her left.

Aggie just got a fatherly nod from Prince Bernard. He didn't seem too enamoured with young Aggie, suggesting that he at least had an age limit on his lechery.

Prince Bernard turned around before the girls could steer him out, his arm accidentally catching Charlotte's chest – although he seemed not to notice. "I wish you the very best of luck, my sweet."

"Why thank you, Bernie," said Madeleina, inclining her head, grateful that the arm-linking had saved her another kiss on her hand.

The relief when Charlotte and Aggie led her betrothed out was immense. Her smile disappeared and her shoulders slumped. The man had stuck to her like a leech all day, in the house and in the gardens. In fact, her only respite occurred when she visited the ladies' room!

Madeleina almost put her head in her hands before remembering her carefully-prepared make-up. Instead, she stood and began to pace the dressing room. She would *not* be marrying Prince Bernard. How could her mother and father think this was a suitable marriage? They had eyes! But how was she to extricate herself? She hadn't yet thought of a plausible way other than downright refusal – and the slurs that would involve. And even then, she'd probably still be forced into it. Inevitably, the plan for appealing to Prince Bernard's sense of propriety had been a non-starter. The man might be fifty-five years of age, but there didn't appear to be anything wrong with his carnal urges.

Madeleina closed her eyes in disgust – just as there was a knock at the door. Maddie blinked. Surely it was too early for Mr Cameron to be fetching her for the performance? She frowned. "Who is it please?"

"A friend," came the response. A woman's voice.

Madeleina looked around her, slightly unnerved. She then decided to take the initiative and walked with a confidence she didn't feel to the door and opened it.

The owner of the voice was quite unremarkable. Small, slight and hunched, maybe five feet two inches tall, perhaps in her mid-thirties, with mousy brown hair which hung lank to her shoulders, and a face that might have been pretty with a bit of make-up. She was also wearing a grey shawl which rather drowned her.

"Can I help you?" she asked, keeping her voice calm.

"No," responded the woman. "But I can help you."

Madeleina frowned. "Help me? In what way?"

"May I come in?"

Madeleina considered for a second. She wasn't due on stage for half an hour, and the woman seemed harmless. Moreover, she was curious. She therefore ushered the woman in. Madeleina then sat on her couch and invited the woman to sit on one of the two chairs in the room.

The woman complied, but then just looked at Maddie, saying nothing. "May I know your name?" asked Madeleina, eventually.

"My name is also Madeleina," she responded.

"Great name," responded Madeleina, eyebrows raised.

"But most people just called me Clair".

"Is that your middle name?"

"No. They call me Clair because I have the Second Sight."

Madeleina looked confused.

"I'm a clairvoyant."

"Ah," said Madeleina. "A jest."

"There's nothing funny about having the Second Sight, Princess."

Madeleina noticed that two of the woman's teeth had gone rotten. "I'm sure there isn't," began Maddie, carefully.

"Do you know what Second Sight is?"

"Yes, it's allegedly the gift of being able to perceive the future. And presumably, you're here to warn me about something in mine."

"No, Princess, that's not why I'm here. I've seen nothing ill for thee."

Madeleina blew out her cheeks. "Phew! You actually had me worried there for a while.

"I'm here about my other gift," said Clair, briefly scratching her nose. Madeleina noticed a raised mole where the woman was scratching.

"Your other gift?"

Again, the woman said nothing. It was ludicrously unnerving. "And does your other gift concern me?" asked Madeleina.

"It can do."

"Well," said Madeleina, leaning back on her couch. "Do please tell."

"You don't want to marry him, do you?"

"I beg your pardon?" She was instantly leaning forwards again.

"He's fat, old, a blatant lecher. It is cruel expecting a beautiful young girl such as yourself – and so talented, too – to marry the likes of him."

"I'm sorry, erm, Clair. But you are speaking way out of turn -."

"I can fix it for you."

"Fix it?"

"You only have to say the word. Ask me to fix it – and I will make sure that you never marry him."

"But how…I mean…what are you saying?"

"I am saying, that if you ask me to influence events such that Prince Bernard finds a new distraction – your busty, raven-haired lady-in-waiting, for example – I have the power to do that."

"Well, I certainly wouldn't inflict him on my friend -." Madeleina cut herself off. "Look, this is preposterous. You can't influence the thoughts of a man you don't know. No one can."

"Any woman can."

Madeleina laughed. "I'm afraid this audience is at an end," she said, now standing.

The woman remained seated. "So, you will marry him. He will de-flower you with great gusto, and when he's got you pregnant with his whelp, he will go and fawn after someone else."

That stopped Madeleina in her tracks. She was torn. All of her senses were screaming at her to send this ridiculous woman away. But Clair's last sentence, brutal though it had been, was probably correct. So, what if? Fantasy it may well be, *but what if?*

"All you have to do is ask," encouraged the woman.

Madeleina sat down again. "I don't believe this, you know."

"Well then, what's the harm in asking?"

"So, let me get this straight. If I ask you to fix it, so that Bernie loses interest and calls off our engagement, you can actually do that."

"I can."

"But how?"

"When you have the Second Sight, you see so many things. Past, present, future. They're all linked. If you don't learn how to control it, it can send you mad. The difference with me, is that not only did I learn how to control my own mind." Clair paused for effect. "But I discovered how to control the minds of others, too. Especially men."

Madeleina just stared at Clair for a good ten seconds, saying nothing. She then dropped her head, a light smile playing about her lips.

"So, you don't believe me," said Clair. "I'm used to that. But if you don't believe me, what harm can it do to say the words."

"You don't hurt the other person?" questioned Madeleina, inwardly berating herself for getting this drawn in. But she *had* to know.

"The other person will neither know nor feel a thing."

This time, the silence lasted longer. Clair's eyes were boring into Madeleina's, but Maddie didn't notice. She was turning over the bizarre suggestion, weighing up possible outcomes. Eventually, she made up her mind. "All right," she said. "I think it's a lot of nonsense, but please go ahead and fix it for me so that I don't have to marry Prince Bernard."

Clair smiled for the first time. It transformed her face – the two rotten teeth aside. "You will not regret it, Princess." And with that she rose, crossed to the door, and exited without another word.

CHAPTER 77 — DRAXAELEN

14th Tertiar, 1789 — Day 105, 14:30

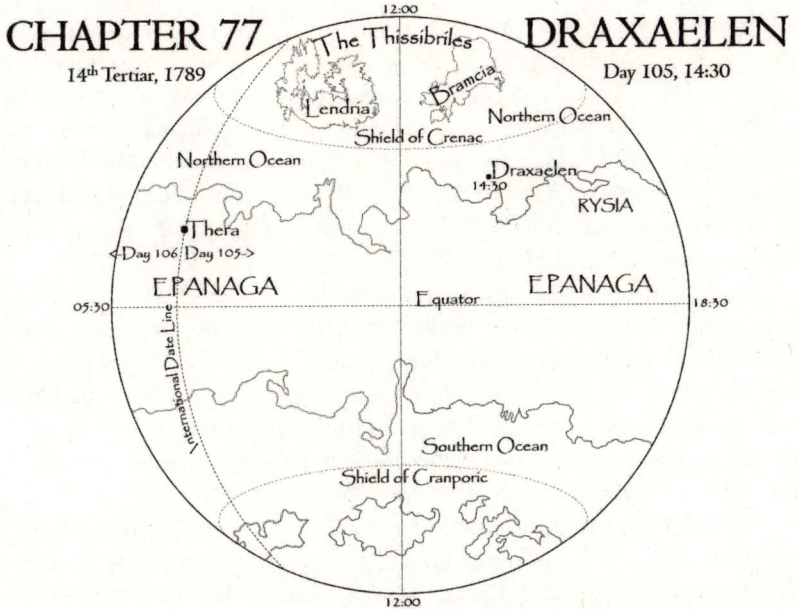

Draxaelen knew that something big was happening. They had been asked to strike oars in the middle of the night; mercilessly in the middle of their meagre rest time. From the few snatches of conversation that he had overheard, and the rumours passing up and down the bays, he had a vague idea what was coming.

General Macrinus had given the biggest clue, back in Alsethonisca, six days ago. He'd overheard him talking about stamping out Rysian raids on Theran commerce. Rysia was an eastern territory bordering the Northern Ocean, and was two to three times as far east from Demonacia as Demonacia was east from Thera. The Rysians were a vassal state of the Theran Empire, but they were a quarter of a world away from the city of Thera and hence difficult to control. Rysian rebels had been raiding ships laden with Theran loot for centuries – and Theran loot it most certainly was, and not the 'commerce' that Macrinus and the Theran *Senate* claimed.

Drax had observed the passage of the sun each day, and he was confident they'd spent six days heading largely east – meaning they were likely to be approaching western Rysia around about now, and would likely be targeting those Rysian galleys which, in turn, had been targeting Theran commercial shipping.

Drax concentrated on the drum-master, drawing his own oar in time with the beat, watching the shadows from the flickering iron candelabras rise and fall across his beating form. Even with his sores, rowing was easy at this pace – although he was sure the pace would soon be increasing.

A shadow fell across Draxaelen's body as one of the whipmasters slowly walked past, scanning right and left, looking at every single rower for any sign of weakness. It was the whipmaster who was missing the lower part of his left ear. Drax could see the one with the shaved head and strawberry birthmark up ahead of him, which meant that the one with the warts on his back was now behind him.

Movement up ahead behind the drum-master caught Drax's eye. He looked, but never once broke his rhythm; it had been three days now since he'd last felt the lash. One of the consuls had descended, and spoke quietly into the ear of one of the two legionaries up ahead. The legionary nodded, then nodded to his partner before the consul disappeared back up onto the top deck. The first legionary then turned to face the galley-slaves and called out what Draxaelen had been expecting. "Attack speed."

Immediately, the drum-master increased the rate of his drum-beats, and Draxaelen and his fellow galley-slaves began to pull on the oars a little faster. Drax found it easy. His six days of 'practice' had honed all of the appropriate muscles for rowing. He had thought them pretty honed before; he knew better now. More importantly, that hideous aching of muscles that had driven him to distraction for the first three days had gone, replaced – almost – by an actual *desire* to row. Drax was good at many things. He was now an expert rower, too, and he was finding a perverse sort of enjoyment in the easy rhythm.

As he and his fellow galley-slaves worked together as one seamless machine, Drax could feel their boat cutting through the ocean at pace. No one was flagging.

Five minutes later, the warhorn sounded. "Ahooooo."

It was answered by at least ten more – giving Drax an indication of how many ships their force comprised. The legionary responded immediately. "Battle speed," he shouted out.

The drum-master increased the beat, and Drax and his colleagues hauled even harder on their oars. From what he knew about this type of operation, Drax was hopeful it would be over fairly quickly.

In the distance, he heard another horn, then another, and then another – but the last had a different kind of timbre; more panicked, less aggressive. For a second, Drax put himself in the position of the commerce raiders. They would always be on the lookout for a Theran backlash, but actually seeing a war-fleet tearing towards you: that must be truly terrifying. Drax briefly felt compassion for the likely lives they were about to take – and then reigned it in. There was nothing he could do about it – and in any case, his revenge was far more important to risk compromising it by not complying.

The Theran horns then blared out again. Times ten.

"Ramming speed," hollered the legionary, sweat dripping from his face almost as much as the toiling oarsmen's. The night was brutally warm and sticky for all.

The drum-beat was now at an intense level, and Drax was hauling on his oar with all of his strength, finding himself breathing hard for the first time in the exercise. Too much more of this, and he would start to flag. He needn't have worried, though. He heard the shouts of panic from somewhere ahead of their boat, and then the roars from the legionaries on the upper deck.

"Brace yourselves," shouted the legionary.

Drax let go of his oars, as did all of his colleagues, and braced his feet against the bay in front. He then leaned forward with his hands over his head not a moment too soon – as a titanic impact from up ahead rocked the entire ship. Seconds later, the two legionaries were back on their feet. "Strike oars in reverse!" bellowed one of them.

Drax and his colleagues did as they'd been trained, whilst noises of chaos from above and ahead filled his ears. Whereas for normal rowing their action took them down and forward and then up and back, the action was now reversed. At first, Drax felt resistance, and envisaged an impalement on the wounded ship that they were struggling to free themselves from. He and his colleagues heaved with all of their collective strength, every one of them with their veins and muscles standing out fit to pop. Then, like a cork being released from a bottle, they suddenly surged backwards, and the reverse rowing no longer met with resistance other than from the water beneath their paddles. That weightless feeling was sweet beyond telling.

A great cheer then went up from above decks. No legionary on this ship was going to die today – assuming they hadn't taken on a fatal breach themselves. Conversely, every single Rysian rebel on the ship they had just rammed, *would* die today – although none at the end of a Theran sword. As for the 'loot' they had effectively reclaimed, the Therans would just leave that to sink along with the crew.

After reverse rowing for around sixty seconds, the legionary commanded them to rest. Like his fellow oarsmen, Draxaelen let go of his oar with relief and fell forward over it, breathing heavily, sweat dripping from his forehead onto the floor. He caught the eye of the man to his right, pulling the high oar. A look of respect passed between them along with a brief nod. They had survived. This time.

A minute later, Maxi Zoninus came below deck, a huge white grin on his dark face. Silence fell over the lower deck, but still Zoninus continued to smile. "My friends," he began. "You were magnificent."

A few galley-slaves actually smiled back and thanked him. Draxaelen kept his expression neutral.

Zoninus turned around. "Bring," he commanded.

Two legionaries then appeared, carrying a cask between them. After they laid it down, Zoninus himself took two huge wooden goblets from a third legionary and opened the tap on the cask, filling each goblet in turn. He then passed it to each of the men positioned alongside the aisle in the first bay, to left and right, indicating that they should drink and pass to their colleagues.

"The finest Acahean red," announced Maxi Zoninus. "For my finest oarsmen."

Draxaelen watched the first two men thirstily guzzle their wine before passing inside to the middle oarsmen, who then guzzled in turn. Draxaelen suddenly realised how thirsty he was and he began to ache for his taste of the red wine. When his turn finally came – Maxi Zoninus dutifully re-filling for each row – the taste was sublime. It had been over a week since he had last tasted wine, although it felt more like a year. It had certainly never tasted this sweet before.

It was a second or two before he realised that Maxi Zoninus was above him, staring at him with his mismatched eyes. "And you, Demon," he said. "You will be the finest of all."

CHAPTER 78   CALIDIUS

15th Tertiar, 1789   Day 106, 11:00

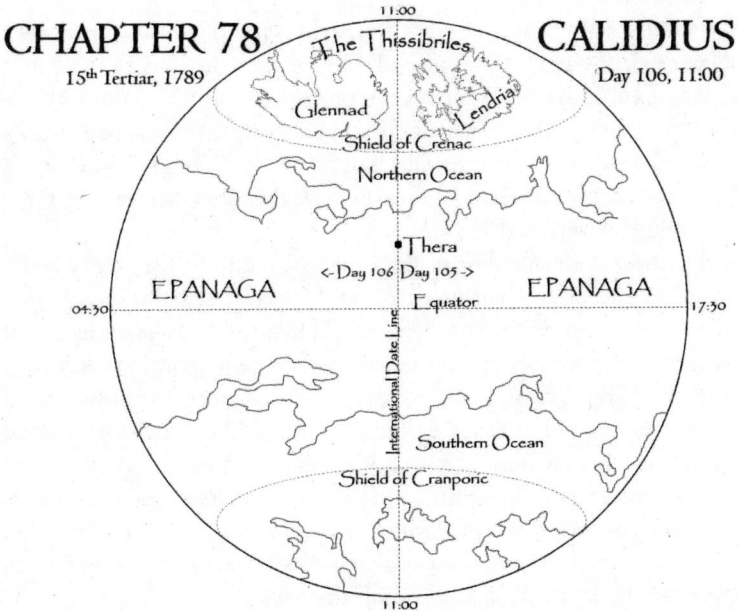

The Senate wasn't due to sit for another two hours, so Calidius had called a session of his secret inner sanctum, held within one of the vaults under the *Aula Regia* – the royal hall of the Summer Palace. The group was comprised of Calidius himself, and four influential members of Theran society whom Calidius knew put duty before career.

To his left at the round table was his uncle, Senator Lucretius – brother of his mother and a member of the Senate for over twenty years. Lucretius was amply equipped to be First Consul, but he was also wise enough to know that this would likely reduce his lifespan, too. Now in his early fifties, Lucretius looked ten years younger than his age, his hair still dark, his tanned face only marked by gentle lines of wisdom, while his imperial robes were plain, white and classy, and avoided the ostentatiousness preferred by other senior senators.

To Lucretius' left was Seutonius, the presiding magistrate over *Derventio* (the western half of the city of Thera), but overlooked several times for the post of Chief Magistrate. Slightly younger than Lucretius, Seutonius had a thinning pate of grey hair but had aged well in every other respect: he was very stocky for a magistrate, well-muscled, and he moved with the fluidity of a much younger man, while his blue eyes always sparkled with vitality and wisdom.

To Calidius' right was Gaitonius, the archbishop of *Navio* (the eastern half of the city), but many-times passed over for Primate – a wise avoidance considering four of the last six had been poisoned to death! Gaitonius was the oldest member of the inner sanctum, at seventy-two. Stooped, with a heavily-lined face, snow-white hair and a neatly-trimmed snow-white beard to match, he also had blue eyes – highly unusual amongst the predominantly brown-eyed Therans.

Finally, the fourth member of the inner sanctum, to Gaitonius' right, was actually a stand-in. Normally, it would have been Calidius' most-trusted soldier, General Macrinus Severus Vitellius, son of one of the oldest and most esteemed houses in Thera. However, General Macrinus was away on a military campaign, and had nominated in his place his most-trusted captain and also his eldest son, Captain Romulus Didius Vitellius. General Macrinus, himself, was only in his early forties, so the fact that Romulus was twenty-nine years-of-age told a story in itself. No longer a boy, though, Romulus was also a veteran of numerous campaigns in eastern Epanaga, but had been severely injured last year in one of Macrinus' campaigns in Rysia. A spear had passed clean through the back of his knee and out the front, shattering the joint and rendering his leg totally useless below the knee. He now walked with the aid of crutches. However, when mounted, he remained a fearsome equestrian; perhaps the best in Thera. He still had one of the finest young military minds in the Theran Empire, too, and so his daily role involved the coaching of legionaries in Thera's military school, where he commanded great respect for one still relatively young.

The rustic table that they were sat around was made of gnarled cedarwood, and its only contents were three pitchers of water and five goblets, which Calidius was now filling for his guests. "Gentlemen," he began, once he had finished pouring. "We sit again to discuss any adverse developments within the Senate, the Judiciary, the Church and the Army. So, Lucretius," said Calidius, turning his attention to his uncle and most-trusted senator. "Are there any rumblings in the *Senate*?"

"There are, I am sorry to tell. Marcus Verus, Lucius Pius and Trajan Caracalla have been observed having frequent whispered conferences, with eyes darting hither and thither. But should someone approach, they make light and their body language changes entirely."

"Do we know the nature of these discussions?"

"The only word of significance that has been passed back to me by my spies is the word 'hoax'. Oh, and also your father's name has cropped up a few times as well."

"Indeed," mused Calidius, stroking his chin. "Well, it's not too much of a stretch to piece that together. They doubt the Nessemi threat and perhaps think I invented it to justify the removal of my father."

"Should we perhaps arrange for another session with Gaius Maurus? I believe he is predicting visibility of Nessemi to the naked eye in the next four or five days. That should wake them up a bit."

"Yes, but they could compromise us in four or five days, too. Our secret cannot get out. Damn it, were they not deterred enough by the fates of Ganatus and Ostorius?"

"Perhaps that is why they only whisper in corners, Your Imperial Majesty," suggested Romulus.

"Yes, but whispers can escalate." Calidius frowned as he considered their next actions. Finally, he spoke. "This is a tricky one, Lucretius, but it feels important, too. Have they been observed talking to others?"

"They talk to others, but my lip-readers have never detected the words 'hoax' or 'Vitasian'. We believe their thoughts and motives are being kept between the three of them."

"Unless their tongues are wagging to their wives, too."

"I hear nothing from the common people who attend church services," said Gaitonius. "And I have my spies in every church. It is likely that if such a dramatic tale had been told, congregations would be worrying about it as a sign of God's wrath and the end of the world."

"It may yet *be* the end of the world, Gaitonius," responded Calidius, grim-faced.

"As you know, Your Imperial Highness, I do not subscribe to that point of view."

"And I am grateful for your faith, Gaitonius." Again, the room fell silent as Calidius considered what to do. "I don't like it," he said finally. "We always knew this could happen. But after Ganatus and Ostorius, can we afford to take action? Five dead Senators in one week would put us on a par with some of Thera's most infamous periods."

"Might I suggest we postpone any silencing for at least two days," said Seutonius. "In the meantime, I set my best lawyers to work, night and day, building career-ending cases against these senators? If they then make a move to recruit more senators, we arrest them, publicly charge them, and hold them in prison for as long as we please."

"And no blood is shed," mused Calidius. "I agree to this proposal, Seutonius. But it must take no longer than two days to compile these charges, and you *must* have evidence and witnesses, too."

"I will try my best, Your Imperial Majesty," said Seutonius.

"And in the meantime, you will increase your watch on these three, Lucretius. I need to know as soon as they appear to be escalating."

Lucretius nodded his agreement. "Of course, Emperor."

"And if they do escalate before the next two days are out, then blood it will have to be. We will make it look like three separate affrays, or muggings or burglaries gone wrong – perhaps one of each. Alas, the rest of the *Senate* will not be fooled."

"But they may well be cowed," suggested Romulus.

"Indeed," agreed Calidius. He pulled his attention back on-track. "Any other matters to report, Lucretius?"

"None. But I will inform you the moment matters change with our three senators, or any other signs of treason are identified."

"Treason, yes. It's the right word, Lucretius. More than ever before in our history." He turned to his magistrate again. "Seutonius. Anything to report from our chambers?"

"Nothing from my half of the city, Your Imperial Majesty, and I have ample spies employed in the eastern half with nothing found to arouse suspicion. Well, not in the sphere of Nessemi, anyway. Petty crime – that's another matter," he added, wryly.

"Information which will be critical when we start operating *Expurgatio*," responded Calidius, hungrily. "Gaitonius?" he said, turning to his archbishop.

"As stated earlier, Your Imperial Majesty, there is nothing from the common people, and nothing from within the Primacy either."

"Excellent, Gaitonius. And Romulus?"

"I expected nothing but loyalty from our selected soldiers," he said, referring to the legionaries who had been present at recent *Curia* sessions. "But I have employed around forty spies, and none of their reports give me cause for alarm." He paused before continuing, a wry smile playing about his lips. "I was rather shocked, though, by the level of infidelity amongst our troops, Your Imperial Majesty."

Calidius issued one of his rare smiles, too – albeit brief. "Well, that, gentlemen, is *not* going to be included in *Expurgatio*. Otherwise, we'd likely not have enough men to populate our shelters!"

CHAPTER 79 — MADELEINA

15ᵗʰ Tertiar, 1789   Day 106, 14:45

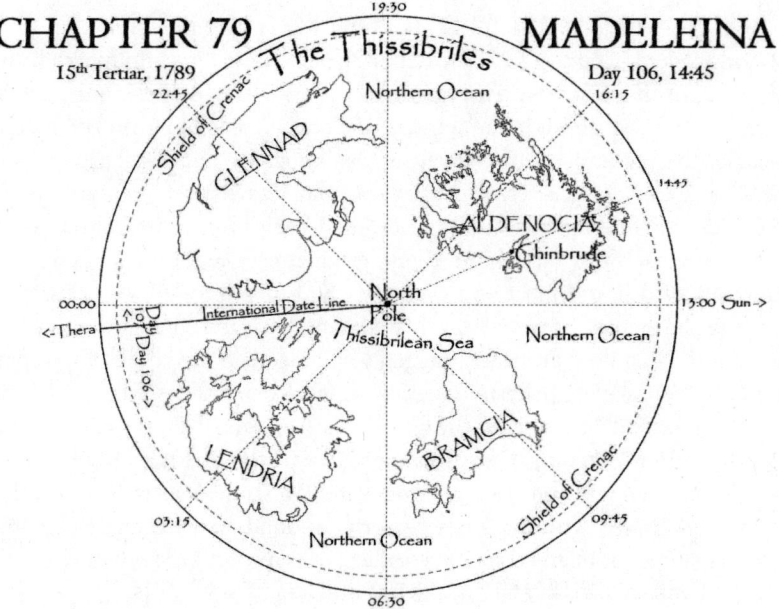

Madeleina was making the most of the first of her two days off. Her tour of Aldenòcia would commence in three days' time, and she would be setting off first thing the day after tomorrow by boat, across the mouth of the Firth of Ghinbrude, and then west for Stormone, where she was due to play at Stormone Opera House.

Today, her mother and father had whisked her off to the annual point-to-point horse races that were run over natural hunting country, two leagues east of Ghinbrude, with the jumps including dry stone walls, some of which dated back to the 16ᵗʰ century. Of course, Prince Bernard was invited too, so Madeleina had ensured that Charlotte and Aggie would be there to act as chaperones. However, it turned out that not only was Bernie highly knowledgeable and enthusiastic about horse-racing, he also knew most of the horses by reputation, and a fair few of the jockeys, personally. He had talked at length about the sport, offering numerous insights, and giving the royal family tips about which horse and jockey to back for each race. As a result, Madeleina was in rather a large amount of credit, which was somewhat embarrassing – although she would most certainly be donating her winnings to a number of worthy causes back in Ghinbrude.

Madeleina wasn't fooled by this slightly enjoyable 'date' with Prince Bernard, though, and he was still eyeing her body far too regularly for her liking. Nevertheless, she still kept getting pangs of guilt for asking that stupid woman, Clair, to fix it for her so that she didn't have to marry him. How could she have been stupid enough to ask? It made her cringe every time she thought about it. Sometimes, she really needed to grow up. As for Bernie, the regularity with which he was knocking back tankards of ale didn't bode well for the rest of the day; the man was forward enough, stone-cold sober, while his appetite for food had been even more voracious at lunchtime. He'd just talked and eaten, eaten and talked, downing copious amounts of fish and meat and savouries, and then a long list of desserts, putting immense pressure on his already-besieged mustard-coloured waistcoat. Maddie then nearly gagged as a hideous image flashed into her mind of that heaving belly-mass descending on her, unfettered.

Eventually, it was time for the final, longest and most-famous race of the day, the Hunt Members' Cup. This race always attracted not only the best riders in Aldenocia, but from all around the Thissibriles as well – with the largest contingent coming from Lendria, a kingdom with an apparently endless supply of talented jockeys. Indeed, a Lendrian jockey had won the Hunt Members' Cup in eight of the last nine years.

The race was run over half a league of open countryside, with the start point over the ridge of the hill to their east. They would see the runners and riders come over that ridge before descending into the valley. They would then lose sight of them for around two minutes as they came up their side of the valley, before the first jockey's cap would emerge over the brow of the nearest hill as he prepared to enter the finishing strait – bringing them past where her party was assembled in the royal enclosure. Following Prince Bernard's advice, they had all had a flutter on the aptly-named grey, Horsed Credit, being ridden today by Richard Brown, one of the best-known Aldenocian jockeys. The general feeling was that this was finally the year for Aldenocia – the last local winner having been The Snail, way back in 1775.

As the time moved towards 3 o'clock, the noise in the crowd began to subside. Everyone was waiting with baited breath for the horn to sound half a league to their east, which would signify the start of the race. When it did, with a lingering "Ahoo", the crowd immediately burst into spontaneous cheering, and everywhere about her there were beaming, expectant faces. Many of the common folk would have betted an entire months' wages on this race, such was its lure and appeal.

A minute or so after the starting horn, Madeleina was convinced she could hear the drum of thirty horses' hooves above the human racket around her. Sure enough, thirty seconds later, the leaders of the race appeared over the far ridge, clods of turf being visibly ripped up even at this distance. Madeleina scanned the caps and colours of the leading jockeys, searching for the amber and burgundy of Richard Brown. "There!" she said, pointing to a jockey on the right-hand side of the pack. Even though it was impossible to tell from this frontal view which jockey was in the lead, Madeleina, Charlotte and Aggie began to jump up and down and shout with excitement. And the noise around her: Madeleina had never heard anything like it before, with ten thousand people bellowing at the tops of their voices.

"Come on Discount!"
"Move it, Huntsman!"
"There he is, Rosy, there he is!"
"Oh, shift your bleedin' arse, Wanderer!"
"We're gonna be rich, Mikey. We're gonna be rich!"

Madeleina had never been so excited in all her life and, like her two ladies-in-wating, was beaming from ear-to-ear.

As the horses and jockeys began to descend into the valley, it was becoming clearer who was in the lead. A pale blue and pink livery on a chestnut was leading the pack. Madeleina had a quick look up and down her programme to spot the colours and saw that the horse was called Lottery Jerry. Behind Lottery Jerry was a jockey wearing scarlet with a blue sash – the programme revealing that the horse was the unfavoured Cure-All – unfavoured because the poor horse had been made to walk all the way from Flundermine in south-east Aldenocia to take part, and was already formally classed as 'knackered' before the start of the race. So much for the experts and tipsters, thought Madeleina. She scanned the leaders again, counted backwards, and worked out that Horsed Credit was currently in sixth position.

Seconds later, the leaders disappeared from view, heading down to ford the narrow stream that ran through the valley and then begin their climb up their side. After another thirty seconds, the trailing horses and jockeys also disappeared from view. By now, though, you really could hear the thunder of the hooves over the human sounds, as the leaders were evidently climbing the valley side towards them, at great pace.

And then they appeared, and bedlam exploded around her. Lottery Jerry was still in the lead, now followed by a jockey in all yellow. The scarlet with the blue sash had clearly fallen away, because there, in third place, around ten lengths back, was the amber and burgundy of Richard Brown on Horsed Credit. Madeleina and her party began to jump up and down like lunatics, shouting until they were hoarse.

There were now only three stone walls between the horses and the finish line. As Lottery Jerry took the first still in the lead, Madeleina was warmed to see the scarlet of Cure-All appear over the brow of the hill in fourth or fifth place. The jockey and trainer would hopefully be getting some reward for their epic journey across Aldenocia after all. But for now, she only had eyes for Horsed Credit. He had taken the first of the three remaining walls, and was beginning to bear down on the second-placed jockey in pale yellow and his horse, which the men to her right were telling her was Mathew's Charity. As Lottery Jerry took the penultimate wall, Horsed Credit was catching Mathew's Charity and was now only around eight lengths behind the leader. By the time the second and third horses took the penultimate wall, they did so in unison, before Horsed Credit began to pull ahead of Mathew's Charity. The distance was now only seven lengths to the leader.

By this stage, Madeleina was baying like a navvy, a state-of-affairs that showed no evidence of refinement as the leading two horses jumped the last wall only four lengths apart. Lottery Jerry's jump was languid; Horsed Credit took the last wall in full flow, huge divots of turf spurting up behind him as he hit the ground and pushed for home, and so Madeleina's hollerings ramped up yet another notch. She was also amused to note that Prince Bernard was now jumping up and down, too, and surprisingly light on his feet given his overburdened frame. Then, Horsed Credit was three lengths behind Lottery Jerry, then two lengths, then one length. As Horsed Credit drew level with Lottery Jerry, Madeleina's vocal cords finally gave out, and so she just concentrated on jumping up and down, her eyes popping out of her head as Horsed Credit forced his way past Lottery Jerry and then crossed the finish line as the winner, seconds later.

The royal enclosure and everywhere up and down the stalls exploded in shouts, cheers and applause. Madeleina actually found she had tears of delight rolling down her face as she hugged Charlotte and Aggie. It had been one of the most exhilarating experiences of her life – on a par with the refined rapture invoked from performing with her concertos. She even had a smile for Prince Bernard, who took advantage of the general euphoria and lifted her off her feet, spinning her around twice.

"Ooh, Prince Bernard," she said, as he set her down, hands still on her upper arms. Annoyingly, she couldn't remove the smile from her face. Bernard just looked back at her, a huge smile on his face, too – but then the smile froze. Something was wrong. Madeleina felt it instantly and she immediately went cold. There was a terror in his eyes now. The next second, Prince Bernard was doubling over, clutching his chest. *It's only indigestion*, Madeleina told herself. But then, as Prince Bernard attempted to straighten up, he began to jerk, clawing desperately at his cravat, whilst his face had already turned beetroot red.

"Oh my God!" exclaimed Madeleina. She was still holding on to his arms. "Somebody help me, please!" she cried, desperately looking around her.

Charlotte and Aggie were with her, their hands wringing helplessly, no idea what to do, otherwise all around her, cheering punters carried on acclaiming the winner, oblivious to the drama unfolding closer to home. However, as Prince Bernard fell untidily to the floor, a few other surrounding racegoers turned around and their faces soon reflected the same concern and horror.

Madeleina was now kneeling and holding Bernie's hand, trying to get him to talk to her, but all that was coming out of her betrothed's mouth were strangulated gasps and incoherent spluttering. It was all-too clear what was happening, and the shock brought natural tears to Madeleina's cheeks. She was briefly aware of her mother kneeling to join her, an expression of horror fixed across her face, too, and then a man was with them claiming to be a doctor. He quickly ripped open Prince Bernard's over-tight waistcoat, loosened his shirt and stock, but before he could administer any treatment, Prince Bernard's half-exposed body arched once more and then lay still.

Madeleina stood up and stepped back, her hands covering her mouth. She couldn't stop looking at poor Prince Bernard's bulging eyes.

Then she remembered the woman from the night before. It hadn't occurred to her until that point…but when it did, it hit her so hard that she began to feel light-headed. Her whole torso began to tingle with pins and needles, and the next thing she knew, she was falling herself…

CHAPTER 80 — EMILYA

16th Tertiar, 1789 — Day 107, 15:30

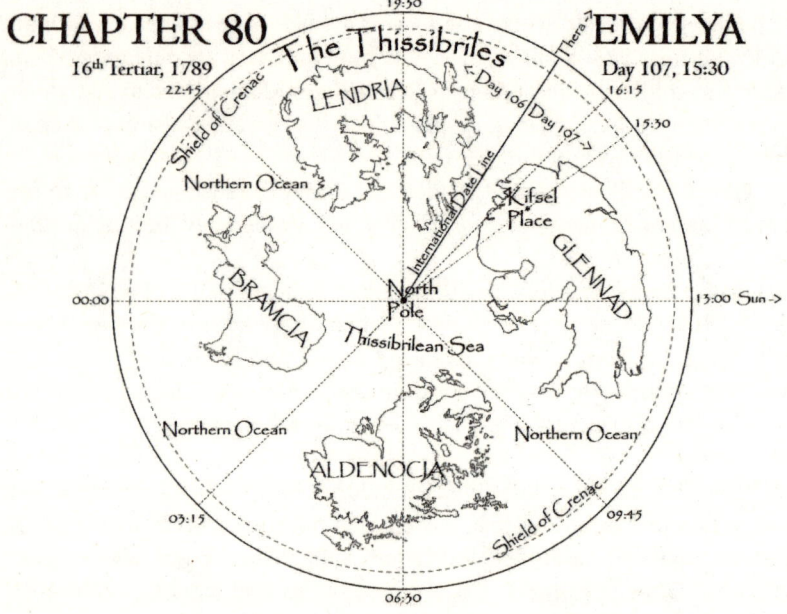

The views had become more breathtaking, the higher they climbed, until yesterday morning, when they had awoken to slate-grey skies and a seven-degree drop in temperature. Wrapped up in thick, warm capes, they had later turned their hoods up as a steady rain had begun to fall, and by the time they'd made camp last night, Emilya had been soaked to the skin.

This morning had offered further grey skies, although the rain had stopped and by lunchtime, the cloud had begun to break up. Now, blue skies were sharing the canvas with fluffy white clouds, while the views were every bit as crisp as the air they breathed. More importantly, Emilya could now see the settlement of Kifsel Place ahead of them, in the middle distance, although it only appeared to be comprised of a dozen or so wooden houses.

Their approach to Kifsel Place had put them on a northerly bearing, and it hadn't been until they'd wound their way to their right, that the village had come into view. Then, as they headed back in a south-easterly direction, Emilya's breath was taken away. The wooden settlement was totally dwarfed by the impossible-looking Kifsel Place monastery. Whereas the village was laid out on a relatively level shelf of land, the monastery rose above it on five different levels, with each set of buildings comprised of walls which appeared to grow upwards out of the five distinct stacks that they inhabited. Emilya wondered what served for foundations – although the buildings looked solid enough, clinging to the top of their stacks. Above the monastery, there were no more discernible levels; just a solid, near-vertical mass of rock, disappearing up towards the sky. There was no wonder the monk's found peace in a place like this, thought Emilya, and she couldn't think of anywhere better to remain out of the reach of Prince Magnus.

As their path levelled out a little, Elyse swung her backpack off and dumped it on the ground. Emilya gladly did the same, suddenly realising how out of breath she had become.

"It's the altitude," said Elyse, puffing a little herself.

"You'll soon get used to it," said Jared. The farmer's son wasn't remotely out of breath, noted Emilya.

"How high are we?" asked Emilya.

"About five thousand feet," said Jared.

Emilya raised her eyebrows. "So, we're only three thousand feet off the height of Dawkids and Keplif Scale then?"

"That's right Emilya," said Jared impressed. "They're to the north," he said, pointing to the mountains behind them, where the first of the snow-topped peaks could be seen. "But you can't see them from here."

"As discussed last week, Emilya," began Elyse, "I've half a mind to take you there. The monks run an annual 'Cleanse the Spirit' expedition to the summit of both mountains, and this year's is due in a few weeks' time. I've done it twice myself, and it would be one of the most-lasting memories of your life."

"I would love to do that," said Emilya, her voice full of wonder. "Assuming it's safe, that is."

"The monks are expert climbers, Emilya. No risks are taken, and the expeditions are only undertaken in the warmest months of the year during good weather. If the weather breaks on the way up, they make sure a position of safety is found to ride out the bad weather, and then will most likely lead the expedition back home. I was very lucky on my two expeditions, as we had beautiful weather for all six days, both times. So, I've summitted both, twice."

"I've summitted twice as well," said Jared. "Dad and I go every other summer, but we've been turned back on three occasions. It's frustrating and disappointing, but always the right call."

"What are the monks like, Jared?" asked Emilya.

"Wonderful people," said Jared, instantly. "Warm-hearted, kind, will do anything for you."

"It's just that I'd heard stories of the odd rotten apple," said Emilya.

"Hundreds of years ago, yes," admitted Jared. "What have you heard about? The Mad Abbott?"

"Was he the one who tortured and executed three quarters of his brethren?"

"Yes, Abbott Byard. He was abbot in the mid-fourteenth century. He thought himself the most pious man in the Four Kingdoms, but saw sin in everyone else. His methods of torture to extract confessions were gruesome, and his executions were even worse."

"I wouldn't mention Abbott Byard when we get there, Emilya," said Elyse. "Even though that happened four hundred years ago, the monks are still ashamed of that period in their history."

"Right, come on ladies," said Jared, shouldering his back-pack again. "We don't want to get caught on these mountains in the dark."

Emilya shuddered at the thought, even though dusk was several hours away.

It took another fifteen minutes to reach the first building – a wooden outbuilding or shed which looked to be full of chopped wood. Jared nodded ahead. "We'll stop at the hostel tonight. It's the only one in Kifsel Place, so it's known simply as 'The Hostel'. I don't foresee any issue with you staying with the monks, but I thought it would be the right thing to do to give the innkeeper and his wife some business – as they only really thrive in the middle of summer when Glennadians arrive to take climbing holidays."

Elyse smiled at Jared. "You really are a most considerate person, young man."

Jared blushed and looked at the floor, but still managed a shy smile and shrugged. "That's just how my parents brought me up to be."

"Looks like we've been spotted by the way," Emilya said, nodding up the path towards the main part of Kifsel Place settlement.

Elyse and Jared looked up to see a middle-aged man with curly brown hair and a thick beard observing them from around a hundred yards away. Alongside him was a middle-aged woman, her hair tucked into a coif and her entire body covered by a thick brown shawl. Emilya, Elyse and Jared waved in unison. Oddly, the middle-aged couple did not return the gesture, but just turned around and walked into the largest building in the settlement which, like all the others was made of wood.

"They don't seem very friendly," said Elyse. "The last time I was here, the place was being run by a really bubbly woman."

"Ah, you mean Bess?"

"Yes, or Big Bess, as she's also known," said Elyse, winking once at Jared.

Emilya saw Jared's complexion change again – this time to the colour of a ripe tomato, so she didn't require an explanation. Emilya rolled her eyes, before the trio made their way towards the only hostel in Kifsel Place, and hopefully a hot meal and a soft bed for the night.

CHAPTER 81 — MADELEINA

16th Tertiar, 1789   Day 107, 14:45

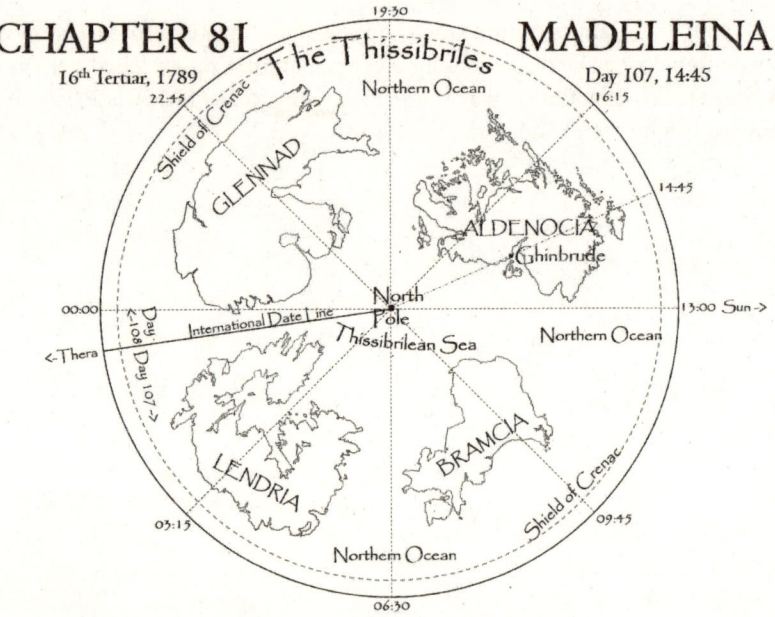

Madeleina was sitting alone in her drawing room, although she had her two cats for company. Each had a chin in her lap and she was gently stroking both whilst they purred a concerto all of their own making. Their presence soothed Madeleina, and she was in sore need of soothing – because whenever she closed her eyes, all she ever saw, were Prince Bernard's own bulging pair beseeching her for help.

Prince Bernard had been pronounced dead shortly after his collapse at the races, and although her mother and father, her ladies-in-waiting and palace officials constantly flapped around her, concerned for her loss, Madeleina could think only of that woman. She was thinking of her now. Those two rotten teeth, the raised mole on her nose, her hair, mousy, hanging lank to her shoulders. She thought of her over-sized grey shawl. But most of all, she thought of her words. *There's nothing funny about having the Second Sight, Princess.* Although that wasn't why she had visited Madeleina. *I'm here about my other gift.*

It had sounded a ridiculous statement at the time, and Madeleina had almost laughed. She had not treated the woman seriously until she'd said: *You don't want to marry him, do you?*

That had reeled her in, as had her next offer: *I can fix it for you. All you need to do is ask.*

And she *had* asked. And when she had noticed Prince Bernard looking other ladies up and down at the races, a tiny hope had stirred, albeit immediately squashed by inner pragmatism. *Don't be ridiculous. The woman was a fraud.*

And then, Prince Bernard had died – from what appeared to be natural causes: a heart attack. For much of the time since his death, sensible, rational Madeleina had found herself half-believing in the supernatural, until pragmatism intervened.

It's just a tragic coincidence.

Madeleina hadn't told anyone about the woman. She had considered telling Charlotte, but decided not as that would feel like an admission to being part-responsible for Prince Bernard's death. It would appear callous, at the very least.

"Oh, Lord, I'm being stupid, aren't I?" said Madeleina, tickling the tabby under the chin. The tabby's smile appeared to grow wider. "Oh well," she added, now tickling the cheek of her black and white. "Duty calls. Mother and father tell me that my tour must go ahead – at least until the funeral, next week." At that, Madeleina gently eased herself out from under her two cats and stood, whilst the cats now closed up to warm each other.

Madeleina checked her pocket-watch. She was supposed to be at the Ghinbrude Palladium at 15:00 to supervise the safe encasement of her grand piano, ready for the voyage to Stormone, tomorrow morning. Of course, people would understand if she didn't show up, but right now, she needed to keep busy to help take her mind off yesterday's events. Her mind made up, Madeleina went looking for Mr Rose, their head coachman, and Mr Leah and Mr Cape, the palace security guards who were due to accompany her to the Palladium. Mother and father had asked to tag along, or to send Charlotte and Aggie with her, but Madeleina was having none of it. "I'll go on my own. I'm not good company at the moment."

Forty minutes later, Madeleina walked through the grand front doors of the Ghinbrude Palladium. "Princess!" gasped Fraser Cameron, surprise and concern etched on his face. "I wasn't expecting you after your -. May I offer my deepest condolences, Your Royal Highness."

"Thank you, Mr Cameron. It has been a difficult time."

"If there's anything I can do?"

"No, thank you, Mr Cameron." She looked across towards the main auditorium, and the stage to where her grand piano was waiting to be stored inside an enormous container. "I see you're ready to pack her. I'm just going to the dressing room first though. I left some music in there as well as some clothes."

"Yes, Princess, they're in the third cabinet on your right as you enter."

Madeleina thanked him and indicated that the two palace security guards, Leah and Cape, should follow. However, when they reached the door to the dressing room, she wanted to be alone inside, given it was where she'd made possibly one of the worst mistakes of her life. "Please," she said, turning around. "Wait out here. I'll be about five minutes."

Both security guards nodded, and took up their positions as Madeleina entered her dressing room and shut the door behind her. She stood still, but managed a brief smile as she remembered her nerves on that first night. Thereafter, this place had been special. She was sad to be leaving, even if it wasn't likely to be forever. So deep was she in thought that it took her two seconds to realise that she wasn't alone. The woman was sat on the couch. *Her* couch. But she looked different. Her clothes were better; of a higher class. Her hair had been washed, brushed and styled. And there was no mole on the nose!

The woman – Clair – smiled – revealing only white teeth.

Madeleina instantly knew something was amiss. There was something else that was different about the woman, too. It nagged briefly, before she placed it. It was her demeanour. It was totally different. There was no deference. She was looking at Madeleina almost insolently.

"You did it then," she said. The voice also sounded different; more cultured than two days ago.

Nevertheless, Madeleina's blood ran cold. "Did what?" she whispered.

The woman smiled – and was instantly far more attractive than Maddie would have believed possible, two days ago. "You know very well what."

"I only have to call out," said Madeleina. "There are two palace guards behind that door."

"I know there are," said Clair, closing her eyes. "Leah and Cape, I believe."

Clair opened her eyes again as Madeleina's jaw dropped. "How do you know that..."

The woman merely smirked and raised an eyebrow.

"Second Sight, I suppose," said Madeleina, warily.

"Who else do you want dead, Madeleina?"

The question took Madeleina off-balance, but still shocked her to the core. When she recovered, she felt an anger stirring. "I don't want anyone dead!" she snapped. "I didn't want *him* dead, either."

"What? The poor fat prince?" said Clair, faking concern, her bottom lip pushed out. Her face then changed in an instant, now cold and calculating. "You told me to fix him!" she accused. "And I did."

"No!" exclaimed Madeleina. "I did not! Not like that, anyway."

"Prove it!"

Madeleina went white. *What was happening here?* Her senses were screaming at her to call her security guards, but a warning voice was also telling her that would be a mistake. "I *asked* you," accused Madeleina. "I *asked* you if you could fix it for me so that Prince Bernard would lose interest. And you said that you could."

"That's right, Princess. I was merely agreeing to the fact that I could – if I so chose – manipulate Prince Bernard into falling for someone else. But you didn't tell me to actually *do* it, did you? You just asked if I *could* do it. And I answered truthfully."

Madeleina glared at the woman. "I also asked you if you would hurt the other person – even though I thought it was a ridiculous question."

"And do you think it ridiculous now?"

Madeleina narrowed her eyes. "Well, if you did do it, you lied about that bit. Prince Bernard was in agony when he died."

"For all of sixty seconds," responded Clair, flippantly.

Maddie began to get angry again. "What kind of a person are you?"

"The kind of person who now owns you," responded Clair.

"Owns me!"

"If you don't do as I ask, I will expose you for naming Prince Bernard's death."

"And every single magistrate in Aldenocia will deride you for the fraud that you are," sneered Madeleina.

Clair ignored her. "Who else do you want dead, Madeleina? All you have to do is think it. Prince Marco, for example. I know you don't like him. He beats your older sister, the Princess Gabriella, doesn't he? Think him dead, Madeleina," urged Clair. "*Think Prince Marco dead*. Or what about poor Mr Cameron?"

Madeleina put her hands to her ears, trying to block out the sound of Clair's voice. "I will *not*," she cried. But even as she was saying the words, an image of Marco being shot in the forehead seeped into her mind…so she pushed it away…only for it to be replaced by another of him drowning, another of him falling to his death.

Madeleina shut her eyes and began to babble and wail. The next second, the two palace guards burst into the room, concerned at the noises of distress coming from their princess.

"I'm all right," she said, composing herself. "The woman was just leaving."

"The woman?" questioned one of the guards.

When Madeleina turned around, the woman had gone.

CHAPTER 82 — EMILYA

17th Tertiar, 1789   Day 108, 09:00

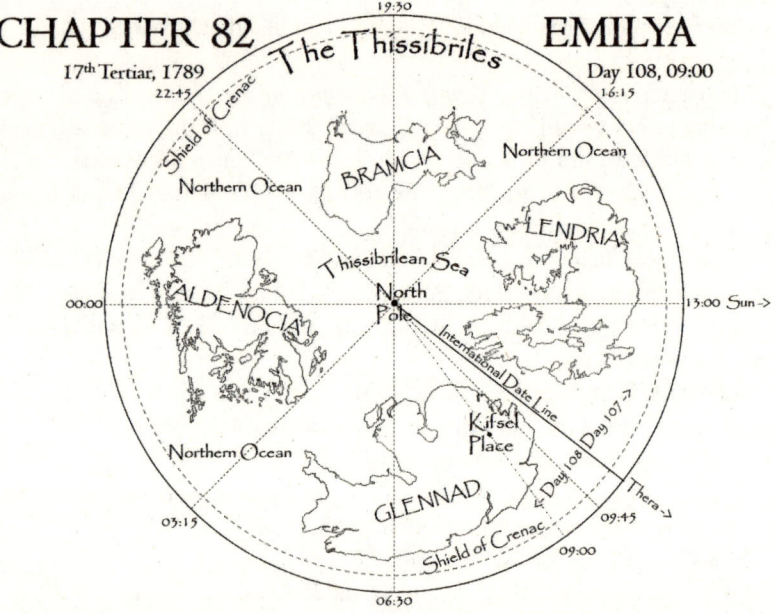

The early-morning scene in the Umbrican Mountains was extraordinary. Emilya, Elyse and Jared had just left the hostel, where they had enjoyed a hearty breakfast, and appeared to have stepped out onto the roof of the world. Wispy clouds were drifting up the mountains and past them, but the valley to the north-west through which they had climbed yesterday wasn't visible – as it was completely filled, wall-to-wall, with a featherbed of clouds.

The clouds were actually below them, this morning!

By contrast, all of the peaks above them reared jaggedly up into a clear-blue sky, while dominating to the south-east, above where they were standing, was the gravity-defying monastery, miraculously perched on top of its five stacks.

Emilya looked nervously at the path that led to the monastery. It looked to be less than an arms-width wide and there was no barrier on the outer edge; it just dropped, vertically, for more than a thousand feet to rocks, way down below.

Elyse put her arm around Emilya. They were both wearing long cloaks that they had purchased in Earl's Leet, and which covered them from head to toe so that their presence at the monastery would be acceptable for the monks. "Are you ready for this then, Emilya?"

Emilya put both of her arms around Elyse. "As I'll ever be." In truth, she was daunted by the prospect of entering a male-only institution and was exceedingly grateful that Elyse was accompanying her.

"I'll come with you to the entrance," said Jared. "But then I will have to take my leave of you."

Elyse turned to their tall, young and polite guide and offered her right arm – which he took with a shy smile. Elyse looked left at Emilya. "We appear to be blessed with wonderful young men, Emilya."

"And middle-aged ones, too," pointed out Emilya.

"Oh, him," said Elyse, a distant smile flitting across her face. "He'll do, I suppose," she added.

Emilya laughed at that. "You so love him, Elyse."

"I so do not," she laughed back. That musical laugh of hers. Sadly, Emilya suspected she wouldn't be hearing it much at the monastery as it would be wholly inappropriate.

Their arm-linking only lasted the remainder of the main path. Once they took the branch to the monastery, it was single file all the way to the monastery doors. As they progressed – Jared first, Emilya in the middle and Elyse bringing up the rear – Emilya couldn't help but peer over the edge. She noticed that the clouds hadn't congregated below in this particularly tight gorge, and was vaguely disappointed at that.

"Stop it!" said Elyse, noticing what she was doing.

"It's making me dizzy," replied Emilya.

"Exactly. So, stop it!"

"Yes, sorry, Mum!"

Elyse laughed at that.

Despite the warning, Emilya looked again. The tops of the trees seemed half a world away down there, while a mountain stream cascaded noisily down the rocks on the other side of the gorge before tumbling through a gap in the trees. There were also large birds cruising around on the rising air currents not too far above them that Emilya was finding disconcerting. Largely black, they had a bald pink head and a pink neck, and let out harsh periodic caws. "What kind of birds are they, Jared?" she asked, nervously.

Jared stopped and looked up. "Vulture eagles," he replied. "They look big and nasty, but they don't attack people. They feed mainly on smaller birds, rodents and carrion."

Emilya shuddered. They looked ugly. Very out of place in this wonderful setting. Emilya noticed that the closer they got to the monastery, the more birds there were. Jared read her thoughts. "The monks feed them all sorts. Particularly the monastery rats."

Emilya shuddered again. "No one told me there were going to be rats in the monastery."

"You didn't ask," quipped Elyse.

"What sort of self-respecting rat lives on the top of a mountain, anyway?" she moaned.

"Mountain rats!" replied Jared, without any trace of humour.

"And I suppose mountain *rat* size is in a similar ratio to mountain *bird* size around here?"

Jared stopped and turned around, forcing Emilya to almost bump into him. "I thought you said you hadn't been here before?"

Emilya looked at Jared, hard. He was stone-faced, but Emilya could just see a tiny twinkle in his eye. She exhaled, loudly, with exasperation. "Why does *everyone* have to take the piss out of me?"

"Language, Emilya!" scolded Elyse, eyes also twinkling.

"Yeah," said Jared, now smirking, and leading on again. "And outside a monastery too!" he threw back over his shoulder.

Emilya soon saw the funny side, though, and apologised.

When they were three-quarters of the way along the path, Emilya saw a wicket gate open in the huge double monastery doors, and two monks stepped out. They were simply garbed in long brown hooded robes, with a piece of rope tied around their waists. Both waited patiently, with their hands clasped together. When they realised that they had at least two former visitors, the face of the monk on the right broke out into a delighted smile. "Miss Elyse! Master Jared!" he said, as they arrived on the narrow plateau of ground on the lowest stack. "How wonderful to see you both again. Have you come to cleanse the spirit?"

"We certainly have," agreed Elyse. "Emilya, may I introduce you to Brother Stephen. As you have probably gathered, we are already acquainted – from both of my previous visits here."

Emilya could have brained herself, as she did an involuntary curtsy – made all the worse by Elyse putting her hand over her mouth to stifle her laughter. Both monks bowed their heads in greeting to the newcomer, and Emilya was disappointed to note that neither of them was sporting a tonsure. She then scrutinised them both. Brother Stephen was the taller of the two, brown-haired and affable, while his dark-haired colleague, whom Brother Stephen introduced as Brother Clarence, was a good half a foot smaller, and twice as wide, but had a winning smile on his pudgy red face, which was made to look all-the-odder thanks to two enormous black slugs for eyebrows. Emilya would have placed both men in their thirties, and she wondered what had driven them both to give up so much, so young.

"Are you staying until our next Cleanse the Spirit expedition?" asked Brother Stephen. "Because we don't leave until the 41st of Tertiar"

"I'll be going back to the farm immediately," said Jared. "But father and I will be back for the 40th.

"And if it isn't too much trouble," Elyse was saying, "Emilya and I would both like to stay until then, and maybe for a little beyond?"

"Of course," said Brother Stephen bowing his head again, only his eyes betraying his curiosity.

"And it goes without saying that we will work throughout our time here," said Elyse. "Any tasks you care to hand us – although I must tell you, that my young friend here is a very talented baker from Ghantiss."

"Ah," said Brother Clarence, happily. "You have come to the right place then, my dear. Although you are a long way from home?" he added, another small question-mark audible in his tone.

"The monks have an *enormous* kitchen, Emilya," said Elyse. "And you won't believe the size of their ovens."

"We do indeed," said Brother Stephen. "Bread is one of our most lucrative exports, but we're always open to new methods. This sounds like a most promising arrangement. The abbot will be most pleased."

"And how is Abbot Geoffrey?" asked Elyse. "He was bearing his years marvellously well when I last visited – what, eight years ago now."

"He is still strong," confirmed Brother Stephen. "Although at seventy-one years of age, his knees are giving him some discomfort, thanks to years in these mountains. Of course, he never complains."

"And does he still tend his psychic garden with great fondness?"

"He does indeed, Miss Elyse. He does indeed."

"What's a psychic garden?" asked Emilya.

"I'm sure the abbot will show you later and explain. But it's a riot of herbs and spices…and plants of a certain nature," finished Elyse with a degree of mystery.

"All of which helps in our endless quest to improve Glennadian medicines," said Brother Stephen. "Now, please, if you would follow me, I will see if I can arrange an audience with the abbot. He had taken a rest, earlier, following Matins, but he is likely about his duties now."

"Erm, this is where I must leave you," said Jared awkwardly. He held his hand out to Elyse, who ignored it and gave him a huge hug, followed by a big kiss on his right cheek. "I can't thank you enough, young man. You have been a wonderful guide. Please be sure to thank your mother and father for loaning you to us."

"I will," promised Jared. He then held his hand out to Emilya, but for once in her fifteen years, she decided to ditch teenage awkwardness, and gave him a big hug too – and then kissed him on his *left* cheek. "Take care on your way back, Jared."

"I will," he replied. "I look forward to seeing you both again, soon."

Emilya felt a lump in her throat as she watched the farmer's son begin to re-trace their steps along the narrow path. She was getting very fed up of goodbyes. Shaking her head sadly, she turned back to the monastery where Brother Stephen gave her a friendly smile, and once again gestured for her and Elyse to step through the wicket gate. As they passed through, Emilya whispered to Elyse: "What's Matins?"

"It's a brotherhood vigil from 3 a.m. until dawn," she responded.

"Ah," said Emilya, not really a deal wiser. "That'll be a long vigil in the depths of winter then," she said.

"Your young friend is very sharp," said Brother Clarence, clearly having overheard the exchange.

Whilst Elyse agreed, rather proudly, Emilya's attention was elsewhere. Having stepped through the wicket gate, she had to admit to being a tad disappointed with what lay behind it. Attentive as ever, Brother Clarence had noticed. "We have only functional buildings on Hector," he explained. "Our ecclesiastical buildings are higher up on the third and fourth stacks, which we call Bowers and Bedford, respectively. I take it your companions explained the names of our five stacks?"

"They did, yes," confirmed Emilya. "I believe Abbot Hector was the first abbot here from 1266 to 1282. He was followed by Abbot Bloomer who was abbot from 1282 to 1300. Then there was Abbot Bowers from 1300 to 1308, then Abbot Bedford from 1308 to 1314, and finally, Abbot Stamps from 1314 until," Emilya screwed her face up as she tried to remember the last year Jared had taught her, "1330, I believe."

"Well, 'pon my soul," said Brother Stephen, looking at Emilya in a whole new light.

"Ditto," added Brother Clarence, equally impressed.

Emilya beamed – and then got a familiar whiff of baked bread. "Ah," she said, finger raised and her nose twitching. "Now that's a smell I know well. One of these buildings must be the bakery."

"Indeed," said Brother Clarence. "In fact, this rather functional-looking building to our left is the kitchen and the buildings to the front are the refectory and parlour, respectively. We also have the buttery and our wine cellars on Hector as well."

"As it is still early, and you aren't weary after a day of travel, perhaps you would like a tour of the monastery?" asked Brother Stephen.

"That would be wonderful," agreed Emilya. "Although I don't want to disturb anyone at prayer."

"Of course. We will only escort you to appropriate areas. But as the guest quarters are at the top of the pile, we would be passing most of the sites of interest, anyway."

"I can't wait to cross one of these bridges," said Emilya, wide-eyed.

"Well, if you would like to follow me," said Brother Clarence, "the first bridge is through here." He then led Emilya and Elyse, with Brother Stephen bringing up the rear, through a narrow gap between the refectory and the parlour. When they came out the other side, Emilya could see the opening to the first bridge. She had a quick look to her left where several other functional buildings could be seen on Hector, but her focus was already on the rope bridge ahead which would take them across to Bloomer. The first thing that occurred to Emilya was that it didn't look very robust. The second thing was how much higher Bloomer was than Hector – and it was soon clear that once you crossed to the other side, you ascended a series of zig-zagged steps that had been cut into the north face of Bloomer and which led up to an entrance, around forty feet above them. And again, no barrier.

"It's all right, Emilya," said Elyse. "It's quite safe. Watch these two monks coming the other way."

The four of them waited at the threshold of Hector and watched the two monks reach the foot of the steps. They then casually grabbed the top of the rope bridge on both sides and walked across without breaking stride. Emilya noted that the first monk was probably in his early forties, having receded dark hair and a rather sinister-looking goatee beard, which was unusual for a monk. But it was his dark eyes which spooked her. They were so dark, they were black, and they held no warmth whatsoever as he skewered her with a withering glare. And then they had swished past and were gone. Emilya was so disconcerted that she hadn't even noticed what the second monk looked like.

Elyse leaned in to Emilya and whispered in her ear. "Not all monks are in favour of visitors, Emilya. Particularly visitors with breasts."

"Oh," was all Emilya could say. The encounter had quite taken the wind out of her sails.

"You'll have to forgive Brother Cyrus," said Brother Clarence. "He is particularly resistant to change. But he is a very dedicated farmer who births most of our piglets and foals."

"And the farm is where we are going next," said Brother Stephen. "If you would like to lead on across the bridge."

Elyse went first, hands on both sides, and Emilya followed nervously, taking care not to trip over her long cloak. They were across in seconds, and the bridge had remained perfectly firm – although Emilya had resolutely *not* looked down, this time.

"Now then, ladies," said Brother Stephen, as they began to ascend the zig-zagged steps. "This next level will hopefully enchant you considerably more than the last."

CHAPTER 83 — ALICYA

17th Tertiar, 1789 — Day 108, 18:45

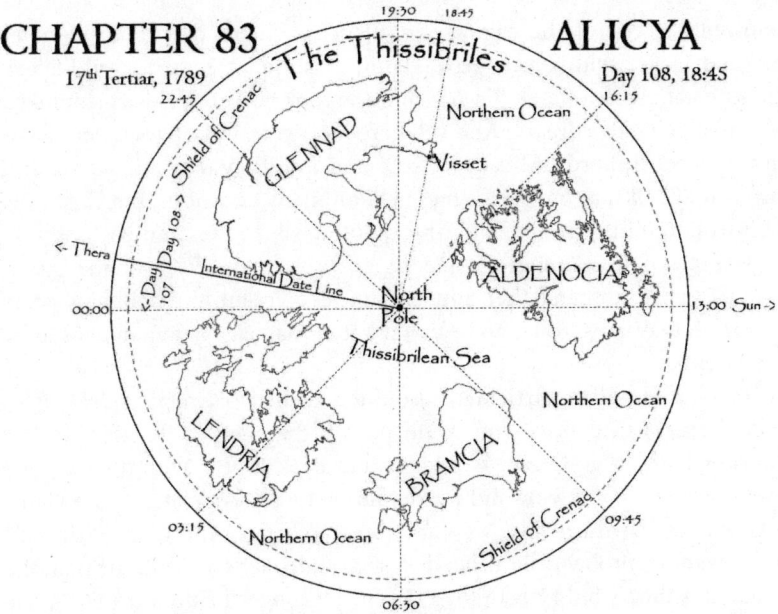

Visset Manor was not a palace, but Alicya could see that Lord and Lady Visset's standard of living wasn't so very far short of royalty. The three-storey manor house was certainly on the large size, and very imposing. It was built of a handsome greyish-yellow stone with hipped Bramcian slate roofs, and one's eye was immediately drawn to the grand portico entrance, fronted by six long and rounded stone columns. On top of the pediment were three large statues and a large flagpole, flying the black and white flag of Wrenko. The portico with its six columns was mounted above five archways, and these were flanked by sweeping balustraded staircases that curved around to provide access to the front entrance. Behind the columns were eight bays each boasting large sash windows, while further buildings fanned out to each side.

Alicya took all of this in as their carriage drew up on the gravel forecourt – which was already populated by three similar carriages and their grandly-attired guests. Other fine suits and stunning ballgowns were making their way towards the main entrance behind the columns.

Gawain's coachman dismounted and walked around to Alicya's side of the carriage. He opened the door, and offered his hand to help her out. Alicya's lilac-gloved hand was returned, and she stepped out onto the forecourt, thanking him for his assistance and for a smooth journey. Gawain followed her out of the carriage, resplendent in his dark blue, double-breasted jacket with black velvet trim, pristine white stock and black tricorne hat. As he offered his arm and she took it, Alicya's heart skipped a beat. It all felt like a dream. And yet, here they were, walking sedately, arm-in-arm, towards Lord and Lady Visset's mansion. They were about to attend the kind of ball that the palace had held on many occasions, but this time, she was not a little girl, peeking through the balustrades and wishing that she was one of those ladies; nor a teenager, forced to drink lemonade and sit and talk to her mother, father, aunt and uncles all night; and neither was she the property of the Crown, to be doled out in marriage to a man chosen by her parents.

This last factor, in particular, accounted for her soaring mood. She was free. There was no price you could put on that feeling. Tonight, in her stunning lilac ballgown, she would gavotte and cotillion with the man she loved. She would sip wine and make idle chat with associates and patients of Gawain, not with royals, MP's and palace officials. And then, at the end of the evening, probably light-headed, she would go home with the man she loved, and they would make love. As for no longer being a princess, she really couldn't care less. The only regret was that her poor mother and father must be grieving terribly. And so, she did the one selfish thing that she always did when heartache surfaced: she looked at Gawain, knowing he would look back, and give her that gentle smile. And he did.

As they glided around the left-hand staircase, an impeccably-attired grey-haired couple were exiting the opposite staircase. Both faces cracked into wrinkled smiles when they saw them. "Gawain, my boy," said the man. "I had hoped you would be here."

"Hello, Doctor Jukes," replied Gawain, warmly shaking the man's hand. "And Mrs Jukes. You look a picture," he said, bending down and kissing both of her cheeks. "Alyona," he said, turning to Alicya and using their agreed alias. "This is my mentor from medical college, Doctor Jukes, and his wife, Darya – who makes quite the finest scones in all of Wrenko. Doctor Jukes, Darya: may I introduce you to Alyona, my second-cousin from Ghantiss."

"He exaggerates, of course," said Darya, exchanging kisses with Alicya. "Alyona, what a pretty name. What's the origin, if I may ask?"

"It's actually Aldenocian. My grandfather was from Ghinbrude."

"Was he indeed! My mother was from Ghinbrude as well. They may well have known each other!"

"Indeed," said Alicya, as she and Gawain began to steer the Jukes' towards the entrance. Alicya sought her memory to change the subject. "Am I right in thinking, Darya, that Lord and Lady Visset have the most candelabra in all of Glennad, bar the palace at Ghantiss?"

"They do indeed, my dear. The reason being, that they have the largest ballroom in Glennad – after the palace, of course."

"Oh, I can't wait to dance there," enthused Alicya, before nodding towards Gawain. "Even if it does mean dancing with my cousin."

"My dear, there will be plenty of eligible bachelors around, this evening. George Douglas, the banker's son, for starters. Their family is absolutely loaded. And it's also rumoured that Lord and Lady Visset's son, Charles, has had a falling out with his fiancée, the Lady Elizabeth Wardlow. So, he may be on the market, too."

"Yes, but can they dance?" asked Alicya, as they approached the commissionaires. Gawain and Doctor Jukes were already handing over their invitation cards, and the four of them were ushered through.

"Well, perhaps you should find out," suggested Darya, as they found themselves in a vast entrance hall. There was an enormous staircase twenty yards further back, in the centre of the hall, but Alicya's eyes were drawn to the two equally enormous entrances to the ballroom beyond. As the four of them glided across the hall and entered the ballroom, Alicya stopped in disbelief. "It's actually *bigger* than the palace ballroom," she said, rather awestruck. "With *more* chandeliers!"

"You've visited the palace ballroom?" asked Darya, intrigued.

"Oh, yes, of course. I live in Ghantiss, and have been invited to the palace for afternoon tea by the Princess Alicya on several occasions. She and I share a love of horses and compete in the same shows."

"Wow!" responded Darya, impressed. "But maybe this ballroom size is an illusion. This room is full and hence may seem larger, whereas I'm assuming the palace ballroom was empty when you saw it."

"That's a very good point, Darya, you may be right," responded Alicya, actually thinking that it was likely to work the other way around.

"Can I interest you in wine and canapes, my dear?" ask Darya.

"Absolutely," agreed Alicya, who happily took the proffered glass and took a sip. "Mmm! That's nice."

With Gawain chatting away with Doctor Jukes, Alicya was quite happy talking to Darya, when her eye was caught by an attractive young woman with jet-black hair but very pale skin and severe scarlet lipstick, and wearing a black ballgown that revealed a very prominent cleavage. She was walking slowly towards them, wine-glass in hand and a mocking smile on her face, with eyes clearly only for Gawain. "Well, if it isn't the redoubtable Mr Rabbit," she said, interrupting Gawain and the doctor's conversation.

"Ah, yes, it is I," confessed Gawain with a sheepish smile. Alicya immediately sensed history here. "How lovely to see you again, Ashlyn."

"Oh, save me the fibs, Gawain," she responded, but still with that mocking smile. "Tell me: are you still hacking bodies after midnight?"

Gawain gave a large false laugh at that. "Ashlyn, please," he said, through gritted teeth.

"Oh, your secret's safe with me, Rabbit," she said, tapping the side of her nose. She then turned to look at Alicya. "Well, aren't you going to introduce me to your glamorous companion, Rabbit?"

"Erm, Rabbit?" questioned Alicya with a half-frown, half-smile.

"A personal secret," said Ashlyn, smiling sweetly. The look in her eyes was anything-but sweet, though.

"Erm, Ashlyn, this is my second-cousin, Alyona, from Ghantiss. I believe you already know Doctor and Mrs Jukes."

Ashlyn moved in to kiss Alicya on both cheeks. "Ah, a second-cousin," she said, before pulling back to inspect Alicya. "Excellent. This means that I won't need to poison you, Alyona!"

Despite such bluntness, Alicya couldn't help but laugh. "I...I don't really know what to say to that," she responded, at last.

"Oh, just ignore me, Alyona," said Ashlyn, winking at Alicya. "Gawain does. You'll soon get used to my ways. But we must chat later. I want to know *all* of the childhood gossip on young Rabbit here." And with that, she floated off towards another group of guests.

"Erm, I do apologise for that," said Gawain. "I really should have forewarned you."

"Oh, she's a *dreadful* woman," said Darya, quite put out by the whole lurid display. "And right now, she's probably only drunk about a tenth of her planned intake for the night."

"Yes," agreed Doctor Jukes, in a drawn-out way. "She's George Douglas Senior's daughter, by the way – George Junior's sister. Quite the wealthiest family in Visset after the Lord and Lady of the manor."

"Well, she's very beautiful," said Alicya.

"And deadly," responded Darya.

Alicya was dying to find out more about this Ashlyn, but it wasn't really appropriate in front of Doctor and Mrs Jukes. Fortunately, she was offered an outlet, as the string quartet on the raised dais to one side of the room had struck up a nice little gavotte. "Ah," she said, setting her empty wineglass down onto a passing tray. "Would my favourite cousin care to indulge me?" she asked, offering her arm to Gawain.

"But of course," he responded, and with a smile to the Jukes', they glided off to the dance floor where they joined a multitude of the rich and prosperous of Visset and where another couple immediately formed up a quartet with Gawain and Alicya. As they stood face-to-face, Gawain bowed and Alicya curtsied. They then moved towards each other, gently hopping and skipping in time to the music, and took each other's hands.

"So, who is Ashlyn, Gawain?" asked Alicya, a mild, neutral smile playing about her face.

They parted, each retreating a couple of steps, arms floating out to the side as they hopped and skipped to the beat, before moving towards each other again. "She's George Douglas' daughter," responded Gawain.

Alicya rolled her eyes, but Gawain was immediately turning to his right to face the other lady in their quartet (and she to her left to face the other gentleman), moving forwards, and then backwards – where they turned to face each other again. "That's not what I meant, and you know it," she said.

But Gawain was now off towards the other gentleman where they swapped places, and then she skipped and swapped places with the other lady, so that she and Gawain were face-to-face again. He remained silent, and Alicya sensed he was composing an appropriate response. She therefore waited until they were back in hold again. This time, she merely raised her eyebrows.

"She and I were engaged," admitted Gawain – just before all four of them came together in a circle. Seconds later, they were moving into a side-by-side position to demonstrate their solo footwork, whilst the other couple moved away to each side to give them room. This latest phase of the dance required them to alternate between face-to-face and side-to-side, and the conversation followed the former steps.

"When was this?"

"Seven years ago."

"When you were seventeen?"

"Yes, and she was sixteen."

"Too young!"

"Didn't I know it."

"Who finished it?"

"I did."

"And she still loves you?"

"Of course she doesn't. You heard the way she spoke to me."

"Oh, yes. I heard the way she spoke to you."

"What's that supposed to mean?"

At this point, they had to part to opposite sides to allow the other couple to display their solo footwork. When they eventually came back to each other, Gawain's words melted her heart. "I love you with all my heart, Alicya. A thousand times more than I ever loved Ashlyn."

Alicya couldn't help her beatific smile. *Now* she could enjoy the dance.

CHAPTER 84　　　　　　　　　　　　ARRAN
17th Tertiar, 1789　　　　　　　　　　Day 108, 09:45

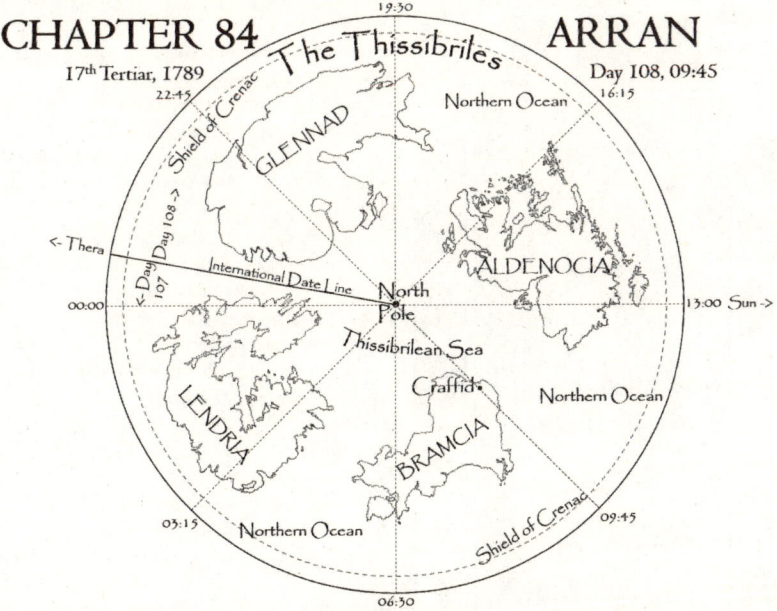

It was Arran's first time in Craffid, although not his first visit to Bramcia, having spent two separate family holidays in Byastwerthy Bay, and that fateful holiday in Natterspy when he was eighteen years old. He had never dreamed that he would return to Bramcia on such grave business.

The person Arran felt most sorry for was the Bramcian Prime Minister, David Grey-Doogell. He had recently announced two days of national mourning for the many miners who had been killed in a dreadful colliery fire at Cabrenar – although Grey-Doogell and his counterparts from Glennad and Aldenocia were already aware that the secret emergency meeting called by Lenahan Driscoll, was 'to impart the gravest of news'. Having suggested that each team bring its Astronomer Royal, it was likely that they had guessed the nature of the crisis if not the magnitude.

The venue was David Grey-Doogell's cabinet office in central Craffid. The conference table had been set for thirty-six places, slightly less than planned – this because the Aldenocian's were comprised solely of the ruling Republican politicians. It would appear that the message of 'all party representatives' had not resonated in Aldenocia. They, like Arran and his Lendrian compatriots, had arrived in Craffid yesterday, with all being accommodated in the city's most expensive hotels at the expense of the combined purse of the Lendrian and Bramcian governments.

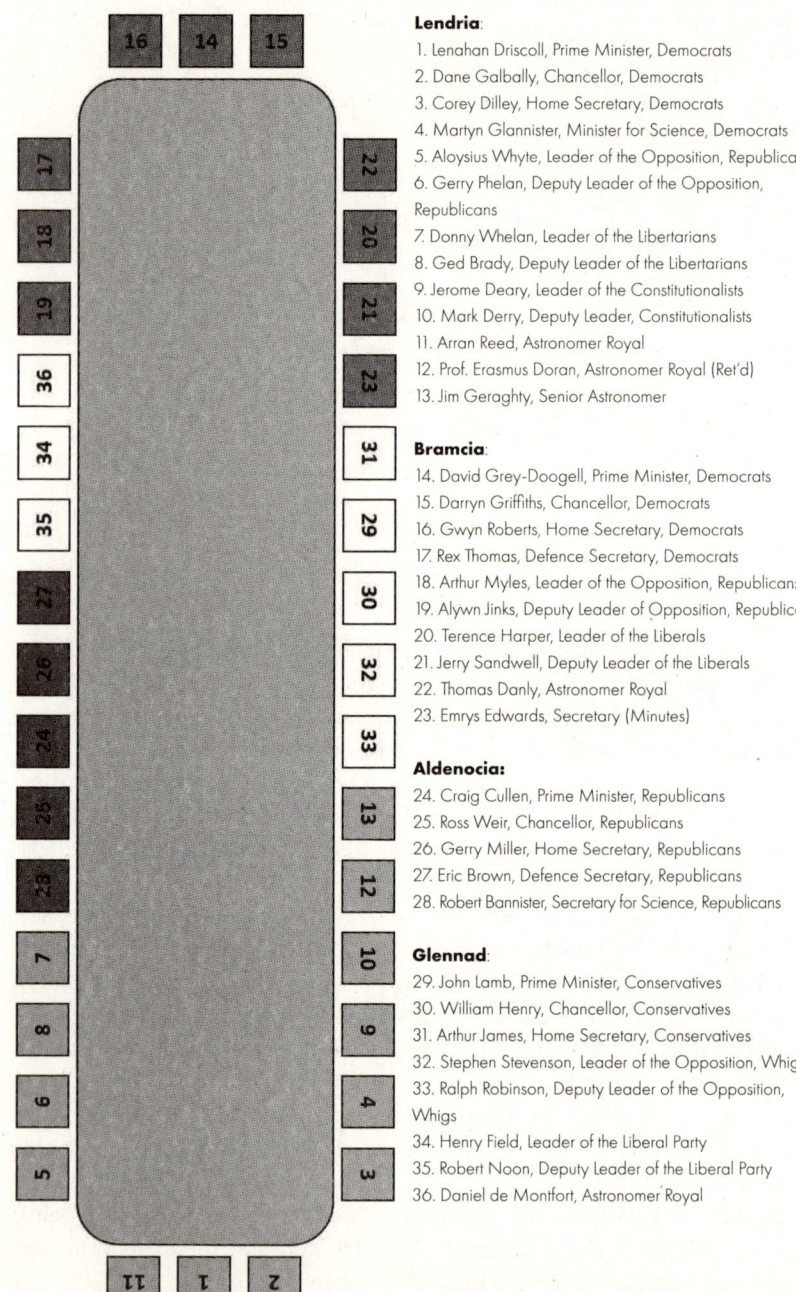

Lendria:

1. Lenahan Driscoll, Prime Minister, Democrats
2. Dane Galbally, Chancellor, Democrats
3. Corey Dilley, Home Secretary, Democrats
4. Martyn Glannister, Minister for Science, Democrats
5. Aloysius Whyte, Leader of the Opposition, Republicans
6. Gerry Phelan, Deputy Leader of the Opposition, Republicans
7. Donny Whelan, Leader of the Libertarians
8. Ged Brady, Deputy Leader of the Libertarians
9. Jerome Deary, Leader of the Constitutionalists
10. Mark Derry, Deputy Leader, Constitutionalists
11. Arran Reed, Astronomer Royal
12. Prof. Erasmus Doran, Astronomer Royal (Ret'd)
13. Jim Geraghty, Senior Astronomer

Bramcia:

14. David Grey-Doogell, Prime Minister, Democrats
15. Darryn Griffiths, Chancellor, Democrats
16. Gwyn Roberts, Home Secretary, Democrats
17. Rex Thomas, Defence Secretary, Democrats
18. Arthur Myles, Leader of the Opposition, Republicans
19. Alywn Jinks, Deputy Leader of Opposition, Republicans
20. Terence Harper, Leader of the Liberals
21. Jerry Sandwell, Deputy Leader of the Liberals
22. Thomas Danly, Astronomer Royal
23. Emrys Edwards, Secretary (Minutes)

Aldenocia:

24. Craig Cullen, Prime Minister, Republicans
25. Ross Weir, Chancellor, Republicans
26. Gerry Miller, Home Secretary, Republicans
27. Eric Brown, Defence Secretary, Republicans
28. Robert Bannister, Secretary for Science, Republicans

Glennad:

29. John Lamb, Prime Minister, Conservatives
30. William Henry, Chancellor, Conservatives
31. Arthur James, Home Secretary, Conservatives
32. Stephen Stevenson, Leader of the Opposition, Whigs
33. Ralph Robinson, Deputy Leader of the Opposition, Whigs
34. Henry Field, Leader of the Liberal Party
35. Robert Noon, Deputy Leader of the Liberal Party
36. Daniel de Montfort, Astronomer Royal

Arran was ushered to his place – an honoured position to the left of Lenahan Driscoll, at the head of the table. Despite his nerves at having to address the most powerful men in the Thissibriles, Arran looked around with interest. What he saw was a room dominated by the enormous mahogany conference table, the top of which was covered by a green cloth – Lendrian Green, thought Arran, which was rather appropriate – while the mahogany chairs were classily upholstered in brown leather. A series of floor-to-ceiling windows brought in plenty of light behind him and also to his left-hand side, although the latter set were separated by a grand fireplace in the centre of that long external wall. All floor-to-ceiling windows were flanked by long, dark red drapes. Meanwhile, the internal wall to his right contained two separate double-door entrances to the conference room, while elsewhere there were numerous paintings, porcelain and various other items of expensive mahogany furniture.

At present, delegates were looking at the large seating map on the wall between the two double-door entrances, memorising their number, and then hunting around the table for their numbered seat; others also took the opportunity to exchange grim handshakes, but didn't engage in conversation. As one of a trio who already knew they would be at the head of the table, Arran, Lenahan Driscoll and his Chancellor, Dane Galbally, had been amongst the first seated. Arran noticed that the Bramcian Prime Minister, David Grey-Doogell, was also in place at the opposite end of the table, with two gentlemen sat either side of him. Their eyes briefly met. Grey-Doogell gave him the shadow of a smile and a brief nod. Arran thought that he looked very tired. *The poor man would be getting even less sleep after he learned of the catastrophe facing them all.*

After further jockeying, the last delegate sat down. That was the cue for David Grey-Doogell to stand. Silence and expectation descended upon the room. "Gentlemen," he began. "Welcome to this extraordinary meeting of our nations. I must first confess to having prior knowledge of the reason for our gathering," he said, surprising Arran. "You will soon be briefed by Lenahan Driscoll and his team, but let me first reassure you: this is not a wasted journey. And when the invitations talked of mandatory attendance to discuss the gravest of issues, I can assure you that this was totally necessary. You will soon understand why. I am therefore not going to draw this introduction out. I am not even going to go around the table and introduce everyone. Suffice to say that we have our Lendrian contingent at the opposite end of the table, my own Bramcian contingent at this end, our Aldenocian colleagues to the right here – and the remaining delegates – on both sides – are from Glennad. Each contingent contains our respective Astronomer Royal – which I would imagine is a major clue as to where this is all heading.

"I would now like to invite Lenahan Driscoll, the Prime Minister of Lendria, to explain why we are all here today. Lenahan," he said, right palm facing upwards, before re-taking his seat.

Sat to Arran's right, Driscoll eased back his chair before standing, the chair's cushioned feet making a very apt sighing sound against the plush red carpet. Arran noticed that Driscoll's hands were slightly shaking – prompting his PM to place both hands on the table in front of him to steady them. "Gentlemen," he began. "I wish to God that I didn't have to make this speech. But it is vital that we tell you what we know, so we can all prepare for the future together. I won't prevaricate. The world faces a catastrophe. Right now, out there," said Driscoll, pointing to one of the windows to his left, "there is an asteroid, half a league wide, and it is heading straight for Thera."

As Arran expected, there was an outpouring of consternation and questions, despite many having already guessed the subject matter.

"I know, I know," said Driscoll, holding up both hands.

"Are you totally sure, Lenahan?" asked a grey-haired, impeccably-dressed man, down the table to their right. He spoke with great intensity.

"Sadly, we are 'totally sure', John," responded Driscoll, with equal gravity. Arran banked the fact that this must be John Lamb, the Glennadian Prime Minister. The two long-standing Prime Ministers were old friends and had introduced much mutually-beneficial international policy over the years. "Obviously we will be getting further opinions from your own Astronomer Royal, but three of my leading astronomers have concluded that, beyond any doubt, this asteroid will hit Thera on 1st Quinar."

Even greater consternation greeted this announcement. Again, Driscoll waited for the hubbub to die down. "I hear all of your questions gentlemen, and my team will answer them all before the astronomers of our four countries pool their resource, and try and understand as much as they can about the threat that faces us. But before they do that, I trust you understand now why we had to invite the heads of all parties, from all countries?"

A murmur of agreement greeted that statement, although the five Aldenocian Republican politicians squirmed a little uneasily in their seats.

"There was scepticism from some of my Lendrian political colleagues," continued Driscoll, briefly glancing to his left towards Aloysius Whyte. "But they were soon won over by my astronomers and their charts, and I am delighted to say, that every single man from Lendria here today, has not breathed a word of this to anyone: not even to their wives. As our story unfolds, you will understand why that is essential for everyone here, too." Driscoll followed that up by meeting all eyes in a sweep around the table.

"Now, as I can see a few of you are already starting to look rather queasy, I must tell you that we do have great hope for the future. Yes, there will be, at the very least, immense devastation, somewhere on our world. But we are optimistic that life here in the Thissibriles, and indeed elsewhere on Thera, will go on."

"You mean there's a chance it might not?" asked a thick-set, keg of a man to Arran's left. Arran noticed that although he was completely bald on top, he had thick brown curly hair at the back and sides.

Driscoll eyed the man steadily before responding. "Aye, Mr Cullen. There is a small possibility that this could be an extinction level event."

The room went silent. Great timing, Ocateshia, thought Arran. I bet you're about to hand over to me now.

"I would now like to introduce you to my compatriot, Arran Reed."

Arran held in his resigned sigh, and took his cue to stand.

"Arran, poor chap," continued Driscoll, patting him on the back, "has only been in the post of Lendrian Astronomer Royal for a handful of weeks – but it is he who spotted the danger, and it is he who has hopefully bought us enough time to prepare. For that, we should be extremely grateful. Arran will now take you through events that led to him discovering the asteroid, how he tracked it, how he plotted its course, and how he sought second and third opinions from experts regarding trajectory and impact. He will then explain the science and the various permutations that may face us, depending upon where the asteroid strikes, and what the ramifications will be for our planet for each scenario. He will use props to help demonstrate what we know…and he will also cover what we *don't* yet know.

"Once you are all briefed on the science, Arran will hand back to me and my team. We have already devised detailed plans as to how we will prepare for this catastrophe in Lendria under each scenario, and we will gladly share these plans with you. But for now, it is over to Arran Reed," said Driscoll, gesturing with his left hand and taking a seat.

Arran nodded to two Lendrian assistants by the fireplace to his right. They brought forth a large globe of Thera and an enormous easel with huge sheaves of paper draped over it, each containing painstakingly composed drawings to compliment his briefing.

"My esteemed colleagues," began Arran. He was immediately aware of everyone's undivided attention. "This all began on 13th Primar. I was observing a red giant in the constellation of Onori, when it became partially occluded – by something much closer to home in our own solar system. None of the planets or known objects were anywhere near that bearing at the time, so I was puzzled. Using our strongest telescope, I was able to see that the object in question was hundreds of millions of miles away, and which I estimated to be around half a league in size.

"At the time, I wasn't concerned; indeed, it was another eight days before I decided to look at where it had moved to. That was when I produced my first chart, plotting the object's trajectory. Again, I wasn't concerned. I went back to look another nine days later, and plotted its course over those initial seventeen days. This was when I first felt compelled to look on a daily, basis. At that time, its trajectory was missing Thera by millions of miles – bearing in mind that 'millions of miles' is a small margin in interstellar terms. But then, I notice a slight change in trajectory, that would bring it into line with Thera's orbit around our sun – perhaps having been struck by a smaller object itself to alter that trajectory. Worse still, against odds of several billion to one, Thera was moving towards the point in our orbit that the object would likely cross. So, what had been hundreds of *millions* of miles apart, was now being whittled down to hundreds of *thousands* of miles apart. And at half a league in size…"

Virtually every head around the table nodded or shook at Arran's tail-off, most of them with grim expressions on their faces.

"Anyway, by Day 98, I needed a second opinion – so I sought out my illustrious predecessor, and mentor, Professor Erasmus Doran, who is seated away to my right," said Arran, raising his right hand in the professor's direction. The professor raised his own right hand in acknowledgement. "And this is largely what I presented him with," said Arran, turning to the massive easel and pulling over the first enormous piece of paper. It showed six charts, arranged in two rows of three.

"I also have these smaller copies for everyone," said Arran, picking up a sheaf of paper and handing half to Lenahan Driscoll to his right and the other half to Aloysius Whyte to his left. Arran paused as the charts were passed around. "I would hope the charts are self-explanatory, but let me point out a few things. Firstly, George is my name for the asteroid. I'm afraid that when I realised it was a 'nasty' in the making, I named it after a particularly nasty bully I went to school with!"

The comment raised a few half-smiles. The charts were hypnotising everyone else as they digested the enormity of their content.

"Clearly, the yellow dot in the centre is our sun, the blue ellipse is our

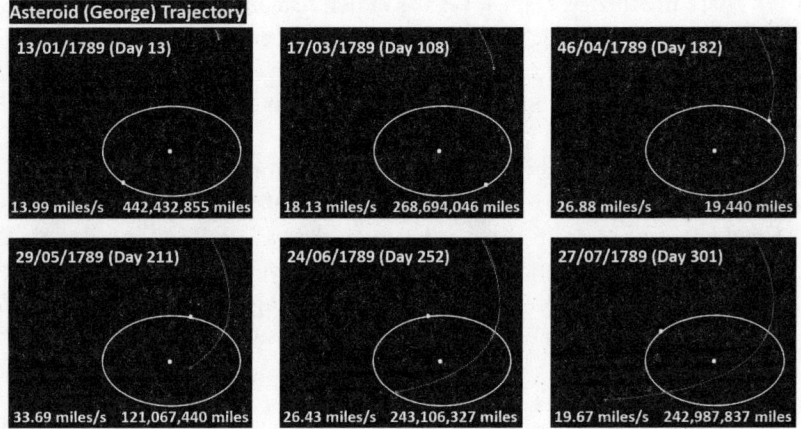

orbit around the sun, and the blue dot is Thera. The pink dot is George, and the pink trail maps George's trajectory. Clearly, the sun, Thera and George are not to scale. The dates and speed speak for themselves, whereas the distance on all charts, is the distance from Thera to George, and is measured in miles, as are all astronomical maps in the Thissibriles. If you are unfamiliar with miles, one league is equal to around three miles. So, divide by three for the distance in leagues.

"You will see that the second chart represents George's position today – as well as our own. It was ten days ago, on Day 98, when I first recorded that gentle swing in trajectory, which now – ten days further on – is even more pronounced. This has enabled me to predict the full swing through our orbit – should it, God willing, miss us – and then its route past the sun and then heading back out to our outer solar system.

"You will not, I assume, need me to explain chart number three?"

A stick-thin, middle-aged delegate further down the table to Arran's left stood up. Arran noted his wild grey hair and a monocle hanging loosely around his neck. "Daniel de Montfort," he said, his voice clipped and educated. "Glennad's Astronomer Royal. You have all intermediate charts, Arran – for every day since, what, the middle of Primar?"

"I do indeed, Daniel, and I'll be very happy to share them with you and your Bramcian counterpart, Mr Danly."

"And might I also ask," said de Montfort, his right hand now stroking his chin. He then looked straight at Arran. "The origin of George – the asteroid belt, presumably?"

"That's my theory, Daniel, yes. It's either a small asteroid forced out of the belt by Rufus Macula's gravity field, or it's a meteoroid fragment of one of the asteroids following a collision with another."

"Which then pitched it towards the inner solar system."

"Highly likely, yes."

"And, alas, Tarmia's gravitational field wasn't strong enough to suck it in?"

"I'm afraid it didn't pass anywhere near Tarmia's position on its orbit, Daniel."

As Daniel de Montfort re-took his seat, another middle-aged man sitting at the far end on the right also voiced his agreement with the likely origin of George. Arran noted that his left arm was in a sling and that he had remained seated. "I'm Thomas, by the way," he added, running his good hand through his bubbly brown locks. "Thomas Danly. Arran," he said, pinning him with a keen and intelligent gaze. "We obviously need to study these charts together, and take a look at George through our own telescopes. But I just wanted to say that even if this proves to be off kilter and we're not in the danger you fear, you've done the right thing by escalating this to Mr Driscoll, and Mr Driscoll has done the right thing by escalating to this forum."

"Thank you, Thomas. I have certainly not borne this burden lightly."

"And now it is a burden shared," interceded Lenahan Driscoll, still seated. "Yes, we may be fortunate and this thing shifts trajectory, or it will move slower or faster from its present position than we are estimating and miss Thera. But we need to prepare in case it doesn't. Arran is now going to explain more about where, when and how George may strike."

"Thank you, Mr Driscoll," said Arran, as he re-positioned the globe on the table. "Before I go on, Mr Driscoll just mentioned an important factor. My astronomer colleagues will be aware of this, but when objects enter an inner solar system and get closer to the sun, their speed increases. You can clearly see this from the charts. My calculations are based on measuring past speed by distance travelled, and the rate at which George is speeding up as it approaches our orbit. Once again, I will welcome validation from my Glennadian and Bramcian colleagues, and..." he said, turning to the Aldenocian delegates to his left, "will Charles Baxter not be joining us today?"

"We appear to have under estimated the importance of this meeting, gentlemen," said Craig Cullen, Aldenocia's Prime Minister, rather bashfully. He stroked his thick brown moustache, nervously. "I can only apologise. But we do have Robert Bannister here, our Secretary for Science. I would like you to involve him in all George-related discussions, please. Robert graduated from Ghinbrude University with a first in Applied Science – albeit twenty-five years ago – so he won't be as useless as the rest of us!"

"I look forward to learning more," said Bannister, also of middle age but with deep-set worry lines etched into his craggy face. "But please, you must continue about the mechanics of this asteroid strike."

"Thank you, Mr Bannister. Now, the globe," said Arran, spinning it slowly on its axis. Like the one back in Driscoll's office, it was populated with land and oceans around the northern hemisphere, and just a blank white space for the bottom half. "If George does strike Thera, our best hope is a strike in an ocean in the southern hemisphere," he said, rotating the globe and dragging a finger around the featureless lower half. "Of course, there may not be such a thing – and the southern hemisphere may be comprised solely of land – although that's highly unlikely. But assuming the asteroid hits southern hemisphere land, then the strike could well be an extinction level event."

As expected, that elicited multiple reactions. One question was asked the most, and once the hubbub had died down, it was asked again by the balding Craig Cullen. "Arran, please explain what you mean by extinction level event"

"Yes, of course. Well, a land-strike of that size, at the speed it will be travelling, would destroy everything within a one-hundred league radius. However, it could also destroy *all* animal life on Thera within a matter of weeks – as the sheer volume of rock and earth displaced would go into orbit around Thera and block out the sun's rays. Without the sun's rays, all plant life dies. Without plant life, all animal life dies."

The reaction around the table was profound. Some were cursing, others were praying, and at least three had their heads in their hands. Arran remembered Lenahan Driscoll's initial reaction: *My daughter is only four years old.*

"I'm sorry," continued Arran. "But there is no point in me trying to give you false hope. If the asteroid strikes land – anywhere on our world – it will most likely result in mass extinction. As Mr Driscoll said when I first broke the news to him, this asteroid could hit the South Pole bang on the nose, and even we at the north pole will likely die, eventually. Although that isn't a certainty – we will come to that shortly."

"Wouldn't the scale of the blast impact and resulting effects depend on other factors, though?" asked Daniel de Montfort. "Like the angle of impact, the resulting wind-speed generated by the blast-front, the terrain upon which it impacts, to name just three."

"Absolutely, Daniel, yes. But I have to present from a worst-case scenario."

"Of course you do, my boy," responded de Montfort, his friendly affectation reminding Arran of Professor Doran. "But I look forward to sharing theories and modelling as more data becomes available."

"Agreed, Daniel. As to our chances, our best is a Southern Ocean strike, our worst is a land strike – anywhere on Thera. That leaves the middle scenario – which is a strike in the Northern Ocean."

"And it's around half a league in size?" asked Thomas Danly."

"Yes, Thomas. A mile and a half wide."

"And it will be travelling at 26.88 miles per second – so, around 96,000 miles per hour or 32,000 leagues per hour?" asked de Montfort, re-checking the calculations on his notepad.

"Also correct."

Silence greeted these two facts as those present visualised such a monstrous event. "As you are all no doubt imagining, the effects will be absolutely catastrophic," confirmed Arran.

"But not extinction-level," said de Montfort.

"Correct again, Daniel. At least for a Northern Ocean strike."

"But still catastrophic for us," confirmed Driscoll. "The Therans in northern Epanaga, of course, will just pull back fifty leagues from the coast. They don't need to lose anybody at all. Thankfully, we do have high ground on all four main islands, and that is where everyone will make for if we know it's going to be a Northern Ocean strike."

"And I suppose," began Thomas Danly, rubbing his bubbly brown locks again, "that you're not going to know *where* it will hit Thera, until much nearer to impact time?"

"Correct again, Thomas," said Arran. "We suspect we will know two or three weeks before impact. We should also know the *angle* of impact as well – as Daniel alluded to earlier. However, we do hope to identify the hemisphere and octant of impact by early-to-mid Quarternar.

"So," concluded Arran. "Those are the options facing us. Mr Driscoll is now going to explain to you how Lendria is planning to approach this disaster, based on both a land strike and a Northern Ocean strike, and how it would make sense to coordinate our actions."

As Arran sat, relieved that all had gone to plan, Driscoll stood, cleared his throat, and began to explain how Lendria was planning to cope.

CHAPTER 85   WILL

17ᵗʰ Tertiar, 1789   Day 108, 17:00

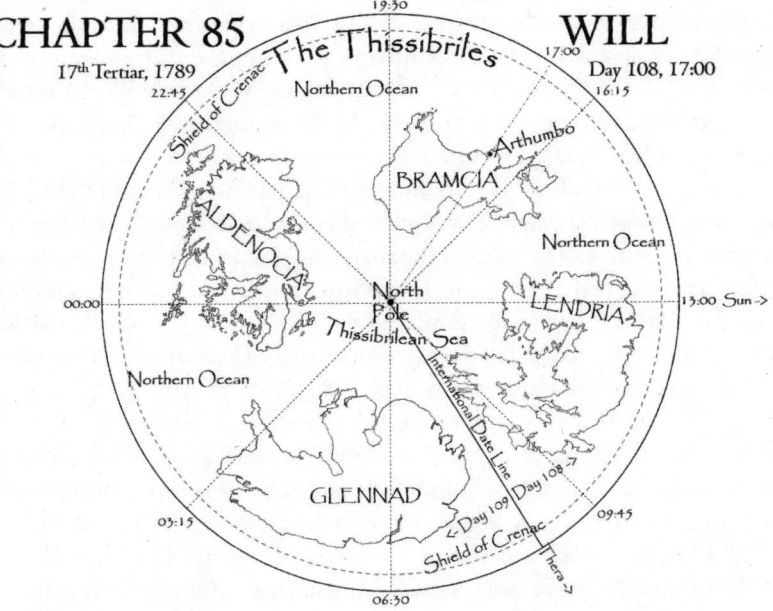

According to Nate Turner, the port they were now rowing into was Arthumbo. They had spent most of the last three fair-weather days hugging the coastline of the vast Byastwerthy Bay, with its long, sandy beaches, whilst heading largely in a south-westerly direction. Will reckoned they must be a long way south of Cabrenar now – which made him think of his Mam again. She was probably inconsolable, having likely buried one son with the other missing, assumed dead. So, why wasn't he making every effort to get back to her?

Will had spent much of the last three days going over why he hadn't run in Perebkom when he'd seen that poster. He had no answers. Meanwhile, he had begun to talk to Nate Turner more and more – learning about the history of mining in Cabrenar all the way back to Theran times over 1,300 years ago. Nate had told him all about open-cast mining and near-surface mining, which had been fashionable between the 13th and 17th centuries, and how the first deep shaft coal mine had been sunk in 1722, albeit much shallower than Cabrenar – which, in turn, was only half as deep as the largest and deepest coal mine in Bramcia, twenty leagues south-west of Cabrenar.

Turner had also told Will everything he knew about the Cabrenar disaster of 1779 in which Will's Da had been killed. Turner had been five hundred yards away above ground and had witnessed the infamous secondary explosion which had blown the lift back up the shaft and rammed it into the headstocks. The blast had thrown him to the ground and saved him from serious injury from flying debris. Will also learned of the rescue attempts, and how many rescuers had perished, too.

"Were you one of the men honoured?" he had asked, out of the blue. Will knew from his Mam, that Queen Joanna, had visited Cabrenar to award bravery medals to many of the surviving rescuers. At that point, Nate Turner had stopped rowing and had started fingering something around his neck. Will had had to force himself not to focus on the object, lest he give away his returned sight. "I was," Turner said. "I keep it against my skin at all times – to remind me of how lucky I was."

"Can I hold it?" Will had asked, looking into vacant space.

For a second, through his 'blind' eyes, Will had seen a look of uncertainty flicker across Turner's face. But then he'd pulled the chain from around his neck and placed it into Will's hands. For a brief moment, Will had felt an irrational urge to toss the medal over the side of the boat. Instead, he'd run his thumb over the surface of the medal, tracing the outline of the Bramcian dragon while his eyes had read what it said. "Are these words?" he'd asked, rubbing his thumb over them.

"Yes."

"What do they say?"

Turner had paused, briefly. "For Valour," he had replied in a cracked voice. Indeed, throughout this entire trip, Turner had been brimming with emotion, whilst also being protective and attentive towards Will. Nothing about him matched those insidious rumours.

Will had handed the medal back and asked Turner if he had been to his father's funeral. He had. "Was it a good service?" he'd asked.

"They were all given a good send off, Will. We even had the Prime Minister for two services on one day."

"How was my Mam? At my Da's funeral?"

Turner's face had creased in pain at that question. Was this an insight into what was driving Nate Turner? He might only be twelve, but Will knew deep sorrow when he saw it. Will couldn't help but feel for the middle-aged miner. He also knew that Turner's wife had died of cholera three years ago – perhaps that was why he was reacting the way he was to all of this talk about death and funerals.

Turner had eventually replied to Will's question. "She was in shock," he had said, quietly. "But she's a brave lady, your Mam."

Will had stopped asking questions about his Mam and Da after that, and the conversation had become educational again. Turner had described many of the great characters he had known down the years, and Will had listened to every word. *Perhaps this was what having a Da would have been like.* He then berated himself. This was also the man who had driven his brother to run away whilst holding a naked flame, and he was therefore the man who was responsible for the likely deaths of Robbie, Dylan and all of those other miners. That was the point that Will knew he was going to run, the next time they made landfall.

Will was pulled out of his reverie as Turner gently bumped their boat up against the stone harbour wall in Arthumbo. The first thing Will noted about Arthumbo was that behind the harbour to their right, the land climbed steeply, with six levels of houses. Off to the left, though, houses had been built up a narrow channel, which Will took to be a river emptying itself into the western flanks of Byastwerthy Bay, while at its mouth, there were various boats beached on a sandy inlet. Will figured this was his best route for escape – to run up whatever path existed alongside the river and try and follow the valley inland.

As these thoughts ran through Will's head, Turner was mooring the rowing boat to the harbour wall. "We'll need to climb up an iron ladder, Will," said Turner – perhaps trying to catch Will out. But Will had trained himself well, and looked 'blindly' in the wrong direction.

"Will you guide me?"

"Of course," was Turner's response. "Are you ready?"

"Yes," responded Will, standing and holding out his hands.

Turner took hold of his arms and steered him towards the iron ladder. Turner then positioned himself behind Will and said, "Now reach out. That's right. You've got it. Now climb up it."

Will was gripping the iron ladder before him that was as clear as day to his recovered sight, and he almost smiled. But "got it" was all he said. He then began to climb, making sure he had the right amount of uncertainty that a blind person might have. Turner then climbed up behind him, encouraging him all the way to the top.

Once they reached the top, it was only a short walk to Arthumbo's promenade. As they walked, with Turner steering Will with a fatherly arm around his shoulders, Will's eyes were darting backwards and forwards – looking for the best escape route, trying to spot the local militia or officials… and also looking out for more of those posters. He then spotted a grocers' shop, and just managed to bite his tongue to prevent himself from pointing it out. Instead, Turner did it for him.

"I see the grocers' shop, Will. There's a bench facing the harbour. I'm going to lead you over to it. Here we go. Can you feel that?"

Will made a play of reaching out with his hands to find the bench. "You want me to sit here and wait?"

"Aye, Will. I don't like what I've got to do now, but we're starting to run low on funds – and I can see fresh apples and pears out front. This bench is about fifty strides away, so if this goes wrong, you'll hear it all. I'll have to claim us to be father and son paupers and beg them to take mercy on us. No one will be heartless enough to leave a blind lad on his own, without his father. But if it goes right, I'll just walk casually back to you and then we'll go and collect some fresh water from the river that runs down into the bay. You all right with that?"

"I don't suppose I have much choice, do I?"

Turner half-smirked at that. "Nay, lad, I don't suppose you do."

As Turner turned his back on him and began walking towards the grocers, Will's heart began to thump. This was the moment. The path towards the grocers curved to the right, but in the middle of the bend there was another path heading off left – presumably towards the river. As Turner began to traverse the bend, Will found he was standing up; almost as if these were the actions of someone else. The boy then started off with a fast walk, his eyes drilled onto Turner's back…but still, Turner didn't turn around. Turner was now approaching the grocers, and Will was approaching the left-hand turn. Just another ten seconds, and he would be up the road and out of Turner's sight. But then, perhaps a sixth sense alerted Turner and he turned – to observe an empty bench. His face registered panic for a split-second – and then he saw Will. The look changed from panic to despair and then anger. Will registered all of that in a split-second, and then he was off.

Turner had no chance. Whilst Will's own breathing had returned to normal several days ago, he could still hear a permanent rattle in Turner's chest and his legs were no match for a twelve-year-olds, either.

As Will ran, houses on both sides passed in a blur. Approaching another corner, Will took a quick look over his shoulder to see how far back Turner was – and cannoned straight into a burly young man in a chunky fisherman's jumper who had just opened his garden gate and stepped out onto the road. They both went down in a heap – although Will was back on his feet in a second. But so was the man.

"Stop him!" screamed Turner from way down the road.

The man just grabbed Will's coat before he could get out of arms-reach.

"You a little thieving git, are you?" he asked. Will noticed the man had several missing teeth.

"Let go of me," shouted Will, and he tried to kick the man's shins – but the man just stepped backwards and Will's legs weren't long enough to connect. Will was still struggling in the man's grasp when a wheezing Turner caught up with them.

"Thank you," he gasped to the man. "And no, he's not a thief. Just a runaway."

"Liar!" shouted Will.

"Oi!" said the fisherman, cuffing Will across the back of his head. "You show respect to your elders."

"That'll do, mate," said Turner. "I'm his uncle. He keeps running away from his Mam. I was supposed to be taking him back."

"Liar! Liar!" repeated Will. "It's *you* I'm running away from!"

"Pah!" said Turner, rolling his eyes. "You look after 'em and this is all the thanks you get."

"Yeah, well, you can sort out your differences without me," said the fisherman. "I'm late for me evening shift." And with that, the man hurried off down the street in the direction of the harbour.

"Why do you do that, Will?" asked Turner, in a voice deep with pain.

"Are you seriously asking me why?"

"But I'd never do you any harm, son. I want to look after you."

"What with no home, no money, no food and a stolen boat?"

Turner just looked downcast at that.

"What do you want from me?" asked Will.

"I want to put things right, son."

"How?"

"I don't know. But I can't hand you in, can I? They'll likely hang me."

"So, you think I should play along just to keep you from the noose?"

Turner was quiet for a while. "I don't know what to think," he said, eventually. "I should have stayed in Cabrenar and handed you over. But I ran because of the rumours."

"What rumours?"

"Unfair rumours." Turner looked skywards, his eyes brimming. "I was suffering. After my Alice died. Suffering in silence, I was. And they gave me this kid as an apprentice. Mikey Laing, his name was. Came from a notorious family. Was playing me up from minute one. And his work-rate was poor, too. The total opposite of your Dylan."

Will frowned, now confused. "What happened?"

Turner looked up to the heavens again and sighed. "I lost my rag with him. Sometimes I can't control my temper. I clouted him around the back of the head. I'd had enough of his cheek. The little bastard had started calling me a kiddie-fiddler. Except he couldn't prove it. But neither could I prove otherwise."

Will was quiet now, digesting this new information.

"The thing is, son," continued Turner. "These rumours – they stick. Especially coming from a family like the Laings. They didn't give a fig about the impact on my reputation. So, they started putting it about in the pubs that I'd been touching up their Mikey. Again, no one could prove anything. And little Mikey played along, spouting a pack of lies. Life was a living hell. And I'd done nothing wrong."

Will remained silent. He was even starting to feel guilty for running. And for his doubts about Turner.

"Eventually, Jed Morris decided to take no action – no doubt convinced by my brother-in-law, Stan. So, you can imagine where I thought things were going with young Dylan doing a runner."

"But *why* did he do a runner?"

Turner paused again, agonising over his next words. "Because of what I told him."

"What do you mean? What did you tell him?"

"The truth."

"What truth?"

Again, Turner was agonising. "Me and your Mam. We knew each other – back in the day. Even when she was courting your Da. And afterwards, too."

"After what?"

Another pause. "After they got married."

Will was stunned. *His Mam? And Turner? They were friends?*

"I didn't always look like this, son," said Turner, indicating his grimy, unshaven face and straggly hair.

"I don't understand," said Will shaking his head. "What are you trying to say?"

"I've lost one son, and I'm not going to lose another."

"I didn't know you had a son, Mr Turner. I'm sorry if you lost him. But what's that got to do with me?"

Turner looked at Will and smiled. "Because you are the other son, Will. I'm your real Da."

CHAPTER 86   MAGNUS

18th Tertiar, 1789   Day 109, 10:30

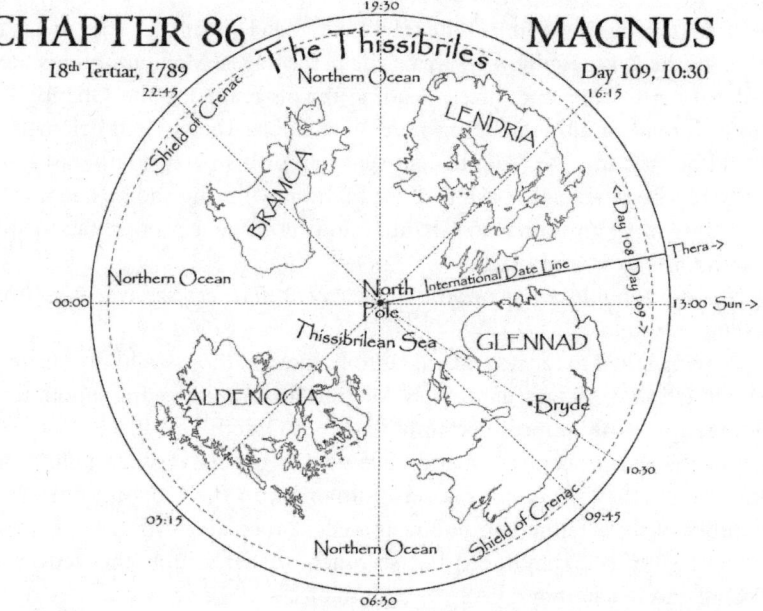

Four days had passed since Magnus had shot Harry Black's lackey in the rear. The fugitives should have been ripe for the taking, but nothing had gone right since. The Earl's Leet militia captain he'd sent up towards Roth's Cave had never returned, meaning he and his two men had probably been ambushed, leaving Magnus torn with indecision. Clearly, at least one of the four renegades had gone up that path. Two was most likely. But which of the other three fugitives had accompanied their injured companion? Or perhaps three had gone to the cave and just one man had led the four horses down into the valley. Or had *all four* gone up to Roth's Cave, and the tracks they were following had been made by four other horsemen?

He could have sent another three or more men back, but the risk had been losing them as well, whilst whittling down the main party, and Magnus was determined he wouldn't be held up again by bandits. So, in the end, he'd decided to stick with the evidence – which was the tracks of four horses. One of the militiamen believed that two of the tracks suggested mounted men and the other two unmounted. If he was right, Magnus would have bet on Oscom and Black taking the horses, with Black sending his other lackey to look after the injured man – effectively cutting them both loose. That's certainly what he would have done. But then again, they might be following the two lackeys!

Two days later, they'd lost the tracks completely after the renegades had taken to the River Rednewt. Playing the percentages, Magnus and his men had bet on Oscom and Black heading downstream for the Ghantiss to Brygmis road, and then making a break for a port. The obvious destination would be Brygmis, so Magnus had sent half of his party south-east once they'd reached the relative safety of the highway, while he had turned north-west, intending to return to Ghantiss and mobilise a proper nationwide search for Oscom and Black.

It's one thing evading twenty men, Oscom, but let's see you hide from several thousand.

Having failed to locate and kill Oscom, though, they would now have to go public about Alicya's 'abduction'. Magnus had mixed feelings about that, although it would almost certainly flush out Oscom and Black. Within a day of the announcement, they'd have posters up in every town, and not only would they have every local militiaman on the lookout, but every member of the Glennadian public as well, as they did love their princess. Magnus smirked. They loved her so much, that if a mob chanced upon Oscom and Black, they'd likely be torn to pieces.

At present, Magnus was in the centre of Bryde. From his school history lessons, Magnus recalled that, in 1720, Bryde had become famous as the location of the first mill to harness the power of water to drive cotton-spinning mills. Multiple mills now flanked the River Rednewt which passed right through the middle of the town and churned out thousands of garments for the Glennadian people.

Magnus and his men were about to mount their horses, bound for Ghantiss, when he noticed a street performer singing and playing a lute in the market-place with his back to them. Magnus briefly noted that the man had long straight brown hair flowing down his back, but was completely bald on top, while his mustard-coloured tights made his thin legs look like those of a chicken. Nevertheless, there was quite a crowd gathered around him; children sat cross-legged at the front and adults from all walks of life stood behind. They were all having a good old belly laugh at the performer's songs, too.

Magnus briefly considered listening for a few minutes, as he was in sore need of some light-hearted entertainment. Instead, he turned to address the remaining captain of the Earl's Leet militia. "Well, Gotch," he began. "I can't blame you or your men for our failure to turn up these brigands. On the contrary, I have appreciated your support these last six days, and I wish you and your men a safe journey back to Earl's Leet." Magnus then held out his hand, which was firmly grasped by the strait-laced Gotch.

"I'm sorry we couldn't turn them up too, Your Royal Highness. Obviously, we will continue to search in the Earl's Leet area and we will get word to you as soon as possible if we learn anything of importance – or better still, if we catch the brigands."

"Thank you, Captain. And thank you to you all," said Magnus, nodding at Gotch's men. "I fervently hope that you find your three men, safe and well. If they are not, then I will ensure that Oscom and Black's executions are drawn out that little bit longer."

With that said, the Earl's Leet contingent nodded their thanks and then wheeled their horses around and set off for the Rednewt Valley path that would take them back home – leaving Magnus alone with Marler, Gage and his two surviving palace soldiers. "Well," said Magnus. "How long do you think it will take us to get back to Ghantiss, Marler?"

Marler didn't appear to be listening. Instead, he was paying close attention to the entertainer in the market-place.

"Are you ignoring me, Marler?"

"No, Sir. I think you might want to hear this."

"What? Hear the song -."

Marler actually had the temerity to shush him at that point.

As I was going to fair Earl's Leet, a shocking sight I saw, came the dulcet tones of the performer, drifting towards them on the wind. Magnus immediately tuned in to what Marler had already rumbled.

For just before where three roads meet, I peered through carriage door.

Magnus indicated for one of the soldiers to take the reins of his and Marler's horses.

Twas like a scene from comedy, or Glennad's daftest farce.

Magnus gestured with his head to Marler in the direction of the performer.

For I kid you not, I caught a glimpse of the Prince's hairy arse.

As the performer delivered that line, Magnus and Marler were around thirty paces from him. As soon as the last two words were out, the men in the crowd erupted into guffaws of laughter, and the women into high-pitched cackles. However, both men and women were totally outdone by the children, who screamed with laughter to hear such a rude word sung in public. The uproar was also luring locals from all over the market square to converge rapidly on the performers' little stage to see what they were missing. Meanwhile, Magnus' face was now twisted with fury, as the performer struck up his second verse – which contained the same first two lines as the first verse.

As I was going to fair Earl's Leet, a shocking sight I saw,

By now, Magnus and Marler were a dozen paces from the stage, but were obscured from the crowd's view by the milling citizens of Bryde.

For just before where three roads meet, I peered through carriage door.

Marler put a hand on Magnus' arm to stay him from going any nearer.

The bare-butt Prince was sobbing loud, robbed by Harry Black.

No matter how much better Magnus had become with anger control, this was a humiliation too far. What was more annoying was the fact that the scenario being painted by the performer was wholly inaccurate. *He had clothed himself in Gage's rags to avoid this, dammit!* And he had most certainly not been seen naked by the public!

Unaware the world could see his Royal sac and crack.

Magnus shrugged Marler's hand off his arm and made to surge forward, but Marler grabbed his arm again. "Sir," he began, in his ear. "You can't win here by wading in."

Magnus also noted the vaguest hint of amusement in Marler's face. It did not amuse him in return. By this stage, though, the blissfully unaware performer was off on another verse.

As I was going to fair Earl's Leet, a shocking sight I saw,

"Wade in or walk away, you'll only make it worse, Sir," clarified Marler.

For just before where three roads meet, I peered through carriage door.

"What do you mean, Marler? I can't allow this."

"Oh, help me, help me," cried the Prince; I need shirt, pants and sock.

"You need to play along with them, Sir. Make it seem like you're in on the joke. The punters will respect you for it. They might even love you for it."

And as he turned around to plead, we clocked the Royal cock.

As Magnus thought on Marler's words, vast gales of laughter were engulfing the market square, and delaying the commencement of the next verse by up to a minute. During this time, Magnus gradually began to see the sense of Marler's words. He could do this.

"What you can do, Sir," continued Marler, "is walk up behind the performer and just sit on that vacant seat of his. He won't see you – but the crowd will. They'll most likely die of belly-laughter if you do that."

"My dear Marler," began the Prince, now suitably calmed, but with a new feral look in his eye. "I do believe I've under-judged your talent." And with that said, Magnus stepped up the three steps onto the mini-stage, and plonked himself down on the vacant seat, right in the middle of the performer's next line. Magnus then crossed his legs, folded his arms and kept his expression neutral.

As I was going to fair Earl's Leet, a shocking sight I saw.

If the reaction to the punchlines had been gales of laughter, the apparent appearance of the subject of the song caused hurricane-levels of paroxysm. Unaware of his co-stage performer, the singer clearly thought that the crowd were just getting even more into his brilliant little song.

For just before where three roads meet, I peered through carriage door.

Magnus raised his eyebrows, cocked his head and pursed his lips, and the wall of laughter went up another notch. The singer was now having to delay his next line, and when he delivered it, he had to positively bawl at the top of his voice to be heard; meanwhile, his lute may as well have had no strings, such was the overwhelming noise in the market-place.

The Prince was crying open now, sobbing great big squalls.

Magnus put both fists to his eyes, and rubbed them in mock-crying mode and then thrust out his bottom lip, while members of the audience were now actually throwing themselves onto the floor, incapable of remaining upright.

And with each racking sob he flashed his swinging Royal balls.

At which point, Magnus stood up and threatened to open his royal breeches. It was at this point, though, amid the tumult of laughter, that the singer cottoned on to the fact that people were pointing not at him, but *beyond* him. When he turned around and saw who his co-performer was, the poor man simply fainted, crushing his lute in his fall. Magnus then took a bow and exited back-stage.

It was said for many decades after the event, that three people had indeed died laughing that day.

CHAPTER 87   CALIDIUS

20th Tertiar, 1789   Day III, 11:00

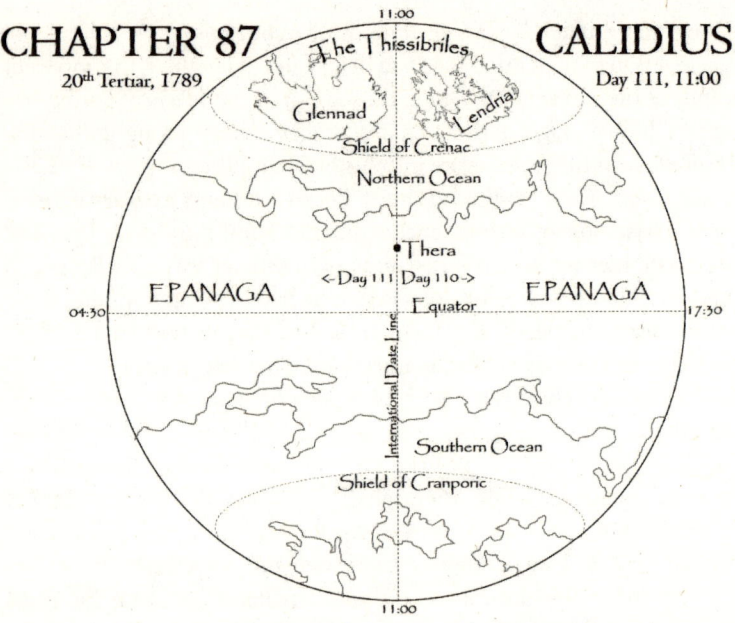

Calidius was running another of his inner sanctum sessions, except this time, his informants were swollen by one more member to five, with the return to Thera of General Macrinus Severus Vitellius, following a glorious and largely bloodless overthrow of rebellion in Demonacia.

"And you say that General Draxaelen had no idea until you stepped off the ship?"

"I suspect the penny dropped slightly earlier than that, Your Imperial Majesty, although by no more than thirty seconds. I believe he saw my face as our ship was docking."

"By which stage your land forces were approaching the harbour?"

"Exactly as planned, Your Imperial Majesty."

"And your legendary reputation grows, my friend. Incidentally, you can dispense with the honorary titles in this forum, Macrinus."

The general issued a rare smile. "Thank you…Calidius," he said. "Although I must admit that I was very sore at missing your coronation."

"You merely missed the Arch-Primate prattling on, whilst indulging in an orgy of self-aggrandisement. No offence meant, Gaitonius."

The white-haired seventy-six-year-old archbishop of *Navio* merely raised his hand and rolled his eyes.

"And elsewhere, it would appear that I have missed much and more," said Macrinus, his eyes flitting from Calidius, to his son, Romulus, and back to Calidius again.

"I do hope your son hasn't broken his vows," said Calidius, his expression quite unfathomable.

"He has told me nothing Calidius – other than he was relieved at my return and that matters were serious. Although given the abrupt nature of my recall, I had already worked that out for myself."

"Excellent. Thank you, Romulus. Your loyalty is appreciated."

"In unity, there is strength," chanted Romulus.

"Indeed," agreed Calidius. "General," he began. "I am sure you have been wondering which foe in all of Epanaga, can so-challenge the might of the Theran Empire, that I have to recall my best officer from the field. Well, the answer to that is – none. Not on our planet. Our 'foe' comes from beyond the stars."

Macrinus frowned, unclear where this was going.

Fifteen minutes later, his frown was even more intense – although Calidius could see that his agile brain was already addressing their predicament and no doubt adjusting to combat each of the three likely scenarios. "So, we won't know for sure, for many weeks?"

"That is correct, General."

"And in the meantime?"

"This is where you come in, my loyal friend. We have a movement that we are about to put into operation, which we are calling *'Expurgatio'*. I need you to lead *'Expurgatio'*, General – as I need a leader with a strong stomach, someone whose loyalty is beyond question, and someone who understands why we need to prepare for this testing time by ridding ourselves of dead wood. Ironically, if it should turn out that Nessemi is to strike land, we will merely have done the dead wood an advanced favour. If it strikes ocean, and the majority of this world's inhabitants survive, then we will have done the Neo-Theran Empire a large favour instead."

"What would you have me do, Your Imperial Majesty?"

"*Expurgatio* will consist of six separate cleansings. These will be as follows."

Macrinus was quickly briefed on the six purges, against lepers, the insane, prisoners of war, thieves, prostitutes and those who dealt in narcotics, and he thoroughly approved. Indeed, thought Calidius, he had greeted the task with the relish he had been hoping for.

"And you say that Edict 1 will be proclaimed on the 30th of Tertiar?"

"That is the plan. Ten days for you to prepare. I shall place whichever resources you need at your disposal."

"Are you up to the challenge, son?" asked Macrinus of Romulus.

"Unswervingly, father."

"I will make the imperial office available for you to use as a base for your operations, General," said Calidius. "I shall also be paying you regular visits to keep abreast of plans and progress. Please feel free to use me or my influence wherever you feel it is needed. Oh," said Calidius, raising a forefinger. "And there is one more thing, General."

Macrinus looked at his emperor and raised an eyebrow.

"The six edicts are the public-facing side of your operation. In between executing the six purges, please feel free to execute whomever else you feel is not suitably serving the Neo-Theran Empire. There will be no questions asked. All I shall need is a briefing – ideally before execution."

This time, the smile on Macrinus' face lingered for much longer than a second. "And is there any limit to the scope?"

"I would appreciate advanced knowledge of any *senior* figures in our society, but I trust implicitly in your judgement, so don't expect any resistance from me."

"Thank you, Your Imperial Majesty. I shall not let you down."

"Oh, I'm counting on that, General." Calidius' own smile also lingered.

CHAPTER 88   JAKE

20th Tertiar, 1789   Day 111, 12:00

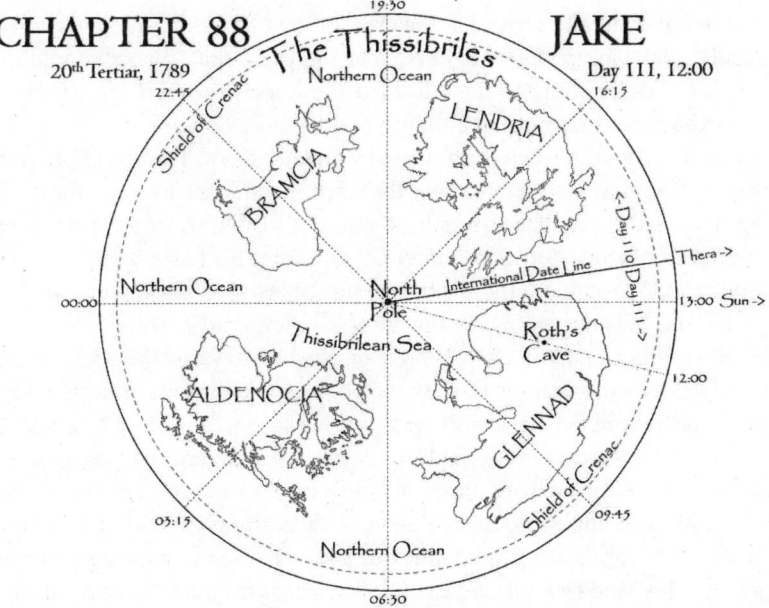

The death of the three Earl's Leet militiamen had been on Jake's conscience for the last six days – although never more so than when, having buried them, he had run down the hill to check for other signs of pursuit, only to find three horses tied to a tree, patiently awaiting the return of their riders.

With a clear view of the valley to the south showing the coast was clear, Jake had given a couple of whistles: the signal for Turnip to limp back down the hill again. Having disposed of the immediate threat, they had decided against getting holed up in a cave with only one entrance, and would only return after six days for their rendezvous with Harry and Swede. Since then, they had spent their time in the valleys to the north-west of Roth's Cave, and the Esou Valley to the north-east. They were now walking back up towards the Esou Aqueduct, Jake mounted on a fine black horse and Turnip on a bay, while Jake loosely held the reins of the third horse, a chestnut filly, which walked sedately in between them. Turnip's wound had not become infected and had begun to heal nicely, such that he was now more prone to bouts of good humour.

In the last six days, they had only had to hide on a couple of occasions. It seemed the Earl's Leet authorities had put their faith in Magnus and his posse apprehending the outlaws, and had presumably gone back about their business of maintaining the most peaceful settlement in Glennad.

When they finally arrived at the crest of the path, alongside the ruined aqueduct, Jake jumped off his horse and indicated that Turnip should do the same. "We're going to have to lead the horses through the woods – unless you fancy being cut in half by a low-hanging bough."

It took an hour to reach Roth's Cave by foot, thanks to Turnip's improving mobility. The cave was set just above the treeline inside the top of a limestone crag, but as the cave faced north, it was not visible from the path nine hundred feet below. "Let's see if anyone's at home," said Jake, tying his own mount and the spare mount to a bough on the last tree before the cave.

"It looks big enough to take the horses, matey," said Turnip.

"First things first, old chap," said Jake, striding towards the opening. As he walked into the shadow of the cave opening, he looked upwards into a space that resembled the inside of a cathedral. The ground-rocks which gave entry to the cave were angled steeply upwards, and had been worn smooth by the footwear of thousands of visitors over the centuries. The combination of angle and smoothness, with nothing to hold onto would test the most sure-footed of people, but Jake was used to balancing on the deck of a ship, and he managed to spring upwards from foot to foot without too much trouble. Turnip ended up ascending on his hands and knees – and even then, he found himself sliding backwards on a couple of occasions.

"How do you do that? he moaned, after finally making it and now standing again.

"Do what?"

"Your mountain goat impression."

Jake laughed, then turned and shouted into the back of the cave: "Hello." The echo took a while to die away. Silence greeted them.

Jake turned back and looked out of the cave entrance. Of the cave, all he could now see was blackness, caused by the stark contrast with the brilliant sunlight beyond with the cave entrance framing a pretty picture of green trees, green hills and blue sky. When he turned back to look into the depths of the cave, he could see nothing for a while until his eyes gradually became reaccustomed to the gloom. "No one here but us brigands, old chap. Let's see if we can find this sub-cavern that Harry was on about."

With Turnip in tow, Jake moved cautiously towards the back of the cave, then doubled back and followed the wall to their right-hand side. Jake was looking for the narrow fissure that Black had described. *"You have to walk past it, and then look backwards for a crease in the wall."*

Jake spotted the crease. He squeezed into it and then crouched down – and sure enough, to his right, there was an opening. However, without a candle, it was pitch black wherever the low tunnel was heading. "Well, it's here," he said back over his shoulder. "But I don't fancy going any further without light. So, if you wouldn't mind backing up, old chap."

Turnip did as he was asked, and Jake managed to shuffle out backwards. "Chances are we'd remain undetected in there," he said, as he stood up again. "But I still say I'd rather not get trapped in a place with only one way in and out."

"Me too," agreed Turnip with a shudder.

They suddenly looked at each other, sharply. They'd both heard a scuff or a footfall or something dropped – and the sound had come from the sub-cavern. Jake indicated with his head that they head back for the entrance. "Let's go and get the horses fed and watered."

Two minutes later, when they had negotiated the lethal slippery slope at the front of the cave, Turnip said: "I didn't imagine that, did I?"

"Certainly not. Although it could have been an animal."

Turnip looked dubious. "What kind of an animal would live up here?"

"A goat perhaps. Or a bat."

"A goat wouldn't be able to get in."

"My money is on a bat then. Or a person."

"But who?"

"Someone else trying to evade the law, perhaps."

"You don't suppose Prince Magnus' men are lying in wait, do you?" asked Turnip, suddenly alarmed.

"Well, if they are, it's the worst plan in the history of mankind."

Turnip laughed at that. "Aye, that it is," he agreed.

"I suggest we just sit out here and wait. If they or it comes out, then we'll know."

"And if we have visitors from below?"

"I'll hear them coming long before they reach the treeline."

It was two hours later when Jake heard the sound of approach from below. He gestured to Turnip to ready his pistol, whilst he unholstered his own and slipped silently down the path. Whoever was coming wasn't making any attempt at stealth, so it was unlikely to be any pursuers. Ten seconds later, Jake made out the dulcet tones of Harry Black. Ever-suspicious, though, Jake hid behind a bush and kept the safety catch off his pistol. Eventually, Black's significantly toned-down roughspun outfit revealed itself, leading two horses, followed by Swede leading the other two. Jake moved out of hiding onto the path and nodded at the horses. "Would you believe we've got seven now?"

"Ah, they sent three men back, did they?"

"They certainly did."

"I take it we don't need to worry about their former riders."

"You take it right."

"Ha! You're as much a wanted outlaw as I am, now then."

"Seems I am," agreed Jake, ruefully. "I take it you have a few stories to tell yourself."

"I do indeed," agreed Black. "Although we did not have to spill any blood. We did, however, lay eyes on an extremely duped prince of the realm, who was last seen heading for the Ghantiss to Brygmis highway."

"Did he have a party of eighteen."

"He did indeed," confirmed Black.

"Good, that means he didn't send anyone else back. Anyway, follow me," he said, holding out his right arm ahead. "We can settle down in this clearing and share updates."

Later that afternoon, as they shared a light meal of skewered squirrel and hard bread, Jake remembered something. He looked around first, taking in the approaching dusk. "We have another guest, by the way."

Black and Swede both looked all around them. "Another guest?" questioned Black.

"Yes – in your sub-cavern. Although we're not sure if it's animal or human at present. But my money is on the latter.

"Intriguing," said Black. "And clearly very unsociable, too."

"Would you want to share supper with the likes of us?" asked Turnip, turning both palms up.

"Talk of the devil," said Swede.

Jake looked to the mouth of Roth's Cave. Stood at the top of the slippery section of rock was a rather pathetic sight. Judging by the child's height, the boy was only seven or eight years of age. He wore filthy rags and his hair was long and unkempt. Jake stood slowly, and slid a portion of squirrel meat off his skewer. "Are you hungry?" he asked, loud and clear.

The child looked at Jake intently for several seconds, and then nodded.

"I'll put it on this rock here," said Jake moving forwards and placing the meat on top of a rock before retreating back to their campfire.

The boy hesitated for several seconds, clearly not trusting strangers, but hunger eventually won out over trust. Agile as a monkey, he hopped down the slippery section, picked up the chunk of meat, sniffed it once and then popped it into his mouth. He chewed for several seconds before swallowing. The child then looked at Jake and smiled.

"Would you like some bread as well?" offered Jake.

The boy didn't need a second invitation. Overcoming any fear, he closed the distance between them in six lithe hops, and took the bread from Jake's outstretched hand. Once the bread was devoured, he looked at Jake again and smiled.

"Would you like water as well?" asked Jake. The boy nodded, so Jake gestured to Turnip to pass over his water cannister. The boy drank thirstily.

"Well," said Jake, when the cannister was handed back. "Do you have a name? I'm Jake, by the way. The man sitting on the rock is Harry. And, you're not going to believe this, but these other two gentlemen are called Turnip and Swede." Both men raised their hats to the child, who smiled again – but still remained silent.

"I wonder if he's mute?" suggested Swede.

"Maybe that's what we should call him," added Turnip.

"What, Mute?" asked Swede.

"It's good enough for me until we find out his real name."

They all turned to look at Mute – who just smiled back again.

CHAPTER 89　　　　　　　　　　　　　　WILL
20th Tertiar, 1789　　　　　　　　　　　Day III, 16:30

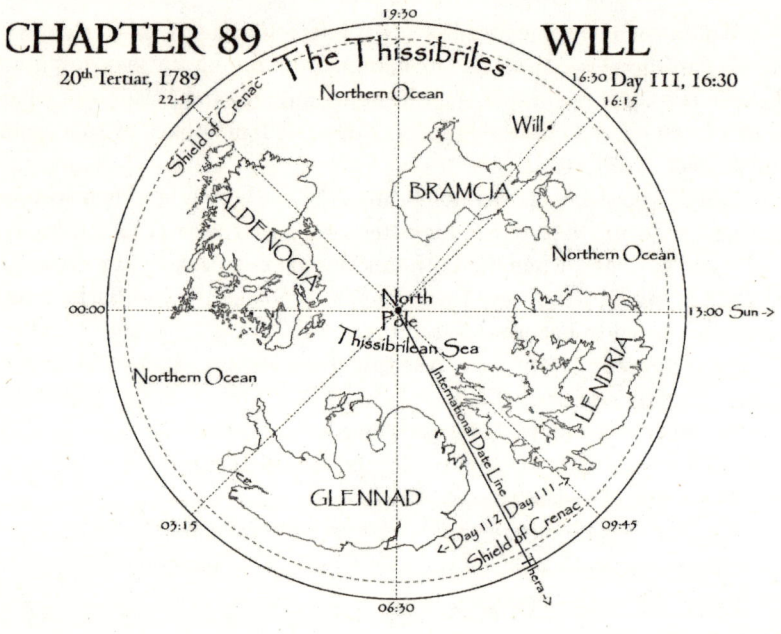

"You're not my Da! My Da died in 1779. You'll never be my Da!"

On reflection, Will wished he had remained calm, despite the enormity of Turner's claim. Turner's pain and grief had worsened at Will's reaction – but was it really for the reasons he claimed? Then again, Will knew the Laing family. The father was a convicted thief, who had been given a second chance at the ironmakers factory, Cabrenar's only other major workplace besides the colliery. But Laing Senior had proved divisive – fellow workers either loved him or hated him. And his kids were always in trouble, particularly Mikey Laing. Three years older than himself, Mikey Laing had dished out a couple of thick lips to both Will and Dylan in the past, and was a well-known pilferer himself. He also lied habitually – which explained why allegations against Turner hadn't been acted upon. But like Turner had also said: mud sticks. The Laing family would have known that when they made their accusations. And despite the dropped charges they had apparently continued shouting vile names at Turner in the street, throwing dog faeces at his house, and inciting others to either shun or victimise him.

It had taken three days, but eventually, Will had begun to reconcile his conflicting emotions and the conflicting angles of truth. Alas, in that time, events had moved beyond Will's control.

That first evening, Turner had pulled off his most significant theft, to date – perhaps fuelled by recklessness following Will's snub. In a secluded and wealthy part of Arthumbo, he had strolled up to a moored cutter, as bold as brass, boarded it with Will and their also-pilfered supplies, and then cast off. No one had batted an eyelid, although at the time, Will had doubted that Turner would know how to sail a cutter. He was soon proven wrong. "It's all about the wind, Will," he'd muttered, that first evening. The only words he had spoken all night.

With his sight back, Will had watched Turner closely. He had first taken a fabric cover off the main sail, grabbed the head of the main sail and slotted it into a groove on the single mast. Turner had then grabbed another rope at the end of the boom (he would later learn this was the halyard), connected that to the main sail via a hook, pulled out the slack from the halyard and secured it to a metal fastener.

Will had then watched with fascination as Turner had pulled on the halyard, which began to release the main sail, bit by bit, slowly unfurling and riding up the mast until it was billowing away in the face of a medium-strength southerly wind. Finally, Turner had rigged up the jib sail at the bow, which was also soon billowing in a starboard wind. Then he pulled the tiller to the left to steer the boat to the right and out south-east into the bay. And that was that. It had taken under ten minutes to get the cutter operational and Arthumbo was already receding behind them. Will couldn't help but be impressed by Turner's maritime know-how. Not bad for an old coal miner.

The next day – Day 109 – Turner had been a little more talkative, and had explained the various sails and how they worked. He'd also explained how sailing at 45 degrees to the wind was known as close-hauled, at 90 degrees was beam-reach, 135 degrees was broad-reach and 180 degrees (the same direction as the wind) was downwind.

"How do you know all this stuff?" Will had asked. "Where did you learn to sail?"

Turner had looked at him hard for several seconds, but then his face had softened. "My Da taught me."

Will could tell from Turner's reaction that his father was no longer alive. "I'm sorry, I didn't mean to…"

"That's fine Will. You can't imagine me young, can you? But yes, my old Da was a sailor, Will. I was born in Brottapolt. Me and Mam moved to Cabrenar after he died."

Will's eyes must have asked the question he couldn't bring to his lips.

"He died with all hands in a terrible storm in 1756. They were shipwrecked off the coast of Glaesyne, not too far from here. After the tragedy, they built the lighthouse there to twice its former height."

"I'm sorry," Will mumbled. "For your loss."

There had been a few moments of silence, before Will had voiced a special interest of his. "I've got story-books back home about lighthouses. I've always wanted to visit one."

Turner had actually smiled at that. "Well, maybe I'll grant you that wish, Will. Now that we have our own boat!"

The following day, there hadn't been the slightest breath of wind, and hence Turner had dropped anchor in the bay. This was when Will had asked a question that had been bugging him since the start of their voyage. "I get how being downwind can propel a boat, as the wind is blowing directly into the sails – so, they billow and propel the boat through the water. But how does the boat move where you want it to when the wind's blowing across us, or we're heading directly into it?"

"Those directions have names, Will."

Will had screwed up his face at that, before rattling off close-hauled, beam-reach, broad-reach and downwind.

"I'm impressed, Will," Turner had said. "Your brother was a quick learner as well." *His other son?*

That had caused an awkward pause, but then Turner had answered the question. "It's because wind and water work as two forces against each other, Will. Wind is pressing against the sails above, while at the same time, water is pressing against the keel and the rudder below. You know what a keel and rudder are, son?"

Will ignored the affectation, but at the same time, felt a pang of loss for Davy Sheerin, who had regularly tested him just like this, and also called him 'son'. Given that he hadn't been below ground during the blast, it warmed Will to know that Davy would still be alive. He then pulled his focus back on track. "They're both underneath the boat, aren't they? And the rudder is at the back."

"Spot on, Will. The keel is moulded under the middle of the boat, and is a thin flat object that looks a bit like an upside-down fish's fin. It's fixed in place and doesn't move. The rudder sits underneath the rear of the boat, and can be moved left and right by this tiller," he'd said, patting the long stick in the cockpit that he used to steer the boat.

"Anyway," continued Turner. "Those two opposite forces – wind and water – are working against each other, and that's what makes the boat go forward. But when you're downwind, you don't get the same forces. You can move forward, but that's simply because the sails are driving you forward. We actually move fastest when we're at 90 degrees, which is?"

"Beam-reach," answered Will, immediately.

"Aye, it's at beam-reach that you get the most force from the wind reacting against the force from the keel in the water."

Today had been another day without wind, but it finally returned in the early afternoon. By around 16:30, it was clear that a storm was heading in from the west. Turner decided to try and avoid the storm by pointing the boat due south, at ninety degrees to the wind. "Here we go, Will," he said, turning the tiller to starboard. "Which direction are we going in now, young man?"

Will checked the weather vane at the top of the main mast, and observed the flags on the rigging which were now blowing to port. "Due south, I'd say," answered Will. "So, we're beam-reach."

Nate Turner smiled again. "We'll certainly be making a sailor out of you, young man."

Despite all that had happened in the last thirteen days, Will actually beamed. Then he realised what he was doing; Dylan, Robbie, Davy and then his Mam all flashed through his mind. Turner noticed and tried to keep Will from brooding. "Would you like to steer, Will?"

Will looked at Turner blankly for several seconds, but then tuned in to what he'd said. "Can I?" he asked, his face suddenly transformed into a picture of wonder.

"Hop into the cockpit. Now, take hold of the tiller. That's right. Now, at the moment, we're heading due south, and pretty fast."

"Because of the pressure of wind on the sails and water on the rudder and keel. A beam-reach?"

"Absolutely correct, young man. Now, move the tiller to port."

Will did as he was told, moving the tiller to the left, and he felt the boat begin to turn to the right.

"We're now turning into the wind, and we're going to go *across* the wind so that both sails move from port to starboard."

Will kept his hand on the tiller, guiding them to the right and to the west into the growing head wind, and observed the sails begin to flap agitatedly. Meanwhile, Turner had released the port jib sheet, then grabbed the starboard-side jib sheet and secured it – and sure enough, the boom swung across from port to starboard, and the sails were now filled with the westerly wind – or a port wind, in this particular case.

Will felt like he was floating on air. *He was actually sailing.* He was navigating a boat, by sail, on the Northern Ocean. Never in all of his twelve and a half years had he imagined he would ever get to do anything like this.

Turner then instructed him to turn the tiller to the right, so that they could re-embark on their southerly bearing, and a minute later, the boom had swung to the other side and a starboard wind was inflating the sails. Will wanted to whoop with joy, but forced himself not to. There was still that sickening sense of confusion. This man, who claimed to be his father, had already guided him on the most incredible journey; from ascending the little-known six-hundred foot downcast shaft back in Cabrenar, to sailing an expensive cutter on the Northern Ocean – and with the promise of a visit to a lighthouse, as well. How many fathers had done that for their sons, back in Cabrenar? Or any other mining village for that matter? Why would Turner do that if he wasn't telling the truth? Will now found himself *wanting* to believe Turner's tale. It would make sense of everything. And surely, if it was all true, his Mam would forgive Turner for kidnapping him? Turner's only misjudgement had been telling Dylan the truth about his parentage, although he couldn't have known how Dylan would react.

Will sneaked a glance at Turner and noticed he was looking to the west, an expression of concern on his face. "What's the matter, Mr..." he was going to say "Turner", but realised he was now confused as to what he should call the man.

Turner turned his head away from the west to look at Will. "Just call me Nate, Will. Nate will do fine." He turned back to scan the western horizon. "As to what's the matter, this storm looks like a bad one, Will. See those black clouds how they run from the south-western tip of Bramcia all the way to the southern horizon."

Will followed Turner's finger as he scribed an arc from north-west to south-west.

"I'm a little concerned that we won't be able to escape that by heading south, and I should have turned back for Bramcia. Although, that said, we'd never have made it back to the coast before the storm reaches us. We're way too far out. And in any case, the rules under these circumstances are to stay away from the coast."

"But look south, Nate," said Will. "The clouds aren't anywhere near as black, and that looks like sunlight on the sea to me."

"Aye, it may well be, son," said Turner, grimly. "But we won't be going that far. Not if we want to stay alive."

It suddenly hit Will what Turner meant. "The Shield!"

"Aye, Will. The Shield of Crenac. We're about five leagues from it."

"What does it look like?"

"I've only seen it once. My Da took me when I was nine years old, and when Mam heard, she scolded him bad. He never took me again."

"Can you see anything?"

"Oh yes! Where it touches the ocean, the sea is a chain of unbroken eddies; some of 'em are lethal whirlpools, too, that can suck you down. And the air above! It really does crackle and fizz. But above everything else, there was this compunction."

"A compunction?"

"Yes, it's difficult to explain. You know it's deadly, and that should stop you in your tracks. But it still draws you in. I remember being mesmerised."

"Can we go and see it now, please?"

"Will, the last place we want to be in a storm is next to the Shield of Crenac. We could get forced over it if the storm is violent enough."

"But if we turn back north, the storm hits us. Turn east, it will overtake us. And west, we ride straight into it."

Turner looked intently at Will for a few seconds. "South is our best option," he agreed. "The clouds are heavier and darker to the north. But I'm not going within a league of the Shield until the storm has passed over."

"Just tell me how I can help, Nate," said Will. "I presume two pairs of hands are better than one."

Turner actually smiled at that, and ruffled Will's hair the way that Davy and Robbie used to do. The thought made Will briefly wistful, but eyeing the oncoming storm, he knew he had other priorities right now.

"Well, at present," said Turner, "there's nothing to do. We're making good speed due south." Meanwhile, Will was scanning the southern horizon, looking for signs of Turner's description. All he saw was open water, though.

The storm caught them twenty minutes later. As it approached, the sails became increasingly inflated to port, while the boat rocked about, buffeted by increasingly larger waves to starboard. Looking straight into the storm, to the west, Will could see that it was indeed darker to the north-west, but they certainly weren't going to escape unscathed to the south-west, either.

"How far are we from the Shield," shouted Will, above the wind and rain.

"A league and a half," shouted back Turner. "I'm going to turn us into the face of the storm now, Will."

"The face of it?"

"Aye – it's the safest position for a ship, Will. We can't afford to face it side-on, otherwise we might get flipped over by a large wave. I'm going to go for a close-hauled approach on the port side."

"So, 45-degrees into the wind to port."

"Aye," confirmed Turner.

Will then watched as Turner pushed the tiller to port and, despite the increasing buffeting from the waves, the boat turned to the right – until they were almost looking into the heart of the storm, a few degrees to their right. Rain lashed against Will's face, and he brushed his wet hair from his eyes, while the boat began to ride up and then down the incessant flow of waves. Will could instantly see the logic of the manoeuvre as despite the rise and fall, the bow of the boat was cutting through the crests of the oncoming waves. It was clearly a dangerous predicament – but it was also exhilarating.

For the next half hour, they had been so intent on steering the boat through the storm, that they had failed to notice their significant drift to the south-west. They were now through the worst of the storm, but the waves were still choppy, and the boat was still riding up and down them as they continued to cut through the swell. For the first time in half an hour, Will allowed himself to look to the south. The skies were leaden in that direction, and without any landmarks to measure by, there was no way of telling how far they had drifted. However, Will's eye was drawn to an unusual eddying of water to port, several hundred yards away. He looked west, then east and saw that it was a linear feature as far as the eye could see. He immediately grabbed Turner's arm by way of warning.

"What?" exclaimed Turner, who then allowed his gaze to be directed towards the unusual phenomenon.

Will could now see that not only was the *water* eddying, but the spray *above it* was eddying as well. And the air above that had an almost imperceptible shimmer to it. Even more bizarre, there seemed to be a consistent current of water up and down the feature that was independent of the storm and wind-blown waves and which was moving the water in a largely anti-clockwise direction.

Turner stared at it for just two seconds before grabbing the tiller and pushing it to the left. But the tiller jammed. Turner stared at it in horror – and then put both of his hands to it and pushed hard. It still didn't move. Something had caught in the mechanism.

Will immediately understood the significance and ramifications, and he added his own weight to the tiller. It still wouldn't move left.

Both Will and Nate whipped their heads around to look south. They were only a hundred yards or so north of the eddying effect now, and closing in on it fast. Will shut his eyes, and tried not to imagine what it was like to feel all of your organs shutting down, one after the other.

CHAPTER 90 — MADELEINA

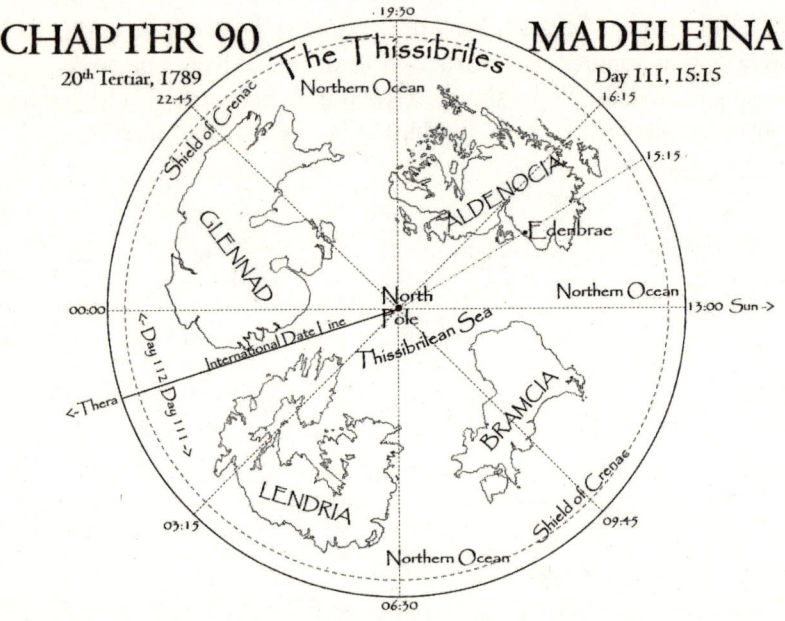

Madeleina was finally beginning to relax. It had been five days since the awful experience at the races and four days since that dreadful woman, Clair, had reappeared in her dressing room at Ghinbrude Palladium. Madeleina was convinced there was another way in and out of that dressing room, and that was how the woman had done her apparent vanishing act – but she hadn't bothered to press the issue with Mr Cameron or either of her guards, lest they think she was going mad. There were certainly times when Madeleina thought she might have imagined it all. Other times, she had to reprimand herself for feeling a sense of relief. Prince Bernard had been a lecher, for sure, but he was also charming, and certainly didn't deserve to die.

Despite all that had happened, though, the performance in Stormone last night had gone well. Indeed, for that hour and ten minutes, the concerto had taken her away from all of her worries. Alas, as soon as the performance was over, she had started fretting about Prince Marco again.

Madeleina sighed. She was being ridiculous, of course. Nothing was going to happen to Prince Marco. It was beyond absurd to believe that someone could *think* another person dead. Nevertheless, yet another unprompted image of his pending death forced itself into her mind.

Madeleina stood and looked around her. Their hotel in Edenbrae was stunning inside, which made up for the dour look from outside – the hotel having been constructed of granite, as had most other buildings in the town. Madeleina had the advantage of being on the fifth floor and her window looked due north, giving her a view over the top of the mass of granite towards the Thissibrilean Sea, which was as calm as a millpond today, albeit light-grey due to the skies above. To the north-east was the beautiful island of Lulm, and Madeleina fancied she could just about make out the main settlement of Mootberry on the island's south-west coast. Due north, there was nothing but hundreds of leagues of sea to the North Pole and beyond there to Lendria on the other side of the world.

Thoughts of Lendria brought back images of Bernie's bulging eyes. Sighing, Madeleina decided to call up Charlotte and Aggie. She was grateful to her mother and father for allowing them to travel with her, as they had helped lighten her mood at times – despite public taxes paying for their presence. This fact would not be lost on the militant Republicans, nor their firebrand right-wing, the ultra-anti-royalist Abolitionists. Although the Republicans ultimately believed in an elected head of state – and which would almost certainly be a President of some description and not a King or Queen – the majority of their party were still respectful of monarchic tradition, and allowed it to continue, albeit with funds and privileges significantly curtailed since they had come to power, three years ago. Neither had they tabled a bill to abolish the monarchy as they knew very well it would not be accepted by the House of Representatives. However, with the public stirred up by the Republican manifesto's obsession with the cost of maintaining the royal family, the monarchy was now effectively on trial. This was one of the reasons why Madeleina's tour was going ahead, as they were providing a service to the public and the income was being shared between the Royal and Republican purses. Of course, the Abolitionists wanted nothing other than the unilateral dissolution of the monarchy and Madeleina and her family thrown out onto the streets of Ghinbrude. Times were certainly tense in Aldenocia, these days.

Madeleina sighed again. Whereas the Republicans were currently in government in Aldenocia, both Bramcia and Lendria were ruled by the much easier-going Democrats, while Glennad didn't even *have* a Republican party, as far as she knew. Naturally, many royal cutbacks had been made in the last three years and posts sacrificed – the price they had to pay, according to the Republicans, for the survival of the royal family, and Madeleina was grateful for her two remaining ladies in waiting. Perhaps their tenuous position would change if the Democrats were voted back in, next year. In the meantime, they would remain under intense scrutiny. Thankfully, the

PM and his leading ministers were currently away at some important conference in Bramcia – otherwise they'd likely have an official sticking their nose in at Edenbrae, right now.

Madeleina was also grateful for the presence of the Head of Royal Security, Jed Wallace, and several of his men who were accompanying her on tour – although if she believed what her gossiping ladies-in-waiting told her, Wallace hadn't been keen on the tour going ahead at all, for security reasons – this based on the growing popularity of the Abolitionist movement in north-east Aldenocia. Thankfully, her tour was heading in the opposite direction. Wallace hadn't let his unease show to Madeleina, though. And with his six foot three inch frame, a great spade of a dark brown beard and built like a kilted wrestler, Jed Wallace was a very reassuring presence. Having said that, there were shocking stories from across the water that Wallace's Glennadian equivalent, John Nash, had been murdered, for reasons yet to be established. Maddie had wondered if that murder was behind the current Bramcian conference, but Wallace had assured her that it wasn't – although Wallace, himself, did not know the reasons for the emergency conference either.

Opening her bedroom door, Madeleina asked the guard outside, Stokes, if he would mind nipping downstairs and asking Charlotte and Aggie to come up to her room. Stokes kept a straight face when he nodded, but Madeleina knew very well that he was jumping at the chance – given he and Charlotte were always making eyes at each other.

Five minutes later, there was a knock at her door, and Madeleina was surprised to see the towering Jed Wallace accompanying her two ladies-in-waiting. His face looked concerned. "Is there a problem?" she asked.

"I have some bad news for you, Princess. This has not been a good week. I'm sorry to tell you that your brother-in-law, Prince Marco, has been killed in a tragic accident."

Jed Wallace could not have expected the impact his words would have on Madeleina, and he had to dive forwards full-length to break her fall and prevent her smashing her head on the tiled bedroom floor.

"Princess Madeleina!" Her name was being repeated over and over. She forced herself to open her eyes, and Jed Wallace's concerned face slowly swam into focus.

"Thank the Lord," said Wallace, a rare half-smile playing on his lips. "You had me worried for a while there, Your Royal Highness."

"Oh, I'm sorry," she said, trying to sit up.

"Take your time, Princess," said Wallace.

Madeleina was now aware of Charlotte and Aggie flapping about in the background. For a few seconds, she was unable to remember what had happened. Then the shock returned. "Prince Marco!"

"It's all right, Princess," soothed Wallace. "I'm sorry. I should have asked you to sit down. The news must have come as a terrible shock, particularly after what happened to Prince Bernard only five days ago."

A terrible shock, thought Madeleina. *You don't know the half of it.*

"How did he die?" she managed to croak as she rose shakily to her feet.

"It was a tragic accident, Princess," said Wallace, his hands steadying her. "He was rock-climbing in the Morin Crags, and sadly fell to his death. It is said that he died instantly and did not suffer."

Madeleina didn't know what to say to that, so remained silent. *"Think Prince Marco dead."* And Maddie *had* thought it. Many times. Including death from a fall. "Thank you, Mr Wallace," she eventually managed to say. "Please. My bed. I need to lie down."

Wallace did as he was asked, with a little bit of fussing from Charlotte and Aggie, too. As Madeleina nodded to him that she was all right, Wallace responded. "I shall inform the stage manager at the Edenbrae Hippodrome that you are not well enough to perform tonight, Princess."

"Please don't do that, Mr Wallace," said Madeleina, rather sharply. "I'll be fine in an hour or so. There's plenty of time to recover and prepare for tonight. I won't let the people of Edenbrae down."

Wallace frowned at that. "Well, if you're sure," he said dubiously.

"I'm quite sure, Mr Wallace."

"Perhaps you should reassess in an hour then, Princess."

"Very well, Mr Wallace. I shall. I would now like to shut my eyes and relax for an hour – alone, please."

Dismissed, Wallace and her two court ladies exited her bedroom, each carrying similar looks of concern. Left alone, lying on the bed, Madeleina put her hands to her face and remained like that for a full two minutes. "Come on," she whispered, eventually. "You are not this stupid. You can't *think* a man dead. The notion is totally absurd."

Nevertheless, Madeleina could not escape the facts. She had named Prince Bernard: he had died a day later. She had imagined Prince Marco's death: four days later, he was dead. She needed someone to confide in. Wallace was the obvious person to tell. He was the palace fixer. But how could she explain any of this to him and sound rational at the same time?

Madeleina let her hands fall to her side, shut her eyes and encouraged her mind to drift. Within a minute, she was dozing, and her dreams soon placed her back in Ghinbrude Palladium. It was daytime, and she had been rehearsing. She was making her way down the silent corridors to her dressing room to leave her sheet music somewhere safe. The rest of the palladium was eerily empty except for the manager and compere, Mr Cameron, and a couple of female cleaners. She was reaching out a gloved hand in front of her to push the dressing room door open but it wouldn't budge – and so, instead, she just passed straight through the solid wooden door into the dressing room beyond. Fully expecting Clair to be sat at her dressing room table, she was not to be disappointed. But when the woman turned around, the face was a grinning skull, skinless except for a little patch on the nose where a raised mole was visible, while only wisps of white hair were stuck to her scalp. "You're too late!" cried the apparition.

An instant later, there was the sound of a single gunshot from the auditorium. Madeleina whirled around and exited the room, noting that the door had now completely vanished. When she entered the auditorium, she found the two cleaners fussing over the prone form of Mr Cameron. He had been shot in the chest, and blood was pumping through fingers that were hopelessly trying to stem the flow. Cameron looked at Madeleina – not with his own eyes – but with the bulging eyes of Prince Bernard.

Then he died.

Madeleina woke up in shock, her heart racing, her skin clammy. Her main emotion was one of dismay: she could now no longer find respite in sleep, either.

CHAPTER 91 — EMILYA

23rd Tertiar, 1789   Day 114, 13:15

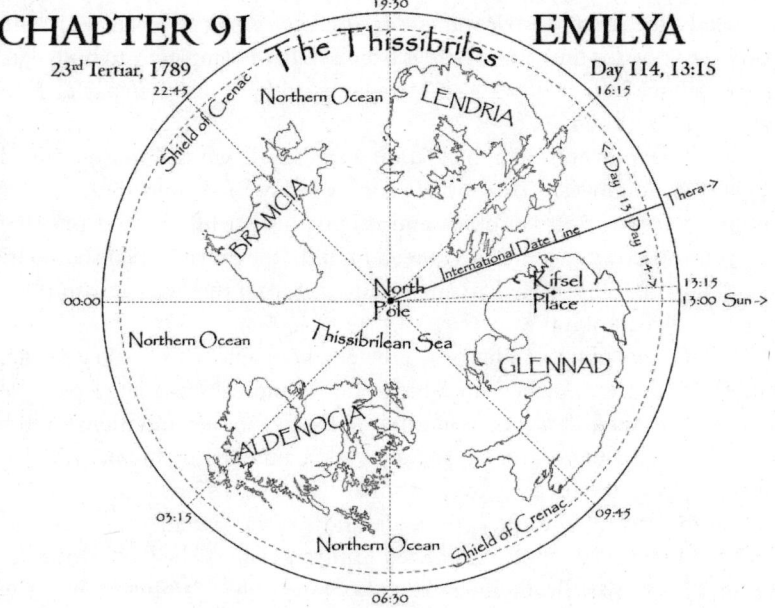

Emilya was rolling her last loaf of bread on one of many worktables, the sleeves of her borrowed monk's robe turned up three times, and her apron looking 'plain daft' over the top – that being how she had described it to Elyse. She had an audience of intrigued monks who, five days ago, had questioned her decision to add a pinch of sugar to her water and yeast mix, as well as the addition of salt to the initial flour-well that she had made. "The sugar leads to a slightly darker crust," she had explained, "while the salt makes it a bit more, well, saltier."

Right now, her dough was of a perfect consistency after ten minutes of kneading, and so she began lining a glass bowl with a thin layer of vegetable oil. "This is to help develop a little more flavour," she explained as she placed the dough into the bowl, "and the dough is now ready for the first proofing, so we're going to leave it to rest and rise for two hours," she said, taking the bowl and placing it in one of the coolers. "Again, this method helps to bring out more flavour."

Emilya then lifted a similar bowl out of the cooler. "This one has had its two hours now – see how it has risen nicely. But we need another proofing. So, if we just sprinkle some flour onto the worktop first, and then roll it to get any air out of it. There we go," she said, rolling and kneading the dough into the shape of a bread bun, before depositing it into a handy bread mould. "I'm now placing this damp cloth over the top of the mould to give the bread a nice humid environment in which to rise. We'll just leave it here on the worktop for now…and here is a mould that I completed an hour ago. As you can see," she said, taking off the damp cloth, "it has risen perfectly to the top of the mould."

Various expressions of appreciation were issued, whilst Emilya donned a pair of oven gloves. "This mould is now ready to go into the oven for baking for around thirty minutes, and as I put this one in," she said, opening the oven and slotting in the latest bread mould, "the previous loaf should be just about right," she added, as she removed it from the oven and shut the door with her right hip.

Further murmurs of approval greeted the sight of the baked bread. Emilya lifted it out, picked up a bread knife, and carved a large piece of crust off the end and a couple of other slices, before passing them round. "And that's all there is to it," she said, as a number of monks nibbled approvingly on the bread. "A very similar method to yours but with a few extra quirks that I hope you agree adds a little extra flavour."

A polite round of applause greeted Emilya to which she gave a graceful curtsy. Meanwhile, Brother Stephen was positively beaming at his new student. "Well brothers, I trust you appreciate the efforts of Miss Emilya. Brother Edric, are you happy to complete the last batch of loaves today?"

A middle-aged, unremarkable-looking monk nodded with a smile on his face. "I most certainly am, Brother Stephen. I can see this new line being even more successful than our current line."

"Excellent. And thank you again for your time, Miss Emilya. I believe Miss Elyse is waiting for you for lunch in the refectory."

Whilst removing her apron and hanging it up on her own special peg, Emilya had mixed feelings about leaving the bakery. All of the monks here were kind and pleasant, and appreciated her assistance; they appreciated *her*. It was wonderful to feel useful – just as Elyse was proving useful in the infirmary, she learning from the monks' methods of treatment and pain control, and they learning from hers.

As Emilya approached the entrance to the refectory, her heart fell as she saw Brother Cyrus approaching from the bridge. He had presumably just come down to lunch from Bloomer where he looked after the gardens, the fish ponds and the monastery animals. As ever, his black eyes were penetrating and she saw them looking her up and down with disdain, making her skin crawl and her hackles rise at the same time – before he disappeared into the refectory.

Elyse was waiting for her just inside the refectory entrance, clad in a much better-fitting robe which, even though it covered her from head to foot, did not really hide the fact that she was a woman. "Good day?" she asked.

"Wonderful," replied Emilya.

"The smells from inside are particularly enticing today," said Elyse, as they walked side-by-side into the long rectangular refectory. Three rows of benches spanned almost the length of the building, all heaving with hungry monks, although there were a few spaces left for two to sit. At the top end, monks were serving a variety of delicious dishes to a queue of waiting brethren.

"I thought we could perhaps read in the orchard this afternoon," suggested Elyse, as they joined the queue. Both ladies had afternoon's off, courtesy of being up with the lark to bake bread in Emilya's case, and to tend the sick in Elyse's – the sick being either human or animal.

"That sounds lovely," said Emilya. Truth be told, she had only been at Kifsel Place Monastery for six days, but Emilya was already a little bored. She was also more intimidated than she let on to Elyse by the handful of monks who clearly resented their presence here.

As they queued, Emilya was looking at the back of Brother Cyrus' head, but even though his eyes were facing forwards, the sensation remained that he was still somehow looking at her. Having collected his lunch, Cyrus seated himself with two other monks who were freaking Emilya out: Brother Gerald and Brother Obadiah. Of the two, Gerald was cold but courteous, but Obadiah was a blatant lecher. He was an ugly man, too, with a high forehead and pockmarked cheeks. Annoyingly, and despite Brother Obadiah's open lechery, the trio had piously remonstrated with the abbot at the presence of women in the monastery being against God's will; yet every time Elyse was around, Emilya caught Brother Obadiah looking at her lasciviously with his hungry, deep-set eyes. Emilya was sure that if anyone asked Brother Obadiah to describe Elyse Dolmen's face, he would have had no chance. He probably didn't even know the colour of her hair!

Half way through lunch, Emilya saw Brother Cyrus lean across the table towards Brother Obadiah and whisper something in his ear. Obadiah's reaction was to turn and face them, a hungry look on his features as he leered at Elyse's back – before locking eye contact with Emilya. As ever, Emilya immediately looked away, a shudder travelling down her spine. She'd tried smiling at these three in the first two days at the monastery in an attempt to win them over, but if anything, her smiles had appeared to make them even more hostile.

Sensing Emilya's unease, Elyse began talking about Edwyn. Emilya was having none of it, though, and cut across her. "Elyse," she began.

"Oh," responded Elyse, rather surprised at Emilya's firmness.

"I don't like it here."

"Just ignore them, Emilya. Brother Stephen and Brother Clarence aren't like that, neither is Abbot Geoffrey, nor ninety-nine per cent of the other monks here. And the monks in the kitchen like and respect you – for your baking talents, and nothing to do with you being a girl. They're lovely, peaceful, harmless men, just wanting to live a quiet and productive existence away from the world and its myriad sins."

"And them?" she said, nodding at the distasteful trio.

"I'm afraid there are good and bad everywhere, Emilya. Even in a monastery. It's a fact of life that wherever you look, there are strains of malice. But would you rather be sat here, in this spectacular place, baking bread in a huge kitchen and helping out with the animals every day…or back in the palace at Ghantiss as Prince Magnus' plaything?"

"I'd rather be stood in my *father's* bakery, baking bread. Or helping Emrys and Edwyn run the commune."

Emilya's right hand was resting on the table-top, and Elyse put her hand on top of it. "I'm sure you would, Emilya. But until we're certain that Magnus has lost interest in you, you're better off here. You should try and relax and make the most of it."

"Huh!" was all Emilya could manage.

"We can go elsewhere if you like," said Elyse, changing tack. "But please try and hold on until the Cleanse the Spirit expedition to Dawkids and Keplif Scale. It's a once-in-a-lifetime adventure, Emilya, and you will be so glad that we stayed. And you'll get to see Jared and Clyve again."

"I'd rather see Edwyn."

Elyse patted Emilya's hands and smiled at her. "And you shall. In two-or-three months' time when Magnus has lost interest. As I've told you before, he's probably already fixated on someone else, by now."

Emilya nodded, but without smiling. She knew plenty of nice, good and honest men – but the other sort was beginning to stir a strong antipathy inside her. *The world would be a better place without them.*

Cultivating these thoughts, Emilya was positively glaring at Brother Cyrus and his two cronies, so when Cyrus next turned around and locked on to her, she didn't look away, channelling what she hoped was animosity back in the goateed monk's direction. Thus began, in the middle of a peaceful monastery refectory, an intense battle – and if Brother Cyrus felt any surprise at Emilya's sudden boldness, he didn't show it. His two companions also noticed, and were looking backwards and forwards at the two combatants, but despite the peripheral movement, Emilya did not drop her eyes from Brother Cyrus'.

"Stop it, Emilya," whispered Elyse.

Emilya ignored her. The staring match went on.

Elyse therefore decided to take matters into her own hands. She stood up and faced Brother Cyrus, hoping his eyes would track to her. They didn't. At that, Elyse couldn't help herself. "Oh, for heaven's sake, grow up, Brother Cyrus! She's only a child!"

Elyse had spoken much louder than she had planned, and the refectory went largely silent, save for a now-muted buzz at the serving hatch. Not only were Emilya and Elyse the only two women in the hall, they had now drawn irreversible attention to themselves. Elyse's actions had, however, broken the concentration of Brother Cyrus, and Emilya felt some satisfaction at her little 'victory'. Not that Brother Cyrus looked bothered. On the contrary, he looked smug and triumphant at having lured Elyse into embarrassing herself, while he now appeared to be the injured party.

Elyse, meanwhile, had moved rapidly around to Emilya's side of the benches, had encouraged her to stand and was now steering her from the refectory. When they got outside, Emilya shook herself free of Elyse's hold, and for the first time, Emilya saw impatience and a tiny hint of anger in Elyse. "I told you to stop!" she said.

"Well, you didn't have to stand up and attract everyone else's attention, did you?"

Conscious that there were other monks moving around the yard, all staring at the two remonstrating women, Elyse put her arm around Emilya and steered her towards the bridge over to Bloomer. Despite being within a whisker of resisting, Emilya allowed herself to be led across the rope bridge and up the steps carved into the side of the second stack at Kifsel Place monastery. She was halfway up before she realised her anger had negated her nervousness at crossing the bridge.

They arrived on Bloomer in between the stables and the piggery, an area which was thankfully less populated than Hector, below them. By this stage, Elyse's annoyance had melted away and she held Emilya to her and kissed her forehead. Emilya still kept her arms truculently by her side. "Ooh, you are such a little warrior at times, Emilya," she said, kissing her forehead again. "Poor Edwyn if he marries you."

"Why should he get away with it?" demanded Emilya, finally finding her voice, but ignoring Elyse's diversion.

"He's not actually done anything, though, Emilya. Other than look."

"What I mean is, that all of the other monks are nice and kind and considerate. Why would they have someone like that here?"

"I doubt Abbot Geoffrey turns anyone away, Emilya. And just because a monk has taken his vows here, it doesn't necessarily mean they're a kind or pious man. Neither does it necessarily mean they have lived a good and honest life prior to coming here."

Emilya was about to respond, when she noticed a monk observing them from the shadow beneath the stable roof, a long-handled brush in his hand. For some reason, she sensed it was the monk she'd first seen with Brother Cyrus, six days earlier, but by now he had moved further back into the shadows and busied himself with his mucking out.

Emilya nodded towards the stables, but by the time Elyse turned around, the monk had his back to them. "Another of Cyrus' cronies?" whispered Elyse.

Emilya nodded, now looking a little crestfallen. "I'm sorry, Elyse," she said. "I couldn't help myself."

Elyse smiled. "Well, it's what makes you, you," she said, touching Emilya's cheek. "What say you go and beg some bread from the kitchens, and we make do with that for lunch. I'll pop up to Bowers and grab two books from the library, and we can meet in the orchard in twenty minutes."

Emilya finally smiled. She knew the situation in the refectory could have been avoided, but she still felt fully justified – and not a little proud – that she had actually stood up to Brother Cyrus. "Good plan," she said. "Brother Stephen will likely give me some buttered scones, too, and maybe even a jar of strawberry jam."

"Ooh, lovely," responded Elyse.

Emilya turned to head back down to Hector, but then turned back and caught Elyse's arm before she headed for Bowers. Elyse looked surprised. "I love you, Elyse," said Emilya.

Emilya saw Elyse's eyes water, and she pulled Emilya into an embrace. "And I love you too. Tiger," she added, whilst ruffling the back of Emilya's unruly dark-auburn hair.

CHAPTER 92   ARRAN

23rd Tertiar, 1789   Day 114, 16:30

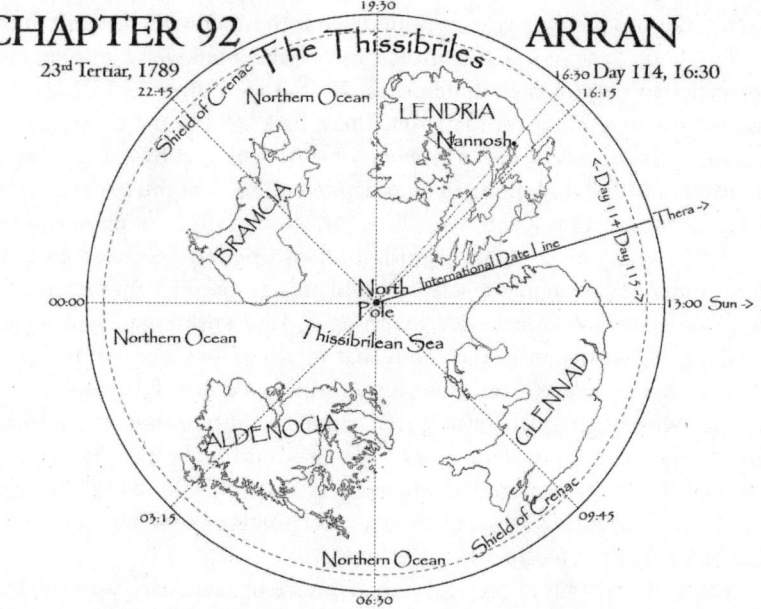

Laden with bags from his long trip to Bramcia, Arran pushed open the front door with his foot. The first thing he noticed was a letter on the doormat. *Ella's handwriting.* Squeezing through the door, Arran dumped his bags onto the hall floor, and scooped up the letter. He pressed the envelope to his nose and, sure enough, it smelt of Ella's perfume. Walking through to his sitting room, he placed his finger underneath the envelope flap and gently opened the letter, taking care to minimise the damage to such a precious possession. His heart began to beat faster as he read the contents. She loved him with all her heart and agreed that they must meet. She was tentatively suggesting Arran take the two-day Olindo Bay ferry from Nannosh to Olindo on 41st Tertiar (Day 132), as Mal was away with the boys at his brother's home in Brytan for three days, starting on the 42nd.

Arran sat down in his most comfortable chair. Were they really going to do this? Or was it just words, and come the 40th Tertiar, common sense would prevail and they would call it off? Ella was someone else's wife, after all. The mother of someone else's children. What right did he have to see her?

Then, Arran remembered George. Amid the excitement and promise of meeting Ella, he had actually forgotten for a while that the world could end in sixty-nine days' time. He had forgotten despite having just returned from a tense but productive two-day conference with ninety-five per cent of the leading politicians in the Thissibriles; formidable men who had remained constructive despite their differences. By the time they had drawn the conference to a close on Day 109, there had been a tangible sense of camaraderie between the members of the four nations and even a smattering of the dark humour that defined all four countries; even from the Aldenocian contingent!

Arran was proud of his contribution of briefing delegates on their predicament in a pragmatic, scientific and orderly manner. The fact that the notoriously volatile Aloysius Whyte was already onside had sent a clear message to every man in the room that the time had come to put party tensions to one side. Nevertheless, Arran still hoped that if they did survive this catastrophe, that whatever government would be running Lendria in the aftermath – coalition or otherwise – it would be headed by Lenahan Driscoll. The man was calm, intelligent, resourceful, willing to listen to all arguments and able to sympathise with most points of view; all the qualities that you needed in a leader.

Driscoll had calmly presented their future options. He had explained how he planned to address each of the potential disaster scenarios in Lendria, and although there was a healthy debate, with other ideas being pushed backwards and forwards for a couple of hours, all four sets of politicians eventually agreed that Driscoll's plans were the ones to go with for each nation. "Although there are three scenarios, gentlemen," Driscoll had begun, "there are only two that we need to prepare for. A strike on land, or a strike in the Northern Ocean. Because we don't know the topography south of the Desolation, we have to assume the worst, and treat any strike in the southern hemisphere as a strike on land. If that is where George strikes, and we don't subsequently experience the blocking out the sun's rays, we will know that there *is* a Southern Ocean, after all, and we in the north can all thank our lucky stars. Literally."

There had been a round of muted amusement at that point.

"But, although we have two scenarios to prepare for, preparations for a land strike will differ, depending upon *where* on land that George is going to hit. This is where things get complicated, so I will come back to that shortly. Firstly, I will deal with a strike in the Northern Ocean.

"If George is going to hit *anywhere* in the Northern Ocean, the effects will be catastrophic for our ports and coastline settlements. They will all be destroyed – and not just by the enormous waves generated. Areas closer to the impact will also be obliterated by the blast front which Arran predicts will generate a wind-speed of seventy leagues, or two hundred-plus miles per hour, perhaps more – albeit losing intensity the further it spreads out."

A few heads had gone in hands at that point, but Driscoll had continued. "This means that much of our shipping will be destroyed – although we are planning to portage a selection to safety in the hills, as we will need boats in the aftermath. Of course, shipping will be way down our list of priorities. People will come first. So, once we know beyond any doubt that we're getting a Northern Ocean strike, we make the announcement immediately, and we withdraw all populations to high land and remove anyone within fifty leagues of the ocean impact point and subsequent blast effect."

"What sort of a height would we expect the waves to reach?" David Grey-Doogell had asked.

Driscoll had deferred to Arran at that point. "Anywhere between one hundred and three thousand feet," he had answered. That had traumatised every man in the room who didn't already know the theory. Arran had gone on to talk about the wave-height depending upon the angle of asteroid trajectory, how deep the ocean was where it struck, the configuration of the shelves around the Thissibriles, and the squeezing effects of channels and straits between the four nations. He had finished by stating that they would be modelling and sharing the effects of the impact as soon as they knew the *point* of impact.

"Obviously," Driscoll had continued, "the islands closest to the impact will suffer the most. But all four islands will have their coastal areas inundated because those giant waves will flow *around* the islands and through the channels *between* our islands. So, regardless of where the asteroid strikes, land or sea, we need to start constructing shelters on all four islands immediately. As we don't currently know *where* it will strike, we build shelters in *all* of our upland areas. If we have an ocean impact, *all* of those shelters will still be used by those displaced from their homes. However, if we have a *land* strike, its impact point obviously dictates shelter usage. For example, if the asteroid is destined for Lendria, well, there may not be any hope for any of us, anyway. Certainly, most of fair Lendria would be destroyed by the impact and resulting blast-front. So, common sense says that we all head for the furthest point inside the Shield of Crenac that we can get to – which in Lendria's case, is Aldenocia. Similarly, if the roles were reversed, Aldenocians would make for the shelters on Lendria. This is another reason why we all need to work together. However, I don't need to tell you gentlemen how chaotic such a circumstance would be. But it is a circumstance that we all must prepare for."

That had triggered a huge debate about the right locations to build shelters, the depth to which to build them, who would be admitted, the limit on numbers, and selection policies based on ability, skills, experience, or even a national lottery. Discussions also raged about the logistics of shipping hundreds of thousands of people across the Thissibrilean Sea, within a limited period, with time running out, minus any portaged boats. Driscoll had repeatedly stated that he didn't have all of the answers, and that's why the conference had been called. There had been a number of arguments, but generally, cooperation was excellent and the camaraderie had gradually built from that point.

Driscoll had also pointed out that a land strike in the Thissibriles was the absolute worst-case scenario, and that a land strike outside of the Thissibriles was a significantly better option, logistically, because all islanders would travel to shelters only on their own island, and there would be no cross-channel chaos on the Thissibrilean Sea. Whether their race survived or not, that was another matter.

Arran's thoughts returned to Ella. If the future of their race was to be in danger – and it was the most likely scenario, given the enormous land-mass of Epanaga – should he break his vows to Lenahan Driscoll and tell Ella, but swear her to secrecy? For sure, if he did tell her on the 42nd Tertiar, she would likely leave Mal and come and live with him along with her sons. Because for all they knew, they might only have another fifty days left to live at that point.

It was in that moment that Arran understood something, very clearly. If George hadn't been out there, and the world was to continue unblighted by catastrophe, then had he been offered the choice between living until eighty but never seeing Ella again, versus spending fifty healthy days with Ella before he passed away, well, there was no contest. Arran was certain they would be the fifty happiest days of his life.

CHAPTER 93 — ALICYA

24th Tertiar, 1789 — Day 115, 13:45

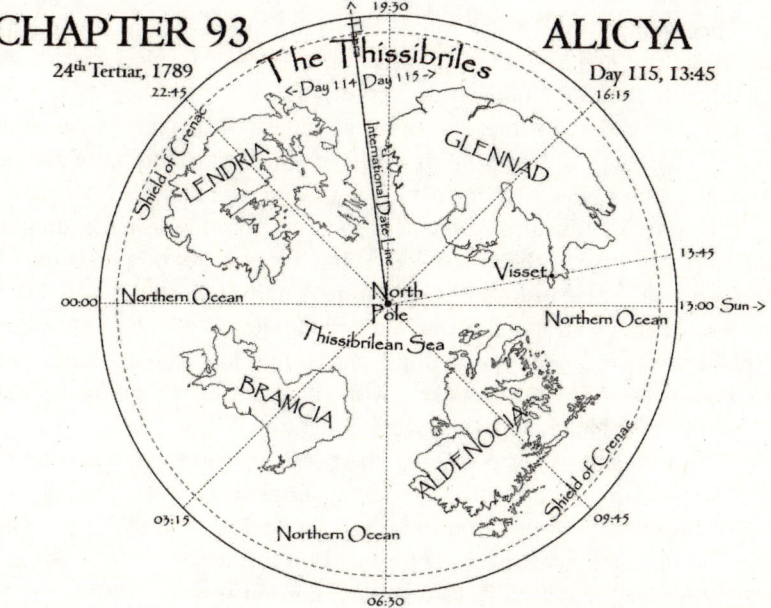

Alicya felt that the man following her wasn't even trying to hide the fact any more. Then again, she had turned around, smiled sweetly and waved at him half an hour ago. She wasn't worried about her tail, though, as the man clearly wasn't a professional, and hence wasn't anything to do with the palace; had one of Mr Nash's men been engaged, she would have been none-the-wiser. No, this fellow was a rank amateur – and Alicya had strong suspicions as to who might have hired him.

She therefore went into her favourite bakery on the promenade, determined to buy herself a cream cake and then sit and eat it whilst facing the sea and reading the novel she had bought earlier that morning. She fancied two hours ought to bore the man into going away.

As the bakery doorbell rang on entry, Alicya put on her biggest smile for Mrs Norris. However, Mrs Norris was not smiling back. "Mrs Norris?" questioned Alicya, curiously. "Is anything the matter?"

Mrs Norris folded her arms defiantly and scowled. "We don't serve your sort in here. I suggest you leave, now."

Alicya was taken aback, and glanced in confusion at the customers who were sat eating various pastries at the four tables in the small bakery. All eyes were on her. She laughed, nervously. "Is this some kind of a joke?"

"A joke, ha! No, it's certainly no joke to be carrying on with your so-called cousin and soiling the reputation of a decent neighbourhood."

"I beg your pardon!" began Alicya, now quite rattled. Damn the woman's impertinence – and in front of an audience, too. Alas, Mrs Norris was back at her before she could follow up.

"Oh yes, you stand there, in all your finery, with your oh-so-posh accent," she said, her face wrinkled in 'bad smell under the nose' mode. "And all the time, you're having it away with your own blood."

This time, a murmur of agreement went up from the seated audience. Alicya looked hard at their faces, searching for evidence of a hoax, but it clearly wasn't. These ordinary people were genuinely hostile towards her. She felt herself go all hot and was suddenly finding it difficult to breathe. She therefore did the worst thing she could have done under the circumstances, and exited the bakery without putting up any sort of defence – and with horrible mutterings ringing in her ears, too.

With her hand to her pounding chest, Alicya paused for a second to catch her breath before heading for her favourite bench. After a minute or so, her breathing returned to normal and she looked around for the man who had been following her. She spotted him further up the promenade, leaning against the statue of a former naval great of Visset. This time, it was her tail who waved – although his smile was anything but sweet.

Too flustered to cope with the attention, Alicya gathered up her skirts and headed in the direction of Gawain's apartment. However, before she'd even left the harbour frontage, some middle-aged woman in servant's clothing had the temerity to half-shout something at her. And the word sounded remarkably like "whore".

Enough was enough. She was a princess, little though these ignorant commoners knew it, and even if she *was* Gawain's cousin from Ghantiss, that gave these people no right to talk to her like this. She turned to the woman, noting a red complexion that hinted at over-indulgence with alcohol. "What did you say?" she asked, advancing rapidly on the woman. Her moves seemed to spook the woman, who immediately began to back-pedal, but then she was joined by several other commoners, all women. And the things they were saying! However, Alicya had suddenly gone deaf to them all, as she'd spotted someone else of far greater significance further down the promenade.

Brushing the commoners aside, Alicya set back her shoulders and advanced towards the smirking Ashlyn. "You," she said, on approach. "This is your work."

"Is it?" she asked, impudently, fingering one of her many black ringlets beneath her expensive bonnet. "I have no idea what you're talking about, my dear."

Alicya was briefly lost for words. She'd taken an instant dislike to the woman at Visset Manor, but she had kept a civil tongue in her head for Gawain's sake when Ashlyn had tried to stir things up later that evening at the ball – no doubt having scrutinised the way that Gawain and his supposed cousin had looked at each other all night. However, Alicya was damned if she was going to let Ashlyn play the moral superior over her in public. "Your reaction to rejection is pitiful, Ashlyn," she scoffed. "I actually feel sorry for you."

That got rid of the smirk, and Alicya felt a brief rush of triumph. Ashlyn narrowed her pitch-black eyes. "You really don't want to make an enemy out of me, my dear."

"It's a little late for that. So, stick this in your pipe and smoke it, Ashlyn. I love him. He loves me. I'm not his cousin. *And* we're going to get married."

With that said, Alicya glared once at Ashlyn and then hurried away in the direction of Gawain's apartment before anyone could see her tears.

CHAPTER 94   DAVY

24th Tertiar, 1789   Day 115, 10:00

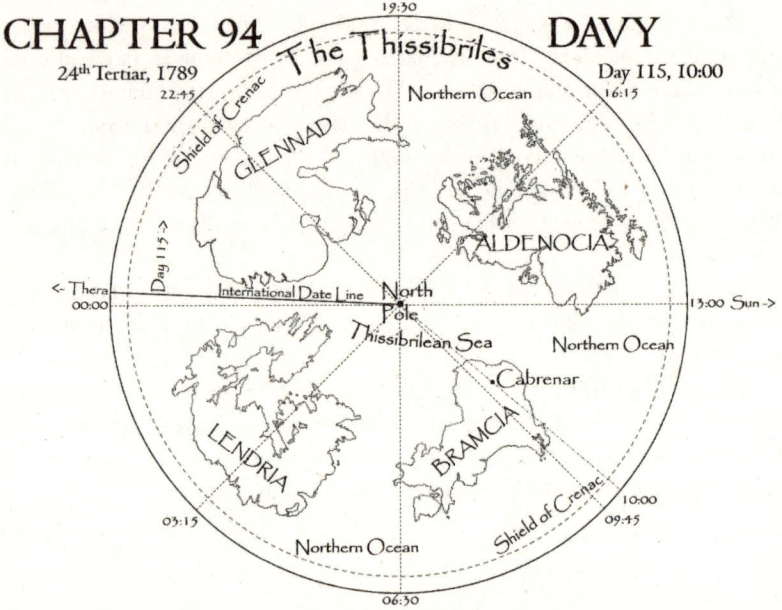

"I'm sorry, ladies and gentlemen," said Jed Morris, raising his hands. "But as you know, we had to flood the mine to put out the fires. The experts are telling me it will take four months to drain the galleries, and at least another two months before they're safe to work again."

A large outcry greeted this last statement at the Miners' Welfare Club in Cabrenar. The wooden building was absolutely crammed; not only were all seats taken, but those standing were wedged together like sardines, too. One voice was then heard over all of the others. Davy recognised Daff Duncan's tones immediately. "Are you telling us then, Jed, that we're all out of work for at least six months?"

"He's saying that the mine is out of action for six months, Daff," said Stan Eckersley. Stan was flanking the mine owner, Jed Morris, at the table on the raised stage, with Vin Ellis, chief engineer on the other side.

"Well, it amounts to the same thing, man," complained Daff.

"Aye," swelled the response from most of the miners present. Davy's voice wasn't one of them. He had been part of the team that had flooded the mine two weeks ago – as had Daff Duncan, for that matter. They both knew the mine was going to be inoperable for some considerable time, which was why Davy had made alternative plans. Seems as though Daff hadn't, though.

Jed Morris was half out of his seat, both hands raised again, trying to calm down the audience. "We do have the benevolent fund, though," he began.

"Aye, but that's for the bereaved, Jed," shouted Josh Goose.

"That's right. Us survivors won't see a penny of that," said Pat Martyn. "It's folk like Carys Russell and poor Edyth Lowe who needs that money."

"I know, I know," said Jed. "The benevolent fund was set up by the Prime Minister who has also agreed to organise a football match in Craffid in honour of those who died. The proceeds are to go to those in need who suffered as a result of what they're calling the Cabrenar Colliery Disaster. I take 'those in need' to mean all of you – not just the bereaved."

"All right, so they raise a few hundred bob by getting a few celebrities to punt a bag of air around a field," said Job Law. "How's that supposed to support two hundred families for over six months?"

A bellow of agreement went up from the room. Davy squeezed Daisy's hand, and indicated that they should leave. Daisy gave him a worried nod, but fortunately they were near the back, and the standing miners and their families parted to let them exit. Everyone present knew that Davy and Daisy were due to get married at midday, so no one questioned their loyalty by leaving early.

"I thought they'd give us trouble," said Daisy.

Davy put his arm around her and kissed her on the forehead. "They're all good people, Daisy. Good people in terrible times. I suppose I ought to tell you that I've said no one is to buy us any wedding presents."

For a second, Daisy looked like she was going to be cross at that, but then her eyes just filled up and she hugged her husband-to-be. "You're such a good man, Davy Sheerin. But what are we going to live on?"

Davy guided Daisy over to one of the wooden benches arrayed around the triangle of grass that was the village green. He took both of her hands as they sat in the shade of a willow and looked into Daisy's watery eyes. "I've known for a couple of weeks that there's going to be no work here for a while, love. A few of the other blokes have, too. So, I wrote a letter to the biggest slate mine in Bramcia, at Keeyola, down south. That was about ten days ago. I got a reply today. They've offered me a job, love."

Daisy's hands flew to her mouth, and for a few seconds, she didn't know what to say as the ramifications of her fiancé's words sunk in. The first words she uttered were, "My Mam and Da. Carys."

"I know, love," said Davy. "But they'll understand, honestly, they will. And if it doesn't work out at Keeyola, we can always come back here in six months and I can work Cabrenar again. But at least in the meantime, to answer your original question, we'll have something to live on."

"But how will we afford a house?"

"The slate mine provide houses to their workers and take their rent directly from their wages – just like they do here. So, they've got a house lined up for us, too."

"I don't know what to say," said Daisy. "I mean…it's wonderful news, truly it is. Why didn't you say?"

"Too much going on, what with the funerals and the salvage and the general grieving. It didn't seem appropriate to be seen to be thinking of ourselves ahead of others. And, I don't know," he added, shaking his head sadly. "I'm thrilled to be marrying you, love, but my heart's broken in other places for Robbie, and for Dylan, and for Will. Moving away for a bit won't do me any harm."

Daisy lent into Davy and put both arms around him. "When do you start?" came her muffled question.

"In just under two weeks."

Daisy untangled herself to look at him.

"Well, Keeyola's as good a place as any to have a honeymoon, love! The area around there's said to be beautiful. We could even climb Onsdown. They reckon you can see all of Bramcia from the top. You do want to go, don't you Daisy? And, I mean, you still want to marry me, don't you?"

Daisy cupped Davy's cheeks and kissed him on the lips. "Of course I still want to marry you, silly. It's just been a lot to take in. But twelve days it is. It will be like a whole new start. I'll see if I can get work too. New home, new job, new location."

"And a new husband, too," said Davy.

This time, their kiss went on.

"Oi, you two!" cried Eric, landlord of the Red Dragon, who was wheeling a barrow past them with a barrel on it. "I've told you before about doing that in public!"

Davy and Daisy reluctantly parted, both smiling sheepishly at Eric.

"Anyway," said Eric, "haven't you got a wedding to be getting to?"

"He's right," said Daisy. "And I'll need all of my two and half hours to make myself beautiful."

"You still OK for the reception Eric?" asked Davy.

"That's what this is for," said Eric, nodding at the barrel. "I've got another six to bring around, yet."

"I'll not keep you then, Eric. And thanks – for laying on the food and drink."

"It's my pleasure Davy Sheerin. I've watched you grow into a fine young man. Giving you two a send-off is the least I can do – particularly under the current circumstances.

Two and a half hours later, Davy was waiting at the altar of the small wooden church that served the village of Cabrenar. Once again, a building was filled to the rafters with locals, many who had been crammed into the village hall, earlier that day. Mr Merkins was playing the bridal march on the church organ, everyone had stood, and Davy turned around to see his Daisy walking towards him on the arm of her proud father. Davy had loved Daisy all of his adult life, and for a few years before at Sunday School. But he had never before seen her looking as beautiful as she did today. She was wearing a slimline, full-length white dress of silk with slim, full-length lacy sleeves, and she was holding a posy of white, pale pink and dark pink roses, while her sister, Carys, was sombrely holding the three-foot train at the back, dressed in pale yellow. But Daisy's nicest touch was the crown of fresh daisies, sitting vibrantly around her classically curled blonde hair and above a flushed youthful face that was beaming with complete happiness.

Davy Sheerin offered up a silent word to a God he had thought might have deserted them all in the last few weeks, and he thanked him from the bottom of his heart for the most beautiful girl in the world.

CHAPTER 95 — MAGNUS

25th Tertiar, 1789 Day 116, 12:45

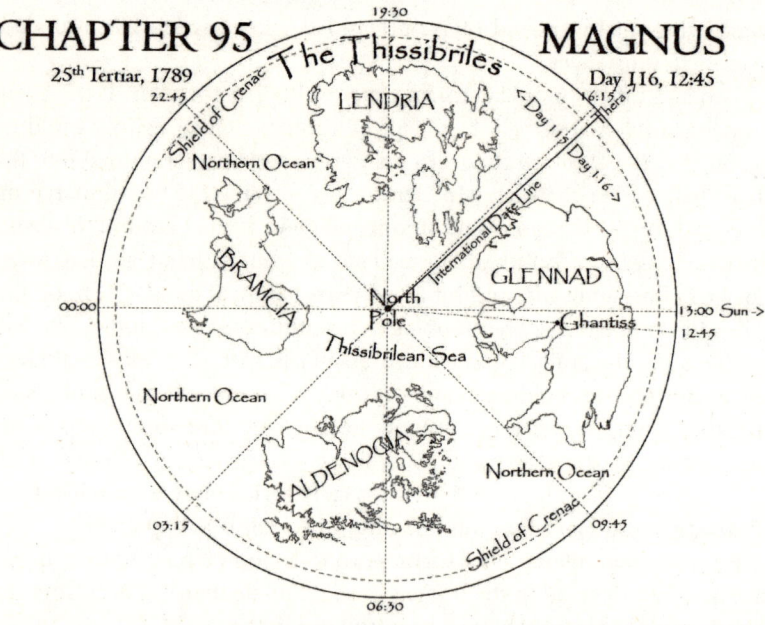

Magnus had been back in Ghantiss for five days now, a time spent largely mobilising the Glennadian army and preparing to engage over ten thousand troops to track down Oscom and Black. He had the full blessing of his desperate parents and the government, all now agreed that this was the only way to get Alicya back.

Right now, though, Magnus was at the rear of a hastily-erected stage in the centre of Ghantiss' enormous marketplace. The entire city was aware that a 'major announcement' was being made by the Glennadian royal family at midday, so hundreds had converged on their famous marketplace, with its awnings, fountains, statues and sculptures while the endless flower-beds offered a riot of Spring colour.

Magnus was spending these last few moments running over his speech – although his strategy was to get into the same zone that he had in the palace council room, nearly three weeks ago, and hope that the emotion stirred took a similar course. Seconds later, he was on stage, resplendent in his blue and gold military regalia complete with Commander-in-Chief bicorn hat which bore the anchor sigil of the Glennadian Navy – the latest in a series of hats which continued to hide the ugly scar that had been inflicted by Freya Colin's knife.

Magnus raised the loudhailer to his lips, and an expectant hush fell over

Ghantiss marketplace. "Citizens of Ghantiss," began Magnus. "I have grave and terrible news for you."

A murmur of disquiet passed across the marketplace. Magnus lowered the loudhailer waiting for the crowd to settle down again. Lots of people were shushing others and some were already getting fractious. Eventually, silence was restored. Magnus raised the loudhailer again. "I am beyond grief to have to tell you." He paused, partly for effect, partly because his voice had genuinely begun to catch. "That my sister, the Princess Alicya," he paused again, "has been kidnapped."

As the crowd exploded in a thousand expressions of consternation, Magnus found himself actually breaking down. He had no idea where this had come from, but he was willing it to continue. Eventually, the crowd marshalled its own silence, yet still Magnus delayed, struggling to find the words. Eventually, he pressed on. "She was taken..." he sobbed once, then recovered. "She was taken from us, three weeks ago..." Another sob followed, and Magnus' hand holding the loudhailer flopped by his side, while the crowd hum began to ramp up again.

Sir John Russell, the ever-solemn Lord High Constable, walked quickly onto the stage in his own formal black and gold regalia and gently took the loudhailer from Magnus. Russell turned to face the masses gathered before him. "Ladies and gentlemen, please," he shouted. The crowd finally settled down again. "Please, this is a terribly distressing time for the royal family. I will tell you myself what I know, and when Prince Magnus has recovered, he will tell you the steps we are taking to address this terrible situation. But first, I must ask you to keep quiet whilst I explain what has happened."

Once again, the crowd fell silent.

"As Prince Magnus has already explained, Princess Alicya has been kidnapped. She was taken on the 5th Tertiar; twenty days ago. We realised she was missing later that night, but a thorough search of the palace grounds did not reveal her whereabouts."

As the crowd volume ramped up again, Russell let the loudhailer drop again to his side, a look of extreme irritation on his lined face. When the crowd murmur dropped again, he spoke his mind. "Ladies and gentlemen. I shall not ask you again to remain silent. If I have to stop talking one more time, then we will terminate this announcement. You will then find out what has happened via an official written announcement which will be circulated tomorrow."

This time, the silence was total. When he next began talking, John Russell told them everything. He told of the Let Us Prey session that triggered the whole catalogue of events. He told of how Prince Magnus was deeply repentant and would never again indulge in such activity. He told of how an ex-naval captain, but more recently-convicted murderer, Jake Oscom, had opportunistically taken advantage of the situation, and blackmailed the Prince for his part in the shameful bout of Let Us Prey. He told of how John Nash, the former Head of Royal Security, had advised Prince Magnus against paying the blackmail money of a thousand guineas. Of how when the money wasn't paid, Oscom went on the run, murdering magistrate Humphrey Horrocks. Russell then told of the circumstances under which Princess Alicya went missing: the bogus laundry men, the murder of Nash and the used chloroform pad in the Princess' bedroom.

By this stage, the crowd were struggling to take in the audacity and horror of this cowardly attack on their beloved princess. There was then great consternation when Russell revealed that they hadn't yet received a ransom note, and that this had obviously left the authorities deeply concerned, and the royal family frantic with worry and grief.

It was at this point that a now apparently-recovered and composed Prince Magnus took the loudhailer back from the Lord High Constable. "I am deeply repentant for my involvement in these tragic events; involvement which appears to have triggered everything. I have done everything in my power since then to make amends and to capture Jake Oscom. We did get an early lead that Oscom was heading for Ghenetenos. I took a party of men to track him down – but it was we who were ambushed, not Oscom. And Oscom did indeed have accomplices – as we had suspected. And the leader of his accomplices, was none other than," Magnus paused for effect: "Harry Black."

This time, the crowd couldn't help but vent their anger. Magnus allowed that. It was all going perfectly, so far. When the latest hubbub had died down, Magnus raised the loudhailer again. "And not only did they ambush us, but they killed three of my men – loyal soldiers of our realm. They then stripped us bare, burned our clothes and took our weapons. Of course, they could have killed me, too. But I believe what Oscom and Black were doing by leaving me alive, was to taunt me, extend my suffering...and also to deliberately humiliate the royal family. But most of all, to make me suffer for not paying that original ransom.

"Anyway, with a company of Earl's Leet militia, we did briefly pick up their trail in the south-eastern Bleaklow Hills, where they murdered three more soldiers. But that was the last time I saw either Oscom or Black. Since then, no one has seen either of them, or their two accomplices. And worst of all, no one has seen my dear sister, either."

Magnus paused, pretending to hold back another sob, before carrying on. "I am now coming towards the end of this announcement. You must understand that this has been a daunting prospect for me. To lay my foolishness bare to the nation. And I *was* a fool playing a foolish game. And then John Nash and I were fools for not taking Oscom seriously. The palace guard are also culpable for letting bogus laundry men both in and out. But I have not chastised or disciplined them, because they are no more guilty than I am. We all make mistakes. For our combined mistakes, we have paid an excruciatingly heavy price. But in the last three weeks, I, personally, have matured. I am not seeking approval for that, nor am I seeking forgiveness for what I have done. All I want is my sister back, and that is the main purpose of this announcement. Obviously, we had to give you some context – and this we have done with brutal honesty.

"As to next steps, this is where all of you come in. This is where every man, woman, boy and girl in this nation of ours comes in. Jake Oscom and Harry Black were last seen in the region between the Bleaklow Hills and the Rednewt Hills. But that was over a week ago. They could be anywhere in Glennad now, but we at least remain confident that they are still on this island, in hiding somewhere.

"Anyway, as a small force, we came close to capturing these men. We kept a low profile in case a national campaign endangered the life of the Princess. But as we've still had no ransom, we have now had to mobilise the army. We have no choice. But with ten thousand soldiers to call upon, we are about to take this kingdom apart to find Oscom and Black, hoping against hope, that we will also turn up our precious princess – alive and well. My precious sister."

Magnus paused for a few seconds before continuing. "In the next week, we will be circulating across the country, over twenty thousand posters showing the likenesses of Oscom, Black and their two accomplices. All I would ask of you, is that if you see anything, or know anything, please present yourself to the Ghantiss Council House at the earliest opportunity with your information. But please, ladies and gentlemen. Please do not waste our time with worthless information. That won't help anyone, and it certainly won't help Alicya.

"All that leaves me to say, is to first thank the Lord High Constable for stepping in when I faltered. Thank you to my loyal palace guard for a valiant effort to ensnare Oscom and Black over the last eighteen days. And finally, thank you to each and every one of you who have come here today to listen to this announcement, and for keeping so respectfully quiet throughout. I hope you now appreciate why we called for this public announcement. It was vital that you all heard the facts from those at the centre of this crisis, as we cannot afford skewed messages that may hinder our future progress. As stated earlier, written accounts of what has happened and how we are going to approach bringing these men to justice, will be circulated over the next week-or-so, and extensive coverage will appear in *The Daily Chronicle*, *The Glennadian Times* and other regional newspapers. Thank you very much for your understanding, ladies and gentlemen. And please, finally, may I ask you all to say a daily prayer for the safe return of our princess. Thank you."

As Magnus walked calmly off-stage in something of a trance, the noise in Ghantiss marketplace went off the scale. Magnus didn't care. He knew that between himself and the Lord High Constable, they had achieved what he had set out to do and more. From this moment onwards, Jake Oscom and Harry Black were dead men walking, and he was already absolved of the murder of his sister.

It was time for a private celebration!

CHAPTER 96 — MADELEINA

26th Tertiar, 1789
Day 117, 12:30

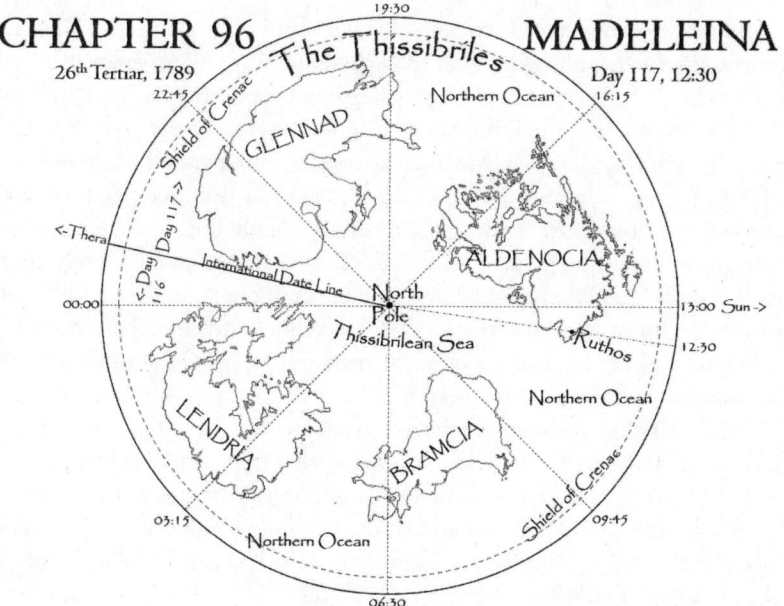

Madeleina watched their boat cut through the surf, deep in thought. In four days, she would return to Ghinbrude, by fast coach, for Prince Marco's funeral before resuming her tour at Yunderoa on 34th Tertiar, delaying each subsequent concert by seven days. It would significantly inconvenience venue managers with rearrangements, but it couldn't be helped. For the journey to Ghinbrude, she would be accompanied by Mr Wallace and two of his men, while her tour manager and his hands would continue to move instruments and equipment to Yunderoa and then wait there for a week until she returned from Ghinbrude – perhaps relaxing and enjoying the sea air on the rugged west coast.

As for Prince Bernard's funeral, Madeleina felt relief and guilt in equal measure for not having to travel to Lendria to endure his service and burial. Given she had been betrothed to him, it would look odd, or worse, terrible, that she would not be in attendance, but the Lendrian royal family had requested a small private ceremony and she wasn't complaining. Poor Bernie, though. *Those awful bulging eyes.*

Madeleina closed her eyes and tried to think of something, anything else. An image of a buttered scone covered with a thick layer of raspberry jam availed itself – unsurprising, really, as she'd just scoffed two of them for dessert. Given they were approaching the western resort of Ruthos, she at least had a new destination to help take her mind off funerals. And despite recent shocks, travelling by boat to each venue was still an enjoyable and rather exciting experience. She could see that beyond the harbour walls of Ruthos, there was a small but tidy town, dominated by the church which sported a fine needle spire. Most of the houses were painted white or were of light grey stone, giving the resort a fairly cheery aspect. As ever, there was a reception committee of locals clustered around the docking area, all intrigued to see their princess and her orchestra disembark, while children were always fascinated by the large wooden containers that were rolled off or carried from the boat to the concert venue, and which contained a number of rather large and expensive instruments; not least of which was Madeleina's enormous grand piano.

Madeleina felt the displacement of air as she was joined at starboard by the enormous bulk of Jed Wallace, his spade-shaped brown beard blowing in the wind. "Are you feeling relaxed, Princess?" he asked in his broad brogue.

Madeleina closed her eyes and let the wind blow in her lightly-freckled face and through her untied fair hair. "I am, thank you, Mr Wallace. But I'll openly admit, that it has been a trying few days."

"Brave heart, Princess. Meanwhile, you just make the most of the freedom of travel and the joy that your music brings you."

Madeleina opened her eyes, turned to Wallace and smiled. "We are lucky to have you, Mr Wallace."

"The honour is all mine, Princess," he responded, giving her the rarest – but briefest – of smiles back.

As the boat cruised serenely into Ruthos Bay, they stood there in silence looking at the approaching town, both with their hands resting on the wooden hand-rail before them. Internally, though, Madeleina wasn't quite as serene as she appeared.

Do I tell him about Clair?
No, he'll think you're mad.
But what if I'm not?
You can't think someone dead, you idiot!

Thirty minutes later, they were all disembarking in single file, including Madeleina's twenty-strong orchestra. The tour manager and his hands remained on board, ready to unload the heavier musical instruments. Madeleina and Wallace were approached first by the mayor of Ruthos and went through the usual introductions and pleasantries. The mayor then introduced them all to a short and stout man with a beetroot-red face and a shock of frizzled ginger hair. "Welcome to Ruthos, Princess Madeleina.

My name is Lochie Kyle. I'm the manager of the Ruthos Coliseum. I can't tell you how honoured we are to have you with us."

Madeleina smiled back at him, having noted that his accent was even broader than Jed Wallace's. "It's a pleasure to be here, Mr Kyle. My orchestra and I can't wait to perform in the Coliseum. I've heard so many tales about its legendary acoustics."

Madeleina couldn't have said anything more pleasing to Lochie Kyle. He puffed out his chest and positively beamed from both eyes and shiny cheeks. "Aye, she's a grand old lady, that she is."

"My itinerary tells me, Mr Kyle," cut in Jed Wallace, "that the concert is due to start at 19:30 hours. We will aim to arrive three and a half hours before that at around 16:00 hours, if that is suitable for you?"

"Oh, you can come down whenever you're ready, Mr Wallace. We'd be ready for you now, if necessary."

"Well, naturally," began Wallace, perfectly rolling his 'r', "we first need to get the Princess and her orchestra settled in at the – one moment," he said as he inspected his little black notebook, "ah yes, the Belle Vue, I believe is the hotel in which we're being accommodated."

"Aye, that's right," said a smartly-dressed newcomer, who introduced himself as the hotel owner.

"Well, I'll take my leave of you now," said Kyle. "And I look forward immensely to demonstrating our acoustics to you later this afternoon."

"Thank you, Mr Kyle," said Madeleina and Jed Wallace, in unison.

"Oh, and before I go," said Kyle, turning back around. "I must offer my condolences about Fraser Cameron. Our paths crossed many times and he was always the consummate gentleman. Terrible business. Shocking times we live in."

Madeleina frowned, confused, having no idea what Lochie Kyle was talking about. It was also clear that Jed Wallace had no idea either, so he immediately took control of the situation, not wishing to upset his princess, especially not in public. For such a huge man, he gently steered the diminutive Kyle to one side, where they proceeded to converse in low voices. Had the message not been so worrying, Madeleina would have probably chuckled at such a contrasting pair.

As Wallace and Kyle conversed, Charlotte and Aggie moved forward to support the Princess, both wringing their hands with distress, having also heard Kyle's condolences. It was then that the likely significance of Kyle's words sank in, and Madeleina felt those now-familiar sensations encroach; a hot flush travelling up her body and a buzzing sound beginning in her ears. She held on to Charlotte, desperately trying not to attract attention to herself. Thankfully, with some controlled breathing and the fresh sea air, the symptoms began to recede.

By the time Jed Wallace came back to them, Madeleina was already prepared for the news. Wallace explained that there had been some kind of burglary gone wrong at Ghinbrude Palladium, and poor Fraser Cameron had come across them and been shot dead.

Rather than feeling faint, this time Madeleina felt completely numb. Her mind had already flitted back to the dream she had had in Edenbrae. *Fraser Cameron, shot in the chest, blood pumping through fingers that were hopelessly trying to stem the flow. And those eyes. Those bulging eyes.*

"Mr Wallace," said Madeleina, her voice perfectly calm. "You and I need to have a long chat. In private."

Half an hour later, Madeleina and Jed Wallace were sitting drinking tea in the penthouse suite of the Belle Vue Hotel. Recognising the likely seriousness of the chat, Wallace had insisted that his three agents be present as well, and they stood to attention behind him. All nicely settled, Wallace asked Madeleina to begin.

"The first thing I want to say is that I'm not going mad. I have *not* imagined any of these things, and I now strongly suspect that malicious forces are at work."

Wallace nodded, his keen blue eyes fixed on Madeleina's, his agile mind ready for anything.

"I also refuse to believe in the supernatural – for that is what these... these *forces* would have me believe."

Again, Wallace nodded. "In your own time then, Princess."

"It all started, twelve days ago in Ghinbrude, just before one of my performances…"

And Madeleina proceeded to tell Wallace everything. He didn't interrupt once, but his eyes maintained a hawk-like focus until she had finished. He then began to ask questions. "So, the first time. Why did you not call in the guards, if you don't mind me asking, Princess?"

"Leah and Cape were aware she was there; it was they who let her in."

"But you chose not to call them in, even when you felt this woman was a crank?"

"It's hard to explain. She was so…unremarkable in appearance, that I didn't feel threatened by her. Yet, at the same time, there was a hypnotic aura about her. I just didn't feel compelled to raise an alert."

"All right," said Wallace. "So, what happened next?"

"Well, as you know, the next day, Prince Bernard died. I mean, you can imagine the sort of thoughts that were going through my mind," said Madeleina, now becoming flustered. "I actually thought that it was my fault," she said, as her eyes began to brim.

Jed Wallace leaned forward and put his hand over Madeleina's. "You've done nothing wrong, Princess. And you're right, there's nothing supernatural here. My instinct is already telling me that this is some kind of a criminal or Abolitionist plot."

Madeleina looked up at him sharply, her watery eyes suddenly full of shock. "Do you really think so?"

"I need to clarify a few points first, Princess. But I have agents everywhere, and we hear of many plots and counter-plots – almost all of which never bear fruit – or even get off the ground, for that matter."

"I can't tell you how much of a relief that would be…if…if…if it wasn't down to me…" Madeleina tailed off, feeling rather foolish.

Wallace patted Madeleina's hand again. "You are completely blameless here, Princess," he encouraged, before switching back to his questioning. "Now, you mentioned earlier that this Clair's appearance had changed for the second encounter? Tell me more about that."

"Yes, it was the day after Prince Bernard's death. I was collecting my sheet music from Ghinbrude Palladium. Again, I took Mr Leah and Mr Cape with me. I asked them to wait outside the dressing room. I can't explain why. Protocol, perhaps – because a dressing room is private. Anyway, what happened next is the most difficult thing of all to explain – unless there is another entrance and exit to that dressing room."

"The woman was already there?" asked Wallace.

"Yes, sat on my couch, as bold as brass. And looking very different."

"Describe her to me."

Madeleina described how the first time she had been dowdy, with mousy, shoulder-length brown hair, two rotten teeth, a raised mole on her nose, and a grey shawl. But on the second occasion, she had been well-dressed, her hair styled and vibrant, white teeth and no mole; taller, somehow. But above all, her manner had been different.

"In what way?" asked Wallace.

"There was no deference like there had been the first time. She was openly insolent."

"Hmm," said Wallace, deep in thought. "Please explain further."

"She accused me of doing it."

"Of killing Prince Bernard?"

"Essentially, yes," said Madeleina, starting to become flustered again.

"It's all right, Princess. Please keep calm. You're doing extremely well."

"I handled it better at the time, Mr Wallace. I was actually annoyed with her. Told her I'd call the guards. And then she did that thing again."

"Thing?"

"Threw me off-balance. She said: 'Leah and Cape, I believe.'"

"She knew the names of your guards?"

"Yes."

"How interesting," said Wallace, now completely gripped by the unfolding mystery.

"Of course, she claimed she knew through Second Sight."

"Pah!" was Wallace's response. "What happened next?"

"She threw me again. Asked whom I next wanted dead."

"And your response."

"I got cross with her. I told her I didn't want *anyone* dead, least of all Bernie. She responded by mocking me and then accusing me of 'fixing him'. That's when she turned the tables on me and started moving towards blackmail. She ended up saying something like she owned me."

"Did she indeed," said Wallace, a grim look on his face. "My Princess," he said, looking her in the eye. "You have nothing to be afraid of or ashamed of. And you are almost certainly right about this being blackmail. This woman is clearly a predator. And a very good one, too, by the sound of it. So, what happened next?"

"She said that if I didn't do as she asked, she would expose me over Prince Bernard's death."

"And what did she ask?"

"Well, that's the strange thing. She didn't ask anything of me." Madeleina set her jaw to a firmer line. "But what she did do, was to suggest that I should – and this is weird – that I should *think* or *will* the death of Prince Marco."

Wallace greeted this revelation with silence. His own jaw stiffened beneath his great brown beard, and his eyes blazed with intelligence. Eventually, he spoke. "I name this woman, Clair, to be a murderess, Princess. A murderess, or an accessory to murder. At least three times. And she has attempted to gain some kind of a hold over you in the process by making you feel guilt over these deaths."

"But I *did* think of Prince Marco dying. In lots of different ways. I just couldn't help it. And one of those deaths I imagined was through falling.

And then he died when rock-climbing."

"All this woman did was put images into your mind. You can't kill a person with thoughts."

"That's what I kept telling myself."

"And you were right, Princess. Let me guess. She also mentioned Mr Cameron, yes?"

Think Prince Marco dead. Or what about poor Mr Cameron?

Madeleina lifted her head to look at Jed Wallace, and nodded, tearfully.

Again, Wallace took her hand. "They're just parlour tricks, Princess. Don't criticise yourself over falling for them. You're only very young."

"But what about Prince Bernard's death. It was only a heart attack. You don't think…"

"I don't think anything, as yet. I would love to have one of my men at the post-mortem, though, but it is probably too late for that. Prince Bernard's body was repatriated two days ago. But I shall ensure that we pass on our suspicions to the Lendrian authorities. In the meantime, Princess, you need to relax," he said, patting her hands again. "This is now all over for you. You won't be troubled by this Clair again."

Wallace's kindness made her well up again and she was furious with herself – both for crying again and for being ensnared in Clair's web in the first place. After a few seconds, she recovered, and a kind of release gradually came over her. "So, what this means is…"

"Exactly, Princess. You've done nothing wrong. And when I catch these black-hearted plotters, they will wish they had never been born."

CHAPTER 97   JAKE

28th Tertiar, 1789   Day 119, 12:00

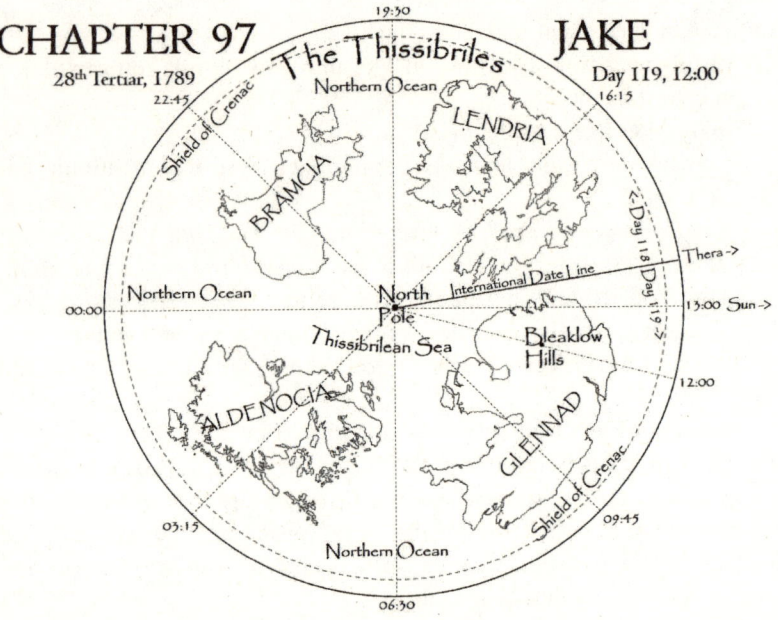

"Mate, you can't call him Mute," said Swede.

"Why not? It's what he is, isn't it?" retorted Turnip.

"Exactly. Which makes it very rude."

Turnip brought his horse to a stop. "Since when have you been bothered about protocol and etiquette?"

Swede also stopped. "You can't call him Mute."

"All right, how about Newt, then?"

"Newt?"

"Why not? Unless that's offensive to small amphibians, of course."

"Which he clearly isn't, and so it's acceptable."

Jake chuckled to himself. He was getting quite partial to Turnip and Swede's banter. Meanwhile, the young orphan they were discussing rode silently alongside them. The boy had said nothing throughout the last eight days, although he seemed to understand them well enough and had answered all questions with a nod or shake of the head, or number of fingers – eight in the case of his age. Through this form of communication, they had established that he had never known his father, his mother had died earlier this year (but of what, they could not establish), he had no brothers or sisters or other relatives, but had lived with his mother in Earl's Leet. And he knew how to ride a horse.

"Poor little mite was probably cast out when his Mam died," Turnip had suggested, several days ago.

"But why come all the way up here?" Swede had responded.

"Probably safer than the town – you know, for a little kid on his own and all."

"But Earl's Leet is the safest town in Glennad!"

"That's 99 per cent true, Swede," Harry Black had interjected. "But it's the other one per cent that a child has to worry about."

"What! In Earl's Leet?" exclaimed Swede, genuinely put out. "That's scandalous, that is Harry. Is there nowhere safe in this rotten kingdom?"

"The highways, perhaps?" Jake had offered, wryly.

"Ah, well, you see, that's different that is, Oscom," began Swede, finger raised. And he and Turnip had then gone off on a rangy argument as to why the highways didn't count and were fair game. Jake had already forgotten what their justification had been. As for the last eight days, they had been spent weaving aimlessly around the southern Bleaklows, surviving on rabbit, squirrel, the odd deer…and some rather tasty freshwater salmon.

"Do you reckon they've given up?" asked Turnip, breaking into Jake's thoughts.

"No!" chorused Jake and Harry Black.

"But we aint seen no one other than that patrol, three days ago," whined Turnip.

"Yeah, we could have used that time to get Newt here down to the authorities in Earl's Leet," added Swede.

"Except someone in the authorities could be in the one per cent," responded Jake.

"Well, we can't have him riding around with us," moaned Turnip.

"Of that, I'm inclined to agree," said Black, "as we're not going to remain unmolested in these hills for much longer. We've got a major price on our heads thanks to you two for killing those three soldiers."

"Not to mention the other three when we ambushed the Prince at Earl's Leet," added Swede.

"What do you think, Jake?" asked Black.

"I don't think Prince Magnus is the type to give up. Sooner or later, they'll come back looking where we were last seen."

"And the boy?"

"I maintain there is a risk in handing him over to the Earl's Leet authorities. But there is somewhere else he would be safe."

"Your friends at the farm?" guessed Black.

"Exactly. Although Clyve and Meg are not likely to thank me. It's an enormous thing to ask of someone."

"Does this mean we're likely to have another taste of the lovely Meg's honeycakes?" asked Swede, his eyes as wide as a child's.

Jake turned to look at Harry Black, who just rolled his eyes. "Maybe you will, at that," answered Jake. "I suggest we head north, down the pass," he said, pointing to a steep decline between two hills. "That should bring us out on the Ghintonoll road. Could do with a disguise of some sort, though."

"I suggest we stay short of the road then, and send Turnip and Swede into Earl's Leet to either buy or acquire some new clothing."

"Why us?" chorused Turnip and Swede.

"Hello?" said Black, leaning his face towards Jake's and indicating the two of them. "The two most wanted faces in the kingdom."

"He's always got an excuse, that Harry Black," moaned Turnip.

"Yeah, and to be frank, Harry, me and him aint far behind you two in the wanted stakes," whinged Swede.

"This is true," said Black, reconsidering, and turning to Jake. "Do you think we might be able to impose on your farmer friend a teensy bit more? For suitable garments, I mean?"

"Aye, but you'll be paying him for them."

"Oh, Mr Oscom!" exclaimed Black, his face falling. "Do you have *any* regard for my reputation."

"No," responded Jake, flatly.

Black made a face, but then it suddenly lit up. "I have the perfect solution!"

"Oh lawks," said Turnip, his face all of a worry. "I don't like it when he has 'perfect solutions.'"

"It will save you a trip into Earl's Leet, you ungrateful wretch, so listen up. Clyve runs a farm. We have two spare horses. Three if we give him Newt's."

"Very good, Harry," responded Jake. "But you'll still pay him for the clothes as well."

Harry Black was virtually spluttering with indignation. Finally, he managed to sort his words out. "But those three horses will be worth a fortune, man."

"Aye," agreed Jake. "But they're not ours to sell, and I was planning on giving them to Clyve long before you came up with the idea."

Having had enough of the banter, Jake tapped his horse into a trot and headed towards the northern pass, leaving three bandits looking miserably at each other – before they and Newt headed off in tow.

It was two hours later when they found the building site – although they heard it first. For around fifteen minutes, the sounds of construction had drifted up the pass on a cold northerly wind – sawing, hammering and banging, and occasionally what sounded like small explosions.

"Any idea what that is?" asked Jake to Black.

"None. There was nothing in this pass the last time I rode up it."

Jake frowned, but for now, curiosity was outweighing caution. They soon came to a bend in the pass to the left, and on a plain below around half a mile to their west, there was a vast construction site on another plateau not dissimilar to the one Earl's Leet had been built on. Rows and rows of triangular joists were pointing up into the air, with varying stages of wall and roof development around them, and the site was awash with construction personnel.

"Looks like they're building a new town," said Black.

"But this is even more out of the way than Earl's Leet," said Jake. "At least Earl's Leet is on a highway of sorts. We've still got another six hundred feet to descend to get down to that road, and the only way up here is this narrow pass. How did they get all that equipment up here?"

Before Harry Black could reply, another explosion rocked the valley, and the five of them observed smoke coming out of one of the limestone caves that ran along the southern edge of the construction site. The four adults in the party looked at each other blankly, no one offering an opinion. Eventually, Jake spoke. "Well," he began. "I've half a mind to head over there and ask the foreman what they're up to."

"If you did that, Jake, my friend, then you really would have half a mind," said Black, drolly. "Come on. Let's leave them to whatever it is they're building. Maybe Clyve and Meg will tell us what they're up to."

"If they know, Harry. This is very much out of the way."

"Well, no doubt we'll find out in time. Let's get out of sight before someone takes an interest in us."

Nodding, but still puzzling over the site, Jake tapped his heels to his horse's flank, and the five of them continued on down the pass. When they arrived at the point where the pass met the construction road heading west, they found their answer to the construction traffic riddle. The path had been widened and gravel packed, meaning that horses and carts would be able to transport equipment up and down the lower part of the pass. Once again, Jake puzzled at the mystery of such a remote and inaccessible site and, moreover, the cost.

By the time they turned into Clyve and Meg's long farm driveway, it was starting to get dark. Like before, though, both Clyve and Jared Swan came out to meet them.

"Now, don't take this the wrong way, Jake," began Clyve. "But I'd rather hoped we'd seen the last of you lot – although I see you've got a new recruit there."

"Aye, he's the reason we're here, Clyve."

Jake was just about to explain when a flustered Meg came running out. "You can't stay here, you lot. In fact, you can't even be seen here. You'll have us shot, too."

"I'm afraid she's right, Jake," said Clyve. "You've been busy since we last met, I understand."

Jake looked at Turnip and Swede and gave them his best frown.

"Don't you come that with me, mister," said Turnip. "You killed one of the militiamen near the Esou Aqueduct."

Jake grimaced at the accusation. "Yes," he muttered, painfully. "Thanks to you landing us in a perilous predicament, I had no choice."

"I didn't know Magnus was going to shoot me up the arse, did I?"

"Gentlemen, please," interceded Harry Black. "This isn't helping. Clyve, Meg," he said, turning to face them with his best winning smile. "Your friend, Jake Oscom here, has taken every precaution to prevent loss of life. In the unfortunate event of us being captured, I will make it clear that he had no part in *any* of the deaths."

"There's no need for that, Harry –," began Jake, before Meg interrupted them.

"That's as maybe," she stated. "But you still aren't coming into my house, and you need to get off my land. Now."

"Meg, love," said Clyve, raising his palms in a placatory gesture.

"And don't you 'Meg, love' me neither, Clyve Swan!"

"Meg," said Jake, firmly. That got everyone's attention, including a startled Meg. "Let me explain our position. It will take two minutes, and then we will leave."

"But what about –," began Swede, before Jake stopped him with a sharply raised hand.

"I'll cut to the chase. We've been hiding in the southern Bleaklows, and we came across this young man in Roth's Cave," said Jake, gesturing towards Newt. "He never knew his father, his mother died earlier this year and he has no other relatives. He would have been handed over to the Earl's Leet authorities, but he left Earl's Leet for the hills because he was scared – of what, we don't know, although we fear that we perhaps do. He has no home.

He's extremely obedient, useful with his hands, knows how to ride – and he needs a home. A farm would be perfect."

Jake could already see Meg's face melting as she looked at the skinny boy on a horse that was far too large for him.

"We also bring you his horse, and these two strays as well," added Jake.

"Now please don't tell me that those are…"

"They're not marked, Clyve," responded Jake. "No one can prove anything, and if anyone ever questions you, just say you found them roaming your fields without any apparent owner and you took them in for their own protection."

"You used to be an honest man, Captain."

"Aye," said Jake, sadly. "I miss that man."

Meg meanwhile had walked up to the boy. "What's your name, love?"

All she got back was silence.

Jake dismounted and walked over to stand beside Meg. He put a hand on her shoulder. "He doesn't speak, Meg. At least we don't think he does. And we've had him with us for eight days now."

"Oh, the poor little mite," said Meg, her eyes beginning to glisten.

"But he does understand us," added Jake.

"Would you like to come inside and see our dogs, young man?" she asked. "There's Mitzy, Rollo and Luther, and little Theo is now doing splendidly as well."

Newt gave her a gentle smile and nodded. Poor Meg's chin gave up its struggle. "Oh, come here, little man," she said, holding out her plump arms. Trustingly, Newt held out his arms, too, and allowed Meg to lift him off his horse. He looked up at her and smiled, so Meg ruffled his hair. "Does he have a name."

"Ah," began Jake.

"Newt," said Turnip.

"Newt!" exclaimed Meg. "What sort of a name is that?"

"Don't ask," said Jake. "Meg, if you are going to take him in, I'm sure he'll tell you his name, in time."

"Of course I'm going to take him in, you scoundrel. You knew darned well I would, too."

Jake had the decency to look bashful at that accusation.

"Jake," said Meg, softly. "I'm sorry about not accommodating you."

"That's fine, Meg. We understand."

"Don't worry about leaving…Newt…with us. You did the right thing. You couldn't leave him all alone up there. There are wolves, for starters. This just proves that you're still a good man at heart." Meg then kissed Jake gently on the cheek.

"Is there anything you need before you move on, Jake?" asked Clyve.

"Yes Clyve," began Jake, carefully. "We need clothes. For disguise. Farmers clothes would be perfect. We thought that between you and Jared, you might have enough, so…"

"Listen," began Clyve. "I'll tell you what we'll do. It's getting dark now, but you see that path off to the side there," he said, pointing.

Jake nodded.

"About two hundred yards down there, you'll find an old cowshed on your right-hand side. There's straw in it – probably not fresh, though. Travellers use it to sleep in without asking. It's yours for the night. Go there now, and I'll send Jared up with some clothes later. Jared can also tell you all about his hike up to Kifsel Place with Emilya and Elyse."

Jake's memory flashed back to that moment when they'd said goodbye on this very driveway, seventeen long days ago.

"I can't imagine a life without you in it."

"And neither I without you."

Jake dragged himself back into the present, and held his hand out to Clyve. "I will never forget this."

Clyve just pulled his old captain into a bear-hug. "I fear we may never meet again, my friend," he said, patting Jake's back. Clyve then pulled back, and held Jake by his shoulders. "But I wish you all the luck in the world, my friend – wherever life may take you."

After that, a sombre trio made their way to the signalled path, and Meg put her arm around Newt and guided him into the farmhouse. Jake turned around once and saw that Newt had done the same. The child raised his hand and waved. It was too dark to see if he had a smile on his face – but Jake felt certain that he had.

CHAPTER 98 DRAXAELEN

29th Tertiar, 1789

Day 120, 11:00

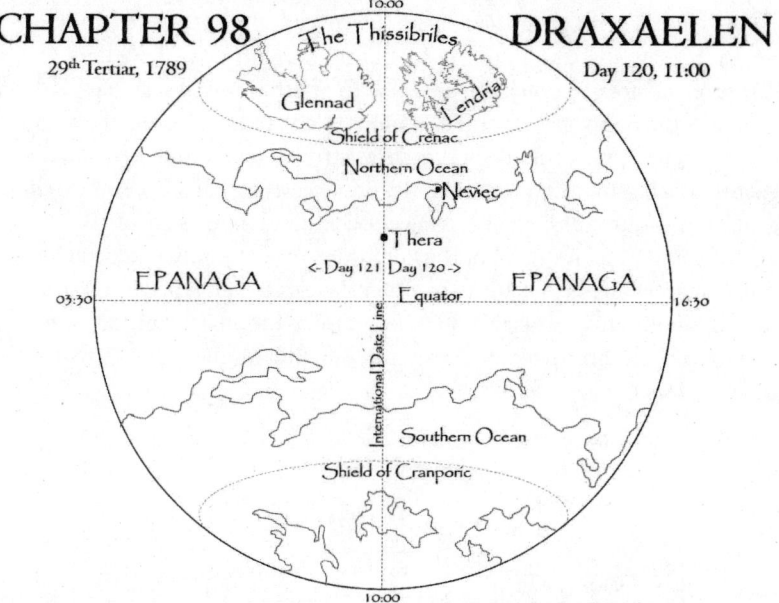

It had taken just under ten days to row the galleys back across the Northern Ocean from Ytre in Rysia to Liatia, where they had docked at the north-eastern port of Neviec – famous for its stunning squares and bell towers. But there would be no sight-seeing trips for Draxaelen and his fellow slaves. Instead, Maxi Zoninus had marched them from the harbour, in chains, for half a league inland, to the outskirts of Neviec. One of the slaves had been brave enough to ask what was happening. He hadn't been quick enough to dodge the club from one of Zoninus' guards. Draxaelen had heard his skull crack. The slave didn't get up, and his limp and increasingly bloodied carcass had since been dragged along the ground by the momentum of the rest of his chain-gang ever since. Nobody had asked any further questions.

Eventually, they were divided up into twenty groups of twenty, with the chains adjusted accordingly. Each group was allocated a Theran official. Draxaelen was in the third group of twenty, and had watched the previous two groups being marched towards a large square-looking, open-topped building for which the external walls were made up entirely of thick, twenty-foot-long wooden poles, side-by-side, each tapering to a wicked-looking spike. They had disappeared through the only doorway in between the spiked poles, which had a large viewing platform rising above it, currently occupied by ten armed sentries.

As Drax and his group were ushered through the open seven-foot oaken doors, he saw that the building was bristling with armed soldiers inside. The internal area was a large square, with another raised viewing platform visible at the opposite end and two more to either side. Inside, the area was divided into a grid of sixteen enclosures, arranged as a four-by-four, one in each corner, while Draxaelen could now see that the walkway extended around all four sides, so that viewers could see into each of the sixteen enclosures. Some, if not all of the enclosures in the top two quarters of the building were already occupied by other slaves, in what Draxaelen estimated to be groups of five – this now making sense of the chain-gang groupings of twenty, as each group would end up populating a set of four pits with five slaves apiece.

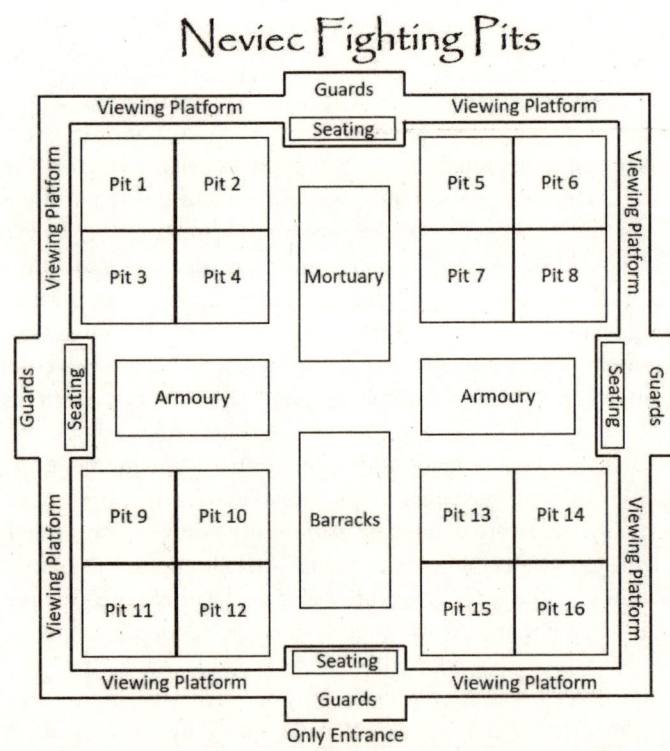

Drax was under no illusions as to what awaited them. These were fighting pits. He had known that at some stage in his life as a slave, he might be cast into a gladiatorial pit, and asked to fight or die. He had not expected it to be this soon, though – less than an hour after disembarking from the boat that he had helped propel a quarter of the way around the world and back. What he had not even considered, was that his opponents might be friends or former Demonacian soldiers. The reality was, though, that they weren't soldiers any more. They were slaves. To be used or abused as Maxi Zoninus saw fit. Draxaelen could see the slave-master dead ahead, standing in the viewing gallery facing the only entrance to the building. Their eyes briefly locked, before the man sat down – confirming that these fighting pits had indeed been built with spectator sport in mind. Some of those spectators were behind Zoninus. Civilians of Neviec, dressed in their finest silks of so many different vibrant colours, each looking forward with relish to the contests ahead. Draxaelen felt sick to his core.

After a short delay, he and his group were unchained, and along with the five nearest slaves, Drax was hustled into one of the rooms in the front left quarter of the building. All of them except one moved to stand at a place apart from their fellows, having realised where this was heading. The other man remained close to Drax, clearly not handling this well. Whereas the other men were upright and alert, this fellow's arms were hanging by his sides and his posture was slumped. Draxaelen then saw the stain begin to spread across the man's breeches.

Laughter above and to his left alerted Drax. He looked up – and saw several faces leering down at them from the left-hand viewing gallery, one of them pointing at the man stood next to him. Drax felt an anger begin to well up. These people, this country, this regime – all utterly inhuman; the main reason why he and his fellow Demonacians had risen up, supposedly supported by comrades from four other countries. *The fake Eastern Alliance*, thought Drax, bitterly.

Elsewhere above him, Draxaelen realised that a row of Theran soldiers had crossbows loaded, raised and pointing down into the fighting pits. The same applied to all other pits. Draxaelen's heart sank. Were they not even going to be given the opportunity to fight fairly? Would those who won suddenly sprout a dozen quarrels? Or would those slaves who the soldiers took a dislike to – perhaps on some whim – suddenly be shot dead through the heart *during* the fight? Nothing from these Therans would surprise him.

Drax then noticed a familiar face eyeing him across the pit. The man's name was Garataelix. He had stood with Drax, Argaeus and Crateuas in

Alsethonisca market square on that fateful blue-sky morning twenty days ago. The man looked lean and fit, and Drax felt a surge of pride that he was one of his own. Like himself, he must have been forced into rowing a galley ship a quarter of the way around the world to raid and kill innocent men, women and children, and then row all the way back to Liatia again. In just twenty days. *How could it only be twenty days?* It felt like half a lifetime.

Drax looked back at Garataelix with guilt. It was his fault the man was here, because it was Drax who had fallen for Leonnatus' lies. Even now, he could hear the casual laugh of General Macrinus as Drax's father and two younger brothers had been crucified in front of him; he could clearly visualise the disparaging look on Macrinus' face as he recalled the rape and murder of his mother and sisters. Drax's blood thumped ever-louder within his skull. And now, these inhuman Therans were going to force him to kill or be killed by one of his own men. For his oath of revenge, it had to be the former. Ideally starting with Maxi Zoninus, sat up there, casting his eyes over his property as a man might look down on a flock of sheep in the slaughterhouse. The man who had branded him, and then relished pressing the red-hot iron into poor Argaeus' already shredded shoulder.

Draxaelen wondered again if Argaeus had survived. He certainly hadn't seen him in the last twenty days. He had been so weak from his injuries, that it would have been impossible for him to have rowed for one hour, never mind twenty days. It was just one more reason why Macrinus and Zoninus had to pay. And once he had executed that pair, the newly-crowned Emperor of Thera would follow; Calidius' coronation being one of the few paltry nuggets of news he and his fellow slaves had been fed in the last three weeks. All three *would* die by his hand. Somehow.

Drax was pulled out of his thoughts by the sound of activity in the adjacent quarter of the great square building – presumably the fourth set of twenty slaves being released from their chains and funnelled into their four fighting pits. With that action complete, all sixteen fighting pit doors were closed, and Drax heard a sturdy bar being placed across the outer side of the door to his pit. Not that any of them would try to escape, as they would be cut down by the many armed soldiers patrolling the inner corridors, or the crossbow-armed soldiers on the viewing platforms above. Drax also suspected that the formidable main entrance door had been closed as well. There would only be one way out of here alive.

Movement from ahead caught Draxaelen's attention. Maxi Zoninus had got to his feet, his finest silks of turquoise and aqua blowing slightly in the breeze. A silence settled over the open-topped building. "Slaves," began

Zoninus, his lisp meaning he pronounced the word as 'Thlaves'. "You have proved your resilience and your loyalty to the Theran Empire over the last twenty days. Thera salutes you for your commitment."

Zoninus paused, and Drax noticed him absently rotating one of his many gold rings around one finger with other fingers of the same hand. "I have always hinted that this day might come. I must confess, I had not expected it quite so soon. But our new emperor has commenced his rule by announcing the greatest, longest and fiercest gladiatorial games in the history of the Theran Empire."

Another pause – and Drax observed Zoninus moistening his dry lips with his tongue. He looked very serpentine. "The best gladiators from each city," he continued, "will be pitched against each other until a few elite victors remain. And then those elite will be pitched against the elite from other cities. Eventually, the best of the best will converge on the Mesocluso in Thera in around fifty days' time, for the greatest contest in our history. That contest," said Zoninus, pausing for effect, "could potentially include any one of you. Even several of you, perhaps. But your journey starts today – in a few minutes' time.

"As for your contests, it should already be clear whom you will be fighting." Eyes briefly met around Drax's fighting pit. "We expect at least one winner from each of the sixteen groups – potentially more, if I step in and stop the contest. I will do this if I think more than one of you is worthy of progressing in this competition. However, many of you will die today. All I ask…is that you die well; with honour."

Zoninus paused again, before placing his hands on the wooden rail in front of him. He leaned forwards slightly. "In terms of rules – there are none. It is simply kill or be killed. Kill by whichever means necessary. Shortly, we will cast five weapons into the first pit. The men in that pit will need to move fast to secure their weapon of choice. That is all."

Zoninus then nodded to a soldier on the walkway overlooking what Draxaelen would later know as Pit No 2. "Let the fighting commence."

The soldier was holding a sack – which he carried to the edge of Pit No 2. The soldier then spoke, loudly and clearly. "You will each move to the side and place your back against a wall."

Draxaelen couldn't see what was happening in Pit No 2, but it sounded as though the command was being obeyed. Drax tried to visualise it by flicking his eyes around his own pit. One of the four walls must have at least two men with their backs to it. Drax's eyes flicked back up to the viewing platform. The soldier was upending the contents of the sack onto the walkway, and two fellow soldiers picked up two weapons apiece – which included a sword, a dagger, an axe and a net. The first soldier picked up a spear. Draxaelen's thoughts rapidly sorted them into effectiveness order. Should his pit be offered the same weapon-set, he needed to grab the spear. Maxi Zoninus then nodded, and the weapons were cast into the pit.

Drax heard the metallic clangs and wooden bangs as the weapons hit the floor and bounced once or twice. There was then a five second silence whilst combatants and spectators alike held their breath. Then it sounded as if all hell broke loose. War cries and shrieks, then the sound of metal on metal, the sound of metal through flesh and bone, and the hideous sound of human screams. And above all of that, the raw sound of soldiers and citizens from the viewing platforms, roaring on the fighters, where money was changing hands in a frenzy as the civilian punters and soldiers bet on a winner.

The fighting lasted for around four minutes. As Maxi Zoninus had not stepped in and stopped the contest, Drax reasoned that there was only one man left standing, while up on the viewing platform, there was a mixture of delight and disappointment amongst the various punters.

Zoninus got to his feet and walked to the edge of the pit, his hands again resting on the bar, his features unreadable. *What carnage lay in that pit below?* As the noise levels diminished, Drax became aware of the pitiful mewling of the wounded from somewhere in Pit No 2. "Finish them!" commanded Zoninus.

Evidently, the command was not obeyed, so Zoninus nodded to the crossbow-equipped soldiers, who all stepped forward and raised their weapons, each pointing down into the pit below. "Finish them, slave!" commanded Zoninus, this time more viciously.

The command was evidently obeyed, this time, as the terrible sounds of human death were soon presented.

A low murmur, generally of satisfaction, echoed around the top end of the building, and then Zoninus spoke again. "Congratulations," he said, addressing the surviving slave down in Pit No 2. "You shall feast like the Emperor himself tonight. Please now drop your weapon."

Two seconds passed, and then Draxaelen heard what sounded like a spear clattering to the floor.

"Please remember this, though. If you refuse to finish your victims next time, you shall die yourself. Immediately."

Zoninus then commanded: "Take the victor out. See that his wounds are tended to first, and then house him in the victor's suite."

Drax realised that Zoninus was addressing soldiers at ground level, who presumably were now unbarring the door to Pit No 2. They would be heavily armed, thought Draxaelen. There would be little opportunity for the victor to use any of the five weapons in that pit – and if he was foolish enough to pick one up, he would soon resemble a porcupine, given the trigger-happy crossbow-armed soldiers up above.

Meanwhile, Maxi Zoninus had walked towards the outside of the building above Pit No 1. This bout went very differently, though. Five weapons were thrown down into the pit again – a different set from Pit No 2's. This batch had included a halberd, a scimitar and a mace, for starters. Drax was also dismayed to see that one of the five 'weapons' was a long-handled whip. He pitied the slave who ended up with that. However, Drax could see that something was wrong by the look on Zoninus' face. First puzzlement. And then anger. "What's the matter?" he asked, sibilantly. "Do you not want to live?"

A pause. And then a gruff response from the pit: "I'll not take the life of a fellow soldier." Four other voices joined him in agreement.

"Very well," said Zoninus, slyly. "Firstly," he began, and Drax noticed him absently twiddling his ring with the fingers of one hand again, "you are no longer soldiers. You are *slaves*. And secondly," he paused, licking his dry lips again, "you are superfluous." And with that, he nodded at the crossbow-armed soldiers. This time, there were ten of them arrayed around the top of Pit No 1; five down each outer side. The first five stepped forward to the edge of the viewing platform and unleashed five quarrels in different directions. Then the next five did the same from a different angle. No further quarrels were required.

Maxi Zoninus looked out over the remaining fighting pits. "I had hoped that lesson would be unnecessary. It's very simple. If you don't fight, you die. If you do fight, you may also die. But you may also live." With that said, Zoninus moved to the top left-hand corner and started to walk down towards Draxaelen's quartet of pits. For a second, Drax's heart leapt into this mouth, but the slavemaster stopped alongside a third of the first quartet of fighting pits: Pit No 3.

As Zoninus prepared to commence fighting in Pit No 3, Drax studied the four other men in his own pit, well aware that they had been doing the same of him. He would not take on Garataelix unless Garataelix took on Drax in return. The man who had wet himself was already dead – although Drax himself would not claim that kill. That was likely to be one of the other two men – whom Drax did not know. The first, to his left, was a fellow olive-skinned soldier, probably from somewhere east of Demonacia. The second, to his right, was a great bear of a man who had the look of an Alglian. He looked like a seasoned scrapper too, given he was missing an ear and had a body peppered with countless scars. Drax recognised him from his own galley crew, but he had never heard the man speak. Not once. Neither had he seen him fight – but instinct told him that this man was a good but brutal fighter.

Encouragingly, the fight in Pit No 3 appeared to have resulted in two survivors, as Maxi Zoninus had stepped in and stopped the fight when two of them were left standing. As in Pit No 2, they were asked to finish the vanquished – a command this time obeyed – and were then allowed to leave their fighting pit, again with the promise of having their injuries tended to and then being allowed to retire to the victor's suite.

Pit No 4 also had two victors. Then, Draxaelen's heart skipped a beat as Maxi Zoninus walked down the viewing platform to his own quartet of fighting pits, stopping alongside what Drax would later learn was Pit No 9. After another fifteen minutes or so, Maxi Zoninus was finally standing above Pit No 12 – his own fighting pit. The slavemaster's eyes briefly touched Drax's and then he was demanding the weapons sack.

Instinctively, all five of them backed up against the four walls in preparation. Even the man who had wet himself had retreated to the wall to Drax's right – the wall beneath where Maxi Zoninus was now standing – although the man was babbling a prayer in whatever his native language was. Drax was on his own on his wall, as was Garataelix opposite him and the eastern-looking slave was to his left, facing Maxi Zoninus. The poor, babbling man with the sodden breeches now also found himself on the same wall with the bear-like Alglian.

Draxaelen's eyes briefly caught Garataelix's again. It seemed as though there was a promise of an alliance there, but even though they were of the same blood, Drax knew he could rely on nothing. *Just grab the spear or halberd, if either are thrown in.*

Then they were out of time. Five weapons crashed to the floor in front of him, and Drax exploded into action, scooping up a sword which had fallen nearest to his wall and keeping his momentum going forwards in a roll, so that he and Garataelix actually crossed, Garataelix having grabbed a similar-looking sword on his dart in the opposite direction. It all happened so fast, that by the time Drax had turned around into a fighting crouch, sword held out before him, blood had already been spilled in the centre of the pit. Surprisingly, it was the eastern-looking slave who had fallen. Half of his head was missing where the Alglian bear had scythed straight through it with en evil-looking battle-axe. The bear was now swinging that axe, single-handedly and had chosen Drax as his next target. He roared as he attacked. Drax feinted to the left but came back right, ducking under the bear's titanic axe-swing, and cutting up and across with his sword, opening the bear from side to side and spilling his entrails into the dust.

He couldn't believe it had been that easy.

As Drax stood, his sword dripping with the bear's blood, Garataelix was withdrawing his sword from the mid-riff of soppy-breeches. Then the Alglian bear fell forward onto his face and twitched hideously in the dust before lying still. Just the two of them left and only twenty seconds since their weapons had hit the floor. There was no chance Maxi Zoninus would halt proceedings so soon into the bout, so the two former Demonacian soldiers circled each other, sword hands to the fore, their eyes locked.

Garataelix attacked first, a high slash to the right, a reverse slash low to the left and a lunge for Drax's mid-riff. Drax blocked the first two attempted blows with his own sword and evaded the lunge, launching a counter attack that was skilfully blocked by Garataelix. Amid their own heavy breathing and the shouting from above, Drax thought he may have heard a smattering of applause, too.

Both men attacked and counter-attacked for another minute, with neither making a mark on the other.

"Come on, men," shouted Zoninus. "No one comes out of these pits unscathed."

His words were prophetic. Just as Drax thought he was finding Garataelix predictable, he didn't move back fast enough from a reverse-slash across his chest, and Drax saw the red line appear before he felt it. Fortunately, it had only been from the very tip of Garataelix's sword.

Adrenaline surged at his near-miss. This was no time to wonder if Garataelix could have gone deeper. As Zoninus had said. It was fight or die. So, Drax fought, with every bit of technical know-how he had at his disposal. After another five minutes, they had both been cut several times apiece, but neither mortally. Alas, despite being naturally graceful and quick, they were both beginning to tire. That was when Zoninus called a halt to the fight. He ordered both men to throw down their swords, which they did. "Good," he said. "I knew you would both be good. You both have fire in your eyes. Now go and get your wounds tended to and then retire to the victor's quarters. You two shall also feast like the Emperor tonight."

A few seconds later, the door to Pit No 12 was unbarred and opened, and a group of armed soldiers ushered them out. They were led towards the only exit, but as they passed through, side-by-side, Garataelix briefly raised his right fist. Drax, to his right, quickly touched his left fist back without anyone noticing. In that instant, Drax knew that Garataelix could have fought harder and nastier – as he could have himself. Alas, Drax feared that next time, he wouldn't be so lucky with his opponents. He might yet need to slay his own men to survive.

CHAPTER 99   JAKE

29th Tertiar, 1789   Day 120, 09:00

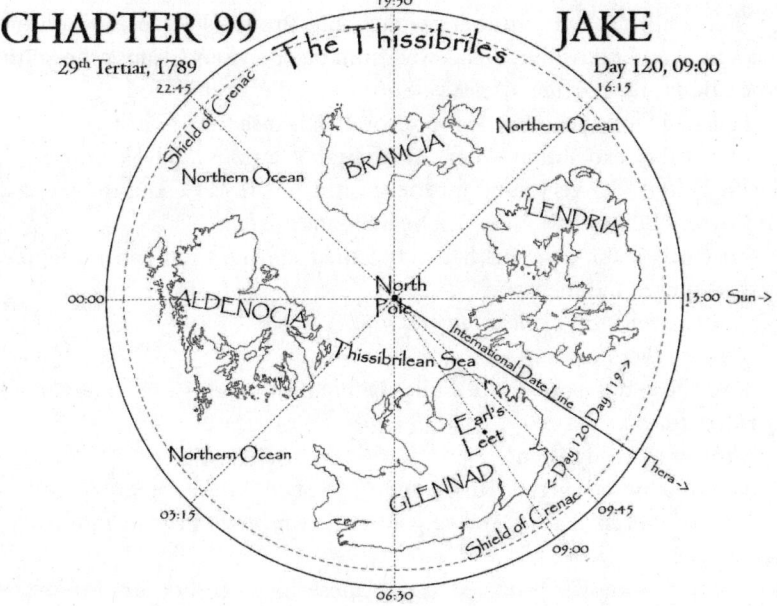

"How do I look?" asked Harry Black, adjusting his brown broad-brimmed felt hat.

"Not yourself," responded Jake, eyeing the rest of Black's farmwear attire: a baggy and grubby smock top, brown rough-spun breeches, grey stockings and black shoes. He also had a loose brown, holey waistcoat yet to put on, and a rough-spun coat that had half a dozen patches of differing browns to cover its holes.

"Excellent," said Black. "You look terrible by the way."

Jake raised an eyebrow at that. 'Terrible' was good. There had been plenty of farm-workers in Earl's Leet the last time they had passed through, with one or two appearing to be as down on their luck as he and his companions now looked, dressed in their farm workers' cast-offs. Jake had been fortunate in the shoe department, though, as his own battered pair fitted nice and snug, whereas the constantly whingeing Turnip's shoes were slightly too small and already pinching.

The four of them had just breakfasted on cold sausage and dry bread, provided the previous night by young Jared Swan. Jake had talked to him at length about his journey up into the Umbrican Mountains with Emilya and Elyse, and it sounded as if the whole thing had panned out perfectly.

"And the monks were friendly?" he had asked.

"Yes, well, certainly Brother Stephen and Brother Clarence were very pleasant. And I know the monks well from our previous Cleanse the Spirit expeditions. They're men of peace, as you would expect."

Jake had looked confused for a second. "Cleanse the Spirit?"

"A six-day expedition where you climb Dawkids and Keplif Scale," clarified Jared. "It's very good for the spirit. Don't worry about the monks, Mr Oscom; Emilya and Elyse will be well looked after."

That had made Jake feel better but their conversation had prompted further images and memories.

"I can't imagine a life without you in it."

"And neither I without you."

Jake allowed the briefest of smiles before his thoughts were interrupted by Harry Black.

"Are we all ready, then?"

Jake and Swede agreed. Turnip didn't. "Not with these shoes I'm not."

"Look!" began Black. "You've got your own boots in your saddlebag, haven't you?"

"All right, I know! I just need to wear these bone-crushers until we're the other side of Earl's Leet. You've told me ten times already."

"Aye, and you've moaned about your shoes double that," complained Swede.

Jake didn't get involved. He went over to where his horse was stabled and walked him out of the old cow-shed that had been their bedroom for the night. Black and Swede did the same and Turnip had to follow suit. Jake looked up at the sky. Another overcast day. The Umbricans rose above them to the east, but their crowns were comfortably hidden in the clouds. *Elyse and Emilya are up there somewhere,* he thought, *hopefully safe and content.*

Their journey into Earl's Leet was uneventful. Four farm workers trotting into town on their horses were about as anonymous as you could get, even poor-looking ones – and even when Jake had raised his battered hat in greeting, he'd been largely ignored, giving them a little more confidence in their anonymity. As they hit the outskirts of the town, Harry Black rode up alongside him. "It's not too late to circumnavigate the town to the east."

"We need those supplies, Harry. And here's a handy stable we can use for the horses."

Five minutes later, they were on foot and heading into the town centre, sticking to the main road which approached from the west. The red-brick houses got progressively finer as they went, before giving way to shops of three storeys, the upper two for accommodation and the ground floor dominated by large glass windows, awnings and vibrant colours. They were approaching the market place, on what appeared to be market day, when they were pulled up sharp by Turnip. "Boss!" he said, a clear note of warning in his voice, his finger pointing towards a billboard which was set in between a tannery and a butcher's shop.

Jake glanced across, and his blood ran cold. He saw a poster which included a fairly decent likeness of himself and Harry Black, with the big black word 'WANTED' splashed underneath it; they'd even captured his off-centre nose, he noted, briefly touching it with one finger. Oh, how life had changed for him, these last three years. *Now he was the joint-most wanted man in Glennad.* Nevertheless, calmness and pragmatism were called for. "Gentlemen," he said. "Might I suggest we split into two groups of two. Swede, you with me. Harry, take Turnip into town and get him to grab the supplies. It can't be you. Too risky. We'll meet you by the statue of Albion Gurch at," he pulled out his pocket watch, "at 10:30. We'll then need to get out of Earl's Leet, pretty sharpish."

Black had now seen the poster himself, and saw the sense in Jake's plan. "Come on old chap," he said to Turnip. "He's right. Let's go and get those supplies. The sooner we're out of here, the better."

As Black and Turnip headed on up the high street, with Turnip still wincing at his pinching shoes, Jake sauntered casually over to the posters. It might be normal for Harry Black seeing his own image staring out from a WANTED poster, but it certainly wasn't for Jake. Nevertheless, when he arrived at the poster, its contents still shocked him. *"Wanted. For the abduction and possible murder of Princess Alicya Havreno of Glennad. Reward for capture: one thousand guineas."* Then in the small print: *"May be accompanied by two other men: one wiry, dark-haired and missing a front tooth, the other of pale complexion, ginger hair, crooked front teeth with a gap between them and likely to be wearing large golden earrings."*

Jake felt a mini-flush of relief that Swede's farmworkers hat covered his ginger hair and that he'd had the sense to remove his earrings, but that was soon overpowered by panic and confusion as the first part of the poster's contents sunk in. Jake remembered something that Prince Magnus had said when they had ambushed him just over two weeks ago. *What have you done with my sister?*

Jake's mind was racing. Was this farce just because Magnus had failed to capture them, and so he now needed a massive cover story to alert the whole country? His sister's fake abduction would certainly stir the passions of Glennadians, and render nowhere on the island safe for them. All Magnus had to do was to get his sister to lie low until someone turned up his quarries, and then he'd reveal it was only a ruse. A case of the ends justifying the means. But what if Princes Alicya had genuinely disappeared? It would be rotten luck for himself and Harry Black, while someone else would get away with a terrible crime.

Interestingly, the poster said nothing about ransom; merely that the Princess had been abducted and possibly murdered. But suppose she *had* been murdered – by Prince Magnus himself – and this poster and campaign was a pack of lies to save his own skin, with Jake and Harry Black the perfect scapegoats? If that was true, it would certainly kill several birds with one stone for Magnus; with the whole nation wound up and baying for blood, there wasn't a court in the land that would spare them the hangman's noose. Whatever the truth, they wouldn't be able to evade a nationwide manhunt for long, not with several thousand soldiers and several *hundred* thousand civilians looking for them. With a sinking heart, Jake knew it would be a long time before he would see Elyse again. And never, if they were captured.

"I can't imagine a life without you in it."

Jake closed his eyes. At least Elyse and Emilya were safe up at Kifsel Place, with the added bonus that the poster hadn't mentioned any female outlaws. With a bit of luck, Magnus was focusing all his attention on himself and Harry – which had been their intention anyway. It just hadn't meant to be this extreme. But if they did escape Glennad, might Magnus then turn his attention to Emilya and Elyse again?

The responsibility he had was enormous.

Jake's thoughts were interrupted by Swede. "Do you mind reading that out to me, Oscom. Only I, erm…I can't, erm…"

"Follow me," said Jake, taking Swede's arm and steering him further into town. "I'll tell you as we go."

Jake's explanation left Swede looking even pastier than normal. "One thousand guineas! That's insane!"

"Aye, there'll be no shortage of takers," agreed Jake, grimly.

Once they were clear of any other incriminating posters, Jake stopped and took out his pocket watch. Still half an hour to go before their liaison with Black and Turnip at Albion Gurch's statue. "Listen, Swede," he began. "It's not a good idea for all four of us to be together – folks are on the lookout for a band of four men. We're damn lucky we didn't get stopped earlier, disguise or not. When it gets to 10:30, if they're at the statue, you go up on your own. Tell them what you know, and suggest we remain in our pairs.

We then make our separate ways to Port Myra. It's the nearest port to here and it's only a two-day crossing to Lendria from there."

"OK chief. Port Myra, you say?"

"Aye. On our horses, we should be able to make it to port in three days if we take it steady. Head out there at a gallop and we'll just attract attention. And when we get there, we don't necessarily need to get on the same boat, either. In fact, I'd suggest that we don't do that in case they're checking every face at every port."

"Right-oh, chief."

"And tell Harry that if we get separated, to try and meet up in the Amber Pelt at Iblund on the south coast of Lendria. He'll like it in there. They sell over a hundred different kinds of Lendrian whiskey."

"The Amber Pelt, you say?"

"Aye, if you forget the name, just think of a fox."

"A fox? Why?"

Jake just looked at Swede for several seconds before Swede got it. "Ah, a fox. Amber pelt. Got you."

Jake and Swede spent the next thirty minutes ambling around Earl's Leet, gravitating towards the market place and the statue of Albion Gurch. There was one brief panic, when two Earl's Leet militiamen were marching towards them, but they didn't give the two farm-hands a second glance. They were also considerably helped by it being market day in Earl's Leet, as the market place was heaving and loud. Sure enough, bang on 10:30, Turnip sloped up to Gurch's statue, alone, laden with several bags – their supplies. He leaned against the base of the statue and took out his water canteen, casually drinking from it.

"Harry's obviously read the poster as well," said Jake. "He's probably already formulated a similar plan. Time for you to go and find out," he said, patting Swede on the back.

"Aye, in for a penny," said Swede, with a big sigh. He then ambled off, just an ordinary farm-hand whiling away a few hours on market day.

Jake watched Swede and Turnip, whilst he wound his way slowly around a number of market stalls. The two outlaws had a fairly long conversation, both remaining relaxed and not showing any signs of agitation. Eventually, the pair shook hands and Turnip handed over half of the supplies to Swede – again, just two farm-hands doing business on market day. Jake moved out to meet Swede and the two of them retreated to the edge of the market place where Swede filled him in.

"Harry's also of a mind to take ship to Lendria."

"I thought he might be. Is he happy with Port Myra?"

"He is – but he is also wary about us all being there at the same time. He's been toying with sending all four of us to different ports."

"I mused on that idea as well. But I then decided that a man on his own is more suspicious than two men riding together. Not many folk travel solo, these days," he said, meaningfully.

"That's true," agreed Swede, rather ruefully.

"Did you tell Turnip about the Amber Pelt."

"I did. He won't forget."

"Right, well. I reckon that if we let them go first, we can follow on an hour behind."

"I'd sooner we went first, boss."

"Ha!" exclaimed Jake. "I bet you would."

Jake manoeuvred himself and Swede through the market stalls again and was pleased to see that Black and Turnip were still waiting in the same place. Black caught his eye immediately and gave a thumbs up. Jake returned the gesture and then nodded his head in an easterly direction, suggesting that Black and Turnip should set off first. Black nodded back and held up three fingers, meaning *see you in three days*. Jake nodded, and with that, Black and Turnip melted away in the direction of their mounts.

CHAPTER 100   ARRAN

29th Tertiar, 1789   Day 120, 13:30

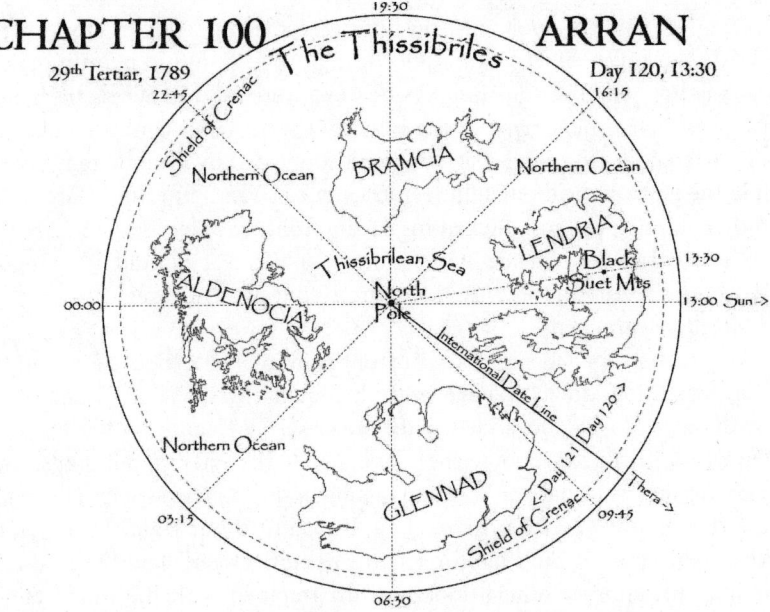

Arran had received his telegram from Lenahan Driscoll four days ago, telling him that he was required to help with the build of the new refuge shelters in the Black Suet Mountains, around forty leagues to the east of Nannosh. He had been expecting it, of course, having volunteered. He had promptly packed his saddle bags and back-pack, and set off at seven o'clock the following day, on Rum Dearg.

Now, over three days later, his dun stallion with the red dorsal stripe was climbing the last part of the incline towards a set of natural limestone caves that faced south-west, and which looked out over a patchwork of green fields and woodland. The whole area was a hive of activity and, as he approached a checkpoint, two soldiers held up their hands to stop him. Arran fished in his jacket pocket, and pulled out his authorisation document, signed by Lenahan Driscoll himself.

One of the soldiers studied the document and then looked hard at Arran, before nodding and handing it back. "Thank you, sir," he said. "Please could you go to the tent at the top of the rise. The gentleman in there will explain where you're quartered, and tell you which section you've been allocated to."

Arran thanked the soldier and tapped Rum Dearg's flank to trot up to the indicated tent. As he went, he passed various soldiers and civilians carrying all sorts of tools and pushing wheelbarrows full of stone. Up towards the caves, he could see and hear people shouting, pointing and gesticulating, while various hoppers of stone were arrayed across the cave entrances. When he arrived at the indicated tent, Arran could see that it had a triangular front and rear, each end supported by a single tent-pole, while the tent was around eight feet in length. Arran tied Rum Dearg to a handy hitching post and ducked inside the front tent-flap. Bizarrely, there was a wooden desk inside with another soldier sat behind it. "Good afternoon, sir," said the soldier. "May I have your name please?"

"Reed. Arran Reed."

The soldier opened the book in front of him and turned a few pages before scanning down a page with his quill. "Arran Reed," he said. "Astronomer Royal," he added, with surprise. "Welcome to Black Suet Mountains, Mr Reed. You have been assigned to the external buildings, sir. What this means is that you will be assisting in the build of wooden lodges, a quarter of a league from here, along the path to our right. When you arrive there, if you could hand over this document, sir," said the soldier, passing him another official-looking card stamped with the four-leafed clover emblem of Lendria and now counter-signed by the soldier as well. Arran quickly scanned the details and confirmed that they were all correct.

"Just to explain, sir, that your quarters will be located alongside the wooden building site. There are stables where your horse will be looked after by our stable-boys. The area also includes a large tent which we use as a dining room – here you will be served three meals a day -."

The briefing was interrupted by a loud explosion, and Arran felt the floor shiver. He was fairly sure what it was and the soldier soon confirmed. "Controlled explosion within the cave system, sir. Happens all the time. Only soldiers and qualified technicians are allowed up there, which is why you're assigned to the external buildings. Sorry about that, sir."

"There's no need to apologise, officer. I suffer a little from claustrophobia so I'd not be too happy with cave duty. Helping put up external wooden buildings is just fine for me."

"Right you are then, sir," said the soldier, before completing his instructions. "There will be another checkpoint tent like this one at the entry point to your development site, and you will be checked in and shown to your quarters. Good luck, sir."

Arran thanked the soldier, exited the tent, untied Rum Dearg and led his dun stallion along the path, on foot. His 'quarters' turned out to be a six-foot tent – although he hadn't been expecting anything more. It was comfy enough inside, with plenty of blankets, and Arran had already been told on arrival at the development site that most of the site's occupants spent their evenings in the large tented dining room, with free access to four different types of Lendrian ale.

Having been shown where his tent was, Arran took Rum Dearg around to the stables – more hastily-constructed buildings, these consisting of open-ended rows of bays for the horses and plenty of fresh straw, but with just a long canvas awning over the top of each bay for shelter. On seeing his approach, one of the stable-boys ran up to meet him and introduced himself as Arthur. He put his hand to Rum Dearg's face and then patted him on the neck. "He's a fine horse, sir." The boy's voice hadn't yet broken.

"Thank you, Arthur. He's also my best friend, too."

"Oh, I'll take good care of him, sir. I'll feed and water him now, and then I'll give him a good grooming."

"Thank you, Arthur," repeated Arran, this time drawing out a silver sixpence. "For your troubles."

"Oh, I couldn't," said Arthur, backing off. "We're already being paid by the government."

Arran ignored him and tucked the sixpence into Arthur's waistcoat pocket. "Like I said," he began, with a wink at Arthur, and then patting the horse's flank. "Rum Dearg here is my best friend."

"He'll want for nothing, sir," said Arthur, leading Rum Dearg to the stables.

Arran watched them go and then took out his pocket watch. It was 14:25. From what he'd been told, working hours were from 07:00 to 18:00, so having dropped off his bags at his tent, he decided to go and look at the construction site – maybe even get involved a day early.

As he headed for the development site, another dull explosion sounded away to the north where the caves were being excavated and enlarged to provide 'worst-case scenario' living quarters. Claustrophobia or not, if the worst-case scenario did come to pass, he would quite happily take his chances in the caves – especially if he was paired with Ella and her boys. Inevitably, a stab of guilt followed; the ramifications of that for Mal didn't bear thinking about. *Maybe it was better to leave them be and take his own chances outside?*

Pushing aside these negative thoughts, Arran focused instead on the development site for the wooden hostels that he was now approaching. The ribs of various buildings were already standing stark, like a pod of gutted whales, although one at the far end did already own a roof. As Arran approached the site, the predominant sounds were of sawing, chiselling and banging along with the shouts of human voices at work. Visually, Arran could see men cutting large sections of wood with huge two-handed saws, while many others were working solo, using various-sized single-handled saws. Elsewhere, men were working wood, chiselling joints, and assembling smaller parts with hammer and nail. The end-results were pillars, posts, joists, studs, trusses and planks of wood of all different sizes, grain and thickness that were being very precisely placed into separate areas where they were being measured and marked up by others.

As he reached the site, a small but stocky man with thinning fair hair offset by a thick fair-haired moustache came to meet him. "Arran Reed," said Arran, "assigned to this site for seven days."

"Please to meet you, Reed," said the man, shaking his hand. "I'm Mallan, the head foreman. You look able-bodied enough to me," he said, looking Arran up and down. "I'm going to hand you over to Mr Mackie, who will give you a rundown on our plans, what we're building and how we're building it. Mr Mackie will then get you buddied up with one of the men who have been here for several days, so you can learn what's required – which is generally arm muscle, sawing up wood to order, and helping get the joists up for these new buildings. Think you can manage that?"

"I'm looking forward to getting started, Mr Mallan."

Mr Mackie turned out to be much older than Arran was expecting and was actually an architect by trade. He still had a full head of hair, albeit grey, and a pair of magnificent grey mutton chops, too. He also had a very distinctive northern Lendrian accent, which meant his speech sounded overly harsh and intimidating. "Are you familiar with why we're doing this wee development here, son?" he started with.

"I am actually," confessed Arran. "In fact, I'm the person who started this all off."

Mackie looked at him, short-sightedly, and then seemed to realise who he was. "Ah, you're the Astronomer Royal, so you are. Welcome to Suetville, son."

"Suetville?"

"Aye, that's what the lads are calling it."

"And do the lads know why they're building this site?"

"Not a clue, son. Even young Mallan there – he doesn't know either."

"Well, what do they think they're here for?"

"Government business, that's all. Need to know. So long as they're getting paid, they're happy. And they're all getting paid more than they would building in Nannosh, Iblund or Dryer. That said, the theory doing the rounds over the last couple of days has been that this is going to be a prison. Before that, it was going to be a loony bin. Tomorrow it'll probably be a top-secret scientific establishment."

Arran pursed his lips in thought. "Well, so long as they don't know the truth of it," he said. "I assume you do know…" he tailed off.

"The potential severity? Aye, son, I do," he added, his lips forming a grim line between his mutton chops. "But I'm praying hard every night for a soft landing, if you catch my drift," he said, winking at Arran.

Arran couldn't help but smile at Mackie, and found himself giving him a comradely pat on the back. "That's the spirit Mr Mackie. Now then. How can I be of help to you gentlemen?"

And off he was led by Mackie to the development site, with Mackie initially explaining how they had been fobbing off the odd local farmer with tales of government business as well.

Later, when back in his tent, Arran lit his one candle, propped himself up on one elbow and began writing his reply to Ella. He didn't see any problem in giving away his current location, so he mentioned that he was involved in a government project in the Black Suet Mountains until the 36th Tertiar (Day 127), and that he would ensure that his next placement would be as part of a similar project in the Ersprin Mountains which was the nearest mountain range to Olindo. He wrote that he would be able to start there on Day 134 or Day 135, depending upon how much time he and Ella would spend together after Day 133. If he were being honest, he was hoping to spend the whole three days with Ella whilst her husband was away with the boys, visiting his brother and his family in Brytan – Arran having finally reconciled with himself that meeting Ella was what he must do.

Where they would go after that, well, that was still totally unknown…

CHAPTER 101 — EMILYA

30th Tertiar, 1789 — Day 121, 13:15

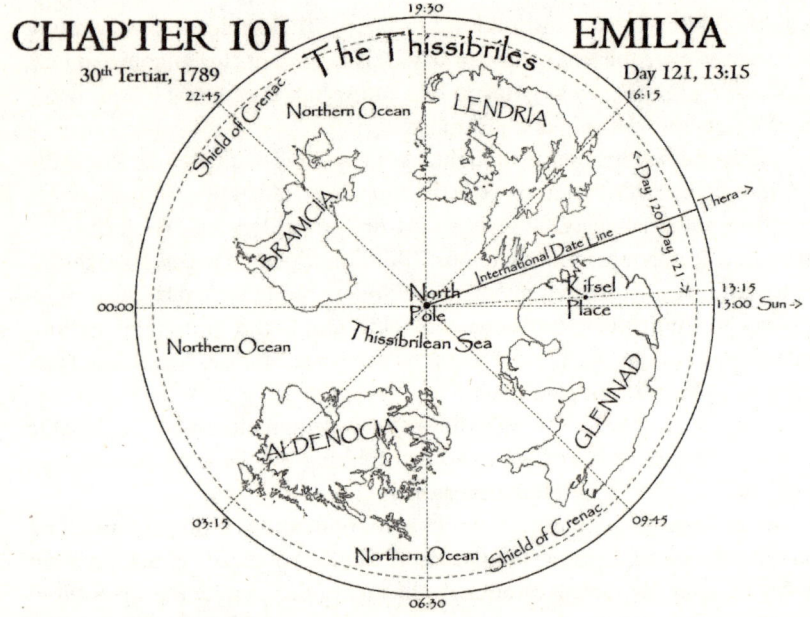

Emilya and Elyse were lunching in the refectory. At Elyse's request, Emilya had been avoiding eye-contact with Brother Cyrus, but that hadn't stopped the stupid man from staring at her, whenever their paths crossed. She just couldn't understand why a fully-grown, middle-aged man, and a *monk* to boot, could be so petty and childish.

They were halfway through their deliciously thick vegetable soup when Emilya noticed a ripple of whispers passing up the refectory. She nudged Elyse, just as the ripple stopped at Brother Cyrus. All he did was turn to look at the two women. Brother Obadiah had also turned around, a leg of honeyed duck in his hand. Emilya was disgusted to see both honey and grease running down both his hand and chin. Elsewhere, the room was buzzing, and Emilya was alarmed to hear Prince Magnus' name mentioned, which immediately set her arm-hairs on end.

Seconds later, Abbot Geoffrey entered the room, the seventy-one-year-old striding fluidly up the centre of the refectory. A hush fell, such that Emilya could hear his sandals slapping against the terracotta floor-tiles. When he reached the top end of the room, he turned and faced everyone. As ever, Emilya was drawn to the sharp intelligence in Abbot Geoffrey's blue eyes, set in a weather-beaten face framed by snowy-white hair which, despite his age, remained thick, curly and vibrant.

Abbot Geoffrey cleared his throat. "I can see that many of you have already heard the news." His voice rang out clear and true. "But for those who haven't…we have been reliably informed that the Princess Alicya has been abducted from the palace in Ghantiss."

A round of consternation circulated. The abbot waited for it to die away before continuing. "This happened over three weeks ago. It was hoped the abductors would demand a ransom. However, this has not yet happened. Naturally, the palace is grieving. They had kept this news from the nation in the hope of either a ransom being offered, or successfully tracking down the abductors. Neither happened and so they have made this knowledge public, and have issued specific instructions to all citizens of Glennad. I will be reviewing those instructions this afternoon, and will pass them on in an update at 20:00 in St Affo's church, followed by a vigil for the princess. I expect all to attend, as we each have a duty in this matter. I will tell more later. May God keep the Princess safe. Amen."

"Amen," concurred all present.

As soon as the abbot exited, the refectory broke out into a buzz of curious chatter. *So much for monks and vows of silence!* Then, with a sudden chill, Emilya realised that Brother Cyrus' eyes had probably been fixed on her throughout the whole announcement. Had she reacted noticeably at mention of the royal family?

Emilya turned to Elyse, who had stayed silent since the abbot's departure. "What's the matter, Elyse?"

"I don't know," said Elyse, placing her hand on Emilya's. "I've just got a bad feeling about this."

"You don't think…" Emilya tailed off, now worried herself.

"That it has anything to do with our business? I don't know. But the timing, Emilya! The abduction seems to have occurred the day after Magnus intimidated your father. The day we set off for Ghenetenos."

"But none of that had anything to do with the Princess."

"I know," said Elyse, with a brief smile. "I'm probably just being paranoid. Which is the fault of Laughing Larry over there," she said, nodding her head backwards in the direction of Brother Cyrus.

"He hasn't stopped looking at us since Abbot Geoffrey arrived," said Emilya, now eyeing him back and not heeding Elyse's warning. "He's not even talking to the other monks or eating."

"Stop looking at him Emilya, please. Let's finish our soup and go and spend some time at the fishing ponds with Brother Clarence. Abbot Geoffrey's announcement will keep for a few hours, yet."

An hour later, they were sat at the edge of one of the three fishing ponds on Bloomer with Brother Clarence. Emilya had taken a lot to Brother Clarence, with his open and honest round face and red complexion, but she still had all on not to laugh at the two huge black slugs crawling across the tops of his orbits. Once again, Emilya found herself wondering what had driven Brother Clarence to give up a life of freedom for a life of servitude and to never being able to take a wife.

"You cast off like this," Brother Clarence was saying, lifting his fishing rod to his right, before casting the line into the pool. The lead weights plopped into the water, making tiny splashes. He showed them twice more before Emilya decided to have a go herself. The first attempt nearly garrotted poor Brother Clarence, but he took it in his usual good humour, and patiently talked Emilya through how to set her stance and re-cast. Emilya's second attempt just about landed in the water to their right, but her third attempt wasn't too far away from Brother Clarence's example.

"That's very good, Miss Emilya," he said, beaming. Emilya couldn't help but notice those two slugs go up by another inch or so. "You learn very quickly."

After another half an hour, both Emilya and Elyse had got the hang of it, although Elyse was adamant that any fish caught would be going straight back into the pond. Satisfied that they no longer needed his assistance, Brother Clarence left them to return to his duties – but after another peaceful half-hour of sitting fishing and chatting, the afternoon took a turn for the worse when Brother Cyrus and Brother Obadiah arrived and took up a position a few yards to their right. Even though she was looking straight ahead and not at the two monks, Emilya could sense Brother Cyrus staring at her and Brother Obadiah looking Elyse up and down…and down and up. Unable to help herself, Emilya turned to look at them – and was alarmed to notice that Brother Obadiah's *hand* was also moving up and down under his robes. He stopped when he realised that Emilya was looking, and immediately liberated his hand. He even had the decency to look a little guilty.

"Just ignore them," said Elyse out of the corner of her mouth.

"But, but…" Emilya just didn't have the words.

Then, to Emilya's amazement, Elyse turned to look at the two monks and smiled, pleasantly. "What's the biggest fish in here, gentlemen?"

Brother Cyrus just glared back at her with contempt. Brother Obadiah's eyes were fixated half-way between Elyse's face and waist. And then, Emilya was astonished to hear Brother Cyrus speak for the first time. "This is no place for a woman." For a big, heavy-featured man, his voice was surprisingly thin and reedy.

"Well," said Elyse, refusing to be put off, "we'll be on our way in a few weeks' time, after Cleanse the Spirit, and then there won't be any more women at Kifsel Place."

A pause, and then the reedy voice again: "Not soon enough," he said, before returning his attention to casting. And that was that. Brother Cyrus didn't bother looking at them again. Shortly afterwards, they decided to pack up for the day, minus fish, and give Brother Cyrus his little victory.

As they walked away, Emilya couldn't stop herself. "Did you see?"

"I see a lot of things out of the corner of my eye, Emilya."

"But Brother Obadiah. He was…he was -."

"Masturbating, yes, I know. I've caught him doing it several times."

"But, but…"

"Close your mouth Emilya, otherwise you'll catch flies."

Several hours later, Emilya and Elyse had taken their places inside the magnificent nave of St Affo's church up on the penultimate stack, Bedford. The church was already packed with expectant monks talking quietly, creating a buzz that was being amplified by the church's extraordinary acoustics. As ever, Brother Cyrus was within eyesight – this time adjacent on the north side of the nave.

For now, though, Emilya was ignoring Cyrus and was looking around her with familiar awe. She had already visited the church several times during the last two weeks, each time taking stock of its stunning architecture, both standard and idiosyncratic. St Affo's was one of Glennad's oldest churches, the core having been built around 650 years earlier, and being added to with each passing century. Given its core age, it had the typical rounded arches of the early 12th century – one hundred and twenty-five of them, according to Brother Stephen; although every time Emilya tried to count them, she always managed to miss a few, and rarely got the same total twice. There were seven bays of rounded stone arches in the nave, with chevrons resting on huge twenty-foot pillars, each over fifteen feet round. Above these arches were the smaller triforium arcades, which opened onto the high-set clerestory windows. When she turned around, Emilya could also see three tiers of arcading in the west tower, which included the capitals of two of its huge pillars which were nationally acclaimed courtesy of their intricate carvings.

However, the church's greatest prize was the Wrothswirk Stone, of Naxos origin and over a thousand years old. It was considered Glennad's most important ancient sculpture and was thought to be the lid from the tomb of St Affo himself, one of the first missionaries to visit Glennad and after whom the church here was named. St Affo was also rumoured to have been one of the authors of the legendary eighth century *Saranti Codex* which had been missing for centuries. Many thought that it had never existed at all, though, especially since the *Saranti Codex* was rumoured to be an ancient druidic text written on the instruction of Saranti, the druidic god of thunder, to warn of future catastrophes. Given St Affo's beliefs and teachings were at complete odds with those of the pagan druids, Emilya wasn't buying the Codex legend at all.

The Wrothswirk Stone was very real, though, and Emilya could see it now, propped up on display against the north nave wall, although she couldn't make out its features from this distance. She had studied it for hours, though, and now knew what each carving represented. There was the Lamb of God washing the feet of his followers, the slain Lamb, the burial of the Lamb's mother with apostles carrying the body on a stretcher and the High Priest being dragged along beneath. There was God in a temple and the *hand* of God pointing down from above, another apostle with a child, a depiction of the Descent into Hell, with God releasing man to re-birth as a babe in swaddling clothes – this symbolising the release of all souls from Hell, with the exception of the Three Betrayers incarcerated in a burning brazier. Then there was the Ascension of the Lamb of God, holding a cross in an oval panel in which he is being conveyed into heaven by four archangels, and the visit of the Angel of Annunciation who carries a scroll in his left hand signifying the Word of God. Finally, in a boat, there was the Lamb's mother and an apostle, she holding the baby Lamb and the apostle holding a scroll, whilst carved upside down across the top edge of the slab – on what would originally have been the side of the tomb's lid – were a series of letters: NEDDMYYYJY.

"What does that mean, Elyse?" she had asked, several days ago, pointing to the series of letters.

"No one knows," Elyse had responded. "Some think they are the initials of some distant king or queen, although having ten names is pushing it a bit – especially with four beginning with the letter Y! Others think it is perhaps a date, but those letters don't relate to any Thissibrilean, Theran or Epanagan numerals. It also might be some long-lost code known only to the ancient inhabitants of these islands."

"Nothing to do with Saranti, then?" Emilya had quipped.

Elyse had merely returned a wry smile at Emilya's little joke.

Emilya hadn't been smiling shortly afterwards, though. Much as she was happy to look at the Wrothswirk Stone and appreciate its craftmanship, Emilya would never touch it again. She had done so, just that once – after Elyse had suggested that she should. Emilya had tentatively touched the row of letters. What had happened next, Emilya was still unsure. But it had been disorientating and unpleasant. For a split-second, it was as if she had been transported elsewhere – to somewhere bad. It may have been a later-infused perception that it was the Hell depicted in the carvings, as that was now the dark place that always popped into Emilya's head whenever she recalled touching the stone. Although, bizarrely, there had been brooding, dark water, too. On numerous occasions since, Emilya had convinced herself that she had imagined it all. Elyse was in no doubt, though, after touching it herself. "A vortex!" she had whispered, in shock. "I never knew."

When Emilya had pressed for more, Elyse had talked of St Affo's church being located at the intersection of another of these energy lines that joined powerful or spiritual places together on Thera. "But I never knew of this one," she'd said again. "An independent object that conducts, too; not a structure with foundations in the earth." She had not been keen to discuss it since. Something about the Wrothswirk Stone had clearly spooked Elyse – and Emilya knew that Elyse was not easily spooked.

Emilya's thoughts were pulled back into the present as, bang on 20:00, the sprightly Abbot Geoffrey entered the nave through the main church doors to the south. Emilya saw that he was dressed in a heavy cream cape that she hadn't seen before, although he had his plain robes on underneath. Before commencing his briefing, Abbot Geoffrey said a brief prayer, his voice echoing off twelfth-century columns and drifting up to the ornate ceiling. He then began the briefing – and Emilya and Elyse's worst fears were soon confirmed. The second that the abbot began talking about Prince Magnus having been caught red-handed engaging in animal cruelty, Emilya had gone rigid with panic – and Brother Cyrus hadn't missed it. She had seen his black eyes lock onto her with triumph, as if this somehow confirmed his suspicions that she was involved in all of this, and that was why they were here at Kifsel Place, hiding from royal justice.

The abbot then expanded upon the incident. Apparently, *someone* had tried to stop Prince Magnus' animal cruelty, and then a former Bramcian naval captain and ruthless opportunist had become involved. It was at this point that Emilya felt Elyse go taut – all keenly observed by Brother Cyrus. By the time the abbot was talking of Jake Oscom's attempted blackmail, Emilya felt Elyse's reaction switch from concern to anger. Emilya took hold of her hand and gave it a reassuring squeeze. *Don't say anything Elyse. Just keep calm.*

There then unfolded a humungous pack of lies, starting with Jake abducting Princess Alicya with an accomplice, whilst disguised as laundry men. *Except Jake had been with them, travelling to Ghenetenos.* So, they were witness to his innocence – for what that was worth. Meanwhile, the lies continued. A huge manhunt had commenced, led by the Princess's poor bereaved brother. Within two days, they had discovered that the former naval captain was on the run from the Bramcian navy after killing a man in Byastwerthy three years ago. More recently, he had allegedly murdered a magistrate in Boserentua.

The mood in the church had now changed to one that Emilya felt must be as angry as a bunch of monks are ever likely to get. Then came outrage, when the abbot revealed that Oscom's accomplice was none other than Harry Black – and that the pair of them had ambushed the Prince at Earl's Leet and killed three of his men in cold blood. Since then, more deaths had been laid at Jake and Harry's door. The only morsel of comfort was that there was no word of any female accomplices.

That didn't help Jake, though. And it was all her fault.

As the announcement finished, Elyse took Emilya by the hand and led her, tight-faced, out of the church, watched all the way by Brother Cyrus. When they passed out of the main south door and into the churchyard, Elyse let out a sob. It was the first time that Emilya had seen her openly upset. She quickly put her arm around her and steered her along the path between the infirmary and the church nave, and then towards the bridge over to Stamps, the top-most stack of the five that made up Kifsel Place monastery, and where their guest quarters were. Once they were a safe distance from the church and about to cross the bridge, Elyse began to vent. "Of all the evil, scheming -."

"Shush, Elyse," cried Emilya. "Someone will hear."

"I don't care," she said, more quietly, as they began to sway across the rope bridge to Stamps. "He's a good man," she called back over her shoulder. "He has a heart of gold. He doesn't deserve this."

Emilya was lost for words as they reached the other side. Elyse turned to her. "How is he going to survive this, Emilya?" Tears were now running down her face.

"He'll go to Lendria. That's what we were both going to do originally."

"Yes, but His Royal Slyness has alerted every soldier and civilian in the country to be on the lookout for him; with hot blood boiling through their veins, too. Princess Alicya is universally loved. How is Jake going to take ship to Lendria – or anywhere else for that matter?"

"He'll find a way, Elyse, I know he will. He's a very clever man."

"He is," said Elyse, wiping the tears from her face. "But the odds are stacked against him. I wish there was something we could do to help."

"So do I," agreed Emilya. "But realistically," she said, spreading her hands. "Even if we went to the authorities and told the truth…"

"Oh, I know," agreed Elyse, who for the first time looked all of her forty years. For once, it was Emilya's turn to embrace Elyse – although the older woman was a good five inches taller than her. When they parted, Elyse even managed a little smile. "Do you know what?" she said. "I think I might start praying in the church, daily."

"You? Pray?"

"Well, it can't do any harm, can it? If there really is a God, it's past time he did something about Prince Magnus, and started looking after good men like Jake Oscom. And innocent little girls like you -."

Elyse broke off. "Just a minute," she said, raising her hand and looking over Emilya's shoulder towards Bedford and the church. "There's someone watching us." She started to walk back over the bridge, but the figure in the late evening shadows by the church's south transept, back-pedalled and disappeared from view. Elyse had stopped halfway across the bridge and Emilya came up to join her.

"Who was it?" she asked.

"I didn't see his face," said Elyse. She sighed. "But probably another of Brother Cyrus' cronies. Well, if nothing else, this latest shock has demonstrated just how insignificant a problem that lot are."

"Unless they get wind of the fact we're connected to this fake plot. We certainly didn't react like the other monks, and Brother Cyrus saw that. I don't like to think of what he might try and cook up."

"He'll have a job to convince anyone that you're involved," said Elyse. "The monks all like and respect you, given what you've done in their kitchens these last two weeks."

"Yes, but we've still not told anyone why we're really here. It wouldn't be too much of a leap to piece this together. I am from Ghantiss, after all. Perhaps we should tell Abbot Geoffrey everything. He might be a powerful ally if we did decide to take on the authorities. We're witness to the fact that Jake isn't involved in this. He was nowhere near the palace on the 5th Tertiar. Emrys, Edwin and everyone at Ghenetenos are witnesses, too."

"So, what's Magnus' game then?" mused Elyse, now steering Emilya back over to Stamps. "Is our judicial system so crooked that they would ignore the testimony of so many people?" Elyse shook her head. "No, it must be a ruse. The Princess is probably lying low for a while, and this is just a ploy to get the whole country out looking for Jake and Harry – seeing as how Magnus failed so miserably to capture them himself."

"Hmm," agreed Emilya, recalling the cold look in Magnus' eyes in that courtyard back in Ghantiss. "Well, it wouldn't surprise me if the scumbag hasn't killed his own sister and concocted this whole cock-and-bull story to save his own skin."

"Emilya, really! You are far too cynical for a fifteen-year-old."

"Well, think about it, Elyse. If it is just a ploy, how does he explain the reappearance of Princess Alicya at a later date?

"Well, assuming she's a part of the ploy, they'll just say that Jake and Harry kidnapped her, but they managed to rescue her."

"If it comes to that, Elyse, we have to take Magnus on. We'll get my Dad involved, and the Colins – particularly Freya. They all know what did and didn't happen in Ghantiss. It will all stack up against him – and by his own admission, this all started with his dog savaging poor Theo."

Elyse pulled Emilya into another embrace and kissed her forehead. "You are such a brave little soldier," she said. "Alas, with much to learn about human nature and injustice."

CHAPTER 102   CALIDIUS

30th Tertiar, 1789   Day 121, 11:20

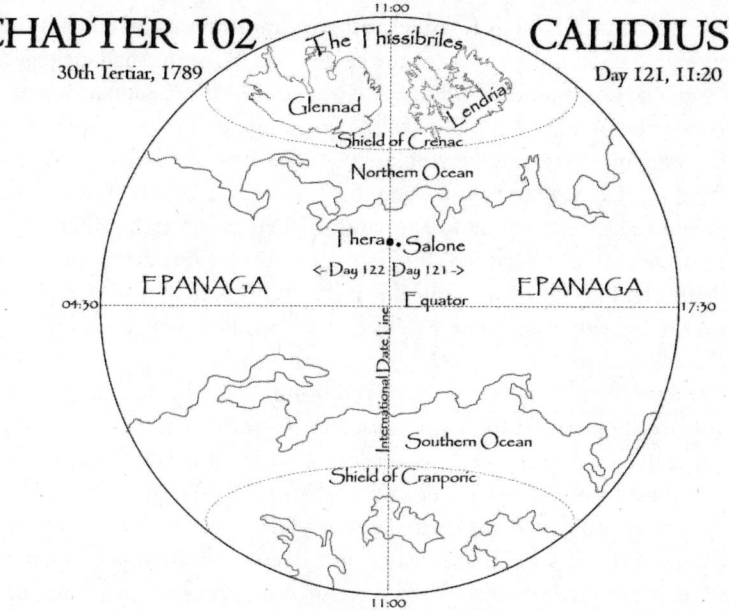

Although he had left the organisation of today's operation to General Macrinus, Calidius was keen to see the actioning of Edict No 1 at first hand. This was why he trotted alongside Macrinus at the head of the unit of fifty Theran cavalry taken from the elite regiment known as the *Celeres*. Their target location was the leper colony of Salone, ten leagues south-east of Thera – and hence, having crossed the International Date Line which ran along the eastern outskirts of Thera, they had travelled back in time by one day! As for Salone, it had long-irked Calidius that the beautiful green Salone Valley was home to such an unsightly collection of humanity. Terraces of cypress, olive and laurel covered the green hills, rising up to the caves which housed the leper colony at the foot of sheer limestone cliffs.

Calidius turned to Macrinus. "I do hope that your son hasn't commenced proceedings early."

"He knows that they have until 12:00 today to disperse east. He won't spoil your fun, Your Majesty."

"He's a good man, general. You must be proud."

"Aye," agreed Macrinus.

Both knew very well that the lepers had neither the will, the strength nor the endurance for a trek east to Maldatia and Acahea beyond – this being from where Calidius had decreed they had come and must therefore return – all part of Edict No 1, issued yesterday morning at 09:00 from the steps outside the *Curia* in Thera. At the same time, Macrinus had arranged for his son, Captain Romulus Didius Vitellius, to lead fifty legionaries from *Legio 14 Victrix*, so that he could make the proclamation to the occupants of Salone in person – essentially giving them a little over one day to leave. As stated by decree, if they were still incumbent today at 12:00, they would be driven from their caves by force. The same applied to the eight other leper colonies dotted about Liatia, which would also have legionaries descending upon them, right now, with very specific instructions issued by Macrinus.

"And the interim executions. Might we pass our time between here and Salone hearing of your, erm, methods?"

"Of course, Your Imperial Majesty. Who would you like to start with?"

"I was most surprised to hear that senator Oscarius had been showing dissent in what he thought were discrete circles. Alas, it would seem that he has disappeared, so we may never know what his objections were. Is this something that you could shed some light on, General?"

"Senator Oscarius had a passion for deep sea diving, Emperor," responded Macrinus looking straight ahead, his expression unchanging. Calidius noted use of the past tense. "Over the years, he had spent much of his personal fortune on a series of diving bells, which are lowered from his boats to the sea-bed by long lengths of chain wound around a drum. Apparently, he was last seen on his latest holiday, heading out into the Bay of Setteri. Later, it was found that the chain on his diving bell snapped. It is thought that he and his colleague in the bell would have suffocated after around an hour, when the oxygen in the diving bell ran out."

"And what do the crew of his boat have to say about this, General?"

"Well, that's the strange thing, Your Majesty," said Macrinus, again quite impassive. "When the rescue service from Setteri found his boat, there *was* no crew. They had all disappeared."

"Oh, that is tragic," said Calidius, keeping his face equally impassive. "Those waters can be so dangerous though. And what of Primate Richarlius?" he asked, switching victim. "It is said that he fell from the belltower of the Intessi Chapel. Do we know what the man was doing up there, given he must be eighty if he's a day?"

"Local reports describe his behaviour as becoming increasingly erratic over the previous two months. His fall was therefore not greeted with a deal of surprise, Your Imperial Majesty."

"Oh, that is sad," said Calidius. "He baptised me, you know. I always felt a kind of connection with him, if you know what I mean?"

"My condolences then, Majesty. A wise man losing his wits is one of the worst of things."

"Isn't it?" agreed Calidius. "And what about magistrate Grecius? Did he really get eaten by his own dogs?"

"Yes, that really was a terrible death. But poor old Grecius had a problem with the Acahean red."

"And how was this vice connected to his death?"

"As you know, the Judiciary celebrate a magistrate or jurist's silver anniversary with a somewhat opulent celebration at the *Villa Magistratus*, in the hills to the north of Thera. It would seem that poor Grecius' celebration lasted for three whole days. His wife and daughters had already left the man's extravagant home in Thera – allegedly due to his love of the Acahean red and its side-effects – and his amnesiac servant had not fed the dogs for a week, leaving them cooped up in one enclosed room of his villa."

"Ah, and Grecius returned home after this celebration, presumably a little worse for wear."

"And unsuspecting of his little canine problem."

"And the amnesiac servant?"

"Disappeared, Your Imperial Majesty. Probably in shame."

"Very probably," agreed Calidius. He then issued a long sigh. "These really are troubling times, General."

"That they are, Your Majesty," agreed Macrinus.

It was another thirty minutes before the Salone Valley opened up before them and, as they turned in a northerly direction, the infamous caves came into view. As they drew closer, Calidius could see figures dotted about, but no sign of Romulus' men.

"Romulus and his men will be encamped in the trees, perhaps a quarter of a league distant from the lepers, Your Imperial Majesty," explained Macrinus. "Although no one can fault them for desire to do their duty, they aren't keen to linger in the same air as the lepers."

"Understandable," approved Calidius.

As they wound their way up through the trees, the subdued noise of the fifty assembled legionaries reached their ears, and Macrinus was soon greeting his son, who had cantered up to them. "Have any left?"

"Very few, father. No more than ten."

"And they headed east?"

"Yes. Very slowly. My trackers gave up after two leagues, which took most of yesterday afternoon. But they were still heading eastwards – and they were not popular with villagers. Several of them were stoned."

"I can imagine. If they really are heading for Acahea, I doubt many – if any – will even get to the Maldatian border."

"It's a fair assumption, father."

"Well, that still leaves us with over two hundred here. Are they all in those caves?"

"As far as we know. As you can imagine, we aren't too keen to find out."

"Well, as we agreed, there will be no need. Do you have the bonfires prepared?"

"Yes father. All is ready."

"Good. We need to get rid of those lepers out in the open first."

"My archers are all in position, as planned."

"Good. Give the order now. I want to be back in Thera by dusk."

Romulus nodded at three of his lieutenants, who headed off: left, centre and right.

"You might want to witness this, Your Imperial Majesty," said Macrinus to Calidius.

"Indeed," agreed Calidius, pulling up a silk shemagh to cover his nose and mouth. Macrinus and Romulus did the same, and the three of them began to advance up the hill. They soon emerged from the trees, and could see the bare rock terraces which fringed the foot of the caves. There must have been thirty or forty lepers, either stood or sat, mostly with their faces to the sun, eyes closed. Very few were engaged in conversation. It was entirely possible that they all knew where this was going and were simply presenting themselves as targets to get it all over with quickly.

Romulus pointed out his archers to the right and left – ten in each group. Another ten were stood before them, each with shemaghs pulled across nose and mouth. All thirty archers reacted to Romulus' appearance and drew their bows in readiness. When Romulus gave the order to fire, the air zinged with the sound of released arrows. Calidius saw one man taken right through the heart, another through the neck and another through his right eye. The thirty archers then nocked a second arrow apiece and finished off the survivors. Within seconds, it was all over, although to Calidius' distaste, a few dying lepers were issuing some intolerable screeching before they expired. But as executions went, it was about as merciful as they came. *They really should be thankful.*

"I'm happy with that," said Macrinus, nodding with satisfaction. "I think a couple managed to get back inside the caves, for all the good it will do them." He turned to Romulus. "Bring the bonfires up."

Before Romulus could give the command, though, Calidius observed two distraught women come running out of the caves. Perhaps those out front hadn't been expecting an ambush after all, as the two women rushed towards one of the corpses, both wailing. Calidius noticed that the younger woman was cradling an infant. It looked very much as if an entire family had been housed here. Father, mother, daughter and an infant grandchild. And all marked with the trademark sores and pustules on their faces and hands. *What could these people possibly contribute to Theran might?*

Calidius was expecting Romulus' archers to put them to death, but that hadn't happened. They were presumably awaiting orders. In the meantime, the mother had stood up from the corpse of her husband and turned her attention to the archers in front of her. Despite the shemaghs, she clearly recognised Calidius' imperial robes and began ranting incoherently at them. She then began to run recklessly towards them, waving her arms and screaming insults.

"Wait!" commanded Calidius, staying the arms of poised archers. "She's mine." And with that, he dismounted, stepped forward, drew his dagger and held it by the hilt. He waited until the woman was twenty yards away, and then unleashed it with all of his strength. It took the woman in the throat, throwing her backwards, but she didn't die immediately. She lay there, twitching her hands clawing at the dagger and cutting her fingers and palms to shreds, whilst her mouth opened and closed without sound.

"Mother!" came the traumatised screech from behind her.

Calidius looked up at the archers to the right, and nonchalantly nodded to them. The woman was impaled five times and dropped to the floor with very little sound. However, her swaddled baby rolled from her grasp, and then continued to roll downhill towards the central group of archers and Calidius, being buffeted and bounced by the passing rocks. The baby was wailing now, and the archers were panicking.

I must not show weakness to the men.

It was Macrinus who put an end to the unfolding drama. He quickly dismounted. He then picked up the Emperor's imperial standard banner, inverted it and impaled the rolling baby with one thrust. He then flung the whole thing away – standard and impaled baby – with a grimace of distaste.

"Get those fires started!" he barked.

Calidius looked hard at the caves. As his men began to drag up the pre-prepared pyres of kindling, tinder and brushwood, he could see other figures now at the back of the cave openings, but none brave enough to come out into the open. As the legionaries hauled the pyres into place at the cave openings, they wasted no time in striking flints to set them alight. The expertly-prepared pyres burst instantly into flame, totally consuming the cave openings. Calidius could no longer see figures through the flames, but assumed they had all retreated to the back of the caves.

The next stage in Macrinus' plan was to engage a series of huge bellows to fan the smoke deep into the cave system. After five minutes of this, Calidius was aware of flitting shadows the other side of the flames, coughing and choking and retching. One figure even tried to run through the flames, but caught fire immediately. Another followed with the same result. Both died, but only after a hideous series of shrieks and thrashings.

When Calidius, Macrinus and their men withdrew an hour later, Calidius had just two regrets. Firstly, there was a small chance that there would be some survivors, if they had found a pocket of air somewhere in the back of the caves – although no one was ever likely to volunteer to check. And secondly, Calidius felt a pang of loss for his favourite dagger. It had been a gift from his mother on his eighteenth birthday and had special meaning – but not that special that he would have retrieved it from the body of a dead leper.

CHAPTER 103 — MADELEINA

31st Tertiar, 1789   Day 122, 09:00

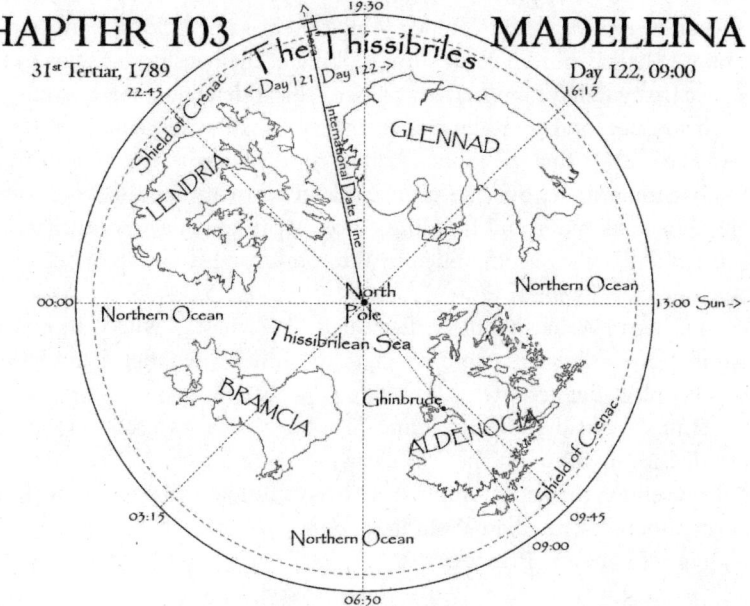

Madeleina sat back in the carriage and closed her eyes, finally able to relax. The funeral of Prince Marco the previous day had been a difficult experience, especially seeing so much grief on show for one who had died relatively young. But at least she no longer had those awful feelings of guilt.

Jed Wallace had kept her up-to-date throughout their two-day stay back in the capital, and it seemed that his suspicions had been well-founded. Madeleina was certain the man hadn't been to bed since they had arrived back in Ghinbrude, two days ago. When she'd asked, he'd told her in that familiar brogue of his that he could sleep for three days in the carriage on the journey back to Yunderoa on the west coast.

Bang on time, Madeleina saw Wallace and his two blue and white-uniformed agents striding towards the carriage, and felt a surge of anticipation. Wallace had told her last night that he would brief her fully as soon as they set off for Yunderoa, and by the satisfied look on his face, the briefing promised plenty of progress.

"And how are you this morning, Your Royal Highness?" he asked cheerfully, as he mounted the single step into the carriage and sat down opposite her on the pristine maroon leather seating. His agents climbed in the other side to occupy the two remaining seats, the carriage rocking back and forth and creaking as they did.

"I am very well, thank you, Mr Wallace," she said, tucking a long strand of blonde hair behind her ear. "But looking at the bags under your eyes, I can see that you have ignored my advice," she added, with a light smile.

"If you can forgive my snoring, Princess, I shall re-acquaint myself with sleep shortly." At that, he tapped on the roof twice with his cane to signal the coachman to set off. The coach, drawn by two splendid greys, gently rolled forward and grand buildings soon began to slide smoothly past to their left and right, accompanied by the comforting clip-clop of hooves on the Ghinbrude cobbles.

"So," began Wallace, shortly afterwards. "We will start with your mystery visitor. Not a 'Madeleina' and not a 'Clair', either. I wonder, Princess, did you ever place her accent?"

"Hmm," considered Madeleina. "The first time, as a commoner, she sounded local, although she was clearly playing a part. The second time, well-presented, her accent might have been a little north-eastern, with that quirky hint of Glennadian about it."

"Eight out of ten, Princess."

"Only eight?"

"Your Glennadian instinct was spot on – mainly because we believe she actually *comes* from Glennad. We think she is the daughter of the Republican leader in Glennad, Ivor Le Mellcrow."

"I didn't think Glennad had a Republican party."

"Well, it does – although they make little impact on the Conservatives, Whigs or Liberals in Glennad. This probably explains why she is over here looking to support a Republican party that not only leads our nation, but which is notorious for its links with the Abolitionist movement on Aldenocia. And I don't need to expand upon what their sole purpose is."

Madeleina shuddered. The Abolitionist movement had been gathering momentum in Aldenocia over the last ten years, as an increasing number of commoners felt aggrieved at their own poverty whilst Aldenocian royalty lived in sumptuous splendour all paid for by the taxes of the masses. This had led to an increasing number of gatherings and protest marches, demanding an end to the monarchy in Aldenocia, and the massive income savings to be ploughed back into public services.

And yet, conversely, whenever she played to the public, she felt nothing but love and appreciation.

Madeleina pulled her thoughts back on track. "And does she have a name, this daughter of the Glennadian republican leader?"

"Olivia, it would seem. Although she drops the 'Le', and is known as

Olivia Mellcrow. Here," said Wallace, withdrawing a sheet of yellowing paper from his leatherbound folder. "I have a likeness of her. This has been taken from a Ghinbrude Library copy of an edition of the Glennadian Times from three years ago. The feature in the newspaper covers her growing republican influence in her home city of Dominniul."

Madeleina took the paper and caught her breath. The coiffured hairstyle, the perfect teeth, the ice-blue eyes. It was all there. She looked up at Wallace, her mouth open in surprise. "This is her," she said, quietly. "The second woman. Or rather the same woman but her second persona."

Wallace nodded his head, expecting that reaction. "I've obviously dug deep on this one. As you know, we have agents all over the island, and Olivia Mellcrow was flagged as a person of interest over two years ago. We can't be certain, but we think she's been in Aldenocia for a year, now."

"A year?"

"Yes."

"Doing what, though?"

"Nothing good. Stirring up locals here. Funding Abolitionists there. And organising those infernal marches pretty much everywhere. She's quite a speaker, apparently. Anyway, around eight weeks ago, she vanished. No sightings have been recorded. No marches. No speeches. No more fundings."

"And no doubt a new woman appeared in Ghinbrude. Dowdy, with mousy brown hair, two rotten teeth, and a mole on her nose."

"Very likely, Princess."

"So, you think she was going to blackmail me to gain some kind of leverage with the Crown?"

"Almost certainly."

"And what about the…" she left it unsaid, afraid to acknowledge that she had played some sort of role in all of this.

"The deaths?"

"Yes," said Madeleina, quietly.

"Well, the death of Fraser Cameron will go down as a burglary gone wrong. I doubt that will change."

"But you think they killed him, purely to make me think it was my fault; to make me think – oh God, I can't believe I'm saying this – but to make me think that I was genuinely *thinking* or *willing* the deaths of others?"

"It's highly likely, Princess."

"How could I have been so stupid?"

"You weren't stupid. You had doubts all along. The woman is an expert and will have fooled all sorts of people throughout her life, some much older and – dare I say – wiser, than you, Princess."

"Stop trying to make me feel better."

"You aren't responsible for the deaths of these people, Princess Madeleina. In any way."

"What about Prince Marco. And Prince Bernard."

"There's a bit of a diplomatic storm over Prince Bernard, Princess."

"A diplomatic storm? I don't understand. I've heard nothing. Are they blaming us for his death? It was a heart attack…" Madeleina tailed off, horrified. "*Was* Prince Bernard murdered?"

"One question at a time, Princess. The diplomatic storm is because of an administrative error. We were told in the strictest terms that Prince Bernard should be sent home and that we were under no circumstances to perform an autopsy. Alas, that instruction was sent to the government and not to the palace, and the government failed to inform on time. Their excuse is that they were tied up with this important inter-island convention, although they're not at liberty to tell me what that's about. But anyway, keen to understand if this was indeed a heart attack, our over-zealous pathologists performed an autopsy on Prince Bernard."

"Ah," said Madeleina. "This probably explains the strange request for a private funeral then."

"Highly likely, Princess. But it also played rather conveniently into our hands, too."

"Are you saying it wasn't a heart attack then?"

"The pathologists originally said that it was. And indeed, they were correct. His heart was badly diseased from decades of unhealthy eating and drinking. But even so, there is usually a trigger for the heart failing. When the pathologists re-examined their blood samples – at my insistence – they found an unusually high concentration of acetaminophen – a substance synonymous with causing high blood pressure. And high blood pressure leads to heart attacks, particularly if the subject is placed into either a highly stressful or highly excitable position."

An image flashed into her mind. *Prince Bernard picking her up and whirling her around. "Ooh, Prince Bernard," she had said, all of a fluster.* Madeleina shook her head to clear the image. "And can this drug be administered orally?"

"It can. Either as a powder or a liquid. My money is on the latter, as Prince Bernard had been seen by a number of witnesses to have drunk a large amount of alcohol on that day."

Madeleina shook her head in disbelief. If this was true, these people were cold-blooded murderers. "And Prince Marco?" she asked.

"A climbing accident. Faulty equipment. Except we've acquired that faulty equipment and it looks like the defects were manufactured."

Madeleina was horrified. "Do you truly believe that this Olivia Mellcrow – and the Abolitionists – have combined to murder three people?"

"More likely than not, Princess, but unprovable. But don't worry. You're perfectly safe now, and I have left my deputy, Ralph Chalmers, liaising with Colonel Marshall of the army to track down Olivia Mellcrow and her associates. By the time this tour of yours is over, we'll either have her or she will have fled Aldenocia."

It took Madeleina some time to relax. The Republicans were a threatening adversary, but at least they tolerated the royal family. And even though matters now appeared to be under control, it was unnerving that a movement aimed at unilaterally dissolving the royal family had gained so much traction and infiltrated so deeply. Madeleina's lifelong cocoon of security had been breached for the first time, and the butterflies in her stomach were of a very different nature to any felt before her musical performances. Furthermore, people had now likely died because of the Abolitionist cause. Someone's husband, father, brother or son. Or indeed, fiancé! It was difficult for Madeleina to comprehend.

In the meantime, Jed Wallace had already begun to snore, peacefully.

CHAPTER 104   JAKE

32nd Tertiar, 1789   Day 123, 09:00

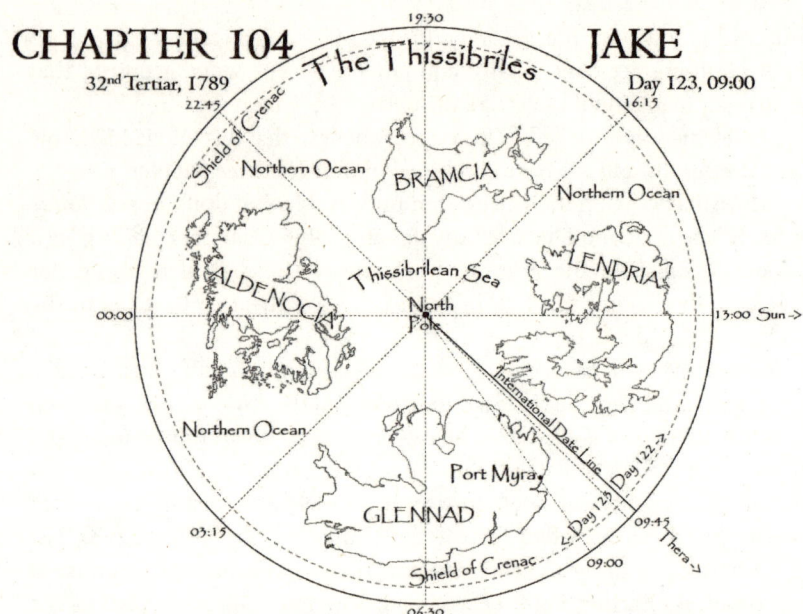

Jake and Swede had camped just outside Port Myra the previous night, still wary despite having made it all the way from Earl's Leet without incident. They were located a hundred yards back from the road, sheltered by a wood of sturdy oaks. It had been raining for a couple of hours now, and despite the tree cover, both of them were fairly damp.

"I must confess, Swede," said Jake, as they nervously walked their horses east. "I was half-expecting to meet Harry and Turnip in these woods. I wonder if he risked going into Port Myra last night?"

"It's possible," agreed Swede. "Harry knows someone in most towns, so they might have had a comfortable bed for the night." He emphasised the point by massaging his stiff neck. "But risky."

Jake wasn't listening. They'd reached a point where the road wound to the left in a north-easterly direction towards Port Myra. As the ground was higher here than out towards the coast, it offered a good vantage point over the coastal road which headed north to meet their road half a league further on. It proved to be a vital advantage, as Jake spotted movement in the distance to the south.

"Get the horses back into the woods," he said, urgently. "There are men coming up the coastal road."

Swede didn't even bother to look. They quickly retreated, tied their horses up in the densest part of the wood, and then inched cautiously out as they approached the road, first crouching and then lying flat in the wet grass. Jake had been right to be cautious.

"Soldiers," said Swede, disheartened, as he spotted the red and white Glennadian uniforms. "And lots of them, too."

"I thought we'd been too lucky. But at least we've spotted them before we went in to Port Myra."

"But as you say, Harry and Turnip might have lodged there last night."

"They might even have booked passage."

"Well, if they have, I hope they've already sailed. There must be over a hundred in that company."

"Aye, I reckon you're right. And the soldiers will likely head straight for the docks, too."

Swede turned his pale blue eyes on Jake. "If they're still there, they've got big trouble."

Jake kept silent as he watched the stream of marching soldiers pass slowly from right to left, their muskets slung over their shoulders, and preceded by six mounted officers gently trotting their horses. He waited until the last red and white uniforms had disappeared from sight. "Come on," he said.

"Eh?" responded Swede, confused.

"Let's see where they go."

"Are you serious?"

"Very. There's an outside chance they won't stay in Port Myra and are headed further up the coast to New Hivetha. If they are, we can still get our boat from Port Myra."

"And if they aren't?"

"Then we're walking into the dragon's den," responded Jake. "Exciting, isn't it?" he added, raising both eyebrows at Swede.

"That's not the word I'd use," said Swede, truculently. "But I suppose we need to know."

"That's the spirit," said Jake. "My guess is they'll also be sending men further up the coast to New Hivetha and Worrab. After that, the mountains almost come down to the sea, so to get any further up the coast, you'd have to take a boat."

"So, all three ports will be overrun with soldiers then." Swede's shoulders slumped.

"I don't call around thirty men per port being overrun, old chap."

"Thirty men, plus the local militia. Plus any other soldiers ahead of that lot," said Swede, jabbing his thumb in the direction of Port Myra.

"True enough. But if Magnus has sent a hundred men to guard these three isolated ports, how many more do you think he'll have sent to Lobstir, Doglinbrint and Luhl? As for the southern ports, they'll be crawling with hundreds of soldiers apiece, and he'll likely have a thousand at Dominniul. No, there may well be soldiers up here – but our odds are still better."

Swede thought about that and then nodded. "You're not daft, are you? For saying you've only been playing this game for a few weeks."

"Three years actually, chap."

"Ah yes, I'd forgotten about that."

"You ready then? Just two poor unemployed farmhands, looking for work in the east coast ports, right?"

"Ooh-arr, ooh-arr."

Jake chuckled. "Let's go, then"

A minute later, the two of them cautiously trotted out onto the road and around the bend until they were heading north east. They soon passed the point where the two roads merged, and where fresh horse droppings evidenced the soldiers' recent passing. From there, the road began to head downhill, and Jake soon got that unmistakable smell of the sea. He immediately felt the draw coupled with a pang of loss for a former life now closed to him forever. A brief flash of anger and guilt followed for the thug in Byastwerthy that had taken all that from him, but he soon buried it. *There's no point crying over the past.*

After another twenty minutes, the road cut slightly to the right and once they had passed through a gap in the hills, there before him was the vast grey slate of the Northern Ocean where it met the Straits of Lendria; Straits which continued north until they adjoined the Thissibrilean Sea. Tucked into the bottom of the valley was Port Myra. It looked prettier than he remembered, particularly the seafront, with long rows of three and four-storey houses either in red brick or painted white. Oddly, there weren't any of the garish pinks and yellows that you tended to see on eastern Glennadian sea-fronts.

The other advantage of being higher up on their approach to the port was that they could see the rest of the town that was set back from the seafront – including what looked like a market square where the one hundred-or-so red and white uniforms were congregated.

"Well," said Swede, bringing his horse to a stop. "That's the end of that then."

Jake also stopped. "What's your alternative plan then, Swede?"

"New Hivetha – seeing as all the soldiers are in Port Myra."

"What about Harry and Turnip?"

"You heard what Turnip said back in Earl's Leet. Harry was considering every man for himself. Right now, that's looking like our best option."

"So, you propose that we leave them then?"

"Aye, and meet up in that pub in Iblund in four weeks' time. The Amber Pelt, wasn't it? If they make it."

Much as Jake hated leaving colleagues in the lurch, he was seriously considering Swede's plan.

"And maybe Harry and Turnip clocked the soldiers, did a runner, and they're already heading for New Hivetha?" continued Swede. "Whilst we stand around here, falling further behind."

"We do appear to be running out of options."

"Aye. And another thing, Mr Masterplan. If we'd galloped all the way from Earl's Leet to Port Myra instead of worrying about attracting attention, we'd have been on a boat to Lendria yesterday."

"Aye," agreed Jake. "Or dead."

"Well, that's as maybe – and I'm not doubting that could have happened. But I say we kick on to New Hivetha now, and we don't spare the horses. Especially now we know that lot are down there."

"Yes, although they'll likely search Port Myra for a few hours. They'll then likely leave a detachment there and send perhaps two thirds of the force further up the coast. Hopefully tomorrow. We could be in New Hivetha before evening and get ourselves booked onto a ship leaving for Lendria tomorrow morning, before they arrive. But it will be tight."

"So, let's go then."

"All right, Swede. You've convinced me. But we don't gallop past Port Myra. We're two poor farmers, trotting on our way north – until we get out of sight of the port and then we make haste to New Hivetha."

"Done," said Swede, and gently tapped his heels to his horse's flanks before Jake changed his mind.

CHAPTER 105   DRAXAELEN

33rd Tertiar, 1789   Day 124, 10:00

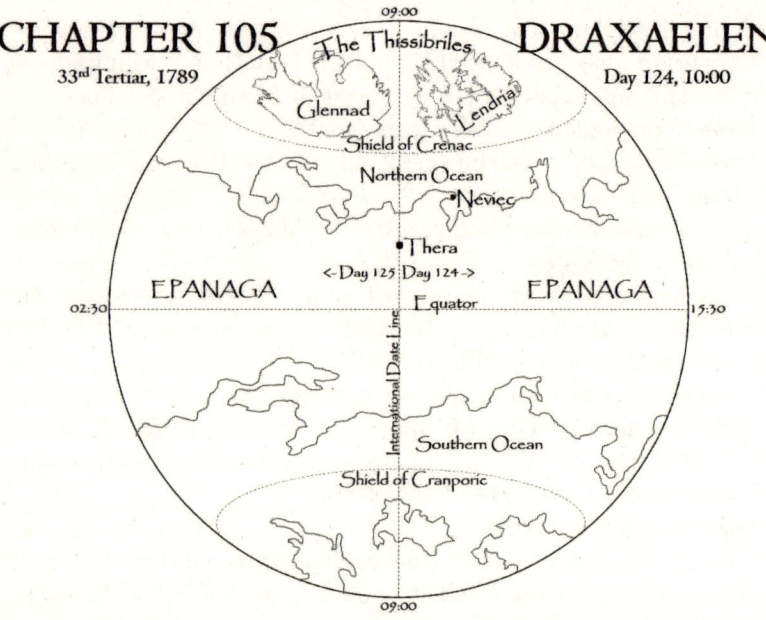

Draxaelen opened his eyes. He was sitting in a comfortable seat in the shaded cloisters on one side of a square courtyard, sheltering from the remorseless heat of the sun. The basking agapanthus and lavender plants lent a heady aroma, and perfectly complimented the gentle sounds from the six tinkling fountains. Neither complimented the brutality of his new profession. Nevertheless, his wounds from the fighting pits, acquired five days ago, were on the mend.

Drax glanced down at his wrists and ankles and was pleased to note that the sores caused by twenty days in chains were also receding, as were the rowing-incurred sores and calluses on his hands. They even had access to mirrors, and with his dark, flowing hair washed and swept back from his forehead, his face clean-shaven, and his intense brown eyes no longer bloodshot through lack of sleep and excessive exertion, he was beginning to resemble himself again.

Similarly, Garataelix's wounds were healing, and his olive-to light-brown complexion was vibrant – as was Drax's own – this following the luxurious skin treatment they had been given by the small army of silent girls in gilded sandals and sheer shifts of white, who had also washed and shaved them, too. Drax had never before been waited upon in such a way, and was slightly alarmed with himself at how good it had felt.

Drax and Garataelix had formed a cautious friendship since their battle in the fighting pits, knowing they could be asked to fight each other to the death at any time. Other than that prospect, life was ludicrously good for them and for the steady stream of slaves converted to fighters who swelled the occupancy of this sumptuous villa on the outskirts of Neviec every day. They now numbered around seventy while this was apparently one of three villas in Neviec housing slave fighters. Of course, the slaves had no weaponry, whereas the fifty guards at the villa were armed to the teeth.

Drax had worked out that of the eighty of his batch of slaves herded into the fighting pits five days ago, around fifteen of them had survived. Just fifteen. Given there were one hundred and eighty galley slaves per ship, and he had rowed back to Neviec with six other ships, the battles in the fighting pits had continued over the next three days. This meant that while there were now around two hundred men living in temporary luxury, the number of those slain would be pushing nine hundred – all for the entertainment of civilian inhabitants of Neviec. It was a senseless waste, even by Theran standards. Why would they give up that many galley slaves? On their return to Liatia, they were all superb rowers. Major assets. Were they that easy to replace? Or had something happened to make galley slaves superfluous all of a sudden? Even more mind-boggling was Maxi Zoninus' claim that these 'selection exercises' were being undertaken in every other large settlement in Liatia, meaning the number of deaths would run into the tens of thousands. It was beyond crazy, and Drax wasn't aware of any other precedent in Theran history.

He shook his head in bewilderment. The last batch of survivors had entered his villa two days ago. To Drax's dismay, neither Argaeus nor Crateuas had been amongst them. Perhaps they were in one of the other two villas. Or perhaps they were still galley slaves somewhere out on the Northern Ocean. Or perhaps they had been taken to another town to fight. Or perhaps…

Movement to his right broke into his reverie. Garataelix pulled up another wicker chair, padded with beige cushions, and sat beside Drax, the wicker creaky loudly as he did so. "Do you still think we'll go another round in the pits?" he asked.

"Gravus is giving nothing away," responded Drax, referring to their fightmaster. "It's entirely possible. It is just as likely that they'll have something else lined up for us, though."

"Aye," agreed Garataelix. "Although Cassius is still saying that we might be allowed to fight in pairs at some stage. They do that every now and then at the Mesocluso, apparently."

"They also make men fight beasts at the Mesocluso," said Draxaelen, perhaps a little too morosely.

Garataelix shuddered. "I'd sooner have the thrust of a merciful sword than be mauled and then eaten."

Drax raised both eyebrows. "Well, what man wouldn't?"

Garataelix laughed at that. "This is true," he agreed.

"We just need to keep believing, Garataelix. Believing that we can keep on winning, make it to the Mesocluso in late Quarternar, and earn our freedom. That's years sooner than I was expecting, three weeks ago."

"Aye," agreed Garataelix. "Will you be training today?" he asked, changing the subject.

"We'd be foolish not to. Although this heat…"

"Will make us even fitter. Too many of the others are drinking wine and ale for fear it will be their last."

"You can hardly blame them."

"They are fools, Drax. Everyone knows alcohol slows your reactions."

"And hopefully dulls the pain."

"Aye, that too."

"Talk of the devil," said Drax, nodding towards the far end of the courtyard.

The top-knotted Gravus was stalking out into the courtyard, backed by six armed soldiers. He stopped in the middle and looked around him. He was a formidable sight. Clad only in gladiatorial sandals and a skirt that ended above the knee, but which was protected by strips of studded leather all around, most of Gravus' magnificent tanned physique was on display.

"As is your choice each day, slaves," he began, in his guttural Cabetian accent, "you can join me now in the arena, or you can stay here, drink wine and ale, and learn nothing. We begin in five minutes."

With that said, Gravus and his soldiers headed past Draxaelen and Garataelix and exited the courtyard through an open archway adorned with a sweet-smelling clematis.

Draxaelen nodded at Garataelix and, under the watchful eye of more soldiers, they followed Gravus, as did several of their comrades. Drax knew very well that the amount of choice and freedom they were being given did not lack method. They were looking for the survival of the fittest. Therefore, every single trick that their fightmaster could teach them might be as valuable as life itself. The lisping Maxi Zoninus had said it true, five days ago. *It is simply kill or be killed.*

Drax had excused himself a day of physical exertion, the day after the fighting pits. He and his fellow slaves had also gorged themselves on food and drink that first night. They'd had beef, lamb, pork and chicken, as well as eel, dace, squid and anchovies. For dessert, they'd eaten the ripest plums, figs, oranges and dates – as well as copious quantities of pastry. And they had soon regretted it. To have consumed so much rich food in such a short period of time, having gone without for so long – there was only ever going to be one outcome. That night, the gullies of the villa had been awash with the consequences. White-robed servants had had the pleasure of cleaning up, the following day. After that, Drax had forced himself to eat and drink sensibly, meaning that he now felt at his fittest since standing in that market place at Alsethonisca, twenty-five long days ago.

The second day at the villa, with his wounds and bruises not quite so sore, Drax had attended Gravus' daily training. As a new face, he had been called out first. "You think you know how to fight, slave?"

Drax hadn't known what to say to that, so Gravus' black eyes had bored into him. "Lost your tongue, slave?"

"I can look after myself," Drax had said, eventually, grudgingly. He knew what was coming next.

His response had made Gravus smile. It wasn't a pretty smile, nor was it kindly. "Then fight me, slave," he had said, opening his massive arms wide. "Hurt me. I am unarmed, as you see."

Manoeuvred into an impossible position, Drax had for some reason taken his silk shirt off – maybe to delay the inevitable. The action had drawn appropriate hoots and whistles from the assembled guards, and from some of the slaves, too. Clad only in his own gladiatorial sandals and some cut-off breeches, Drax faced up to Gravus, who had now moved into a crouching stance. Drax did the same. The two men circled around, eyeing each other, waiting for the other to make the first move. After another ten seconds of circling, it became apparent that the onus was on Drax. That was when an old trick from his youth came to him, and Drax couldn't believe Gravus fell for it. Drax flicked his eyes to his left, and to Gravus' right. The instant that Gravus' eyes moved right, Drax was inside his guard, left hand reaching across Gravus' body to his opponent's left. As expected, Gravus' reflexes were rapid, and he went to defend his left side, leaving the right side of his face open to attack – which came in the form of a whipped right-handed back-fist to Gravus' right temple and an audible *smack!*

Having made his mark, Drax danced back out of reach.

The reaction from those assembled was of surprise and approval. A few even applauded. That didn't go down at all well with Gravus. At around six feet five inches tall, Gravus moved with remarkable speed and grace for a man of his bulk, and once he'd got inside your guard, you were done for. Drax had managed to block half of the punches, but a good five or six had landed – ribs, upper arm, cheek, stomach – after which he'd somehow got turned around and Gravus' massive forearm had been locked around his throat. Drax could hear his own rattling and gasping, but just as his vision had started to go hazy, Gravus had released him and thrown him to the floor.

Gravus then laughed his guttural laugh. "Lesson number one, slave. Never score the first point against me."

Drax clambered gingerly to his feet, rubbing his constricted throat. "I wish you'd told me that before," he croaked.

Gravus laughed again at that and then clapped Draxaelen on the back, forcing Drax to stagger. "That was a good move, slave, a good move. It's a start. But you have much to learn. You need to learn to fight dirty. As I told all of these men here yesterday, before you learn to become an expert with a sword or a spear or a halberd or an axe, you need to use your attached weapons. These," he said, holding out his hands. "And these," he said, tapping both elbows. "And these and these," he said, indicating his knees and feet. "When it is kill or die, and you're in an enclosed space, these weapons may well save your life."

More hand-to-hand fighting had followed, sometimes one-on-one, other times in pairs. By the time they had finished, three hours later, all of them were drenched in sweat, and sporting a multitude of cuts and bruises. None of Draxaelen's hurt as much as the four or five landed by Gravus.

The next day, Gravus had taken them for a four-league run, out in the dusty grasslands to the south-west of Neviec. There were no trees and no respite from the brutal sun. But any man who straggled would likely feel the lash of a guard's whip – guards who ran alongside in lightweight red and gold silk tunics and battle skirts, all supremely fit. By the time they returned to the villa, Drax was the hottest and most sweat-drenched he had ever been in his life, and was grateful for the fresh water that Gravus had laid on for them. Every one of the fifty-or-so slaves that had run with him had made it back, and not one whip had been engaged – perhaps because the rowing and the fighting pits had already sorted the wheat out from the chaff. Drax's bruises from the previous day still ached, and his legs were tired from the hard run, but his legs had also felt strong. If he were to die in the pits, one day soon, he would likely die the fittest he had ever been.

Yesterday, they had returned to hand-to-hand fighting. By this stage, all of the winners from the fighting pits had hauled themselves out of the comfort of the villa's refreshments, bar two whose wounds from the pits were still several days off healing, and two others who had died of their wounds – both inflicted on the bowel, as it happened. That was another useful lesson to have learned – to protect the bowel at all costs. As for those whose training was two or three days behind the rest, they soon found out how costly their absence had been.

Today, three of those men had reverted, and chosen to stay in the refreshments lounge. Drax was grateful for having hauled himself to training just two days after the fighting pits, and annoyed with himself that he'd missed the first day. Those no-shows today, well, they had as good as committed suicide in Drax's book. Gravus was a master at combat, and he taught superbly. Moreover, brutal though he was, he actually seemed to care about their development. When he'd caught Drax looking at him intently, he'd said: "Yes, slave. You are my pupil, and I want you to succeed."

"As this is Day Five of your training," he was saying, now, "and many of you are at different stages of development, I am going to split you into two groups. Group One will be with Annius, there," he said, indicating a man clad similarly to himself, but just a mere six feet tall and considerably less bulky. "Annius will be leading hand-to-hand combat today. Group Two: you have proven yourselves capable at close combat, and although you all still have a long way to go, just for today, you have graduated to weaponry. There will still be much close combat for you to master before your next competition. But today, I want to see how you handle non-ballistic weapons. In other words, steel – although it will only be wooden blades until I am happy that you know how to handle them. Group Two will therefore be with me."

Drax was one of those named in Group Two, which was soon led off to another combat yard. Despite having once been a decorated general in the Demonacian army, Drax felt a swell of pride at being selected for Group Two. He had no idea who Gravus was, where he came from or what he had done in his life, but he appreciated his approval. Drax was even happier when amongst the batch of wooden sparring weapons lying in their dozens against one wall, was the short-bladed sword and small round shield, not so dissimilar to those used by the *Demonata*. Intimidating though Gravus was, Drax fancied his chances if he was selected for demonstration using those. *"Never score the first point against me"*. Well, he might yet make Gravus eat those words. Although Drax would no doubt be profoundly sorry the next time Gravus selected him for an unarmed session!

Drax's thoughts were interrupted as Gravus began handing out short-handled daggers with five-inch wooden 'blades' to everyone. He was soon made to regret his thoughts on sword and shield, as Gravus called him out first for a demonstration. This time, Drax showed no reticence. He accepted the wooden knife handed to him by Gravus with a nod, knowing that the fightmaster would hurt him, but would not disable him.

Surprisingly, though, they didn't go into combat for some time. Gravus got all of the men to line up facing the two of them, and commenced to use Drax as a model. First on stances, manipulating Drax's hands, feet and even hips and shoulders for attacks from the front, the left, the rear and the right, as well as from above and from below. He drilled them on stances for a full hour, all the while under the remorseless sun. But Drax scarcely noticed. He was learning. And he was actually enjoying himself. For the first time in twenty-five days, he briefly managed to forget his grief and hate.

With the long lesson on stances complete, Gravus then instructed his model to face up to him. "I'm now going to come at you from all of those different angles, slave – although you won't know from which angle until I'm almost upon you. Do your best to remember what I have told you. And if you get any opportunity, try and come back at me with your own dagger."

Drax briefly recognised that the roles were different this time compared to the hand-to-hand combat. There, the onus was on the learner to attack. Here, the onus was on the learner to defend. He prepared his stance as Gravus had shown them, and they began to circle each other. Then Gravus attacked with a high stabbing motion to the right. Just as Gravus had shown him, Drax pivoted away in a semi-circle to his own right-hand side and remained unscathed.

"Good," said Gravus simply, already homing in for the next lunge. When it came, Drax was ready for it and pivoted away again. This continued for another five lunges, but on the sixth, Drax did his best to counter, attempting a lightning-quick slash of his wooden dagger to Gravus' midriff. Somehow, Gravus had seen the attack coming, and in less than a second, Drax was on his back, all of the wind knocked from his body and Gravus' wooden knife at his throat. The head fightmaster grinned down at him. "Too slow," he said, as beads of sweat rolled off his forehead and onto Drax's exposed torso. Gravus then withdrew the knife, stood up and hauled Drax to his feet. "Again," he said.

For the next two hours, Gravus had them up, one-by-one. Not one of them laid even the tip of their wooden daggers onto Gravus' exposed flesh, and all of them ended up on the floor with Gravus' dagger at their throats. But watching was every bit as good as participating. For two hours, Drax's eyes had been pinned to Gravus' body, watching the way he glided and pivoted, beginning to see how the dance worked, always with an intense focus coming first from the eyes. That was how he was doing it, decided Drax. Gravus was reading his opponent's next move from their eyes and translating that message into lightning-quick defensive or evasive actions.

The lesson continued until well into the afternoon, with Gravus next showing them the different grips required for each type of attack, how and when to swap the knife from one hand to the other, where to stab to kill, and where to slash to disable. Soon, even after just one very long session, it all began to knit together for Drax, and he found himself looking forward to sessions planned for later that week when they were due to start mini-competitions within the villa.

Wooden weapons only, of course. A rare mercy in this new life of his.

CHAPTER 106 — JAKE

33rd Tertiar, 1789 — Day 124, 09:00

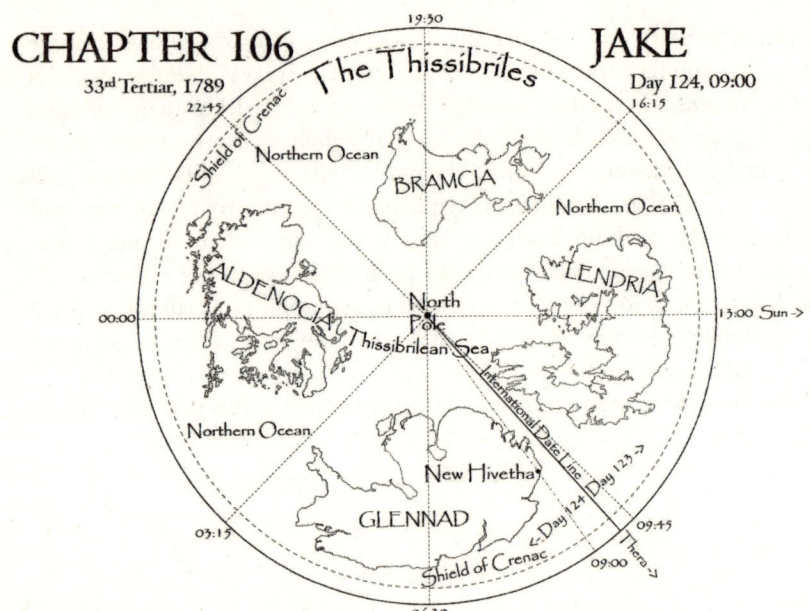

Jake put his pocket watch away. Still another half an hour to go – and only four minutes on from his last check! Trying to appear outwardly calm, Jake scanned the road leading into New Hivetha from the south. Still no sign of any soldiers. They were so close to pulling this off.

Having arrived in New Hivetha at midnight, they had roused a drunken captain and booked passage on his boat, *Four-Leafed Clover*, which was sailing to Spurroth in Lendria at 09:30 the following morning. Having secured their passage, Jake and Swede had sold their horses to the local stablemaster at 07:00 that morning (having slept in his stables the previous night), stuffed all of their belongings and supplies into two back-packs, grabbed some breakfast at a New Hivethan tavern, and then made their way to stand with the other travellers waiting to embark.

So focused was Jake on the south, that he hadn't seen who had joined their queue from the north. Swede nudged him in the ribs and he turned around to look – and groaned, quietly, as he clocked the cowled forms of Harry Black and Turnip, both disguised as monks. *What were the chances of that?* Their eyes briefly met, and Black raised his heavenwards. Nevertheless, if those soldiers could just keep out of New Hivetha for another half an hour, they'd all be away together and no doubt happily regaling each other of their respective adventures from the last four days.

Jake turned back to look at the boat again, a medium-sized merchant sailing vessel with three masts. The captain and his crew were on-board, but still performing their pre-journey checks and preparing the berths below decks. Jake was beginning to fear they wouldn't be away for half past nine when the captain appeared at the top of the gangway, and removed the rope – signalling that the first passengers could embark. Jake let out a sigh of relief. He also allowed himself a tiny smile for the captain's bleary, red-rimmed eyes that were squinting down on his boarding passengers. There was no hiding a traditional captain's hangover!

It took another ten minutes before Jake and Swede showed their tickets to the first mate who was controlling embarkation. Once he had waved the two poor-looking farm-workers through, Jake felt some of the tension leave his muscles. Instead of going below decks to find their cramped berth, though, Jake led Swede up to the stern which was facing south, where they slung their back-packs under the bench. Happily, the highway to the south remained empty.

Jake turned his attention inland. New Hivetha was more spectacular than Port Myra, as the foothills to the Umbricans came down to within half a league of the western outskirts of the port. The hills only rose to two or three thousand feet, and the majority of them were grass and then tree-covered, and nowhere near the clouds, at present. Five leagues further back, to the west, the Umbricans became progressively rockier, and those even further west *were* hidden in the clouds – and would no doubt still be snow-capped, even at this time of the year.

Looking at the Umbricans also made Jake think of Emilya and Elyse.

"I can't imagine a life without you in it."

"And neither I without you."

And yet, here he was, leaving these shores. Would Elyse come to him if he was to be marooned in Lendria? He wanted to believe that she would. She was as fearless a woman as he had known. Although young Emilya ran her a close second.

Jake smiled at the memory of their time together, journeying from Ghantiss to Earl's Leet. Of the banter, camaraderie, warmth and occasional deep conversations. Yes, he had got himself into the biggest crisis of his life. But if rescuing Emilya Luca led to marriage to Elyse Dolmen – and he would ask her to marry him, if she came to find him in Lendria – then everything would be worthwhile, ten times over.

Jake was so wrapped up in his thoughts of a Lendrian wedding, that he had stopped watching the southern approach to New Hivetha, while Swede was busy munching on an apple and facing north. When Jake turned to look south, his blood ran cold. A steady stream of red and white-clad soldiers was marching up the highway, along with just four mounted officers now, but they were already at the southern entrance to the port.

"Swede!" he said.

Jake's tone alerted his colleague who turned around to see what the problem was. His apple hit the deck. After several seconds, he found his voice. "What do we do?"

"If they come on board – and they surely will – we'll be trapped."

Swede unleashed a string of vile obscenities.

Jake checked his watch, although there was no help to be had there. It was 09:18. *They had come so close.*

"What are we going to do?" repeated Swede. "We can't disembark now – they'll see us and it will look way too suspicious."

"Aye, it will," agreed Jake. "There's nothing else for it. We're going to have to go over the side."

"Are you serious?"

"Do you really want to suffer the Prince's justice?"

"You know what, Jake Oscom. You've been nothing but trouble ever since we met you," moaned Swede. "If we'd have just carried on robbing folks on the highways, we'd have been free men now. But oh no, we have to go and hold up the bloody Prince of Glennad, don't we?"

"You enjoyed that," accused Jake.

"Huh!"

"You killed soldiers that didn't need to be killed."

"Well, what if I did?"

"What indeed," agreed Jake. "It's too late now. Would it help if I said I was sorry?"

For once, Swede showed a bit of maturity. He patted Jake on the arm. "Don't listen to me, mate. I know it was all in a good cause. It's just that me and Turnip – we aint never done good causes before."

"I'm sure your reward will be in heaven."

"Don't remind me about Judgement Day, Oscom. I'm depressed enough as it is."

"Looks like Harry's spotted them," said Jake, interrupting Swede's self-mourning.

They both watched Black and Turnip have a quick discussion, cowled heads darting everywhere. They were three couples away from boarding.

"Well, they can't board, or else they'll be as trapped as us."

"Aye, but if they leave the queue now, the soldiers will be suspicious." Jake looked left. The four mounted officers and the vanguard of soldiers were a hundred yards away. "They're actually in a *worse* position than us."

"How do you figure that out? They're on land!"

"Aye, but much as I don't want them to get caught, if they bolt now, it will cause a massive diversion. We can slip overboard to starboard and keep the boat between us and the quayside."

Black and Turnip then made their move. They surreptitiously placed their back-packs to one side and slowly began to walk in the opposite direction, to the north, desperately trying to appear monkish. They had gone around twenty paces when the mounted captain dispatched two soldiers to run after them, clearly suspicious of anyone and everyone. On hearing the pursuing footsteps, Black and Turnip decided to run.

"Go on Harry," encouraged Jake under his breath.

"Leg it, Turnip," whispered Swede.

"They need to make for the hills, Swede," said Jake. "See that path there – behind the church steeple?"

"Aye," said Swede, spotting the broach spire topped off by a golden weathercock. A white path behind it wound its way through the grassy hills before disappearing into the trees, around three hundred feet up.

"Those alleyways down there must eventually lead to that path."

In the next moment, though, Turnip made a fatal mistake. He turned around to see how far the soldiers were behind them – just as a fruit and vegetable tradesman wheeled his barrow out onto the promenade. The instant Turnip turned back north, he crashed into the wheelbarrow, sending potatoes, carrots, apples and, no doubt, turnips and swedes, bowling all over the promenade. Worst of all, he went over the top of the barrow, and came down on the other side on his head, knocking himself senseless. Harry, meanwhile, was several yards further ahead. He briefly stopped to take stock, rapidly evaluated his best course of action, and turned and fled, leaving Turnip to the approaching soldiers.

Jake and Swede watched the developing scene in horror as Black made good his escape and the soldiers homed in on Turnip. Perhaps knowing it would save him from the gallows, the groggy Turnip drew his pistol from beneath his robes – and was instantly shot dead by both soldiers.

As Swede stared, open-mouthed, Jake grabbed him and bundled him over to the starboard side of the boat, which was currently empty, with all passengers watching the drama unfold on the other side. "Put your back-pack on, mate," said Jake, just as two of the mounted soldiers took off in the direction Harry had taken, sending folk scattering out of their way. "We're going to need those supplies."

Swede was still in shock at seeing the death of his long-term friend and fellow-outlaw. "If you want to save yourself," said Jake, "then follow me." And with that, Jake climbed over the rail, and worked his way down so that his hands were clinging onto the deck. He looked down. It was a long drop. He thought once of Elyse, and then let go.

CHAPTER 107 — ALICYA

33rd Tertiar, 1789   Day 124, 10:00

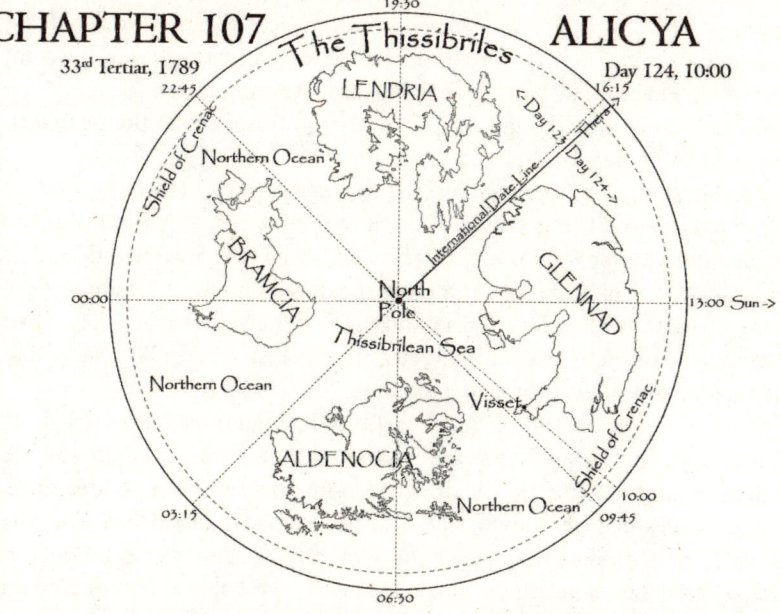

It had been nine days since Alicya's face-off with Ashlyn. She hadn't dared set foot outside Gawain's apartment since, while during the same period, there had been a steady trickle of patients transferring from Gawain to other practitioners. Gawain wasn't remotely bothered. "Less work for me," he'd said. "And of no consequence once I've set up in Sattellus."

Mrs Baker, the housekeeper, had been a comfort, too. Alicya knew that she didn't approve, but she had paused by the front door the day after the Ashlyn incident. "Are you happy, ma'am," she had asked?

Alicya had almost filled up at that. "I'm in love with a wonderful man," she had replied. "How could any woman not be happy with that?"

Mrs Baker had looked at her for several seconds. "That's all that matters then. You take no notice of them, love. It will all blow over in a few days, and folks around here will get used to your arrangement."

Alicya had felt a hot flush at Mrs Baker's mention of an 'arrangement', feeling rather ashamed. "Thank you, Mrs Baker," she'd managed to say.

Three days later, Gawain had returned from work with a copy of the *Glennadian Times* – and another shock. She was front-page news. Or at least Princess Alicya was, hence it was now even more important that she became Alyona from Ghantiss, lest Gawain be arrested and tried for kidnapping a Royal and probably executed for treason. All things considered, though, the development didn't surprise Alicya; it was typical Magnus, and had the potential to completely absolve him. She felt terribly sorry for Jake Oscom, no matter what he may have done in the past. Weaving Harry Black into the story was fairly silly though: Alicya wasn't quite sure how the people of Glennad had fallen for that.

Today, though, Alicya had decided to brave going into town again. Mrs Baker was right. Loving Gawain was all that mattered. What of it if a few small-minded people shunned her or called her names? She was a thousand times luckier than they were, and given the developments in Ghantiss, they were actually helping her by solidifying her new persona! Alicya had therefore resolved to just smile sweetly, if provoked. And as Mrs Baker had also said: *it will all blow over in a few days.*

The reality was, that Ashlyn's actions had amounted to very little damage. A few lost patients and a few nasty comments, that was all. Catching sight of herself in the drawing room mirror, Alicya nodded once. "So, we shall still go into town, Alyona," she coached out loud, before taking down her cream-coloured shawl and wrapping it about her shoulders. It also covered any vague hint of cleavage as well – probably a silly concern on her part, but she felt that she now must avoid any hint of wantonness!

Everything else looked ship-shape. Her pale-yellow dress was understated yet clearly of quality, and nicely complimented the amber earrings that Gawain had bought for her two days ago. As Alicya closed the front door to Gawain's apartment and locked it, she felt a warm breeze ruffle the curls falling over her right shoulder, and she gently caressed them. It was turning out pleasant again, and the creamy-blue sky was dusted here and there with high-level cirrus clouds. The bell on the parish church was just chiming ten o'clock, and the ubiquitous seagull calls resonated all around. Life was wonderful, really. *You just had to have the right perspective.* And so, for the first time since that last encounter with Ashlyn, Alicya decided that she would return to her harbour bench and read. It was a free country, after all.

As had been her daily routine before the incident, Alicya took the same route as normal. Gawain's apartment was set high above the town, and Alicya could see rows and rows of houses before her with their terracotta roofs descending one-by-one to the port. As she crossed the road, she entered a steeply-descending cobbled walkway, fringed by trees, which also descended one-by-one in a similar manner to the roofs on either side. Framed below by the trees was the parish church of St Evis, with its square tower dominated by four pinnacles at each corner, while the sea was spread out like a light blue-green blanket beyond it.

As Alicya headed down the walkway, the church tower gradually disappeared as closer buildings obscured it. She soon reached the point where her walkway adjoined the main high street, two buildings on each corner mirroring each other with grand hexagonal towers topped by peaked turrets – tiled in terracotta, of course.

So far, so good. No abuse.

Crossing the road, Alicya entered another walkway between the high street and the harbour promenade. Called Bedford Terrace, Gawain had told her it had been named after the fourth abbot of Kifsel Place monastery, Harold Bedford (1408-1414) who had been born in Visset and who had allegedly been one of the finest athletes in Glennad in his youth. This terrace was narrower, and was populated mainly by shops. Alicya was in two minds as to whether or not to venture into her favourite antiques shop, when the peaceful ambience was shattered.

"Oi! Missus!"

Alicya turned around to see who was hollering at her – and saw two unkempt boys, probably both aged around eight or nine years old. They both had something in their hands, and they both threw it at her at the same time. Alicya instinctively raised her hands to fend off whatever it was, but as well as slapping into her hands, it also splattered across her face, chest and midriff, and became entangled in her hair. Some of it had also caught in her right eye, and it was immediately stinging.

Then the smell hit her. "Ugh!" By the time Alicya had worked out what it was, the two boys were running away, laughing, also shouting abuse over their shoulders at her. One of them even had the nerve to call her a whore.

Seconds later, the boys disappeared around the corner, and a piece of foulness, slid off her nose and into her mouth. She immediately spat it out, but couldn't stop the retching. On recovering from that, Alicya realised that she still hadn't moved her feet following the attack – with good reason, as any form of movement was likely to exacerbate her discomfort. Far from receiving any help, all Alicya was greeted with was twitching curtains, while a door to the haberdashery shop in front of her actually closed, as if to say: *You're not coming in here, woman.*

After a few more seconds, Alicya's shock at the incident passed, and she began to feel an uncharacteristic anger boiling up inside her. At the same time, her right eye was still stinging badly, so she pulled out a pristine white handkerchief from her sleeve and wiped the corner of her eye. The handkerchief came away brown.

Alicya rarely resorted to bad language, and never in public, but she did so now – albeit under her breath. The anger remained, too; she knew exactly who had put those two horrible little urchins up to this task. Well, if that was how Ashlyn wanted to play it, then two could play at that game. Gawain had plenty of money – and no doubt there were plenty of other grubby little urchins in Visset who would gladly return the compliment if she crossed their palms with silver.

In the meantime, thanks to a complete lack of chivalry in Visset's Bedford Terrace, Alicya began to stalk back up the hill towards Gawain's apartment, her soiled hands held rigidly out to each side. Her anger enabled her to keep her head held high, and woe betide anyone who chose to laugh at her or tell her she deserved it.

Naturally, she drew some shocked looks, but continued stalking upwards, past the twin hexagonal towers and into the wider upper walkway. She was half-way up it when a stout, middle-aged woman took it upon herself to open her upstairs window, and look down her nose at Alicya. "Serves you right," she said, with as much pinched-nosed disdain as she could muster.

Well, thought Alicya. I'll give you a pinched nose, madam. She still had the soiled handkerchief in her right hand, and it was still heavy with substance, having used it to wipe more of the foulness off her dress as well. Without even pausing to think, Alicya hurled it at the woman. Her aim was never truer. Both woman and soiled handkerchief fell back into the room. Alicya didn't bother to remain and laugh or remonstrate, but stalked on upwards, the woman's screeching abuse ringing in her ears.

Two minutes later, she was crossing the road to Gawain's apartment, although her bravado was starting to crumble and her chin beginning to wobble. Fortunately, no one was about, and she managed to extract Gawain's key from her dress pocket. Seconds later, she stumbled into Gawain's hallway and closed the door. For a minute or so, she stood there sobbing, but then she remembered Ashlyn and her gloating face. The sobbing stopped instantly. She *would* make Ashlyn pay for this.

Tentatively, with her nose wrinkled against the smell, Alicya began to shrug herself out of her pale-yellow dress, suspecting that the stains would never come out – and it was such a pretty dress, too.

CHAPTER 108   DAVY

34th Tertiar, 1789   Day 125, 09:00

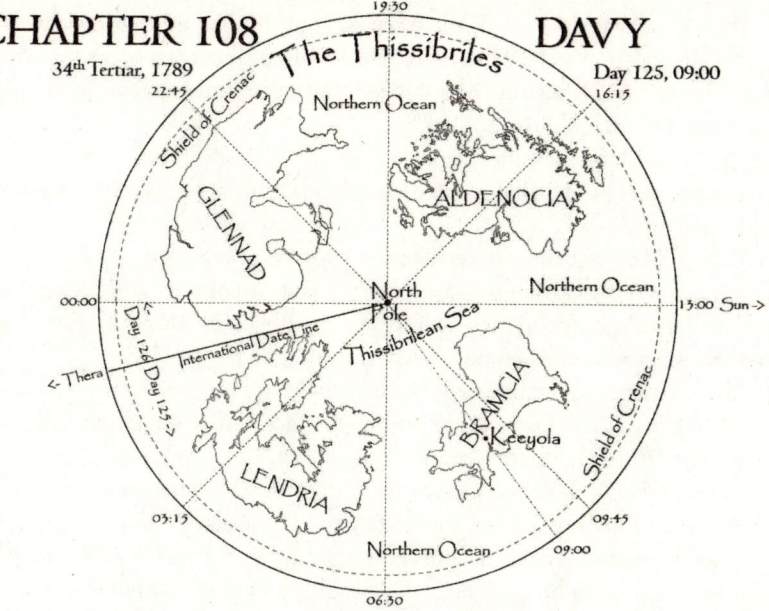

Ten days had passed since Davy and Daisy had married in Cabrenar. They had packed all of their essential belongings over the next two days, and then bid an emotional farewell to friends and family. It had been particularly hard for Daisy to say goodbye to her sister, Carys, who was still in deep mourning for Robbie. The departure and wrench of leaving had hung heavy as they had acquired a lift on a hay cart travelling between Cabrenar and Craffid. It hadn't helped that it had rained all the way, and there was no shelter, while the heavily rutted road had slung poor Daisy from one side of the cart to the other whenever Davy didn't have hold of her. "I've more bruises from one journey than I've collected in my entire lifetime," she'd grumbled.

    From Craffid they had managed to get on another cart to Phanter, and from there, they had booked passage on a ship to Arthumbo, spending almost all of the money that they had left. The boat had taken five days to traverse the east and south coasts of Bramcia, and then it had taken another day – yesterday – to get a ferry around the Hechlar peninsula and up the beautiful estuary to a place called Port Mogdha which had a stunning backdrop of hills and mountains. Davy had then managed to persuade a farmer on the inland outskirts of Port Mogdha to let them sleep in his barn for one night for just two farthings.

So it was, that the two of them awoke, stiff-limbed and with straw in their hair and boots. Nevertheless, Daisy still cuddled up to Davy, who instinctively kissed her on the forehead. "Are you ready to see what this legendary rail incline is like, then?"

"No," was Daisy's simple response.

Davy kissed her fair hair again. "There's nothing to be scared of, love. It works like clockwork."

"They have three or four accidents every year, Davy."

"Aye, when the drum operators aren't paying attention. We'll make sure they are. And the majority of accidents are with slate trucks. It's rare that anything goes wrong when people are travelling in the trucks."

"How reassuring," said Daisy, her face looking even pastier than usual.

"Listen love," said Davy, now cupping her face with both hands. "Would I ever let anything happen to you?"

"I know you'll always look out for me, Davy. But accidents happen. I would have thought that you, above all, would be aware of that."

Davy looked downcast at that. He would never forget his fellow forty-nine coal miners who had been killed in the recent Cabrenar Colliery disaster. Least of all his dear friend, Robbie Russell, and his young apprentice, Will Lowe, who was still missing. But they had to move on. And that was why they were about to climb the hills from Port Mogdha up to Keeyola's slate mine, the largest of its kind anywhere in the Thissibriles. Davy was due to start work at Keeyola in two days' time, and was hoping to be given the keys to their new house before the end of today, as promised in his job offer letter. So far, their convoluted journey had gone to plan. They just had this last leg to go, and thanks to the ground-breaking rail-road pulley system, they wouldn't have to walk all the way up to Keeyola, which was located at around two and a half thousand feet above sea level.

They breakfasted on ground oats and chopped apples, and by 09:45, they were hiking north, with the ground already rising before them. The mountains stood ahead, stark against the grey sky. Looking hard, Davy spotted a channel rising up through the lower half of the hills ahead. "There," he said, pointing.

"I can't see anything," said Daisy.

"You can't see anything from here, but that will be the channel that the rail-road runs up and down."

"I suppose we'd better get this over with, then."

"That's my girl," said Davy, gently rubbing her right shoulder.

It took them another hour of walking with their laden back-packs, which contained only essential clothing and a few personal effects. Like Cabrenar Colliery, the Keeyola Slate Mine Company was providing a house with all of the fixtures and fittings included. Even sheets for their bed. Stuff that they couldn't bring had remained at their parents' houses.

Throughout their hike from Port Mogdha, they had passed horse-drawn cart-loads of slate heading downhill and been passed by supply-laden carts heading back up again, the contents of which would be hoisted up the rail incline to the village at Keeyola. Most of the carters nodded at them and wished them a good day, though not all. "You see," Davy had said on one occasion. "They're just normal people. No different from our families back in Cabrenar."

Sounds of activity became gradually louder the higher they went. What was probably the ratcheting of the trucks as they were constantly hauled up and down the incline came first, along with the crash and bang of slate being unloaded from the iron trucks and loaded into the carts that would then descend to Port Mogdha. And above that, there was the constant shout and call of workers as they supervised and actioned the transportation of their product. The noises eventually became so loud that Davy and Daisy had to shout at each other to be heard.

Both of them were breathing heavily by the time they rounded a corner in the track, and there ahead was a hive of activity at the foot of the railroad incline. A brick-built building around twelve-foot square was situated at the bottom of the incline, while the incline was transporting trucks down the left-hand side and raising them up the right-hand side. Off to the right was a row of cobble-floored stables, home to the army of horses, donkeys and mules that traipsed daily up and down the road to Port Mogdha.

Davy looked back uphill again. The Keeyola Incline Plane looked pretty much as he had visualised it. It was a gravity-balanced incline system – an ingenious invention that had been introduced five years earlier and which enabled the Keeyola Slate Mine Company to ship slate cheaply, easily and quickly down the steep slope from the quarries a thousand feet above them to the mine-owned toll road below. From there, the slate was transported to Port Mogdha, and then distributed all around the Thissibriles. Keeyola slate was recognised as the very best in the archipelago, and demand always exceeded supply – and therefore slate was as good business as any to be in as far as Davy was concerned.

As Davy looked, he could see the incline was constructed in a number of stages. The first stage climbed around two hundred feet to a brake drum above them. It was the cable around that drum which controlled the descent of each slate-filled truck, while lighter empty trucks provided the counter-balance, going in the opposite direction. The full truck at the bottom would get emptied, and the empty truck at the top filled. And so on. Squinting into the sun, Davy could see that the brake drum at the top of the first incline was manned by a brakeman. It was his responsibility to ensure that each truck was properly secured before lowering.

"You see that offshoot about a quarter of the way up, love," shouted Davy, pointing towards an earth-filled emergency siding. "If anything goes wrong, the brakeman pulls a checkpoint lever, and the points are shifted, directing any runaway trucks into the siding."

"Well," said Daisy. "That at least says to me that it's less dangerous going up than it is coming down."

"Exactly, Princess," said Davy, his affectation making Daisy smile, bringing forth those irresistible dimples. Davy squeezed her hand for comfort. They then walked towards the brick building at the foot of the first incline. It had a placard above the main doorway which announced it as the 'Tally House'. The men were busy when Davy and Daisy arrived, so they watched them go about their jobs with interest. It looked as though the man in the broad-brimmed felt hat and heavy drooping moustache was in charge. "I think he's the tallyman," shouted Davy in Daisy's ear.

"The tallyman?" she shouted back.

"Aye, he records the weight of each truck. I was told in my letter that we're divided into teams up above," he said, indicating the top of the incline. "And we get paid according to how much slate we deliver. So, your man there," he said, indicating the drooping moustache, "is a very important employee indeed."

"You're telling me," shouted back Daisy. "What you're saying is, that if he gets his tally wrong, we could be out of pocket."

"Aye, or 'in pocket', if you get my meaning."

Daisy looked at him, surprised. She put her mouth to Davy's ear. "You mean they're not always honest?"

"I've no idea," responded Davy. "There's good and bad everywhere."

Daisy looked worried at that, so Davy gave her a reassuring wink. Meanwhile, the tallyman was overseeing the manoeuvre of the latest truck onto a weighbridge in front of the tally house. A system of levers and counterbalances were being engaged, whilst a small weight was moved along a calibrated bar, which Davy would later find out was a steelyard. The weight of all trucks would be the same and would therefore be deducted from the weight recorded by the weighbridge.

Having done that, the tallyman nodded at the truckmen and they began to manoeuvre the truck towards an embankment where the already pre-cut slate would be unloaded into a waiting cart below. The tallyman went back into the brick building. Davy and Daisy walked towards the entrance where they could see him writing into a lined ledger where he was recording the date, time, wagon number and weight. Once he'd done that, the man with the droopy black moustache looked up and gestured with his head that they should step into the tally house.

Davy offered his hand. "Davy Sheerin," he said. "I'm a miner due to start work at the slate mine in two days' time." They were in a brief lull where no slate was being unloaded and the trucks weren't ratcheting up and down, hence Davy hadn't needed to shout.

The tallyman nodded, but didn't take Davy's hand, leaving Davy lowering it awkwardly. "You can go up in that truck that's just being emptied," said the tallyman. "Should be ready in about two minutes."

"Aye, I'm looking forward to it," said Davy, offering a smile. Daisy offered a weak smile too – but neither smile made any inroads on the implacable tallyman.

"There are eight stages to the incline, in case you're not aware. Same drill on all of them. Wait for a truck to be unloaded, and then you hop in to the empty and climb to the next stage. Good luck," he offered, finally.

"Thank you," said Davy, simply, and led Daisy out of the tally house and over towards the truck which was in the process of being emptied. The noise-level was going up again. The two-man truck team were using a series of chains to slowly unload the contents of the truck into the waiting cart, below. Once done, they righted the truck and wheeled it back towards the incline where they hitched it back up to the incline cable system, with Davy and Daisy following them. Both men had nodded briefly at them before commencing the task, and as the empty truck began to cycle round the bottom of the incline plane before beginning its turn to head back up again, the two men gestured to Daisy and held out their hands to help her into the dusty iron truck. Davy followed suit, and he was relieved to see the two men respond – one with a quick wink, and the other with a thumbs up.

As they began to climb the incline, the creaking, groaning and rattling of the machinery began to work up to a crescendo again, all underpinned by the whirr of the pulleys and thick steel cables. Davy looked up and saw a heavy slate-laden truck descending, right at the top of the adjacent two-hundred-foot stretch. He also noticed a bridge crossing the incline system about halfway up, where a signalman was standing. He was presumably acting as a middleman between the upper and lower stations, passing on instructions to the brakeman above. Davy was unsurprised to note that the signalman was probably about the same age as Will Lowe – triggering a familiar pang of loss.

As they passed the siding on the other side, Davy could see that the end of the offshoot was indeed piled high with earth and sand, its purpose being to absorb the impact of any heavy runaway trucks. Davy nodded at it and said loudly into Daisy's ear: "I'm a fool for telling you this…but there was an occasion a few years back…when a runaway truck was diverted into a siding…but some idiot had temporarily stored a load of explosives there. The blast killed three men and three boys…and, outrageously…the inquest found the brakeman guilty."

Daisy didn't reply to that. She just shook her head in horror.

As they passed under the central bridge, Davy and Daisy waved at the signalman, who waved back. Davy noted that he didn't beam back, like young Will Lowe always had. In fact, he hadn't even smiled. The pang of loss squeezed a little harder. Davy shook his head and tried to think of the future instead. Looking up, he could see the huge wooden drum that sat in between two stone pillars, and the cable was winding around the drum on their side and being released on the other side. The brakeman was also a boy. Davy wondered if the poor brakeman charged over the explosion caused by the runaway truck had been a boy as well. If so, it was twice as scandalous that he had been found guilty.

As they approached the top of this section of the incline, the mechanism slowed down and Davy saw the boy grab hold of a large iron lever, around the height of an average man. It was certainly longer than the boy. The boy pulled on the brake lever with all of his strength and, just as they arrived into the truck's reception bay, the chains stopped moving and they came to a standstill. The boy then dutifully moved across to the truck and helped Daisy out, as did Davy.

"The next port is just above us, mate," the boy said, pointing directly ahead. As Davy looked, he saw a four-man team of slate workers hooking up another slate-laden truck to a ten-yard connecting rail that linked the final section of the downward journey to the penultimate section.

Davy and Daisy thanked the boy, and walked past the four sweating workers, only one of whom noticed them and nodded briefly. Turning around, they stood and watched for five minutes as the young brakeman disconnected the truck they had travelled up in from the system, and wheeled it into a waiting bay where three other empty trucks were ready and waiting to be hauled back right up to the top. The four men then connected their laden truck up to the system, and the brakeman then pushed the great lever away from him to release the mechanism. It all slowly creaked into gear again, and then the latest truck of slate began its final clanking descent, with the four men walking down the steep path alongside it, perhaps intending to watch their truck get weighed at the bottom before being unloaded into a waiting cart.

"What an amazing thing," shouted Davy in Daisy's ear.

Daisy just nodded. It was quite clear there were dangers, and she was likely imagining Davy himself getting caught underneath a runaway truck.

"Come on," he said, indicating a waiting empty truck above them at the bottom of the next section. "Your carriage awaits."

This time Daisy gave him her fullest smile, and Davy's heart melted all over again.

CHAPTER 109   WILL

34th Tertiar, 1789   Day 125, 11:30

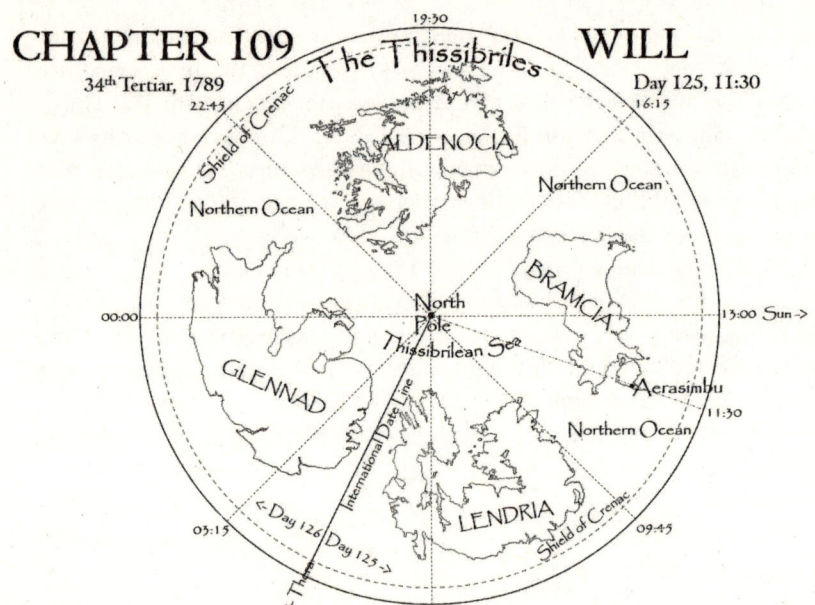

It had been two weeks since their brush with death up against the Shield of Crenac. With the tiller jammed and not able to be pushed to the left to move the boat to the right, Nate Turner had done the only thing they could do. He had turned the tiller to the right and, initially, moved them due south, directly towards the Shield of Crenac. He had then kept the tiller pressed hard right until they turned first due east and then due north, after which they followed a beam-reach bearing back towards Byastwerthy Bay.

Turner had actually laughed at that point. "What am I like?" he'd said, patting his heart. "For a second or two I forgot all of my sailing knowledge and thought we were done for!"

Will had laughed at that, too. It was the point at which their relationship had mellowed. That didn't in any way suppress Will's grief for what had happened to his brother and Robbie, nor his grief for his Mam, nor did it stop him missing Davy. Those things would never change.

From the Shield they had ended up back at the top end of Byastwerthy Bay again, Turner laughing at his errant navigation. "Seems I'm not as good as I thought," he had said.

Having fixed the jammed rudder and picked up fresh supplies from Byastwerthy, the plan was to head south-west and head for the lighthouse off the southern-most tip of the island of Glaesyne. However, they had become enchanted by the estuary that ran north, towards Port Mogdha, with its stunning mountainous backdrop. Will would remember that view for the rest of his life. It had helped that the days were calm, the sun was out and the sky was blue – meaning that the bay was a beautiful blue, forming a stunning contrast with the golden beaches and the greenery on the land. On one day, they had found a colourful shoreline village, with very different architecture to anything Will had seen before. So invigorating had it been whilst walking on a nearby deserted beach, that Nate Turner had uncharacteristically thrown his hands out to the sides, put his head back and shouted: "I am a free man!" Free from his past, Will had supposed – given decades underground and the last few years being victimised for being something that he wasn't.

It had been the mountains that had captured Will's imagination the most, though. They rose right up out of the estuary to the north, while there were hills to the west and east, thick with dark green tree cover lower down and brighter grassy knolls at the top. Will had said that he wanted to run around on top of those hills and climb those mountains. Nate had granted him the former, twice, and promised the latter "one day soon". In the meantime, he had also promised an even better treat, and that was where they were bound now.

By this stage, Will was happy that Nate Turner wasn't a danger to him, although he was still undecided whether he was his Da or not. His instinct told him it was true, as everything fitted. And much as he loved and missed his Mam, the adventures he'd had during the last four weeks had been beyond his wildest dreams. He would still return to his Mam, one day, shocking though that might prove for her, but she'd soon come around and smother him with kisses once she realised that she still had a son. But for now, he was going to make the most of his situation, knowing that he couldn't lose: if they were discovered and handed over to the authorities, he would be returned to his Mam, Nate would hopefully be treated leniently, and Will would still have had an adventure that none of his contemporaries could ever dream of; and if they weren't discovered, well, the adventure would just go on.

Right now, Will was right at the front of the cutter's bow, straining his eyes, looking for the first sight of a building he'd been told was painted white with a red stripe around its middle, and stood seven stories high. He was even more excited now than he had been two days ago when they'd finally arrived at the southernmost tip of mainland Bramcia at the end of the long Nelly peninsula. Nelly stretched out into the Northern Ocean like a forefinger pointing due south, while a protuberance along its east coast looked like the thumb of the hand. The peninsula was named after the ancient Theran philosopher Nellicromas, also known as Nelly, who had once, over 1,500 years ago, stood at the headland pointing towards what was, at that time, the unexplored lands of Eastern Epanaga.

It had been a real thrill for Will to see that point from a boat, and imagine ancient Nelly in his flowing white robes, pointing out towards them. At the same time, Will could turn around 180 degrees in his own boat and look due south himself where he could also see the island of Drybase. The next-most exciting thing had been spotting the island of Glaesyne from between Nelly Point and Drybase – although it hadn't at any time looked like an island until they were able to look to their right and due north up towards the Emani Straits, the narrow channel that ran between mainland Bramcia and Glaesyne. They had put into port at Chalwm the night before last, 'acquired' more supplies and slept on the boat, and then moved further along the south coast of Glaesyne the next day. Then it had been an early start, today, with Nate anticipating rounding the southernmost point of Glaesyne at around midday.

"It's no use straining your eyes, son," Nate said. "Unless you can see through rock."

"What do you mean?"

"It's around the headland. The one with the old church on it," he said, pointing.

"I thought you said no one lived this far south other than the lighthouse keeper and his family."

"They don't."

"But there's a church," said Will, pointing.

"Aye, old and abandoned. No one has lived at Black Rock Village for over two hundred years – since the plague took its entire population. The church, though – that's stood there for five hundred years, and probably will for another five hundred more."

"Ah," said Will, taking in the information. "When will we first see the lighthouse, then?"

"Only about ten minutes before we sail past it."

"And how long from there to Aerasimbu?"

"Another three hours. We'll have to bed down for the night in Aerasimbu, and then make the journey to the lighthouse on foot, unless we can magic up a horse. If we're on foot, we'll not make it to the lighthouse before nightfall in two days' time, so we'll likely be sleeping rough for one night. Is that all right with you?"

Will nodded back. He'd been sleeping rough in the tiny cabin of their boat for the last two weeks anyway, so it was something he was prepared to do if it meant visiting a real-life lighthouse. "And you say we can't get any nearer than Aerasimbu because of the coastline."

"That's right, son. Glaesyne and Nelly Point stick out into the Northern Ocean and are surrounded by leagues of lethal rocks. Plus, there's nothing to break the waves for three hundred leagues to the south. Today is very calm for these waters, but most of the time – certainly throughout winter – they're home to monster waves, especially in a storm when they can spray the cliff-tops a hundred feet high."

"So, there wasn't anywhere suitable to build another town or port or even a village."

"Well, I dare say they could have. But the terrain is inhospitable and battered by winds all year round, so why would you? They certainly never repopulated Black Rock Village. Aerasimbu, though – that's more sheltered, ten leagues further up the west coast of Glaesyne."

"So is there a road from Aerasimbu to the lighthouse."

"There must be. Otherwise, how would the lighthouse keeper get his supplies? I'd hazard a guess it'll be nothing more than a track, mind. So, carriages might struggle, but a horse and rider wouldn't."

It was a quarter to midday when Turner moved them further out into the ocean around Glaesyne Point. "I'm not taking any chances with the rocks," he'd said. For a while, they headed due south, away from land, but when satisfied they were far enough from danger, Turner pushed the tiller to the left to bring it slowly around the headland. And then, perched on a sturdy black rock around thirty yards from the coast, there it was: easily the most magnificent building Will had ever seen.

He had been prepared to expect a tall building, as the lantern room was on the seventh floor...but this was *huge*. As expected, the circumference was much wider at the base than at the sixth floor, with the building gradually tapering the further up it went. Above the sixth floor was a walkway which fanned out above floor six. Railings encircled the walkway, and within, was the lantern room. The sun had come out around ten minutes ago, and the timing was perfect, as the sun's rays were reflecting off the floor-to-ceiling glass at the top, forcing Will to put his hand in front of his face when looking at the top of the structure.

From their current angle, Will saw were single square windows on every level, all looking out to sea. He suspected he would see the same from the opposite side, along with a rectangular-shaped doorway at the foot of the structure – just like his model lighthouse, back home.

Will suddenly noticed Turner looking at him with a kindly smile, and he realised he had his mouth open. He smiled back at Turner and said the only word he could think of. "Wow!" Then he went back to looking at the structure as they rounded the headland and began to head north, taking in every detail. He could even see the keeper up in the lantern room.

As they sailed past the lighthouse, Will walked down to the stern. He stayed there, looking at the structure as it slowly receded into the distance, standing indomitable above the crashing waves. Will was vaguely aware of a white cottage sitting on the mainland around fifty feet above the crashing waves, but it was far too unremarkable to look at compared to the lighthouse. He had also briefly noticed, in passing, that the church on the southern headland to Black Rock Bay was more tumbledown that it had looked from distance. But again, compared to the lighthouse, it was irrelevant.

Eventually, Will tore his gaze from the slowly receding lighthouse and turned back to Turner. "And you're sure they'll let us have a look around."

"Aye, I'm hoping so, lad. Otherwise, we'll end up with a wasted four-day journey on foot, there and back."

Five hours later, they were sat in a harbour-fronted tavern in Aerasimbu, with two steaming hot beef and potato pies before them. Will could tell that Turner was on tenterhooks, clearly still worried that the posters might have found their way down to the opposite end of Bramcia – but they'd seen no evidence of that since they'd docked in Aerasimbu's harbour. It was the absence of posters that had convinced Turner it was high time they had a proper meal. Will's mouth was watering at the smell of the pie, and when he broke through the crust, it got even better. The pie tasted every bit as good as it smelt.

Halfway through their meal, two Revenue men plonked themselves down at their table, both extremely conspicuous in their red coats with gold buttons. Will noticed that one had droopy eyes and the other a rust-coloured beard. Turner nodded to both of them and they nodded back, although Will could tell that Turner was relieved that they hadn't struck up a conversation. No doubt he was on tenterhooks worrying that Will might say something; Will had to admit, it was at the forefront of his mind. But he wanted to see that lighthouse, too much. And in any case, Nate may well be his father. But maybe a day or two after they returned from the lighthouse trip. Maybe then.

As they finished their meals, Will couldn't help but tune in to the Revenue men's conversation.

"Rumour is, they're planning something," said Droopy Eyes.

"They're always planning something," said the other, whom Will had already named as Rusty.

"Yeah, but this is something big, so I've been told."

"You'll be saying they've discovered the source of Envey's Gold, next."

"I'm telling you, it's something big," persisted Droopy Eyes. "That's what I've been told."

"Told by who?"

"By whom?" corrected Droopy Eyes.

"Eh?"

"The correct phrase is, 'told by whom'."

Rusty rolled his eyes. "Just tell me who told you?"

"Ah," said Droopy Eyes, tapping his nose. "We both must keep our informants secret, Badger."

"Chances are," responded Badger, he with the rusty-coloured beard, "that our informants are one and the same, and they've told you and I totally different stories."

And so they went on, both claiming to know great secrets, but neither willing to reveal them to each other. Eventually, Will switched off and yawned. Another day out at sea in all that fresh air had really done for him.

"Come on, young man," said Turner. "Let's see about getting us a room here. You look like you could use an early nigh… and a proper bed!"

CHAPTER 110   MAGNUS

35th Tertiar, 1789   Day 126, 12:00

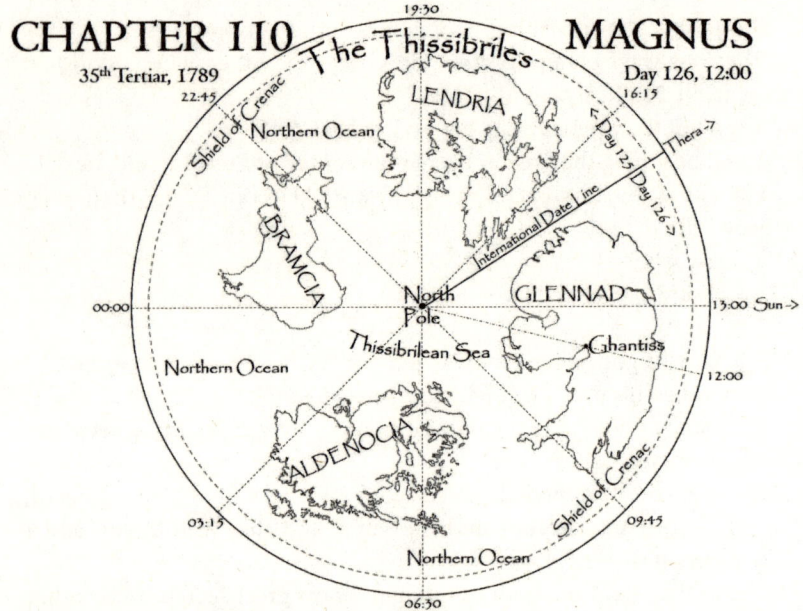

"And they're certain? There is no doubt?"

"None, Your Royal Highness," responded John Russell, the permanently solemn Lord High Constable.

"Right," said Magnus, nodding to Terry, the butler. "Show them in, please."

Magnus then turned to Russell. "How many captains do we have here in Ghantiss?"

"Just Captain Potts, Your Royal Highness. The rest are all out around the country, leading platoons.

As two saddle-weary soldiers were ushered into the palace drawing room, Magnus went over to one of the bookcases and pulled out a rolled-up map from a cylindrical scroll container. As he walked back to the enormous drawing room table, he nodded at the two soldiers who both gave him a salute. Magnus then unfurled the huge map of Ghantiss on the table-top and weighed each side down with paper weights.

"Gentlemen," he said, to the soldiers. "Please take a seat." Both soldiers sat down on the opposite side of the table to Magnus and John Russell, looking very nervous. Magnus noticed. "At ease, men," he said. "As far as I'm concerned, any news is good news." He forced himself to smile. "So, please tell me your names, and then tell me what you know."

"Captain Arnold, Sir."

"Sergeant Knight, Sir."

"Captain?" said Magnus, inviting him to explain.

"Sergeant Knight and I were part of a platoon of one hundred soldiers sent to cover the three most easterly ports in Glennad."

"Port Myra, New Hivetha and Worrab?"

"Aye, Sir," confirmed Arnold. The plan was simple. We reached Port Myra on the 32nd of Tertiar. We took all one hundred soldiers into the port and turned it upside down. We investigated two alleged sightings from locals. Both turned out to be false leads and wasted time."

Magnus rolled his eyes.

"Confident our fugitives weren't in Port Myra, I left twenty men to lock the place down and vet all future boat passengers, and we carried on with the other eighty men to New Hivetha. We rode through the night and arrived just after nine in the morning."

Magnus shifted in his seat, but his eyes remained pinned onto those of Captain Arnold.

"As we approached the port, we could see that a merchant ship was boarding passengers. Obviously, we weren't going to let that go without searching it and forcing the captain to account for every passenger."

Magnus inclined his head, indicating his favour with the tactic.

"As it turned out, Black and one of his lackeys – the dark-haired one – were waiting to board. Dressed as monks, would you believe! Anyway, had we been half an hour later, they would have got away to Lendria."

"And you got them both, Captain, yes?"

"No, Sir. We shot the lackey dead after he pulled his pistol on us."

"And Black?"

"We got held up with the crowds and the lackey shoot-out. Black managed to steal a horse and flee into the mountains. We sent ten men after him; they found his horse an hour later, but no sign of Black."

Magnus' face was beginning to betray his disappointment, but he bit back his anger. "Any sign of Oscom?"

Captain Arnold's eyes darted, uneasily. Magnus was not anticipating good news. "It turns out Oscom and the other lackey had already boarded that merchant ship, Sir – as the captain described two passengers fitting their description. But when we boarded, they were nowhere to be found. We think they must have gone overboard on our blind side. There had been over an hour in between us approaching Port Myra and actually boarding that boat, you see, bearing in mind the distraction of killing the lackey and hunting for Black. So, I'm very sorry, Sir. It looks like that was enough time for them to escape. But we did pick up further leads, later."

"Go on," encouraged Magnus, tight-lipped.

"They must have swum north, as some time after dark, an elderly couple saw two men matching their description, row ashore three leagues north of New Hivetha – in wet clothing!"

"Anyone else see them?"

"Yes Sir. A farmer, further up the coast was held up at midnight by an armed middle-aged man in damp clothing. He took two of his horses and demanded two sets of dry clothing. The strange thing is, Sir, that the man – presumably Oscom – actually paid him. For the horses and the clothing."

"That cuts no ice with me, Captain. Although I dare say Black wouldn't have paid him. But courtesy won't save either of them from the noose."

"Aye, Sir," agreed Captain Arnold.

"And I don't suppose there was any sign of my sister?"

"I'm afraid not, Your Royal Highness."

"Well," said Magnus, rather subdued. "That's pretty much what we feared. She's either being held somewhere, or…"

"Let's not give up just yet, Your Royal Highness," said John Russell, one hand rubbing the back of his neck in frustration.

Magnus turned to look at him, apparently momentarily distracted by grief. He then refocused, apologised and turned to loom over the map again. "So, we know they were here two days ago," he said, pointing at the furthest extremity of the east coast." Magnus bit his bottom lip. "Do you know what, though?" he said, looking up at the Lord High Constable. "They couldn't have been spotted in a worse position for them."

"Aye," agreed Russell. "It wasn't their best move."

"Agreed. Granted, those ports *are* the most sparsely-manned, and it's a shortish voyage to Lendria. But the risk was, that if they got spotted…"

"They only had one place to run," finished Russell.

"Which is here," said Magnus, pointing to the Umbrican Mountains."

"Agreed. They couldn't have gone south because of your platoon, and there was no point going on to Worrab, because the captain's men, here, would easily outrun them."

"The only down-side is that they're on the one part of this island that's an absolute bitch to get to by land, and takes at least four days from Ghantiss even by the fastest boat."

"You're thinking of going after them personally, Sir?"

"Damn right I am, Russell. I want to be there when we catch them."

"But like you say, it's probably four days by sea, and five by land if you go via Luhl and the coastal route."

"I could go via that cursed high road again, through the Bleaklow Hills and Earl's Leet."

"More direct, but much longer to traverse. That could take you five to six days, and if the weather turns..."

"Indeed," agreed Magnus. "So, I shall go by ship...to here," decided Magnus, pointing at Les Antonocca. "We've already commandeered the fastest ship in our navy. If we set off tomorrow morning, which will be the 36th, *Swiftsure* will get us to Les Antonocca by evening on the 39th. I'll take the whole damn garrison from Ghantiss with me, including Captain Potts, and Captain Arnold here shall be their commander."

"Sir," said Arnold. "Happy to serve, Sir."

"And Sergeant Knight?"

"Yes, Sir?"

"I shall need you to go back the route you came as soon as you possibly can. This afternoon. Your horse must be in no fit state to take you, so we'll look after it here. You can take one of my sister's horses. The Lord High Constable will see to that for you."

"Sir," agreed Knight.

"And Sergeant, you will collect men from Luhl, Doglinbrint and Lobstir. I'll make sure you have the appropriate papers. You and your men will be allowed to take free quarter wherever you go. The plan is to blockade that eastern coast from Port Myra to Worrab. There will be no way in and no way out of that stretch of coast for *anybody*, is that understood."

"Perfectly understood, Sir."

"Use smaller platoons to search the mountains as well, but never sacrifice so many men that we can't blockade those ports and lockdown the extreme east of Glennad."

"Understood, Sir."

"Alas, I very much doubt you'll find them with the mountain forays, as they'll go in deep. My money is on them trying to claim sanctuary, here," he said, pointing at the little drawing of a cross. "At Kifsel Place."

"Those were my thoughts, too, Your Royal Highness," said Russell. "And I can see what you're aiming at here."

"Exactly. I'm going to range Captain Arnold's forces along here," he said, drawing his finger across the north-western edge of the Umbricans, "blocking every path in and out of the Umbricans to the west, whilst we will also bolster the local forces at Les Antonocca and Twixelfoe. That will mean a lockdown on the Umbricans to the west, north and east. And then I want you, Lord Russell, to lead another force up that tortuous route to Earl's Leet. Secure the town and then push your men into the lakes and southern foothills of the Umbricans. Again, spread them out and block all paths out of the mountains to the south."

"Leaving them largely encircled in the most inhospitable place in Glennad."

"Exactly. I also need you to send forces to bolster the militia at Kinnslyng, Rhincow, Merroc and West Floot – just in case Black and Oscom manage to evade our western blockade. When we land at Les Antonocca, I shall lead a force of thirty men into the Umbricans, along with Captain Potts, and descend upon Kifsel Place Monastery from the north. If that's where they're seeking refuge, well, more fool them. I shall expect the abbot to give them up immediately. And if he doesn't…well, I shall close down his monastery and arrest the abbot for high treason."

"It's a good plan, Your Royal Highness," approved Russell. "This is as good a chance as we're going to get. Assuming they are hiding out in the Umbricans, I can't see them escaping now."

"Oh, they won't escape, Lord High Constable. It's now just a matter of time."

CHAPTER III — CALIDIUS

35th Tertiar, 1789 — Day 126, 11:20

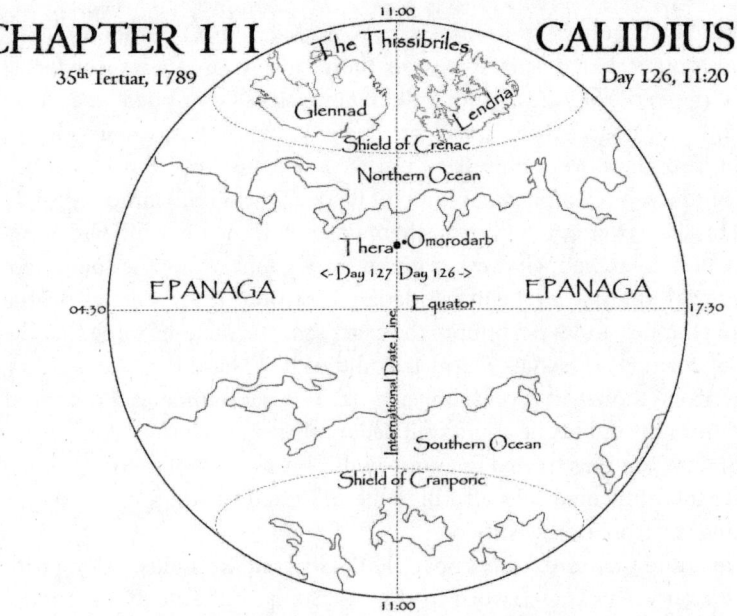

Calidius knew it wasn't necessary to be in attendance, but he wanted to see this latest element of *Expurgatio* acted out first hand again, and he had Lucretius, Seutonius and Gaitonius watching events from within the Senate, the justiciary and the church, back in Thera. So, here he was, having crossed the International Date Line again, accompanying General Macrinus to Omorodarb; the location of only one building – but a building which was infamous throughout the empire.

He had passed Edict No 2 yesterday to an expectant mass gathering in Theodorus' Square. There had been greater expectancy for this edict than for the previous one – and slightly less shock after it was issued. Having sailed through Edict No 1 without opposition, he had felt relaxed, standing above the masses. He had certainly felt little compassion announcing to Therans that they had just twenty-six hours to retrieve their relatives from seventeen lunatic asylums throughout Liatia, if they so wished. It was a largely worthless concession, of course, as only a few would have the time to make the necessary arrangements, even here in Omorodarb, close to the capital. There was no chance for those at the furthest-flung asylums in the country.

As before, squads of soldiers had been sent on ahead to issue 'eviction' warnings in person, on the day of the edict; again, it was Captain Romulus who had been dispatched to Omorodarb. This time, though, armies of soldiers had begun digging mass graves nearby – in Omorodarb's case, around a quarter of a league west of the property, on an area of fertile ground masked from the asylum building by a sizeable wooded area.

Soon, the huge edifice came into view. It was not of classic Liatian architecture; there were no pillars, porticos or pediments. But it was still hugely impressive, simply on account of its size. It was built almost entirely of red bricks – over one million of them. It stood three tiers tall, with long, paired, double-arched windows featured throughout, while the roofs were slate grey as opposed to the usual Liatian terracotta. There were also large wings to the east and west, built to the exact same format, meaning that the building formed a very large C-plan. Calidius had heard that the building had over one thousand rooms, housing one thousand inmates. Looking at it now from his saddle, he could well believe that.

Captain Romulus trotted forwards on his horse to greet them.

"Are there any medical staff still in there?" asked Calidius, his keen eyes scanning the front of the edifice.

"I'm afraid there are, Your Imperial Majesty," said Romulus. "Along with inmate relatives who are sworn to stop us. Some of the medics are more traumatised than their patients. Indeed, some of the lunatics are the calmest people in there!"

Calidius sighed with exasperation. Compassion was acceptable in certain situations. But here at Omorodarb, there was no pragmatic case to be made for it. "It was my wish to save the majority of the medics," he said, quietly. "As they will be invaluable if Nessemi hits land…"

General Macrinus looked across at him. "If we do have a land-strike, Emperor, and by some miracle we survive, there will be no place for lily-livered hand-wringers in the society that endures. Better to slay them now, with all the lunatics and their foolish relatives."

Calidius looked back at his trusted general.

"And besides," continued Macrinus. "We already have our maximum quota of medics for the shelters. If any of these lot are on the lists, we just replace them with grateful medics who aren't."

Calidius smiled a cruel smile. "And there was me wondering if I was being too harsh."

"This is what is behind *Expurgatio*, Emperor. 'In unity there is strength'. These simpering medics will not give you the unity you desire, and they certainly won't provide any strength."

"You are right, General, of course." Calidius turned to Romulus. "You may begin, Captain."

Romulus turned to his two lieutenants. "Antodus, as discussed, you and your squad take the western half of the building; Numerian, you and your squad take the eastern half. Slay everyone, but swords only. No one other than our legionaries are to come out of there alive."

Calidius and Macrinus sat ahorse in silence as the legionaries spread out and surrounded the building. Within minutes, all exits were secured and the order was given to draw their swords and go in. There were no war cries. The Theran legionaries just did their job silently and methodically – moving systematically from room to room. Calidius' eyes followed the screams of living terror followed by death-screams from left to right, and then up a floor and from left to right again. And then up another floor.

The whole operation was carried out in less than an hour, and then they began to drag out the first batch of bloodied corpses, where they were dumped into horse-drawn carts, all lined up in front of the house and destined for the mass graves a mile to the west of the house. Once the first batch of bodies was heading for the woods to the west, Calidius lost interest. "Well, General," he began. "I suggest we return to Thera and see if there are any more signs of the truth emerging."

General Macrinus laughed a harsh laugh at that. "If only they knew how grim the truth actually is."

"Hmm," mused Calidius. "The ignorant may yet be the lucky ones."

CHAPTER 112 — EMILYA

36th Tertiar, 1789 — Day 127, 14:00

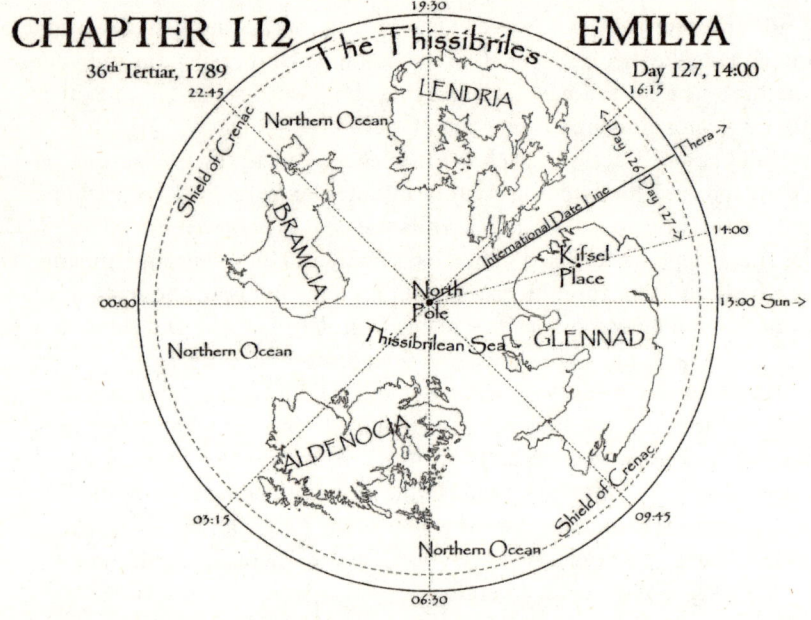

Emilya was lost in thought as she kneaded dough. She had been back to St Affo's church each of the six days since the announcement about Princess Alicya. Each time, she had stared at the Wrothswirk Stone for a long time... but she had not touched it again. And each time, her recollection of what had actually happened when she had touched it became less certain. Elyse had remained evasive about the subject and appeared confused over its presence...or purpose. Elyse had also claimed that she had not touched it again herself, but Emilya was fairly sure that she had. She either still had no answers, or she was protecting Emilya from whatever she had discovered.

Yesterday, Emilya had questioned the mystery inscription again: NEDDMYYYJY. "Perhaps the sculptor's name was Nedd?" Emilya had joked. Rather than the expected musical laugh, Elyse had just frowned – which had only increased Emilya's growing sense of unease.

On a more positive front, there was no evidence, as yet, of any association between themselves and Jake and Harry Black, so that at least meant they could continue their stay at the monastery without any controversy. Moreover, it was looking as though Jake's selfless plan to use Harry Black to lure Prince Magnus away from Emilya had worked a treat – although Emilya had mixed feelings about that. After the abbot's announcement, she and Elyse had been fearing news of their capture, but as each day passed, there was an increasing possibility that Jake, Harry, Turnip and Swede had safely left the shores of Glennad.

Emilya sighed. If news did filter through that Jake had been captured, and charged with crimes against Princess Alicya, she and Elyse had agreed to return to Ghantiss immediately, and raise merry hell. At the very least, they had to ensure that sororicide questions would be asked in public – particularly given that before this incident, Prince Magnus was not loved and often despised. There were all sorts of rumours and claims about his reputation with women, and most folk had believed there was no smoke without fire. In the meantime, the Cleanse the Spirit departure was only five days away, and Emilya and Elyse were still committed to taking part in the expedition to Dawkids and Keplif Scale – so long as Jake remained uncaptured. And, as Elyse had told her numerous times, Jake Oscom and Harry Black were just about the two most experienced outlaws in the Thissibriles. If anyone could evade capture, they could.

This positive vibe helped keep Emilya's spirits up throughout the afternoon on her late shift, as she helped the chefs in the kitchen prepare the evening meal for the monks, with Emilya allocated to preparation of the main course. Tonight, there would be two choices: either herb-crusted pike, or roast partridge, each served with glazed carrots and parsnips and buttered and minted potatoes. The smells coming from the roast partridge were doing nothing to support Emilya's vegetarianism – but, like Elyse, she would make do with extra vegetables and take the fruit salad for starters, and any number of scrumptious puddings for dessert.

With all preparation complete, and trolleys of delicious food being wheeled out towards the refectory, Emilya undid her apron and hung it up on her peg. Brother Mervyn thanked her for her labours and Emilya headed out of the warm kitchen into a much cooler alleyway, given it was now only an hour until dusk. She could hear the low murmuring of monks as they began to file into the refectory for dinner, but given she'd only just finished helping to prepare it, she couldn't face eating just yet – and in any case, she wasn't due to meet Elyse outside the refectory for another half hour. It was a pleasant evening, so instead, she fancied a walk around the ever-fragrant psychic garden.

As she headed towards the bridge to Bloomer, she passed a throng of hungry monks heading to dinner, most of whom smiled at her and bowed their heads. Thankfully, she didn't see the faces of Brothers Cyrus or Obadiah. Arriving on Bloomer, Emilya took a short-cut to the psychic garden behind the piggery and chicken coops. On passing the top end of the huge vegetable patch, she leaned over a low wall to see how the leeks and artichokes were doing. The leeks were nearest, and there was row upon row of squeaky leaves growing upwards and outwards like green fountains. To her right were the artichokes, with slightly darker green leaves, not as tall as the leeks but taking up more ground space. Looking further on, Emilya could make out rows of carrots, potatoes and fennel, while huge clumps of rhubarb grew to one side – all spring vegetables as she had learned in her first week at the monastery.

Smiling to herself at this simple pleasure, Emilya moved on towards the psychic garden. Abbot Geoffrey had told her a couple of weeks ago that psychic gardens used to be known as apothecary gardens thanks to many of the plants being used for their healing properties. He had also proudly told her how the psychic garden at Kifsel Place monastery was the most richly-stocked garden in Glennad, and its seeds were sought and distributed all over the Thissibriles. *"Plants have been a source of healing and nutrition for centuries, Emilya," the abbot had explained. "Sage, rosemary, thyme, mint and borage have been grown here for over five hundred years, and we're still producing ointments, cordials, infusions and purgatives, first and foremost for the treatment of the monks here – particular the elderly or the infirm – but we are also exporting our medicines in large quantities as well. No doubt the shelves of the pharmacies in your own native Ghantiss are filled with our products. I shouldn't wonder if you haven't been administered our medicines yourself as you grew up."*

On recollecting the abbot's words, Emilya felt a surge of nostalgia for her bakery in Irongate. As ever, the memory meant that not only could she smell her father's bread, but she could vividly taste it, too.

As Emilya looked at the riot of plants, flowers and even weeds, she remembered more of the abbot's instruction. *"Yes, Emilya. We grow weeds here, too."* Emilya recalled his friendly smile at that point. *"Plants such as dandelions and thistles are very important in medical herbalism, and they deserve their place in this garden every bit as much as your rosemary and thyme, or your meadowsweet, lemon balm and comfrey."*

Emilya walked slowly through the psychic garden, breathing deeply, enjoying the aromas, as well as the freshness of the clear mountain air and the sound of birdsong as they heralded the end of another perfect day. Could there be a more peaceful place in the entire kingdom?

Emilya was recalling how the rows of plants and herbs, bushes and saplings were grouped according to their healing properties, when she saw movement ahead between some bushes. Frowning, and sensing something wasn't quite right, she was about to turn around when a powerful arm seized her from behind and a strong hand clamped around her mouth. Emilya tried to shout, but it only came out as muffled incoherence. Before she knew it, three monks were manhandling her roughly towards the trees that formed a border between the psychic garden and the fish ponds. Throughout, the hand remained clamped tightly around her mouth, so Emilya desperately tried to keep track of where they were going. Unfortunately, there was no one around, as the majority of monks would be in the refectory or making their way there. A shed then came into view, and Emilya recalled having seen this before: where all of the gardening equipment was kept.

As soon as they were through the door, one of the monks shut and locked it. Still the hand remained around Emilya's mouth, preventing her from calling out. With her predicament worsening, Emilya's legs began to shake. She had to get out of here, so she feigned relaxation, and after a few seconds, the pressure on her mouth lessened slightly. Immediately, she opened her mouth and bit down hard.

The monk behind her grunted in pain, but managed to get a firmer grip on her. This time, he grabbed her mouth so tight that his fingers were bruising the flesh around her lower jaw. Despite the discomfort, though, Emilya felt a brief pulse of satisfaction when she saw the blood running from the back of the monk's hand. She tried to kick back with her heels, but the impact wasn't enough to disable the monk – and in any case, the other two were now moving in from the front. She recognised Brother Obadiah an instant before the monk behind her released his hand – and her head was then jerked upward as he pulled sharply on her hair, enabling Brother Obadiah to thrust a filthy rag into her mouth. It immediately made her gag, but hard as she tried, she couldn't shift it.

"Stop struggling, girl," said the reedy voice from behind her. *Brother Cyrus*. No surprises there. "We don't want to hurt you."

You could have fooled me.

She was led to a chair and thrust into it. She immediately tried to bolt for the door, but this time, Brother Cyrus struck her hard across the side of her face, knocking her senseless. Emilya was vaguely aware of being put back in the chair, and when her senses returned, she realised she was now tied hard to it – with rope around her hands and legs, and also around her upper arms and torso, limiting any arm movement.

Emilya looked at her captors with wide eyes. They were asking the question that her mouth couldn't: *What do you want?*

Brother Cyrus' hypnotic black eyes swam closer. "We want you to leave," he said, reading her eyes. "First, because you are likely an associate of this Jake Oscom, and unless you leave, we will reveal this to the abbot. Second, you must leave because you and your companion are full of sin."

Emilya's eyes must have betrayed her confusion.

Brother Cyrus' eyes blazed back. "Particularly your companion. She is not a woman of God. She delights in leading men astray."

Emilya couldn't believe what she was hearing. If only she could speak, she would tell them that Elyse had no interest in misleading anyone, least of all a bunch of wayward monks.

"Her presence here is driving poor Brother Obadiah to hitherto unknown sins of the flesh."

Oh yeah, thought Emilya. *So, aged around 45, he had never before committed 'sins of the flesh'.*

"Tell me, girl," continued Brother Cyrus, his voice suddenly at her ear and barely more than a whisper. "Have you flowered yet?"

No filthy rag in the mouth could have hidden Emilya's frown of disgust. *What the hell has that got to do with you, you filthy mongrel?*

"Ah, you have," concluded Brother Cyrus.

Emilya noticed Brother Obadiah almost immediately looking at her in a new light. And he was now looking at her barely-noticeable chest, too. Worse still, his hand had disappeared under his robes.

The look of alarm on Emilya's face was instantly noted by Brother Cyrus. "It is not his fault, child. He came here to remove himself from temptation. And yet," he paused, chillingly. "Here you are."

The panic that Emilya had felt before was nothing to what was going through her head now. *Surely it won't happen like this?* Before she knew it, tears were sliding out of both eyes, and all she could visualise were images of Edwyn along with a sense that she had let him down.

Brother Cyrus showed no compassion, but he did at least begin to assuage Emilya's fears. "Do not worry, child. No harm will come to you. You shall go on your 'Cleanse the Spirit' expedition in four days' time. But when you return, you shall leave this monastery the very next day, and never return. Do you understand?"

Emilya looked at him, the fire now gone from her eyes. She merely nodded. If she had her way, they would run away from here right now, given the chance. Brother Cyrus appeared to be reading her mind.

"You will not, however, depart now. And if you go to the abbot with this story, things will end very badly for you and your companion. And probably for the abbot, too. Do you understand that?"

Again, Emilya nodded, albeit unsure whether Brother Cyrus would have the power to overthrow Abbot Geoffrey. But she would nod at anything to get herself out of this predicament. Try as she might, she couldn't avoid hearing the increasing level of grunting coming from Brother Obadiah, and when her eyes deserted her and looked to his face, his whole balding pate was glistening disgustingly with sweat.

"Brother Obadiah," snapped Brother Cyrus. His voice was like a whip. "Stop your sin this instant!"

It was extraordinary, but the command had the desired effect. It was like Brother Obadiah had suddenly snapped out of a trance.

Brother Cyrus ignored him. Instead, he moved across to Emilya and went down on his haunches so that his intense black eyes were on a level with hers. "I'm going to release you soon. But before I do, I am going to give you some sound advice. I pride myself in being a man who can control his urges. Unfortunately, not all men can. Brother Obadiah here is not the only example. We have at least three others who have had to remove themselves from the normal routine here, so that they avoid seeing you or your companion. Brother Obadiah here is not strong enough to do even that. This is why you must leave. However, if you pass on to your companion any news of our little encounter," he said, choosing his words carefully, "then you will regret it," he added. He then smiled for the first time. A cold, ungodly smile, *though*, despite his pretence of faith. "But not nearly as much as your companion will. Do you understand this?"

Emilya nodded again. She had little doubt that Brother Cyrus would carry out his threat. And yes, she was in a terrifying position here, and now had a major dilemma to shoulder alone, but her overriding emotion at the moment was one of relief. They were going to let her go. All she had to do was keep quiet, go on the expedition, and then leave. That was a gift from heaven compared to where she had thought events were heading five minutes ago. And Brother Cyrus knew that. He had planned this whole encounter to perfection. It also briefly flashed through Emilya's mind that she might not tell Elyse *after* they had left the monastery, either. But that was something for her to sleep on over the next few days.

Brother Cyrus was still staring at her – but then he reached out and almost gently took the rag from her mouth.

Emilya remained silent, but couldn't keep the fear from her eyes.

Brother Cyrus then nodded to the other two monks who began untying her. Brother Obadiah immediately went for the ropes around her upper body and his hands instantly strayed to her breasts.

"Brother Obadiah!" snapped Brother Cyrus. "Untie her feet."

Brother Obadiah meekly did as he was instructed. When she was free of her bonds, Emilya looked fearfully up at Brother Cyrus as if to ask if she could get up.

"One moment," he said. And out of the pockets of his robes, he pulled a glass vial which contained a clear fluid. "Witch hazel," he said. "From our own psychic garden." He then pulled out a velvet cloth, soaked some of the witch hazel onto the cloth and then gently applied it to the side of Emilya's face where he had struck her. "This will help to soothe your skin and reduce any inflammation. If your companion – or anyone else for that matter – asks about the bruising, please tell them that you weren't looking where you were going on your way to supper tonight."

"All right," whispered Emilya. "I will." And then, she added two more words, with no idea why she said them: "Thank you."

Witch hazel administered, Brother Cyrus drew back slightly and looked at her. He nodded, and some form of humanity appeared to manifest in those black eyes. "You're welcome," he said.

CHAPTER 113   WILL

36th Tertiar, 1789   Day 127, 15:30

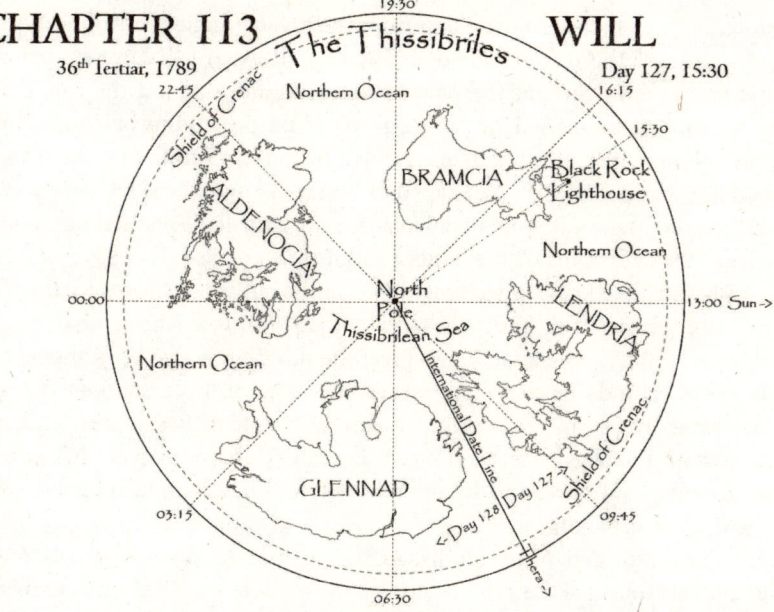

Will's excitement was close to bubbling over as they descended the path towards the rugged southern coastline of Glaesyne. He knew that as they rounded the next bend, they would finally be looking at Black Rock Lighthouse close-up. And from land, this time.

It had been a long, hard trek without horses, and as there were no houses on this bleak, treeless coastal stretch at the end of their country, they had been forced to spend the previous night sheltering in the lee of a clump of gorse. When they had risen that morning, Nate Turner was so stiff he could hardly move, but thankfully, the stiffness along with the aches and pains in his legs, back and neck gradually eased up as their journey progressed.

With each step downwards, the curve in the limestone cliffs ahead began to straighten out. The first thing that Will saw was a rocky bay, and there, nestling around thirty feet above the water was the white cottage he had largely ignored on their seaward passage. Way above it on the headland further down the coast was the old abandoned church.

Will knew that the lighthouse was another thirty yards off the far headland of the bay, although he couldn't yet see that because of the way the cliffs of the bay curved around to his right. But then, very gradually, first the headland, then the bay began to open up…and then, there it was – standing majestically on its stark outcrop of black rocks, with its seven storeys, as before, but much closer now – and from the reverse angle – meaning Will could now see the rectangular doorway as well. Above that were square windows, one on each of the next five storeys, and then, at the top, the lantern room with its floor-to-ceiling glass and the protruding balcony with safety railings. Will recalled being dazzled by the sun shining off the glass when they had sailed past, two days ago. Today, though, the skies were grey and he could make out more detail inside. With a thrill, he realised he could even see the keeper inside the lantern room.

Will and Nate kept on walking downwards, but when they were thirty yards from the cottage, a middle-aged woman with frizzy brown hair and wearing a white apron came out to greet them. Will saw two boys appear a few yards behind. As they approached the woman, Nate shouted out a welcoming "Hello" in an attempt to demonstrate that they were friendly. The woman managed a weak smile. Will realised that they wouldn't have many visitors out here, and so any that they did have would probably be treated with suspicion.

"Hello," repeated Nate, loudly, as the path levelled out towards the cottage. The sound of the sea crashing on the rocks to their right meant that voices had to be raised. "I hope you don't mind. My son has always wanted to see a lighthouse, close-up," he said, waiting for Will to join him at which point, Nate put his arm around Will's shoulder. Will gave the woman his best beam – which worked the way it always did with mothers.

"Well," she said. "You've come to the right place. But you must be a long way from home."

"We're stopping at Aerasimbu," explained Nate. "But as this is a life-long ambition of Will's, we slept rough last night half way between Aerasimbu and here."

"Good Lord!" exclaimed the woman. "You must be keen, young man."

"I'm going to be a lighthouse keeper myself, one day," announced Will.

"Are you indeed. Well, you'd better come in and have a cup of tea then, you and your father. And then we'll see what we can do about showing you around our lighthouse."

"You'll actually let me go inside?" asked Will, his eyes like saucers.

The woman ruffled Will's hair. "How could I refuse a face like that?" she said, her smile now indicating that any suspicions had been banished.

By this stage, the two boys had approached as well, the elder tall, thin and fair-haired, the younger slightly fuller with hair of pale ginger. These are my two sons, said the woman. My name is Kyra. I'm the keeper's wife, and these are our children, Matt and Tom."

Will waved at the two boys, who both waved back.

"Matt is fifteen," said Kyra, "and he helps run the lighthouse with me and my husband, Eric. Eric's up there in the lamp room," she said, turning and waving. Eric obviously hadn't seen them as there was no return wave. "Tom there is thirteen," said Kyra, indicating the smaller lad. "He's learning the ropes with all three of us. How old are you Will?"

"I'm twelve and a half," he said. Keen to learn more, he asked the first of his many questions. "Have you run the lighthouse for long?"

"Yes, we took over from Eric's father, ten years ago, when the boys were very young. It was harder then as we had to do alternate thirteen-hour shifts. Matt then graduated as a keeper on his fourteenth birthday, and we've been down to three 08:40 shifts ever since."

"Did Matt have to train alongside you and Eric then? How long does it take to learn? And how did Eric's father manage on his own? Did he never go to sleep?"

Kyra's face went from open-mouthed amusement to gentle laughter as Will breathlessly asked his questions.

"Steady on, young Will," said Nate. "One question at a time, son."

"I will answer all your questions, Will," said Kyra, placing a guiding arm around his shoulder. "Inside, and over a cup of tea. How does that sound?"

"I'm sorry, Miss," said Will, his face falling. "I guess I've waited a long time for this moment."

"Don't you go making any apologies, Will," said Kyra. "And please don't call me 'Miss', either. Kyra is perfectly all right."

As they walked towards the cottage, Nate and Kyra were exchanging small-talk, and so the younger boy, Tom, fell in beside Will. He offered his hand, which Will shook. "I'm glad you came to visit us, Will. We hardly ever have any visitors here. We get a supply cart from the Company, once a month, and occasional visits from the Revenue to see if there has been any smuggling around our cove. But apart from that we don't see anyone else – and certainly no one of my age. Except for those that we wave to on boats from the cliff-top over there," he said, indicating the high ridge above the right-hand side of the harbour, opposite the lighthouse.

Tom then changed tack. "I'm training now as well, by the way. For the lighthouse. It's been in our family for over two hundred years. Well, I say 'it'. That lighthouse," he said, indicating the seven-storey structure, "was only built thirty-three years ago. As Mam said, Gramps ran it before us. He died last year, by the way."

"Oh, I'm sorry about that," said Will, momentarily distracted. He was thinking about Nate's tale of his Da – potentially Will's grandad – dying along with all hands in that terrible storm of 1756, and which had led to the lighthouse rebuild. He decided to keep that story to himself, given the uncertainty over his family links.

"That's OK, Will," Tom was saying. "He was very old. And he was very kind," said Tom, his eyes distant for a second. "But he was also very content. He loved his job."

"So, will you do a shift when you turn fourteen, Tom?"

"That's the idea. It will give Mam and Da more time together, as we'll do shorter shifts between the four of us. We won't get less money, though, as the Company always pay us the same hourly rate, and it's always been enough to live on. In another two or three years, we'll go back to three shifts, as Matt will likely head off to Aerasimbu for work, and…you know…"

Will looked at Tom without understanding.

"Find himself work in the town and then, you know, find himself a wife."

"Ah," said Will, now understanding.

"Then, maybe in ten or twenty-years' time, when Mam and Da are getting old, he'll come back here with his own family. Or perhaps I will. But one way or another, the lighthouse will stay in the family."

As they stepped into the porch of the cottage, Will couldn't help but notice a strong smell of damp. As Tom shut the door, Will asked about the previous lighthouse, unable to pull his thoughts away from his likely grandad and the terrifying death he must have suffered.

"It was only four storeys high," said Tom. "In those days, there were more shipwrecks than there are today. The Company decided that was because it wasn't tall enough or bright enough. And it was old, anyway. Dad remembered it from being a boy, and Gramps always told me that it was beginning to crumble before they demolished it and built the new one. Imagine that, though – stuck up a crumbling lighthouse when the tide's in and the waves are thirty-feet high!"

Will could well imagine it. The drawings from his childhood books were forever locked into his mind. Images swirled around his head as they were shown from the porch into a fairly large kitchen-dining area, and Kyra asked Nate and Will to take a seat at the table whilst she set to filling up a kettle. She then placed it on a kitchen appliance that Will had never seen before, but which appeared to be heated from a fire below whilst a huge black pipe rose out the top of it and disappeared into the wall above. Tom saw him looking. "That's one of these new-fangled stoves, Will. The

Company installed it for us last year. The lighthouse kitchen is obviously too small for one."

"There's a kitchen in the lighthouse?"

"Of course there is! There are bedrooms, a sitting room, a bathroom and several store rooms. We'll show you them all, soon. It will be low tide in around an hour and we can walk the causeway instead of taking the boat. Mam takes over at 17:20, anyway, so the timing will be perfect."

"So, does that mean that your Mam will work until midnight – and then Matt will take over."

"Aye, that's right, Will," said Matt, also taking a seat and speaking for the first time. Will noted that his voice had already broken. "I'm on nights for a week. I then do a double shift at the end of the week, and we all move forward a shift. It's the easiest way to keep us all on some kind of normal cycle – whatever that is," he added, eyes cast heavenwards.

"Do you go to school, Will?" asked Tom.

"Aye. Well," he said, flicking a glance to Nate. "I did before…before me and my Da took a break. Sunday School, that is."

"Did you work then?"

"Will worked down a coal mine, Tom," interceded Nate. "We both did. But there was a terrible disaster. At Cabrenar. Perhaps you heard?"

Kyra had been listening, and walked slowly across to the table, a look of shock on her face. "The Company brings us newspapers with the monthly supplies. So, yes, we know of the disaster. Were you involved?"

"We were two of the lucky ones, Kyra," said Nate, quietly. The haunted look on his face was totally genuine. "We got out…"

"It's all right, Mr Turner," said Kyra, holding up her hands. "There's no need to explain. The newspapers were overly graphic about the casualties. I can't begin to imagine what you've both been through."

There was silence for a few seconds, and then Matt voiced his curiosity. "How did you get to be down here, if you don't mind me asking?"

"The mine owner was very generous to Will and I," explained Nate.

Will kept quiet, fascinated to see what story Nate would come up with.

"We were working the same seam together, some way from the explosion. As was the mine owner's son. We were all protected from the worst of the blast and managed to climb to the surface via an old downcast shaft. Many of those who stayed down below either died of their burns or of carbon monoxide poisoning."

"Yes, that's what the paper said. How dreadful. It also said they had to flood the mine to put out the fires."

"Aye, well, a flooded mine is no use for mining coal," responded Nate, now improvising. "So, it was shut for a couple of months to drain the water. Some miners found alternative employment. Many didn't. But because we had saved his son, and my father was a fisherman, the mine owner told me to take Will away for a few weeks on his boat which was moored at Phanter. 'Sail all the way round Bramcia,' he said. 'You've earned it.' He even gave us some funds. He's a very generous man, and he took the disaster to heart. Took it personally."

"There's not many men so kind," said Kyra, quietly.

Kyra returned to supervise the boiling kettle, and soon came back with five steaming mugs and some applecakes. The conversation had dissected the cause and effect of the explosion, and had now returned to Will's fascination with lighthouses. "It's because of the books Mam read to me when I was young. The lighthouse stories were the best, especially the drawings. They're fixed in here," said Will, pointing a finger at his temple. "One of the lighthouses was being attacked by a giant kraken. It had its tentacles all over the exterior." Will shuddered at the memory.

"A kraken!" said Tom. "There are legends of a kraken in these waters as well, Will."

Will's eyes grew to saucer-size again.

"And which are only tales," scolded Kyra. "There's no such thing as a flipping kraken. It's all a myth."

Will awoke for only the second morning in over four weeks in a comfortable bed, having shared Tom's the night before. Such terrible things had happened only a few weeks ago, and yet, somehow, Will was content. A sad look then crossed his face as he realised that he was going to have to leave the wonderful lighthouse behind, and the new friends that he had made. Particularly Tom, who for one day, had filled the void left by his twin-brother, Dylan. But Will was determined he would come and visit again. There had also been offers of future employment, but Will wasn't quite sure they were genuine. Perhaps if Matt and Tom left for Aerasimbu and settled down there with wives and new jobs. But then again, it wouldn't be the same working here without Tom.

"You're awake."

Will turned over and saw that Tom was fully dressed. "What time is it?"

"10:30."

"10:30!" he exclaimed, sitting bolt upright.

"Don't worry, Will. Your Da told us that you'd barely had a decent night's sleep since you were back home, so we decided to leave you be."

Will flopped back onto the bed and blew out his cheeks. "Yes, I've missed my bed." He then got a whiff of breakfast. He turned to Tom, his face a picture of dismay. "You've not had bacon and eggs?"

"Don't worry, Will," repeated Tom, this time with a smile. "We've kept yours warm."

Will beamed at the thought. He threw off the covers, which reminded him that he was wearing one of Tom's nightshirts.

"Your clothes are on the cabinet over there," said Tom, gesturing. "I'll see you downstairs in five minutes."

The bacon and eggs were divine. Will thanked Kyra before eating them, twice during, and then again after.

"You must be the most polite and grateful twelve-year-old boy in all of Bramcia, Will," Kyra said, smiling.

"Sorry," said Will.

"Don't apologise. You're very welcome. We don't get visitors here very often, and certainly none as enthusiastic for lighthouses as you!"

Will smiled at that, his mind rapidly running through the magical two-hour tour he'd had last night, before his thoughts were interrupted by Tom asking if he wanted to go rock-pooling. "I must help your mother with the washing up," said Will. "I always help Mam with ours." A sad look flicked across his features.

"No need," Kyra said. "You and Tom go rock-pooling. It's lovely for him to have a companion."

"My Da said we would need to leave early, though."

"That's all been sorted out Will. You're staying another night and you'll leave early tomorrow morning."

Will's face lit up, and the two boys were soon excitedly exiting the house, armed with a fishing net and a bucket apiece.

"Lunch is at thirteen-thirty," shouted Kyra after them. The instruction just about registered as the boys raced down to the waters' edge.

"This is my favourite rock pool," announced Tom, as they arrived at a six-foot circle of trapped sea water. "It's deep, so there are always crabs in here. Look! There's one. And there's another."

"And fish, too," said Will pointing. "And what are they?" he asked, looking at a group of transparent creatures with lots of feet and a blotch of orange on each side.

"Baby shrimps," replied Tom. "But they're too small to eat. My brother catches proper shrimps. He's got a fishing rod made especially for the sea."

Will could tell that Tom was proud of his older brother.

The two boys were still busy rock-pooling as the clock ticked around to 16:00, and the tide was already well on its way out. They had long-since had their lunch – which had been mash and very tasty sausages, stuffed with delicious herbs – and they were now on their fourth bucket, the first three being already full of sea creatures. Nate and Matt had now joined them, having returned from a long walk along the top of the coastal path. "Well," Nate was saying. "That's done wonders for my miner's lungs."

Sure enough, Will thought that Nate's voice didn't sound as gravelly as usual and he couldn't detect as much wheezing, either.

"Although the wind's getting up, I notice."

"Aye," agreed Matt. There's a storm coming from the south-west. I can taste it."

"We'd better turn in then boys," said Nate. "And later, young Will here will get to see waves crashing against the lighthouse in a storm."

"Wow!" said Will, his eyes all agog again.

"But before we go, you boys need to show us what you've caught," said Nate. The four of them then spent the next five minutes studying the contents of the four buckets, with Matt pointing out what each individual creature was to Nate. All the while, the wind got steadily stronger.

Nate and the three boys were all heads down at the northern extremity of the little bay and the furthest part of the bay from the lighthouse, but some sixth sense made Will look up. He struggled to register what he was seeing straight away, as it had been explained to them more than once that visitors in these parts were very rare. But right now, he could see five men crossing the causeway towards the lighthouse – and they were all armed with muskets slung over their shoulders. "Who are they?" he eventually managed to blurt out.

By the time the other three looked up, the first man was across the causeway and racing up towards the lighthouse door.

"I don't know," said Matt. "But I don't like the look of them." He jumped across a number of rockpools, heading in a downwards direction, and then began to run across the bay, his shoes spurting pebbles out in all directions. "Excuse me!" he shouted.

The last two men in the chain turned around at his voice. Both unslung their muskets.

"Matt, get down!" screamed Nate.

The first of the men raised his musket and fired. The bullet took Matt in his right shoulder, and spun him around, dumping him face first into the pebbles. Then all hell broke loose.

The men at the head of the raiding party wrenched open the lighthouse door and disappeared inside. Will, Tom and Nate were all shouting at the same time. And then Kyra came running out of the cottage, saw her eldest son lying prone in the bay, and let out a raucous scream. The other man aimed his musket at Kyra and pulled the trigger. Thankfully, his aim was poor and missed.

In the meantime, Nate was running towards the prone Matt, and the first man was re-loading his musket. He also fired and missed, and a split-second later, two other shots sounded from inside the lighthouse. The second man on the causeway then re-loaded and fired, and his shot took Nate in the left arm, spinning him around. Nate didn't let it stop his momentum though. He staggered a little, but then righted himself to reach Matt. He dropped to his knees and grabbed the boy with his good arm and began pulling him back to the north side of the bay, screaming at his own pain, but not relenting on his pulling. His agony persuaded Will and Tom to run towards them to help – a distraction which had enabled Kyra to go back into the house, and come out running ten seconds later.

The two men had now re-loaded for a third time and were aiming at Nate and the three boys, when the head of one of them exploded in a mass of blood, bone and brain. That pulled the other man's attention from Nate and the boys to where he could see Kyra re-loading a beast of a gun with a splayed muzzle. The man took one look at it and fled for the lighthouse. He didn't make it. The force of Kyra's second monster bullet punched through the middle of his back and left him flopped half in, half out the lighthouse entrance.

Kyra didn't stop there though. She began to run for the causeway. "Eric!" she screamed. "Eric!"

"Get Matt to the safety of those rocks, boys," shouted Nate, pointing to a cluster behind them. "I need to help your mother."

But Nate Turner was out of condition, injured and too far behind. "Kyra," he was shouting. "Kyra, get back. They'll shoot from above."

That stopped Kyra in her tracks, and she looked up at the circular balcony at the top of the lighthouse. It was currently empty. But for how long? She turned back to Nate. "But Eric's in there," she shouted.

"We can't help him, Kyra. There are three armed men in there."

Tears were pouring down Kyra's cheeks now. "But we have to get help. We need to -."

A musket bullet entered Kyra's back and exited via her heart, dropping her forwards, dead before she hit the ground. Other bullets splashed the shore around Nate's feet all being fired from the lighthouse summit. Nate acted upon instinct, and as the men above re-loaded, he sprinted forwards, picked up Kyra's fallen gun and ran back for the cottage as another round of musket balls whizzed past him, spurting up rock, sand and pebble.

From behind the shelter of his rocks, Will braced himself for Nate taking a bullet, but they all missed and Nate managed to reach the house, collapsing behind the porch door. The events of the last two minutes had barely sunk in, yet instinct told Will that Nate had done the right thing in grabbing the heavy-duty ordnance. Without it, they were all dead. Will then saw Nate raise his head to look out of the porch window – and the glass above his head shattered. Beside him, Tom was crying for his Mam, his Da and his injured brother.

Will briefly closed his eyes. *Why did so many good people have to die?* His heart was already aching for Tom's loss but he knew he needed to stay strong. "Don't worry, Tom. Me and Nate will look after you."

Matt had now come around, although he was grimacing in agony. "I'm going to kill those bastards," he gasped.

Will noticed the blood running freely down Matt's right arm and dripping fast from his fingertips. Will's stomach began to turn, so he looked Matt in the eye. "Who are they?"

"Never seen them before," wheezed Matt, before a fresh lance of pain forced him to gasp out loud. He breathed out rapidly for a few seconds to control himself. "But they're probably smugglers. The last letter from the Company warned us there had been an increase in activity in the area."

Will remembered the conversation between the two Revenue men in Aerasimbu. "What are they smuggling? And why would they shoot your Mam and Da?"

"They smuggle anything and everything. And they will have shot Mam and Da because they want that light out tonight."

Realisation dawned on Will. "So that ships run aground?"

"Exactly," gasped Matt. "They'll light a beacon a hundred yards back from the headland."

"And ships will come a hundred yards closer to the rocks?"

"You've got it."

"That's appalling!" cried Will, unable to understand such a lack of humanity.

"What are we going to do?" interrupted a tear-stained Tom.

"We need to get back to the house. There's a proper, long-range musket in there as well as the fowling piece that Mam just used."

Will's mind flashed back to sitting in Eric and Kyra's lounge last night. The musket in question had been mounted on the lounge wall and there had been a case full of musket balls on the top of the fireplace.

"Whilst we have those two guns," Matt was saying, "we've a good chance of keeping those three *murderers* inside the lighthouse."

"Because there's only one way in and out?" asked Will.

"Exactly. They're trapped."

"But how do we get back to the house?"

"We wait here until it's dark. And in the meantime, we hope that if the smugglers leave the lighthouse, your Da picks 'em off, one by one.

"If he's still all right," said Will, looking anxiously across at the shattered porch glass.

The storm increased in severity with each passing hour. Behind their cluster of rocks, the boys were now being lashed by continuous driving rain, whilst the wind was constantly whipping at their sopping wet hair and clothes, making them all shiver with cold. The tide had begun to come in again as well, which meant that the causeway was no longer crossable, and their tiny bay was a constant maelstrom of surging froth. This also brought some relief to Will, as it meant that the smugglers could not approach them for several hours, now. And thankfully, each passing hour had seen the elder son bear his physical pain better. The same couldn't be said for poor Tom's emotional pain, though.

Will's question about Nate's welfare had been answered an hour ago. One of the smugglers had appeared at the lighthouse doorway. It wasn't clear what his intention had been as he had merely heaved his dead colleague unceremoniously away from the door entrance, presumably so he could shut the door. But when he had stood up to survey the scene before him, Nate Turner had put a musket ball right through his throat. Nate had obviously had the presence of mind to grab the long-range musket and musket balls from the lounge – allowing him to demonstrate yet another skill that Will had been unaware of. Nate Turner was certainly full of surprises. Of course, the two surviving smugglers hadn't bothered with the door since then. But they were still up there in the lantern room – although since their companion's death, they had also avoided the open balcony around the top of the lighthouse. This didn't help the boys, though, and they remained pinned down behind their rocks.

As dusk began to fall, it was no surprise that the candles and wick lamp in the lantern room remained unlit. Elsewhere, the headlands began to take on a darker, more-sinister form, and even the dark outline of the old church on the southern headland looked creepy, particularly its square and squat tower.

"I've been thinking," said Matt. "I don't think they intended to come out of that lighthouse, tonight, anyway," he said, nodding at the submerged causeway.

"You mean they would have known the tide would be in by dusk?"

"Yes, Will. Which makes me question what their plans were for my family."

Will didn't say anything to that, still secretly relieved that the smugglers would be staying put in the lighthouse. Poor Tom didn't say anything either, but he had at least stopped crying now. Nothing Will could say could make up for what had happened to his Mam and Da – two lovely people who had shown nothing but kindness to Will and Nate. As for Matt, Will was in awe at how well the older brother was handling both his serious injury and the loss of his Mam and Da.

"Right boys," said Matt. "Now it's dark, I'm going to put my theory to the test. I could crawl all the way to the house, but I don't think my shoulder will let me. So, I'm going to crouch. If I get to the house without incident, you're to come across the same way yourselves, all right?"

"I don't want them to shoot you, Matt," said Tom, holding onto his older brother's hand. "I don't want to lose you as well."

"We both need to be brave, Tom. Can you do that for me?"

Tom looked up at his brother, and eventually, he nodded, miserably.

"Good boy," said Matt. Taking a deep breath, he inched out slowly, in a crouch, from behind the rocks. Nothing happened. He then began to inch slowly but surely towards the house. Will began to count. He had got to a hundred when he realised that the rain had stopped, although the wind was still blowing a gale. He had reached over three hundred when Matt made it to the porch, where he could just about make out Nate greeting him. Will felt a brief pang of concern for Nate and Matt. They both needed urgent infirmary care.

"Come on, Tom," he said, turning to look at his pasty-faced friend. "Our turn now."

Tom was clearly scared, but he nodded once. "We'd best go ten seconds apart," suggested Tom. "You know, in case…"

Will patted him on the back. "Good thinking, Tom. I'll go first."

Five minutes later the two boys were reunited with Matt and Nate. Once the greetings were over, Will mentioned that it had stopped raining.

"Which means they'll now be able to light the beacon," said Matt, with disgust.

"Assuming they've kept their tinder dry," said Nate.

"Oh, they'll have done that all right. This practise has been going on in these parts for hundreds of years, Nate. They know what they're doing. A little bit of wind and rain doesn't stop them."

Sure enough, around twenty minutes later, a brief flicker appeared on the looming southern headland to their left, a hundred yards or so back from the edge, and a similar distance from the dark outline of the old church. Within seconds, the fire had expanded into a blazing fireball.

"Any idea how many men are up there, Matt?" asked Nate.

"Difficult to say. I've heard that smugglers can number as few as three or four – so they each get more loot apiece. Other times there can be dozens. Especially if it's a merchant ship that they're targeting."

"Do you know the shipping schedule for tonight?"

"No, my Da would have told me on handover."

"Do the smugglers usually know."

"Oh aye, they'll know all right. One of 'em is likely from the coastguard. In fact, it's not unknown for their numbers to include Revenue men!"

"You're kidding me?" asked Nate, with disbelief.

"Wish I was, Nate."

"So, we're likely to have company down here, soon, then."

"Won't they only come if a ship is wrecked?" asked Will.

"Difficult to say," admitted Matt. "But up there," he said, nodding to the headland, "they have the shelter of the old church – although most of its roof is missing. But up there, they also know they're not going to get a one-inch calibre musket ball put through their throats. That was a hell of a shot, by the way."

"More tricks from my mis-spent youth," responded Nate, grimly. "But anyway, if they do come down here, we'll likely be trapped in this house," said Nate, worriedly.

"Not necessarily," said Matt.

Nate looked at him, hopefully.

"Aye," said Matt, a brief smile on his face. "It wasn't unknown for former lighthouse keepers to be involved with the smuggling as well."

"Meaning?"

"Meaning, there's a tunnel from our cellars that the smugglers might not know about."

"Where does it lead to?"

"Well, that's the problem," said Matt. "It leads to a cave over there," he said, pointing towards the cliffs facing the lighthouse.

Nate was staring at the spot. Slowly, his eyes narrowed and a strange look passed across his face. "No, it's not a problem," he said. "It's perfect."

Will looked at him as if he'd lost his mind.

"How many smugglers are left in the lighthouse?" asked Nate.

"By my reckoning, two," said Matt – and he suddenly saw what Nate was driving at. "And you're right. It's our best hope. The lighthouse is built like a fortress, so long as we can lock and bar the door. I'll need to see if I can raise a musket first, though," said Matt, flexing his wounded shoulder. A stab of agony coursed through it and he winced. "Otherwise, you'll have to give the second musket to Tom or Will."

"Me!" exclaimed Will. "I've never fired a gun before."

"And how are we going to cross the causeway?" asked Tom.

"We'll take the boat by the cave."

"But the sea!" complained Tom.

"I've rowed it in worse, and it's only a few yards. Fact is, we'll be better off taking our chances swimming the channel than staying here for when that lot come down," he said, nodding at the fiery headland.

"Yes, but you and Nate are injured."

"Which is why we'd better make it in the boat then. I'm not arguing any longer, Tom. Grab the other gun, and let's get down to the cellar. Those smugglers could come down here any minute, now they've got their fire burning. And where's the first place they're going to head for?"

"All right," said Tom. Will felt terribly sorry for him. In the heat of their current predicament, he appeared to have forgotten about his Mam and Da. As far as they knew, his poor Mam's body might have been plucked out to sea – except the tide was coming in at the moment. But that meant a potential dashing on the rocks. Either way didn't bear thinking about.

"Listen, Matt," said Nate. "We also need to take the boat, because we need to grab supplies from here to take over to the lighthouse."

"The lighthouse has supplies, Nate."

"Yes, but if we manage to get across *and* kill the two smugglers in there, we don't know how long we're going to be holed up for. They won't want us raising the alert, will they? So, it may well be a fortress good enough to keep the baddies out, but it's also a prison with only one door – as those villains found out earlier today. And what about ammunition? We're probably going to need a lot of musket balls."

"All right, Nate, agreed. And yes, we've got plenty of ammo."

Twenty minutes later, they were in the dank cellar, amongst crates and barrels and boxes. Will and Tom had been burdened with the sacks of supplies and ammunition as well as being the candle-bearers, as both Nate and Matt couldn't carry a gun and hoist a sack due to their injuries.

Will was asked to put his sack down and take Tom's candle, and then bring the light over to the far wall, where three barrels were stacked: two on the bottom and one on the top. Between them, the injured Matt and Tom managed to get the top barrel off, and then they manoeuvred the bottom two barrels out of the way – revealing a hole in the wall of about three and a half feet in diameter.

"I'll go first," said Matt, although he paused briefly to manoeuvre his shoulder, and spasms of agony crossed his face. He then grabbed his musket and got down on his hands and knees. "Tom will follow, and then Will. Both of you will need to push your sack of supplies ahead of you." With that said, Matt crawled into the tunnel, pushing his musket before him. Will watched Tom follow and then he placed his sack at the entrance to the tunnel along with his candle, got down on his hands and knees, and pushed the sack before him. There wasn't a deal of room in the tunnel, even for a twelve-year-old, so Will was already beginning to worry about Nate.

"Don't worry," called back Matt, reading his mind. "It opens out after a hundred yards."

Will sighed with relief. Several yards in, he could hear Nate puffing and wheezing behind him, along with the scrape of his musket along the rocky floor as he pushed it before him. "They'll soon spot the tunnel…if they go down into the cellar," shouted Nate, in between gasps for breath.

"By which stage we need to be in the lighthouse," floated down Matt's response.

Will was looking around as he shuffled forward, his candle architecting all manner of demonic shadows on the walls. The rocky floor was damp, and he also had to be careful not to kneel on painful rocky protuberances. Up above him, the tunnel roof had a horrible slimy texture to it.

As they progressed, Will was sure that the smell of saltwater was growing stronger, although there was also a constant *drip, drip, drip* of water that was more likely to be fresh water seeping through from above. After several minutes of crawling, Will heard the sound of the sea crashing onto rocks nearby, and soon after, Matt announced that they'd arrived. Seconds later, Will emerged on his hands and knees into a sizeable cavern. He was even able to stand up and hoist his sack over his shoulder.

Nate exited the tunnel next, wheezing and wincing before standing and stretching his cramped limbs. He looked back at the tunnel, blew out his cheeks again and then turned to Matt. "How old is it?"

"We think it's been here for over two centuries."

"From a time when the keeper was on the smugglers' payroll?"

"Aye, probably," agreed Matt. "I assume you've heard the rumour, though?"

"We're not locals, Matt. What rumour?"

"About Envey's Gold. You've heard of Captain Harry Envey, surely?"

"The pirate?"

"Aye, the pirate. Known as the King of the Pirates by many or the Black Pirate – due to his jet-black heart. And never caught, either. Hence, he was thought to have accumulated the greatest amount of treasure of any single man in history – hence Envey's Gold. And because he was highly active in these waters, there are strong rumours that his gold is stashed along this part of the coast, somewhere. I've looked, of course, as did my father and grandfather before me."

"When did he live?" asked Will, his eyes agog at such a story.

"Last century – well over a hundred years ago. Anyway, I can tell you all about Harry Envey once we're safely in the lighthouse. I'll take the lead," he said, turning around. "And we'll need to blow the candles out in a bit," he threw back over his shoulder. Matt then began to move forwards, in a slightly downwards direction. After twenty seconds, Will heard splashing ahead – and sure enough, seawater began to appear under his own shoes, and then briefly over them, before they headed slightly upwards again onto rocks slick with seawater and seaweed.

"We're here," said Matt, presently. "Blow the candles out."

Both Will and Tom did as they were told, plunging them into blackness. After several seconds, though, Will's eyes began to distinguish a lighter blackness ahead of them, and as Matt led them towards it, he began to see the darker shapes of cliffs ahead as well. Then they were suddenly back out in the open, and the wind was immediately tearing at Will's hair and clothes again. The storm hadn't yet abated, but it had remained dry – with the downside being that the beacon above them would still be burning bright.

Will could see that there was a channel of seawater running adjacent to them and it was rushing backwards and forwards with the tide. Off to their right, Will could make out the waves crashing onto the rocks and it was towards there that Matt was leading them. As they edged forwards, the towering dark form of the lighthouse slowly appeared from behind the cliffs ahead of them, much closer now. Will couldn't help but feel it looked ominous in the dark; nothing like its cheerful aspect in daylight, especially in sunshine. Matt held up his hand and got them all to fall back into the shadow of the cliffs.

"The boat is over there," he whispered, pointing to where the rower was tied to a mooring post. Will watched as the rower was tossed about from side to side by the buoyant tide. He reckoned it was about thirty yards across the water to the plug of rock on which the lighthouse stood, but couldn't see how they were all going to fit into the boat along with their supplies. It looked like a two-man boat: one rower, one passenger.

"Can you swim?" asked Matt of Nate in a low voice.

"I can with two arms," he whispered back, holding up his injured arm.

"You and me both then. We're going to have to do this in two runs. "I'll take you over first."

As Matt released the rowing boat from its moorings, and Nate got in along with one sack of supplies and his musket, Will saw the logic of sending Nate first, in case a firearm was called for. Despite his injured shoulder and the choppy surf, Matt coped with the rower – albeit constantly wincing in pain – and the boat was soon butting up to the plug of rocks on which the lighthouse stood. Nate was straight out, musket at the ready – but other than the sounds of the sea and the wind, there were no signs that they'd been spotted. No doubt the last thing the smugglers expected from three boys and an injured old man was an offensive – but soon, all four of them were standing on the lighthouse plug, battered by the wind, while Matt secured the boat. It was not a moment too soon, as the sound of voices on the mainland drifted across to them.

"Quick," said Matt, "round the back of the lighthouse."

The four of them hurried to a point in the shadow of the base of the lighthouse, taking the supplies and muskets with them, and crouched down, whilst the sea crashed against the rocks just ten feet below them, showering them with salt-spray every ten seconds or so. Peering back inland, they saw armed, lantern-carrying figures emerge onto the stony beach. There were around a dozen of them. Four immediately went to check out the house, whilst three others were busy scouring the shore for signs of life. That group were laughing at something on the ground before them. Will's gut wrenched as he realised that they were laughing at the body of Kyra. One of them turned it over with his foot, which prompted another to say something, his words snatched away on the howling wind. There was no mistaking the callous laughter of all three of them, though.

The next moment, Will's heart leaped into his mouth as the lighthouse door opened, and the two incumbent smugglers stepped out, both armed, no more than four yards away from where they were hiding. "Oi! Travis!" hollered one of them, struggling to be heard above the storm. "Watch yourselves! They're armed and dangerous! They've got a long-range musket that shoots one-inch bullets."

The men on the beach immediately became alert and unshouldered their own muskets. "How many?" one shouted back, presumably Travis.

"Three boys and one old bastard," shouted back the man from the lighthouse doorway. "Grandad's injured, as well, as is one of the lads."

"Right you are," shouted back Travis, releasing the safety catch on his musket. "What about the keeper?"

"Full of lead," shouted the man with his back to them, followed by another callous laugh. "Happy hunting boys."

Unbeknown to Will, Matt and Nate had swapped hand signals behind him, deciding who was taking who. The next second, they stepped out, released the safety catches on their muskets, and sent both smugglers to hell from very close distance, one of the deaths being very messy courtesy of the fowling piece that Matt was brandishing. Then, before the smugglers on the beach could gather their wits, Matt and Nate bundled the two younger boys before them, along with their sacks of supplies and were into the lighthouse before their foes could react – although Will did hear Nate hurl an insult at the two dead smugglers, inferring that 'Grandad' was still very much alive and they weren't.

As soon as the door was shut, Matt turned the key which had been conveniently left in the lock. There was also a solid wooden bar standing to one side of the door, which Matt and Nate lifted between them and slotted it into very comforting and sturdy-looking iron brackets. The smugglers wouldn't be bludgeoning this door down any time soon.

Following their burst of activity, Nate slumped to the floor, but Matt's face was exultant. "We did it!" he cried. "We actually did it!" He even went to pick up his little brother to spin him around, before he remembered his injured shoulder. Instead, he just hugged Tom – who had already begun to cry again. That soon sobered up Matt, and realisation came crashing in.

Their Da's in here, somewhere, thought Will, grimly. *'Full of lead'.*

Will's eyes caught Nate's. Nate stood up, grimacing in pain from the bullet in his arm. He put his other hand on Matt's shoulder. "You leave this to me, son," he said, patting him. "I'll make your Da comfortable. And then we need to light the lantern room up, sharpish. Those evil bastards won't be getting their loot tonight."

CHAPTER 114   MAGNUS

39th Tertiar, 1789   Day 130, 18:25

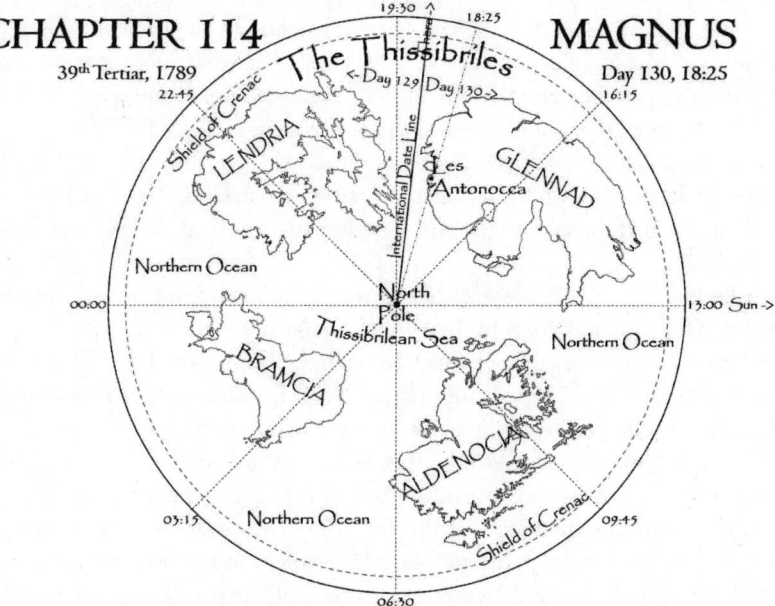

It was late afternoon when the warship, *Swiftsure*, finally arrived in Les Antonocca. As Magnus, Captain Arnold and Captain Potts disembarked at the head of their force of one thousand men, they were met by the head of the Les Antonocca militia, a man with short, jet-black hair and a matching jet-black moustache.

"Your Royal Highness," he said, bowing his head. "We weren't expecting you."

"To whom am I speaking?" asked Magnus.

"Captain Weams, Sir, at your service."

"Thank you, Captain. We're not expecting to be waited upon. I just need two things from you – starting with an update on events here in the east over the last four days. I will then brief you on what myself and Captains Arnold and Potts here will be doing in your neighbourhood over the next two or three weeks, along with my second request."

"Of course, Your Royal Highness. There have been no sightings here in Les Antonocca, and as you can see, we have posters everywhere," he said, pointing out three placards in close proximity. "The local guard are vigilant, meeting three times a day for updates and -."

"Yes, yes," said Magnus, impatiently. "There's no news here. What about elsewhere along this coast?"

"Like us, Worrab and Twixelfoe report no sightings, Sir. The same applies to New Hivetha and Port Myra, and the roads on that stretch of the coast are now totally impassable for Oscom and Black, to both north and south."

"As was my plan, but it is good to hear it is being adhered to."

"The fugitives haven't taken a boat, either, Sir," continued Weams. "All boats are accounted for, while the navy has been patrolling the sea in force, up and down the coast, night and day. For me, that can mean only two possibilities."

Magnus nodded. "They've either gone to ground and someone is hiding them, or they're hiding out in the Umbricans."

"Agreed, Your Royal Highness. The general consensus is the latter as they were last seen in the foothills behind New Hivetha – plus no one would be foolish enough to harbour such wanted men, anyway."

"Thank you, Captain Weams, this is as we'd hoped. As for their next move, they won't exit the Umbricans via Earl's Leet, as by now, the town and the lakes will be crawling with the Lord High Constable's soldiers. This means their likely options are to hike all the way through the Umbricans – which would take around two weeks from south-east to north-west – or they'll be holed up at Kifsel Place monastery. This is why I've got Captain Arnold here who will be blockading the north and north-western exits from the Umbricans; I, myself, will lead a small force to the monastery. This time we *are* going to capture them."

"I sincerely hope you're right, Sir. And that their capture will lead to the Princess being released."

"Yes," agreed Magnus. "We are fervently praying so, too. Tell me," he said, changing tack. "If you were a betting man, Weams, where would you think the outlaws would head for."

"Well, a lot of people are suggesting they'll head for Kifsel Place monastery, as well – and claim sanctuary."

"But you don't?"

"It's possible, Sir, but the abbot's a staunch Royalist. He'd surely never let them in."

"Not if he knew who they were, no. But supposing they can pass themselves off as someone else…"

"I see what you mean, Sir. That is possible."

"It is, Weams, but please don't impart our plans to anyone. I'd hate for them to get tipped off in advance of our visit, if that's where they're hiding out."

"You mentioned two things that you needed from me, Sir?"

"Yes, Weams. I need the loan of two men who know these parts and can safely lead us to Kifsel Place Monastery from here."

"The best mountaineers in my squad are Yarhill and Ginsten. I'll see that they're assigned to you immediately. Will you be staying in Les Antonocca, Your Royal Highness?"

"No, Captain. We've brought tents. We'll be using the last three hours of daylight to get ourselves inland by a few leagues. We're expecting to get to the monastery in four days' time. Does that sound reasonable to you?"

"It's an arduous climb, Your Royal Highness. You'll need every hour of daylight to get there before sunset on the 43rd."

"We intend to do just that, Captain Weams."

"Yarhill and Ginsten will see you right, Sir. They both know the Umbricans inside out."

"Excellent. Please see that they report to me within half an hour. Now, if you'll excuse me, I have my men to organise. We'll be out of your town in under an hour. Just you make sure that no ship sails out of this port until we've got Oscom and Black in custody. Or in a coffin."

CHAPTER 115 — DRAXAELEN

39th Tertiar, 1789   Day 130, 09:30

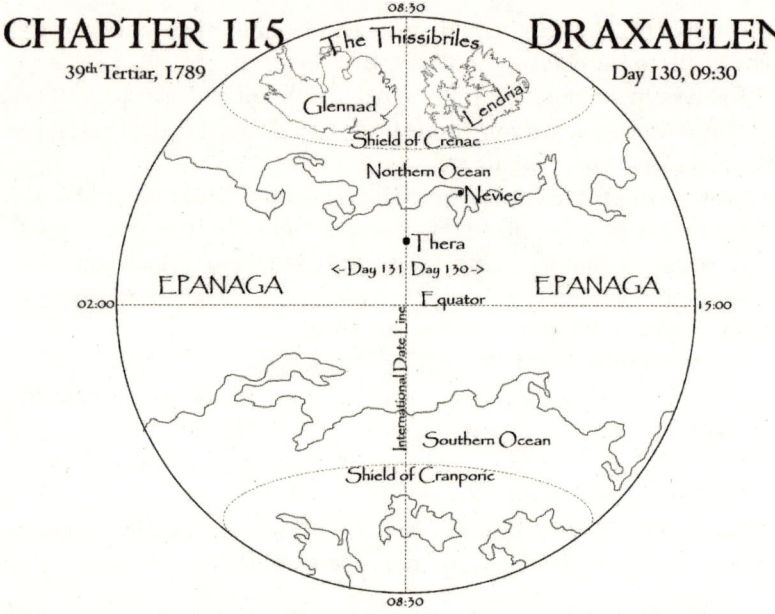

Draxaelen's heart sank as they were marched back to the fighting pits. They had all feared the worst when their chains had been re-applied earlier that morning. Drax had been feeling empty-stomached dread ever since. The last eleven days had been relatively safe, first recovering from injuries received on his previous visit to the fighting pits, and then training with Gravus. The training had been hard, but it had also been a revelation. It had certainly helped take his mind off the series of tragedies that had recently befallen him, and he had actually *enjoyed* most of it. His reward for throwing himself into the training was that he was already twice as fit as he had been before, and three times the fighter.

Alongside the training, the food had been delicious and copious, but Drax had been sensible, always taking the healthiest option and never touching alcohol. As a result, he was lean and mean and it felt good. Or at least it had until the chains had gone back on. He really shouldn't have been surprised. After all, none of them were referred to by their names; they were all referred to as either 'slave' or the number their slave-masters had allocated to them.

It was also evident that it wasn't just his villa compatriots who were being marched towards the fighting pits, as he was now seeing survivors from his own galley and the other five galleys which had returned from

Rysia nearly two weeks ago – all being marched in chains towards the same destination – and all looking very much healthier. The numbers certainly looked about right: close to two hundred slaves.

Eventually, they arrived outside the square building with its one single entrance, where Maxi Zoninus and several other slavemasters were waiting with at least one hundred armed soldiers. They soon began organising the slaves into groups. This time, Draxaelen was somewhere in the middle of the waiting throng, so he was hoping to get a decent idea of what lay in wait *before* he was sent in himself. Drax then heard the sound of crowd noise from inside the building, which immediately banished any hope this would be another training exercise; there weren't going to be any wooden swords issued today.

The first big difference from last time was that soldiers had begun to chain slaves together in pairs – something that had been mentioned several times in the last eleven days as a common tactic, both in the fighting pits and the famed Mesocluso. That immediately got those waiting in line looking around at their fellow slaves, wondering who they might be chained to. Clearly, they would no longer be able rely on just themselves for survival. Drax's tactical mind had already realised that, being right-handed himself, it would give he and his partner a potential advantage if the partner were left-handed – as Garataelix was.

Their eyes briefly met and Garataelix gave Drax the slightest of nods. He had figured it out, too. Then, both men returned their attention to the front. As they watched, just sixteen slaves were chained together as eight pairs, after which they were marched towards the huge main doors, which opened to admit them and then closed again. In his mind's eye, Draxaelen was picturing the blocks of four fighting pits, and he was fairly certain it would be two chained pairs per pit. This hopefully meant just the one fight for each pairing, today – albeit to the death.

With a thrill of horror, Draxaelen realised that even if that *best-case* situation was to play out, that would still leave half of their number dead! They would be down to less than one hundred! His eyes quickly flitted about him. Half of the men around him could be dead before nightfall. Again, one word thundered around inside his brain: Why?

As the minutes passed, the tension in the group outside intensified. A scuffle broke out between two slaves. Both immediately felt the lash of the whipmasters, and dealt themselves a disadvantage in the life-and-death fighting to come. After a few seconds, the doors to the fighting pits opened, and one of the other slavemasters stalked out, a look of thunder upon his face. He briefly conferred with one of the Theran captains, and then walked arrogantly up and down the front third of the waiting slaves. "Please remember that you are aspiring to be professionals," he spat. The look on his face suggested that he wasn't expecting anyone here to achieve such status. "The next slave to even speak," he growled, "will get a sword in their side." And with that, he stalked off back to the fighting pits. Thereafter, the slaves waited in silence.

Shortly afterwards, the noise level from within the building began to ramp up. Unlike eleven days ago, though, the noise for each bout was still ebbing and flowing after twenty minutes, whilst in the middle of that, a single horn had sounded followed by a swell of crowd noise. Those outside tried to visualise what was happening. Draxaelen's initial instinct was that the eight pairs would have been slung into pits 1 to 4, with two pairs per fighting pit. But if that was the case, why was it taking so long for a conclusion to be reached? Perhaps fighting chained to another person severely limited the ability to deal a killing blow? This was an unknown factor, certainly for Drax, as they hadn't trained in pairs back at the villa. This was a major worry, as others assembled here today may have done. And if *both* of a pairing had that experience, they would have a massive advantage.

Following the first horn, the noise had continued to ramp up, and civilians and soldiers could now be clearly heard baying for blood. The noise eventually reached a crescendo, followed by another blast on the horn and then raucous cheering amidst a few boos and catcalls. Thereafter, the noise fell away to a low buzz, almost certainly signifying that the contest was over. But how many were left standing?

Five minutes later, the slavemasters came out again, and eight more pairs were chained together. As they were marched into the building, Drax worked out that he would have to wait another three hours or so for his bout – whereas those at the back of the queue wouldn't get into the fighting pits until early evening – having stood under the blazing sun all day. Severely sunburned and dehydrated, they would then be expected to fight for their lives.

Draxaelen's attention was diverted to the door to the fighting pits, as it opened again. This time, it was the victors who exited; just the four of them, exhibiting a mixture of elation and exhaustion. One of them was limping badly from a nasty-looking gash to his right thigh. Worryingly, Draxaelen didn't know any of the men; they were neither *Demonata* nor did they belong to his villa.

The four men were led away by twelve armed guards – presumably to be returned to whichever villa they were training at. In the meantime, the noise had already begun to ramp up again as the next bout or set of bouts got under way. This time, Drax was visualising all combatants being herded into Pits 5 to 8 at the top right of the building; it certainly seemed as if the noise was coming from that quadrant.

The pattern was much-the-same as before, although the entire bout lasted perhaps six or seven minutes shorter than the previous one. As before, four victors were led out, these seemingly less elated, more exhausted and certainly more damaged. But they had survived. Clearly, twelve of the others who went in with them hadn't, and had presumably joined the first twelve in the mortuary. Drax's horrifying original estimate of survivor numbers was now looking optimistic.

It was 12:50 when Drax finally found himself at the head of the queue. Garataelix was sticking by his left side. Both had resisted efforts of others to jockey their way in between them, and with the whipmasters ever-attentive, no one put up much of a struggle when they were denied. Eventually, it was their turn, and Drax was relieved when the lazy soldiers just chained pairs together who were stood next to each other, without bothering to look if they were well matched. He and Garataelix shared a look which spoke volumes. They were one. As one, they *would* prevail.

Drax and Garataelix's batch of sixteen were soon being herded towards the building. As they passed through the huge wooden doors, Drax looked up to see a mass of civilians and soldiers, encircling the entire complex above, before they were marched towards the top right corner of the building, to pits 5 to 8, above which the baying punters were currently the most tightly crammed in. Money was changing hands at pace. However, when the slaves were all pushed through the entrance to Pit No 7, Drax got a big surprise.

He looked around, temporarily disorientated. He was expecting something of the size of Pit 12 which he had fought in previously, but this space was four times the size. It took him a few seconds to realise that they had opened up Pits 5, 6, 7 and 8 into one huge fighting pit. He then noticed the folded wooden screens at the centre of each of the four walls, and realised that Pit 12s two internal walls must have been made of wood. The retractable walls had also left a giant plus sign marked upon the sandy floor which clearly showed where the subdivisions of the four former pits had been. As Drax took this in, the noises that had preceded the previous five bouts began to make sense. This was going to be a free-for-all.

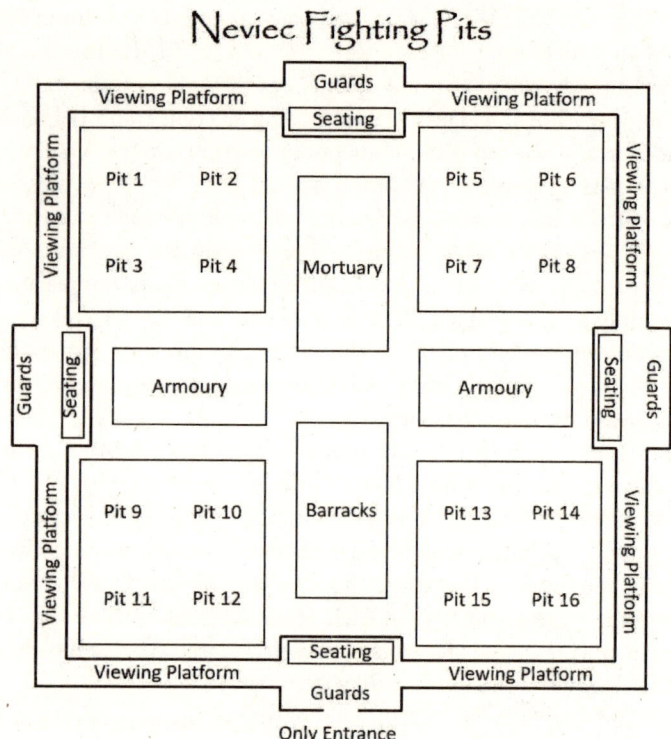

Drax and Garataelix nodded at each before they were led by armed soldiers to the top right of their pit and what would previously have been Pit 6, along with a pairing of slaves they had never seen before today.

As the last-minute arrangements were made, Drax and Garataelix studied their paired opponents. Of the other fourteen men in the room, only three were from their villa. Two were in the Pit 5 space to their right, but Drax had already written them off, as they had trained infrequently back at the villa, whilst eating and drinking themselves stupid every night. The evidence was there before everyone, chained together, with untoned torsos and matching paunches drooping over the tops of their overtight breeches. Their gluttony and laziness would now prove to be nothing but an extended last meal for the condemned. That said, the two slaves facing the two gluttons were very young. Both had tried to grow beards, neither with much success. And although they were toned, there was no bulk – and bulk counted for a lot in an enclosed space, as Gravus had repeatedly demonstrated in training. Clearly, any winner from the other three pits would likely turn their next attention on the winners from Pit 5.

The other person that Drax knew was a young man in the Pit 8 space. Standing at an athletic 6ft 2in tall, he was one of his one-thousand *Demonata*, seized by General Macrinus and Maxi Zoninus on 8th Tertiar. The lad's name, if Drax remembered rightly, was Maurulen. He had no desire to take the life of any of his former men, and he suspected that Maurulen would not want to take the life of his former general, either. With a bit of luck, they would be the last two pairs standing.

Over in Pit 7's space, though, there was a stark contrast. Drax didn't fancy the chances of the two small, dark-skinned Dimunian-looking slaves, as they were up against two olive-skinned giants who hailed from Acahea, judging by the red sun tattoos on their chests. If ever there was a definition of what a seasoned scrapper looked like, they were it. Both torsos were criss-crossed with scars, one of them was missing his right ear and the other had a hideous depression where his left cheekbone should have been, which had dragged his left eye socket down to be around half an inch lower than his other eye. They were clearly the favourites to survive this particular bout; Drax could hear it above, all around them. He even picked up a simple moniker they'd been allocated: The Beasts.

That left the two facing them in the space formerly held by Pit 6. One was young and fair-skinned; even his hair was brown rather than Theran black. Drax couldn't place his ethnicity. The other was much older, easily in his mid-forties. But that didn't mean a thing, looking at how toned and tough he looked. His large hooked nose suggested Alglian heritage and with his large dark eyes, his nickname surely had to be Hawk. However, his skin colour was of a dark brown found in the lands a hundred leagues south of Thera. It was the eyes that chilled Drax the most, though, as they stared at his opponents. They held no fear; this man was confident.

Suddenly, the noise in the building reduced and Maxi Zoninus appeared above them in the gallery – just as he had done eleven days ago. "Slaves," he began, his lisp once again forming the word 'thlaves'. "As well as proving your resilience and your loyalty to the Theran Empire in Rysia, most of you," he said, flicking a glance of distaste towards the Pit 5 space, "have conducted yourselves with honour over the last eleven days. Once again, Thera salutes you for your commitment and application."

Zoninus paused, and as he had before, he began rotating one of his many gold rings around one finger with other fingers of the same hand. "As you now know, our new emperor, Calidius Antoninus Dominius, is glorifying his fledgling rule, with the longest and fiercest gladiatorial games in the history of the Theran Empire. You are already part of this."

Drax watched Zoninus pause and moisten his dry lips with his sibilant tongue. "The winners of today's bouts, here in Neviec, will be crowned Champions of Neviec. We hope to crown four from each batch of sixteen." He paused, wetting his lips again. "As I am sure you have already gathered, this means that twelve of you will not make it today. But you will die with honour. For those who win, you will continue to be treated well, and train with our fightmasters. For you Champions, there will be one more fight before you go on to a stiffer challenge in another Liatian city, where you will face their champions – a wholly more challenging prospect. Fear not of the final fight in Neviec, though," he added with a ghost of a smile on his lips. "Very few of you Champions – if any – will fall during *that* fight. But we will be expecting you to mete out death on a large and brutal scale, as we assess your credentials as true Champions."

Drax and his fellows in the pit frowned at that, struggling to work out what task might lie ahead – should they survive today.

"But we are getting ahead of ourselves. For today, the rules are simple," he said, as pairs of armed soldiers entered through the four doors of the pits below, each carrying two of what looked like short twelve-inch and wickedly-sharp swords, with two small round iron shields apiece. Drax looked across at Maurulen who was already looking at his former general in silent triumph. *Our weapons of choice.*

Each of the sixteen combatants was presented with a sword and shield. "Drax immediately strapped his shield to his left arm and grasped his sword firmly with his right hand. Garataelix was already his mirror image. The weight of both sword and shield felt good. But Drax was under no illusions. This would be nothing like a one-on-one bout. One of them may not be able to go for the kill as it might leave his partner wide open to attack from his opponent. Drax immediately saw the sensible way to start. "We defend for five minutes," he whispered."

Garataelix managed to nod back before Maxi Zoninus was talking again. "The rules are simple," he repeated, once everyone had their weaponry in place. Silence fell over the fighting pit. "First, you will fight only against the other pairing in your pit space, and this fight will be to the death." Drax's eyes flicked to their opponents; he had already noted they were both right-handed. "If you exit your pit space at any time," Zoninus was saying, "our crossbowmen up here will pepper you with arrows. So, please be mindful of your space. You will see that a grid is clearly marked upon the floor.

"When you have won your pit-space bout, no matter what is happening in the other pit-spaces, you will remain in your own space until the horn is sounded. And that horn will sound like this."

Drax watched as a soldier raised a curved ivory horn to his lips, and blew a deep blast lasting for around three seconds.

So that's what it had meant.

"When that horn sounds, all rules will end. Whichever pairs are still standing, you may attack whomsoever you wish. The contest will be ended by a second blast on the horn, when we have either two surviving pairs or four men still standing. Do you understand?"

All sixteen men nodded.

"Very well," said Zoninus. "You all have your swords. You all have your shields. Now, please fight."

Draxaelen and Garataelix immediately went into a dual crouch. Their opponents did the same – as did the other twelve men in the extended fighting pit. At the same time, an explosion of sound descended from above from the expectant crowd, but Drax had already blocked that out and was facing Hooked Nose with intense concentration; Garataelix was facing Fair Skin, similarly.

Inevitably, each fight began in a cagey fashion, with pairings circling each other. Out of the corner of his eye, Drax saw The Beasts suddenly pounce and strike first blood, instantly followed by an agonised human wail and cheering from above. The right-handed Hooked Nose immediately used the distraction to strike straight ahead at Drax's torso, but Drax whipped his shield across and blocked the blow, deflecting Hooked Nose's sword to his right. His evasive action also pulled Garataelix to the right, leaving him temporarily vulnerable – but Fair Skin hadn't grasped that yet. The lesson had been immediately banked by both Drax and Garataelix, though, along with a need for total focus. That said, it was clear that the competition in Pit 7 was already over.

Still circling, it was surprisingly the fair-skinned, brown-haired opponent who struck next. He was also right-handed, and so whereas Hooked Nose was coming in at centre to Drax, Fair Skin tried a slash to the left side of Garataelix's neck – which Garataelix blocked with his sword held in his left hand. Drax could tell the lad's arm was badly jarred by the action, although he tried his best not to show it. And in mirror image to the first strike, this time, Drax had been pulled to his left following his partner's blocking action. Hooked Nose had noticed, too. He smiled an evil smile.

"Try again," he ordered his partner – who duly obliged.

This time, Draxaelen was ready for the pull, and he also knew that Hooked Nose was going to strike – which he did with an overhead slash –

perfectly blocked by Drax's raised shield.

The circling continued, with Hooked Nose and Fair Skin taking it in turn to lunge, slash and chop. Every action was counteracted by Draxaelen's shield and Garataelix' sword, and every action helped build up a picture of the mechanics of two right-handers against a rightie and a leftie.

"Come on, slave," goaded Hooked Nose to Drax. "Show me what you're made of."

But Draxaelen ignored him, all the time circling, all the time watching Hooked Nose's eyes.

"You think you make us tired by forcing us to do all the work, huh? Well let me tell you -." He lunged for Draxaelen in mid-sentence – but Drax had read his eyes and was ready for him. At the same time as the lunge, Fair Skin belatedly tried a slash. It was easily blocked by Garataelix. Gravus' training was proving invaluable.

As they continued to circle, noises of discontent came from above, as the punters had started to focus on their bout. Meanwhile, although he was watching Hooked Nose all the time, Drax could sense that there were casualties in Pit 5, now – possibly one on each side, meaning the experience of the two gluttons had at least counted for something. Elsewhere, the battle in Pit 8 was still in full flow.

Another five minutes on, and Drax felt comfortable. Neither of their opponents looked capable of getting through their defences. Being a rightie and leftie, the bulk of their defence – their shields – were locked together in the centre – meaning Hooked Nose and Fair Skin couldn't penetrate through the middle, and certainly wouldn't be finding his heart; Garataelix did have that exposure, but his sword defence was too good for Fair Skin. It wasn't all plain sailing in this configuration, though. It might actually have been easier if they'd switched sides – Drax on the left and Garataelix on the right. That way, they wouldn't have constantly rubbed and clashed shields and could strike swords at the core of their opponents. But they had soon adjusted; soon understood where best to place the shield, how to balance from one foot to the other.

After ten minutes of cat and mouse, and the crowd now booing raucously, Drax could see worry building in Hooked Nose's face. He was no longer goading. Fair Skin, meanwhile, had grown in confidence with the lack of counter-attack, and Drax felt his concentration was wavering.

It was another two minutes later when Garataelix killed Fair Skin. It was almost as if Drax and Garataelix could read each other's minds. Hooked Nose came in with a particularly savage slash at Drax, but instead of moving his balance to his right to block with his shield, Drax moved to his left, dropping his shield perilously close to his body – but it successfully took the brunt again. Meanwhile, Garataelix had also moved to the left – not the right as Fair Skin had been expecting. As quick as lightning, Garataelix's left-handed sword was underneath Fair Skin's raised right-handed sword, and two-thirds were buried in the youth's side. Garataelix quickly withdrew the sword. Fair Skin looked stupefied and made no sound as he fell to his knees.

The response from Hooked Nose was immediate and savage. He knew this was his only chance – to strike instantly and even the odds. Draxaelen blocked him three times with his shield – low left to block a lunge, high to block an overhead slash to the head and high again to block a wild slash to the neck. When Hooked Nose went for a fourth lunge, Drax was ready. His shield slammed down on his opponent's sword, wrenching it from his hand where it hit the sand, point-first and bounced back up again. With Hooked Nose staggering forwards with the momentum, Drax's sword went straight up into his opponent's gut, under his shield. Hooked Nose staggered once, and dropped his shield arm, his eyes briefly alighting on Drax's. He knew he was dead – and Drax acted mercifully, finishing it quickly – straight through the heart. He then pulled out his sword, the sucking sound totally obliterated by the bedlam of noise from above.

Both Drax and Garataelix then withdrew into the corner of their pit and surveyed the other pits. As Drax had expected, The Beasts were standing over the bodies of the two Dimunians and were presently hurling insults at Drax and Garataelix. Drax knew enough Acahean to know that they didn't approve of their fighting prowess. Missing Ear was shouting something about fornication with a senior family member, and Wonky Eyes was quite convinced of their illegitimacy. Meanwhile, the contest in Pit 5 was difficult to watch. Each survivor had a dead man chained to them, being dragged along the floor like a butchered carcass. Both bodies were dead-weights, but because survivor and carcass pairings were evenly matched, the exhausting battle became protracted, with instinct for survival driving them beyond their energy resources. Had the young lad had a glutton chained to him, he would have been dead. But that was the other glutton's millstone, and because he was out of condition, he was tiring fast. Drax's money was now on the wispy-bearded youngster – as was the real money up above, judging by those baying for him to 'cut open fatso's belly'.

As for Pit 8, all four men were injured – including Maurulen. Drax didn't know how he wanted that bout to turn out. If Maurulen was slayed, it at least meant he didn't have to do it himself. But if Maurulen and his partner won, they might just have an ally in the next round.

In the end, it was the latter theory that would be put to the test. The 6ft 2in Maurulen dealt both of the killer blows to their opponents, and he was clearly in a much healthier state than his surviving partner, who was spraying the sand red from two nasty gashes. Almost simultaneously, the young lad in Pit 5 finished off the glutton with an angled thrust and then sideways slice to his sagging belly. Drax turned away as steaming intestines spilled out onto the fighting pit floor.

The noise above hit an all-time high – but then soon began to drop down as anticipation took over. The question now was: would the horn-blower allow the final victors time to get their breath back? Surprisingly, he did, while above, more money was feverishly changing hands – but Drax didn't look up once. His eyes were fixed on The Beasts and their eyes were fixed on his. They were ready and straining at the leash. They didn't look like candidates for slow circling and sizing up the opposition.

However, when the horn blew, The Beasts charged to their right and inflicted a savage assault on Maurulen and his partner, Wonky Eyes on the right and Missing Ear on the left. Already injured, Maurulen's partner was dead within seconds, blood spurting from several more gashes including a severed carotid artery. Maurulen was holding on desperately, and had already been cut two or three times himself, when Drax and Garataelix sprang to his defence. "Get behind us man," said Drax. Already, their four swords were clashing, but The Beasts were finding their latest two opponents a harder nut to crack, and Drax and Garataelix weren't just defending this time, either. A roar of anticipation went up from the crowd, probably expecting Maurulen to bury his sword into the unprotected backs of Drax and Garataelix. But he didn't. And injured or not, honour didn't allow him to cower behind other soldiers, either. Instead, he re-joined the fray on Garataelix's left.

Outnumbered, The Beasts were now panicking for the first time in the entire contest, and went for the berserker approach. The first killing blow, when it came, arrived from a most unexpected source, though. The right-handed young lad from Pit 5, who they had all temporarily forgotten about, and who had dragged his dead partner with him across to Pit 8, buried his sword under the right arm of Wonky Eyes, coming round at him from his right. Then, as Missing Ear was desperately parrying Garataelix with both sword and shield, Drax did the most dishonourable thing in his entire life: he buried his sword into the left side of Missing Ear and up through his heart. When he withdrew it, the crowd went crazy, Missing Ear toppled to join Wonky Eyes on the floor, and the horn blew for the second and final time.

CHAPTER 116   DAVY

40th Tertiar, 1789   Day 131, 18:00

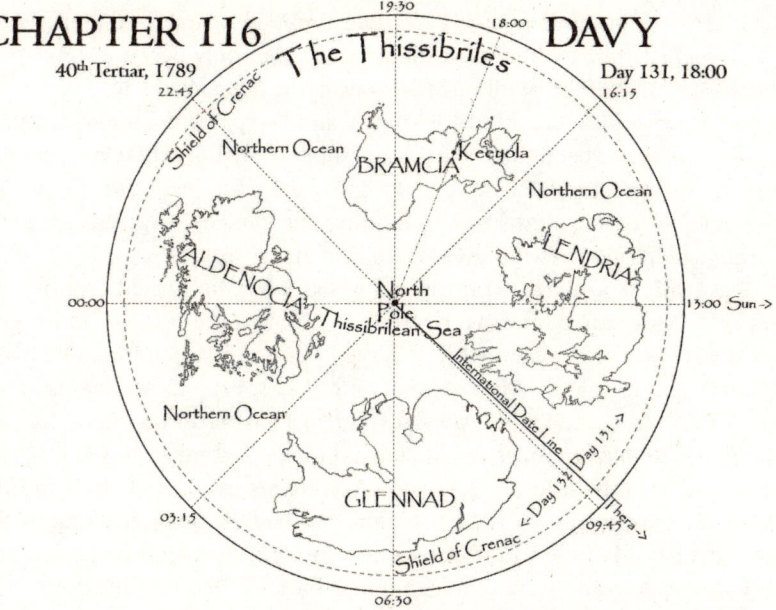

It was the unfamiliarity that Davy hated the most. It wasn't just the mining that was the problem, though. It was the whole atmosphere of the place. Back in Cabrenar, miners had been a friendly fraternity, always watching each other's backs; a real team. Newcomers were properly looked after, placed with an experienced miner and mentored; made to feel welcome. Here, it seemed to Davy that most of the blokes were cold and mercenary and selfish. And those that weren't had to act like they were.

His problems had started on his first day at work. There was a group mentality that wanted to prove that slate miners were better than coal miners. So, every little thing he didn't know or struggled to immediately master, was seized upon and ridiculed or exaggerated – except when his inexperience led to damaged slate; then, the mood became more hostile. It was an experience Davy had never felt before in his life. He had always been comfortable and confident back in Cabrenar as both boy and man. Here, he'd tried to brazen it out, join in and be jocular, but the response was always cold. He was deliberately being made to feel like an outsider, and this had gradually worn away his confidence over the last five days.

Matters had come to a head yesterday. The ringleader of the baiters was a sour-faced thirty-something called Ceri Wickham, who already had jowls, probably thanks to his perpetual scowl. They had been clocking off shift, and half an hour earlier, Davy had dropped a large wedge of slate which had shattered when it hit the ground – but only because someone had nudged him at the point one foot was off the floor. Wickham had been in his face ever since about lost earnings, and Davy was itching to thump the man. They had been stood outside the supervisor's hut, when Wickham's sniping had gone too far. "There's no wonder they lost forty-nine miners if they had twats like Butterfingers holding the candles." Agreement and jeering had immediately followed from Wickham's cronies.

Davy might just have controlled himself when he turned around to confront Wickham, but it was the bloke's smirk that did it. Also, an image of Robbie's face as he had died had flashed into his mind and then he had recalled Robbie's hand as it had gone limp. The smirk on Wickham's face had gone an instant later, as Davy had landed a haymaker on the bridge of his nose. The bloke went straight down, blood spurting from his busted hooter, but within seconds, several of Wickham's mates had piled in on Davy. He did his best to fight them off, but he'd already been thumped around the head three or four times when the supervisor and several senior miners waded in and started dragging men back by their overalls.

Wickham was back on his feet by this stage, holding his ruined nose and whining that Davy had been the aggressor.

"I saw and heard what happened, Wickham," said the supervisor, a thin rake of a man of around fifty, called Matthews. Davy had already noticed he had quick eyes and saw much – for which he was extremely grateful. "It aint no excuse for fighting mind."

"Yeah, but he threw the first punch, Mr Matthews. He's got to go for that, surely?"

"I'll leave that up to Mr Masters to decide. The two of you can come with me, now. Sykes, Roberts. You can come too as witnesses."

And that was that. After only five days in the job, he was being hauled before the slate mine manager with his chances of keeping his job hanging by a thread. Daisy would never forgive him if he was sacked over this. He hadn't even been paid, yet, either. How would they get back home to Cabrenar without money? It all made Davy want to belt the whingeing Wickham once more. And whinge he did: all the way to the log cabin that served as the manager's office, around thirty feet below the main entrance to Keeyola Slate Mine.

"Hello," said Masters, rising from his seat. Another tall and thin man, Masters was also around fifty and had thinning grey hair slicked back. His three-piece finery also left no one in any doubt as to who the manager was around here. "What's this then?"

"Fighting after coming off shift, Mr Masters."

"Fighting, eh?" said Masters, walking around the front of his desk and standing in front of Davy and Wickham. "What have you got to say for yourselves then? You first, Wickham."

"He's a slacker, sir. He don't pull his weight. And he deliberately dropped an expensive slab of slate just before we came off shift."

Masters turned his attention to Davy. "Did you?"

"Why would I do that?"

"Don't be insolent, man. I asked you if you dropped the slab deliberately."

"Of course I didn't. I'm gutted I dropped it. It's not like me at all. But I am still learning, sir." *Someone nudged me, for sure.* But that just wouldn't sit right with Matthews and Masters.

"And what do you have to say to being called a slacker?"

"I'll prove to you that I'm a hard worker, sir."

"Well, your references from Cabrenar were glowing. Work rate, commitment, mentoring. And I hear you earned the King's Medal for bravery in the rescue?"

"Aye, sir."

"What do you have to say to that, Wickham? Does that sound like a slacker to you, man?"

"He still punched me, sir. Sheerin was the aggressor."

"Why did you punch him, Sheerin?"

"Ask him what he said," suggested Davy.

Masters turned to regard Wickham, one eyebrow raised.

"I didn't say nothing, sir. He just attacked me for no reason."

"Tell the truth, Wickham," said Matthews, shaking his head. "I heard what you said. Do you want me to tell Mr Masters myself?"

Wickham looked at the ground, scuffing his feet. "I called him a butterfingers, sir."

"And the rest," said Matthews.

Wickham remained silent.

"I do hope your comments weren't anything inflammatory about the Cabrenar Colliery Disaster, Wickham."

Davy was expecting either Wickham to own up or Matthews to expand on what had been admitted so far. Neither happened – although Davy spotted a knowing look pass between Matthews and Masters. Given Matthews wasn't expanding, Davy felt it would be bad form to expand on his behalf so he remained silent.

"Very well," said Masters, eventually. "Mr Sheerin," he said, addressing Davy, whilst fixing him with a hard stare. "It's not the greatest of starts, is it? Fighting on your – what is it? Only your fourth day?"

"Fifth day, sir."

"Whatever," said Masters, dismissively. "On account of your recommendations, your newness, and your award for bravery, I am only going to give you an official warning. Fighting on Keeyola's premises normally results in dismissal. This will be your one and only warning. If you're back in here inside the next five years, you will be shown the door and you and your wife will be thrown out of your cottage immediately. Do you understand me?"

"Yes sir, thank you for your leniency, sir."

"But you can't -," began Wickham. "He hit me, sir. He's broke my nose."

Masters moved to his left to stand right in front of Wickham. Now it was Wickham's turn to receive the penetrating stare. Masters' voice was icy-calm. "Then I suggest you choose your words more carefully the next time you talk to him. That is all." Masters then turned his back on them and seated himself behind his desk. They were quite clearly dismissed, but just before they trooped out of the office, Masters had a parting shot.

"Oh, and Wickham?"

"Yes, sir," he replied, turning around.

"The same applies to you," he said, now looking up. "If I see *you* back in here in the next five years, you will also suffer the same consequences."

Inside, Davy was still fuming with what Wickham had originally said, and because the man hadn't had the decency to own up to it in front of Masters. That said, he realised it could have ended up a lot worse. Later, when he had calmed down a little more, he realised that Masters had handled the whole matter superbly. In fact, if he'd felt like being remotely humorous, one could say that he'd handled it in a masterly fashion. But humour was far from Davy's mood. As for Masters, at a stroke, he had ensured that no further action needed to be taken this time, but had also ensured that neither man could afford another transgression. For a very long time. That really ought to be it; all over; nipped in the bud. But Davy wasn't as green as that. It was only Wickham who had to tread carefully. The same didn't apply to his cronies.

Sure enough, he'd been barracked throughout today's shift by two of Wickham's toadies, Roach and Smyth – despite not having put a foot wrong, and mining as much slate as those experienced men around him. Naturally, he hadn't reacted at all to the jibes of Roach and Smyth.

When the hooter sounded for end of shift, Davy was surprised when a rather short and ferret-faced miner patted him on the back. "You've done a good shift there, Davy lad," he said. "Well done."

"Thanks," replied Davy, unsure how to take the compliment. It appeared to have been well-meant. As they trooped out to clock off, the man winked at Davy and held out his hand. "Rhys Connor," he said.

Davy nodded at him and shook his hand. "Davy Sheerin. Ex-coal miner, current slate miner."

"Aye, that you are, lad," replied Connor. Like all of the other miners, it was hard to make out Connor's features in the dark and through all the facial grime. But he was well-built, despite his lack of inches, and probably only two or three years older than himself. As they began to emerge out of the entrance to the mine, he saw Connor have a quick look around him. "You've made a nasty enemy there, Davy."

"You think I don't know that," said Davy, with a smirk.

"It was a bloody marvellous hit, though. Where d'you learn to punch like that?"

"Cabrenar Boxing Club. Happy days," said Davy, wistfully.

"Things'll turn around here, mate. I heard Roach and Smyth chipping away at you. Couple of twats, them. Just like Wickham. But they'll get fed up, eventually. They're hoping you're going to snap again. I assume you're on a last warning?"

"Oh aye," confirmed Davy, a half-smile on his face. "But so is Wickham."

After they'd clocked out and were making their way down to the timber-built Keeyola village, Rhys Connor walked with Davy. Davy was wary in case this was some kind of a ploy, but the man seemed pretty genuine. And he must have been chancing it slightly, conferring with the enemy, so Davy appreciated that. And he was quite happy listening to Connor regaling him with a bit of slate mining history.

"The early workings here were just surface pits, you know. But as the miners exhausted the upper levels and kept heading downwards, they soon ended up working underground. They constructed the chambers we worked in today via a roofing shaft, over one hundred years ago, and then followed the slate vein downwards. They then created the horizontal levels to enable us to get at the veins."

Eventually, they came to Connor's road. "This is me," he said. "I'll see you tomorrow, Davy."

"Yeah, listen. Thanks…Rhys. I appreciate this."

"Get away man! We're not all arseholes up here, you know!"

"I'm very relieved to hear it," said Davy with a smile.

As they went their separate ways, Davy felt his spirits rising a little. He'd not made any mistakes, he'd been more productive, and he seemed to have made a friend. And at least Daisy wasn't going to go mad tonight when he got home. There were no fresh bruises on his face for starters!

CHAPTER 117 — MADELEINA

41st Tertiar, 1789 — Day 132, 14:00

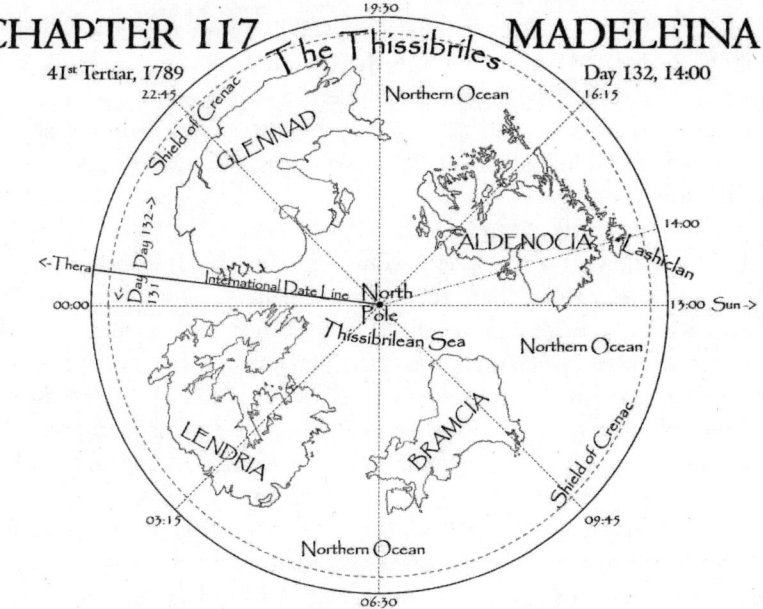

Madeleina could barely contain her excitement. Since getting back on tour following her brief return to Ghinbrude for Prince Marco's funeral, Madeleina and her orchestra had delivered concerts at Yunderoa, Guento and Undress. Each place was located on the wild south-west coast of Aldenocia, but their arrival at each town had brought a warm welcome on docking, and rapturous applause and rousing ovations in the evenings.

Alas, for the last week, the seas hadn't been kind to them, and several of the orchestra had suffered from severe sea-sickness in transit from one venue to the next. Madeleina was one of the lucky ones. Thankfully the rough seas hadn't stopped their brief diversion and an interlude of eight days in the tour, spanning from Day 129 at Undress to Day 137 at Lolapolu. The interlude was to give the orchestra a break and to enable Madeleina to realise a life-long ambition of visiting the famous and myth-shrouded Lashiclan Stones on the island of Wisel. Around half of her orchestra had tagged along on the hop across the Wisel Straits to the island's capital, Wystroona. That had proven to be an even rougher journey, two days ago, and a violinist and a flautist were so ill they'd had to remain in Wystroona, unable to join their intrepid colleagues, along with Jed Wallace and ten of his men, on their two-day hike across the bleak moorlands of Wisel to Lashiclan on the southern side of the island. Madeleina had even enjoyed slumming it in a tent, the previous night, and had been awake and giggling with Charlotte and Aggie until well after midnight. She was certainly glad of their company in the early hours, as the temperature had dropped considerably, and they had all ended up taking it in turns to be the one huddled in the middle. Madeleina wouldn't have changed the experience for the world, though.

Now, it was early afternoon, and Madeleina knew that she would soon be looking down on the oldest stone circle in the Thissibriles; over a thousand years older than the famed Ghenetenos on Glennad and rumoured to be twice as powerful if you listened to Aldenocian druids; apparently, certain gifted members of their community could use the stones to see into the future! Madeleina seriously doubted this claim, but she did wonder if that was where Olivia Mellcrow had got the inspiration for her nasty little Second Sight scheme from. These thoughts were soon pushed aside, though, as her excitement at approaching the stones grew.

As was typical on Wisel, there were very few trees in the vicinity, and all of those were now behind them as they approached the exposed south coast of the island. Everywhere, it was rough green grass and brown moorland, so Madeleina was itching with anticipation to see the blue of the Northern Ocean and the grey of the majestic stones.

"Only another five minutes, Your Royal Highness," said Wallace, his dark-brown spade of a beard blowing in the wind – as it had for much of this tour, reflected Madeleina, wryly. They were walking up the middle of a track that went over a small hillock which was blocking the view ahead, while passing to their right was another white-stone and thatched crofters' cottage with the ubiquitous sheep dotted about on either side.

"I shall be quite the fittest I've ever been, Mr Wallace," she said. "But thanks to you and your boot advice, I shan't be limping back to Wystroona, either."

"Aye, you can't go anywhere on these islands without a proper pair of walking boots, Princess."

"The girls and I have quite got used to them," said Madeleina, each of them lifting their long skirts a foot to demonstrate. "We believe we may try and start a new fashion when we finally return to Ghinbrude."

As ever, Wallace didn't smile at that, but there was humour in his voice. "Aye, I can well imagine that up and down Princess Street."

All three girls laughed delightedly at that.

"Right then, Princess," said Wallace. "Are you ready for this?"

"Ooh, are they coming?" asked Madeleina, her excitement making her voice almost trill.

"Just around this bend…"

Sure enough, slightly off to the left, on a level piece of ground, Maddie saw the tops of some of the larger stones appear. She gave a little shriek of joy, and then more contented noises as with every footstep forward, all of the stones were gradually revealed from top to bottom. Eventually, they reached the top of their hillock, and Madeleina could see them in all of their prehistoric glory, perched on their little ridge, while beyond, the vast expanse of the Northern Ocean had finally appeared, too, its blueness interrupted everywhere by thousands of relatively tame white horses stirred by the constant Northern Ocean winds. It was hard to imagine that there was nothing but three hundred leagues of sea between here, and Northern Epanaga.

Madeleina then noticed that there were already several other people flitting in and out between the stones.

"There are always folk here," said Wallace, spotting them. "This place is a magnet."

"It's probably ancestral," said Madeleina. "An irresistible draw, thanks to race memory."

Wallace just grunted at that.

"What, you don't believe in race memory?"

Another grunt.

They soon arrived at the northern end of the site where Madeleina asked if they could stop and enjoy the sight for a few moments before walking amongst and touching the stones. With Wallace alongside her, she was also joined by Charlotte and Aggie, and two violinists from her orchestra, Iona and Ailsa.

"Well, it's just as the books say," announced Madeleina. "Arranged in a cruciform pattern with the stone circle at the centre. Oh, it's so beautiful. And so *powerful* too."

She flicked a sidelong glance at Jed Wallace. He wasn't buying that either, judging by his impassive face.

"Do you know the history, Mr Wallace?"

"About four thousand years old, aren't they?"

"Five thousand, actually. Doesn't that impress you?"

"Well, yes, I suppose. But they're just stones, aren't they?"

Madeleina was exasperated. "Just stones! Yes, they're just stones. But all aligned with various points on the horizon, giving you sunrise and moonrise at different times of the year. With this stone circle, you could even calculate an eclipse, you know. You could say that it is a forerunner to our modern observatories, but built thousands of years ago."

Wallace did his best to look impressed. "I thought they were used for ritualistic purposes, though."

"They were. This place was also a temple as well as an observatory." Madeleina looked sideways at Wallace and issued a wide smile. Shall we go and walk amongst the ghosts of our ancestors, Mr Wallace?"

"Aye," said Wallace, nodding his head once. "I'd like that."

"Come on girls," said Madeleina. "I'll race you to the centre stone."

And off the girls went, the five of them shrieking with delight and gay youthful abandon. Jed Wallace ensured that his ten agents maintained some decorum, but nodded towards the stone circle, indicating that the other members of the orchestra could go and explore as well.

Madeleina didn't quite make it first to the centre stone, as Iona was tall, lithe and athletic and got there with minimum effort. "It's huge," said Iona, looking up towards the top of the centre stone.

"Well, the books say it's nearly sixteen feet high. I'd say that's about right, wouldn't you?"

"Yes," agreed the strawberry-blonde Iona. "It's round about three times our height, so that makes sense. But how did they get here?"

"Well, that's a mystery," said Madeleina, "as the rock doesn't come from around here."

"So, they actually transported these stones?" asked Charlotte. "Over five thousand years ago?"

"You need to talk to Mr Wallace, Charlotte. He's not so impressed."

"Mr Wallace is very impressed, actually," said a dry voice from behind them, prompting a few giggles from the girls. Wallace was now looking around the stone circle with a new-found respect. "That thing must weigh about six tons," he said, indicating the centre stone.

"Seven tons, actually, Mr Wallace. And as you can see, there are thirteen stones in this circle – plus our seven-ton monolith here in the middle. And then there are five rows of standing stones connecting to this circle," she said, pointing them out, "including these two long rows of stones which run almost parallel to each other towards the north-east. It is thought to be some kind of an avenue."

All eyes turned to look straight up the middle of the suggested avenue. Charlotte was counting them. "Nine on one side, ten on the other."

Madeleina noticed Jed Wallace looking around him. "What's the matter?" she asked.

"Nothing," he said, somewhat distracted. "I'm just wondering where those people went that we saw amongst the stones, earlier."

"Perhaps they've gone down to the shore for a swim," suggested Charlotte.

"Yes, probably," agreed Wallace.

"What's that mound there?" asked the red-haired Ailsa, pointing towards an area of raised ground behind the centre stone, but still within the circle. "It looks manufactured."

"It was," said Madeleina. "It's a burial chamber."

"So, there are bones in there?"

"Yes. And lots of ghosts and ghouls, too," she said, coming at Ailsa with raised talons. Ailsa shrieked and turned to run, with Madeleina chasing her in and out of the stones, both of them laughing and squealing, their skirts billowing out around them and their hair flowing in the wind. Eventually, Madeleina caught Ailsa, but all she did was ruffle up her hair and make monster noises, before both girls fell to the ground in a fit of giggles.

Madeleina then hauled herself to her feet and helped Ailsa up. "Oh dear," she said. "That wasn't very regal, was it, Mr Wallace?"

"I've no idea what you mean, Princess", was Wallace's bland response, although his eyebrows were both raised quizzically.

"Are there really ghosts here?" asked young Aggie, looking more than a little worried.

"There are ghosts everywhere, Aggie," said Madeleina, cryptically.

"What are the legends about this place?" asked Iona. "There has to be legends."

"Of course," responded Madeleina. "The most common legend is that the stones were giants who were petrified for being so ungodly – folk on the island refer to them as 'the false men', although the meaning isn't clear. And then," she said, dropping her voice dramatically, "there's the legend that on midsummer morning, a figure known as the 'Shining One' or Satanri walks the length of the avenue."

A brief silence greeted this revelation, and Madeleina could tell that she had spooked the gathered youngsters around her. Jed Wallace's face remained as impassive as ever, but one or two of his agents were smirking away, enjoying the tale.

"Of course, in later years, particularly on midsummer's day when the Shining One is supposed to appear, this site is sought out by druids from far and wide. During the ceremony, the head druid stands alongside the centre stone from where he recounts his heathen prayers, pleading with Satanri to re-manifest himself and reveal his great secret -."

Madeleina broke off, noticing that Jed Wallace had his hand shading his eyes, even though he was looking to the north-east with the sun behind him. "What is it?" asked Madeleina, her tone immediately serious. Despite her apparent carefreeness, she still hadn't fully recovered from the shock of Wallace uncovering the Abolitionist plot to compromise her – if that was what it was. Hence, whenever Jed Wallace wasn't relaxed, her legs immediately felt unsteady.

Madeleina found herself unnecessarily shielding her eyes, too, to see what Wallace was looking at. In the middle distance there was another crofters' cottage, with smoke blowing out of its single chimney. But Wallace was looking beyond there, where a series of low hills marked the north-eastern horizon – and over those hills there was a path, similar to the one on which they had approached on from the north-west – and on that path was what looked like forty or fifty *marching* men. Madeleina's blood ran cold. "Did you ask for reinforcements?"

"I did not. Men," he said, addressing his ten agents. "Ready your weapons. I don't like the look of this."

The mood in the centre of the stones turned in an instant.

"How long do you think it will take them to reach here, sir?" asked Agent Stokes.

"That's if they're coming here?" said Iona.

"Oh, they're coming here," said Wallace. "We've been damn fools."

"So how long?" asked Madeleina, this time.

"We've got about thirty minutes, I'd say."

"Is there going to be a battle?" asked Ailsa, ashen-faced.

"Not if I can help it," replied Wallace. "They'll surely not shed blood."

Madeleina began to panic. They were so totally exposed here. Wallace was right: they probably had been foolish – and it was her fault again. So determined had she been to realise a childhood dream, she had convinced herself that all the Abolitionists were clustered in the opposite north-eastern end of her country, and that Olivia Mellcrow was now on the run. Also, it was a stretch to assume that she would have been in *this* much danger as an Aldenocian princess hadn't been captured by rebels for centuries; it just didn't happen in the eighteenth century.

Maddie looked back towards the hills to the north-east where the marching men had temporarily disappeared from view as their path followed a dip. Her thoughts were then interrupted by a grating sound behind them. The group turned almost as one, to see an extraordinary sight. An old man, with long flowing grey hair and a white beard was rising from the centre of the burial mound. He had a black cape slung over his shoulders over white robes marked with a black wolfs-head in the centre. He also wore a metal circlet about his head with symbols around it such as the sun and the moon, a goat and another wolf. "Ladies and gentlemen," he announced, with a mellifluous Aldenocian burr. "Please follow me. I have it on good authority that those men are Abolitionists. They will doubtless have one intention."

Madeleina turned to look at Jed Wallace. His face was torn with indecision, looking first at the distant hills to the north-east and then back at what was clearly the head druid of the resident Lashiclan cult. The fact that he had risen up out of the ground was an anomaly to be explained later.

"We can't take on forty men, sir," said Agent Stokes. "And certainly not with a princess and a dozen civilians to protect. I say we take our chances."

"Come quickly," said the head druid, now disappearing back down into what looked like a large black maw in the ground. "There's plenty of room for you all."

Madeleina could see that the altar stone that stood in the middle of the burial chamber had somehow been moved to one side. "Well, I'm not hanging around to get kidnapped," she said, decisively, and she began to walk towards the altar stone.

"Princess, wait!" commanded Wallace. "I'll go first. Stokes, you follow with three more men. Then the Princess and her ladies. Then the rest of you." As Wallace got to the edge of the opening, he shouted down into the depths, "How did you know they were coming? And what is this place?"

"I'll answer all of your questions shortly. Right now, I don't want you to give away our secret – particularly not to Abolitionists."

Wallace turned around to look at Stokes, who nodded once. The five men before her disappeared into the ground, and as Madeleina went to follow, a ladder was revealed leading downwards, along with a flickering light. Wondering if she was about to wake up and find this to be a particularly surreal dream, Madeleina hung one boot over the edge of the opening, and slowly climbed down, Jed Wallace helping her off the last rung and onto a stony floor. As the other four girls followed her down, Madeleina looked around and saw that the tunnel headed both south towards the sea and north towards the crofters' cottage. Each tunnel direction was well-lit by flaming torches held securely in iron wall sconces.

Their party began to fan out as the rest of the agents and orchestra members followed them down. Once they were all down, the head druid climbed back up the ladder accompanied by a brawny young man also dressed in druidic garb, and between the two of them, they manoeuvred a large iron lever set into the wall. As they hauled it towards them, Madeleina heard the grating sound again, and the oblong of daylight began to disappear until, with a loud clunk, the altar stone above them slotted back into its original position.

The head druid climbed down and then stood before Madeleina and bowed. "Princess Madeleina. It is a pleasure to be of assistance. My name is Beric. This is my son, Dareon. And this," he said, indicating the tunnel around them, "is but a small part of the best-kept secret in Aldenocia. If you would all like to follow me, I will take you to our common room where we can provide you with refreshments and," Beric paused, his eyes twinkling with humour, "explain ourselves."

CHAPTER 118   EMILYA
42nd Tertiar, 1789   Day 133, 14:00

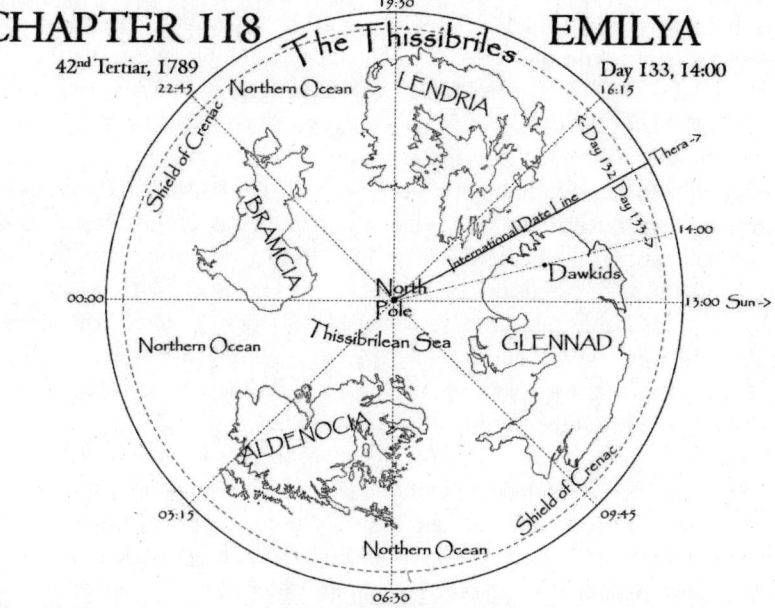

The snow-clad summit of Dawkids was around two hundred feet above them, but the going was getting progressively steeper and tougher as they closed in on its apex. Emilya was in the middle of a chain of heavily-breathing monks and civilians nearing the end of their ascent as they traversed a steep and narrow ridge of snow-dusted scree that only allowed single-file traffic. Conversation had dried up, although most of them didn't have the breath for chatter, anyway.

Emilya looked ahead, but that just made her feel dizzy, so she riveted her gaze back to the ground where scree was skittering down either side of the ridge to both left and right with each trudge forwards; a *long* way down either side. Thankfully, now that it was mid-spring, most of the snow had melted, otherwise only spiked boots would have sufficed.

In front of her, the boots of Clyve and Jared Swan were also sending icy stones skittering hither and thither, adding to the rhythmic noise made by the trudge of many climbing boots on loose rock, her own heavy breathing and the increasingly strong wind. It was an aural combination Emilya would likely never forget.

Clyve and Jared had arrived at Kifsel Place monastery two days ago, before setting out with the group of around forty climbers at 06:00 yesterday morning, led by septuagenarian Abbot Geoffrey. As an ex-officer in the

Bramcian Navy, Clyve had been outraged at the suggestion that Jake had either kidnapped or murdered Princess Alicya. However, he had also imparted the wonderful news that Jake, Harry and his two lackeys were still alive – or at least they had been two weeks ago when they'd turned up out of the blue at the farm with an eight-year-old orphan, and were planning on taking ship to Lendria from the north-east. There had been no further national news since then, other than the search was progressing, while Clyve had assured them there was nothing in the press about any female involvement in the bogus crime. He had even suggested that Emilya and Elyse were probably safe to leave Kifsel Place – news greeted with great relief by Emilya, given her recent experience at the monastery. Emilya regularly recalled those cold, ungodly eyes, and Brother Cyrus' threat in the gardening shed about speaking of their encounter.

You will regret it. But not nearly as much as your companion will.

Emilya didn't doubt the monk for one second – which was why she would be pushing Elyse to leave on their return. She had enjoyed much of her experience at the monastery, but she wouldn't be sorry to see the back of it. Of course, Elyse had sensed something was amiss despite Emilya's best efforts to act normally since the incident. She certainly hadn't bought Emilya's facial bruise being caused by bumping into a low-slung bough in the orchard, and she fancied that Elyse had smelt the witch hazel on her cheek, too. Elyse had shadowed her everywhere from that evening onwards, even swapping her duties in the infirmary for kitchen duties. *She had done what any loving mother would do.* Beautiful both inside and out, despite her baggy brown habit and tied-up hair! Emilya wondered if Brother Obadiah's hands would remain outside his robes once they'd departed. Somehow, she doubted it.

Her thoughts were interrupted by shouts and whoops from ahead, so she steeled herself to look up again. Apart from Clyve and Jared in front of her, it felt as if only sky was around her. Their first epic climb was almost complete.

"Nearly there, Emilya," confirmed Elyse from behind. "Just a few more steps."

Emilya didn't reply as the altitude as well as the exercise was fuelling her breathlessness. As the path neared the summit, Emilya was relieved to notice that the scree was gradually disappearing, replaced by hundreds of jutting snow-dusted rocks, all about half a foot-or-so high, but wedged fairly tightly together. It made the final ascent of three hundred paces-or-so that much easier because of the firmer ground under their boots, even though the incline got a little steeper before levelling out at the summit.

By the time Emilya and Elyse reached the top, it was already home to around twenty people, with a further twenty following on behind. Those above were taking it in turns to touch the cairn at the top, and most were placing scree-like stones around the base of the cairn. "Why are they doing that?" asked Emilya, remembering Jake and Elyse doing it on top of the Bleaklow Plateau for perhaps differing reasons.

"I've got one here," said Clyve, somewhat breathily, holding up a stone in his hand. Emilya noticed that Jared had one as well. "Cairns leave a trail of where human beings have passed. Legend says that when we add to the cairn, not only do we help make it a more significant marker, but we also ensure that our spirit remains long after we've gone."

Emilya felt a shiver run down her spine. Elyse noticed that she was moved and put an arm around her. "I picked one up for you on the way up, darling," she said, handing her a palm-sized stone.

Emilya took it from Elyse gently, thanked her, and then moved in line behind Clyve and Jared, where she placed the stone reverently on the pile. She felt oddly detached as she moved off a little way down the other side of the summit to allow those behind her to place a stone. It was only really then that she began to look around her – and her jaw almost hit the snowy rocks beneath her boots. Again, Elyse saw, smiled and this time slipped her hand into Emilya's. "Something else, eh?"

Emilya began to circle around, three hundred and sixty degrees, keeping hold of Elyse's hand all the way, Elyse turning with her. "I have no words," she whispered.

"Wait till we get to the top of Keplif Scale, Emilya. You can actually see the Lendrian Channel from there, it's so high."

"Is that Keplif Scale?" she asked, pointing to the north, and a conical mountain top that seemed to be even higher than Dawkids.

"It certainly is," said Elyse.

"But, how are we going to get from here to there in one day?"

"With ease," said Jared, joining them with a smile on his face.

"Well, it might be easy for you…" said Emilya, tailing off as she studied the vista to the north. They couldn't have asked for clearer conditions. There wasn't a cloud in the sky which was of such a deep blue it made Emilya want to sing out loud. Mountains rose up all around them, to the north, to the east, to the south and to the west. It was like one vast spiky white tablecloth that had been thrown across north-eastern Glennad, and they were the candelabra in the centre.

Down far below to the west, Emilya could see a path cutting up through the valley, heading back in the direction of the monastery. She could see figures dotted along the path, looking like ants.

"Look down there," she said. "Do you think they can see us?"

"I'm sure they can, if they're looking up," responded Elyse.

Both girls began waving their arms at the procession of people below, and were joined by several of their fellow climbers.

It was at this point that Abbot Geoffrey took over. It was time for The Prayer. For this he asked everyone to sit down cross-legged, clasp their hands together and close their eyes. Emilya did so, and immediately felt more secure with her new lower centre of gravity.

Then, the abbot began to speak, in his warm, kindly voice. "Our Lord Father in heaven, we thank you for the wonder of your world."

Although her eyes were closed, the wonder of that world, seen seconds earlier, was still firmly imprinted upon the back of Emilya's eyelids, somehow augmented by the wind that tugged constantly at the exposed part of her hair beneath her grey woolly hat. She was profoundly aware of where she was.

After delivering that first sentence, Abbot Geoffrey paused for a few seconds, allowing time for all to contemplate his words. Then he spoke again. "We thank you, Lord, for the sun which rises every day, and for the moon and the stars which light our way at night."

Emilya remembered sunsets in Ghantiss and looking in wonder at the brightest of full moons with Edwyn, that wonderful night in Ghenetenos; then counting the stars with her younger sister, Tammy, on her birthday, last year.

"We thank you for the warmth of your sunshine, for the rain which cleanses and sustains life, and for the clear and fresh air that we breathe, every minute of every day."

More serene images were visualised, and with each, there came an increasingly profound peace.

"We thank you for the wondrous creatures that inhabit our island: for the noble horse, the industrious bee and the loyal canine."

Brief images of horses and bees were superseded by an image of little Theo. Not the injured, bedraggled, close-to-death creature that she had scooped up from that courtyard back in Ghantiss, but the vibrant, happy and healthy terrier that Clyve and Jared had talked about. The love and warmth she felt for her little pet, merged with that which she felt for her father, her brother, her sister, for Elyse and for Edwyn. *So much love.* And for true friends, like Jake, Clyve and Jared and for Meg who was showering her little Theo with love some thirty leagues to the south-west of this mountain top; both Theo and young Newt, it would now appear.

"We thank you for your rivers and seas which teem with life and the skies which are blessed with a thousand different kinds of bird."

Emilya thought of Elyse and her diet. If Abbot Geoffrey was right, then weren't the fish and the birds God's creatures, too? What right did they have to eat them? Another layer of warmth and confidence was placed about her, and a sense of knowing that Elyse was leading her in the right direction. Although Emilya suspected that Elyse's God – or rather Goddess – was very different to Abbot Geoffrey's. *Or was she?*

After a few more minutes of beautiful serenity, Abbot Geoffrey ended the prayer. "And finally, Father, we thank you for the goodness in men and women, of the love and compassion that resides in every one of us. And, yet, we would still ask you to re-fill us, right here, right now, with the love and the compassion and the calmness and the peace of your holy spirit. Now and forever more. Amen."

Emilya kept her eyes shut for a few seconds, quite aware that no one was speaking. When she eventually opened her eyes, perched there on top of the world, her eyes met Elyse's, sitting cross-legged opposite her. "Wow!" she mouthed.

People were beginning to murmur now as they came out of their tranquil personal bubbles. "Did you feel it?" whispered Elyse, her eyes shining with love and anticipation.

Emilya nodded her head in wonder. "Yes," she said – although she didn't quite know what 'it' had been – except that over and above the enduring feeling of love, she had had fleeting perceptions of being both receptacle and transmitter. It wasn't something she could explain. But whatever 'it' was, it was still within her, she was quite certain of that.

Elyse reached over and took Emilya's hand, her beautiful eyes glistening. "Welcome to our world, Emilya. She feels you too."

CHAPTER 119   ARRAN

42nd Tertiar, 1789   Day 133, 14:00

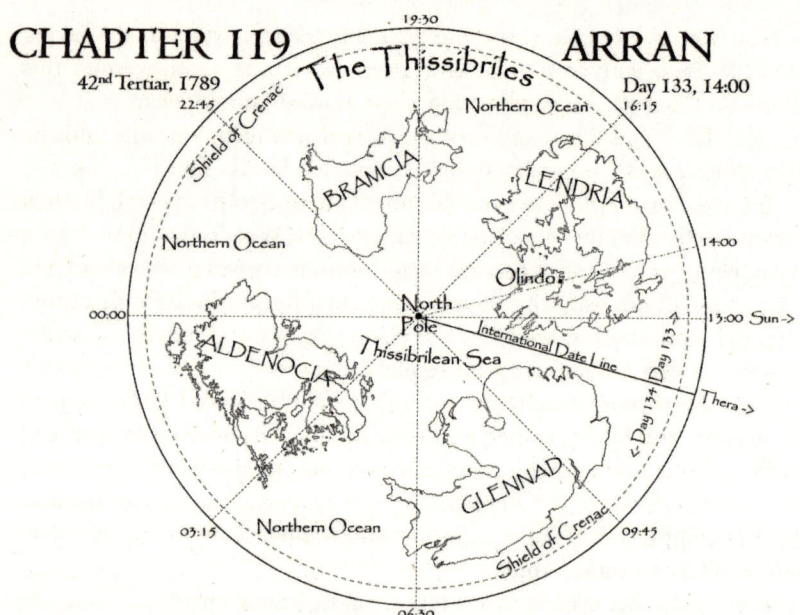

The journey had passed like a dream. The weather had been glorious, and the scenery even better. The Nannosh Inlet had been everything he remembered from his childhood holidays. Lush green trees and vegetation along the shores, interspersed with small villages and ports comprised of mainly wealthy whitewashed houses, and both water and sky a stunning blue. It had been pleasantly warm, too, for the time of year.

Nevertheless, Arran's thoughts had still been dominated by two huge issues. Firstly, an intense sadness that all of this beauty could be destroyed in less than fifty days' time. He had constantly looked at the people around him. Men, women, children. Young, middle-aged, old. Blacksmiths, farriers and endless fishermen. Perhaps, for now, they were the lucky ones in their blissful ignorance.

Secondly, there was Ella. What would she look like eighteen years on? Would her smile still bewitch him? Would the sound of her voice, unheard for so many years, render him speechless? Arran had concocted a thousand sentences with which to greet her. He couldn't remember any of them right now.

The ferry had put into port at Unbild the previous night, but Arran hadn't alighted; he had a cabin on the ferry, and he didn't want to go anywhere that would take him further away from the reunion he had dreamed about almost all of his adult life. Instead, he just willed the minute hand to move on his pocket watch – every movement bringing him closer to that reunion. The fact that it was happening with an extinction level event hanging over the world, somehow didn't lessen the excitement or the anticipation or the nervousness.

Now, as the ferry crossed the last part of the Sound of Ekilek to Olindo, Arran's heart was racing – even more than it had when the boat had first set off at 06:00 that morning, with the air so fresh and the promise so ripe. Most remarkable of all was that the way he felt now was an exact replica of nineteen years ago, that first time he had set out from Gwyala to Olindo. That sense of intense familiarity made it seem impossible that nineteen years could have passed.

The coast to the north-east had first come into view half an hour ago. Of course, as a teenager, he had been approaching from the opposite direction, when he used to sail due west from Gwyala, and then bear north-west into the Sound of Ekilek. But now, as he watched the town and port of Olindo grow larger to the north-east, the sensation of familiarity remained overwhelming.

Then came that constant nag. He was about to meet somebody else's wife. Did he have that right? He and Ella were two people who had loved each other all their adult lives and yet somehow, they had not ended up together. Meeting was probably the worst thing they could do. It certainly was for Mal.

But nothing can stand in the way of true love.

Those words had been spoken by his dear Grandad, around eighteen years ago, after Arran and Ella had broken up. What he was saying was, that if she truly loves you, she will eventually realise that, and true love will reunite you.

Arran smiled, sadly. "You were right, Gramps," he whispered. *But you didn't advise me on the time lag!*

Eventually, Olindo harbour came into view, and Arran could see people dotted along the quayside, watching the ferry come in. All being well, one of them would be Ella. When the ferry turned left inside the harbour wall, Arran moved over to port so he could get a closer look at the crowds. He scanned left and right, and then right and left…and then backed up right a bit. There. In a pink dress, with a parasol. It was his Ella. And she hadn't changed. Her hair was still unfashionably short. And she was wearing a stylish lilac beret that was perched on the back of her head – perhaps a deliberate nod to their first meeting back in 1770.

As ever, she looked perfect.

It also took a few seconds for Arran to realise that he'd actually stopped breathing. He afforded himself a brief smile before exhaling, slowly and calmly – just as Ella spotted him. Her face broke out into a wide smile and she waved, enthusiastically. Arran's heart skipped a beat – before he waved back, realising that he was smiling, too.

The disembarkation took around twenty minutes before Arran was weaving through the throng of people towards the spot on the quayside where Ella had been standing. And then she was there before him. They both stopped walking and looked at each other… and then she ran to him and threw her arms around him.

Arran buried his face in Ella's short blonde hair. The aroma brought about another instant transportation to the same place but a different time. For starters, he had forgotten how tall she was – and so as he held her, the natural blend of their matching height brought about new waves of familiarity. So many special memories of old now played through his mind, some forgotten for so many years.

Eventually, Ella pulled back, but Arran kept his hands on her shoulders. "You look beautiful," was all he could say.

"I am not!" she retorted. "I'm old!"

"You don't look any older, Ella. You haven't aged a bit."

"Are you *blind*?" Look at the crow's feet!"

Love is blind. Another cliché. "You have hardly any. And I like them, anyway."

"You look well, Arran," she said. Her hand touched his cheek. "Age suits you."

"I'm not an invalid yet, Ella."

She laughed at that. "I meant that the mature Arran is very handsome."

"And the teenage Arran wasn't?"

"The teenage Arran was beautiful."

"Beautiful! Not handsome?"

"I've missed you, Arran," said Ella, her face now sad. "So much and for so long. What are we going to do?"

Arran looked at the floor for a second, and briefly closed his eyes before rallying. "I'm going to take you to that tea room on the front over there," he said, pointing towards a harbour-frontage shop painted in pale yellow, with wooden chairs and tables outside.

Ella smiled, sadly. "That's not what I meant, and you know it."

"I am going to take you for tea and cakes, and we're going to tell each other what has happened in our lives over the past eighteen years. Just two old friends, catching up."

"Old friends," repeated Ella with another sad smile.

"The dearest of friends," said Arran. "The very dearest."

"Am I permitted to take your arm, sir?"

Arran held out the crook of his arm. "Why certainly, madam. Shall we?"

Ella smiled her sunniest smile, transporting Arran back in time again. That smile had such warmth. That smile had shown him what it meant to be loved. Truly loved. No one else had ever looked at him or smiled at him like that. Ella's smile hadn't changed in eighteen years. Neither, suspected Arran, had Ella's love. The phrase 'bitter-sweet' did not come close to describing their predicament.

Ella interrupted his thoughts by taking his arm, and they strolled slowly towards the tea room with Ella pointing out landmarks and buildings as they went – anything that had changed in the last eighteen years. Arran tried to listen and take it in but he was in a complete daze.

Eventually, they stopped to gaze around. "It still looks the same to me, Ella," he managed to say. "This place is so special to me."

"And you are so special to me," said Ella.

The words were wonderful; everything he craved. But it was still a knife through his heart. *Why, why, why?* Yet he managed a smile. "As you are to me, Ella."

Ella briefly put her head on Arran's shoulder, and he melted all over again. Any lingering doubts he might have had about his feelings for Ella had already been erased forever – however long forever might be.

CHAPTER 120   CALIDIUS
43rd Tertiar, 1789   Day 134, 13:00

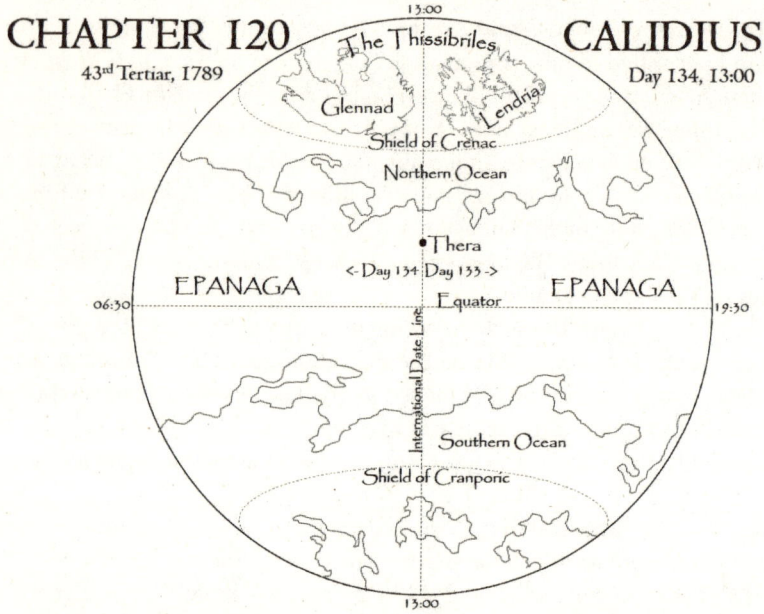

Emperor Calidius Antoninus Dominius took his place on the podium halfway along the northern circuit of the Mesocluso, in between two imperial eagle-topped colonnades which rose to either side of his lavish seat. Immediately, the noise in the arena from fifty thousand spectators grew to a mighty crescendo, while the faces of the white-robed senators ranged along the front of the arena to his left and right displayed various expressions of anticipation and relish.

Calidius smiled, coldly. His idea for a national distraction was already a triumph. Not a single seat spare. All here to see justice meted out. He raised both of his hands, palms facing outwards to signify silence. On their Emperor's command, the audience fell silent.

Calidius paused to collect his words, preparing to launch his latest competition. He then projected his voice as best as he could to take advantage of the Mesocluso's impressive acoustics. "My fellow Therans," he began, his voice echoing around the arena. "As you know…we have launched a national campaign…through which we intend to bring our Empire…to its optimum strength."

Calidius paused, holding out both hands with palms facing upwards.

"In unity, there is strength," chanted around a quarter of the crowd, albeit not in unison.

They will soon get the hang of it.

Calidius took another deep breath. "Three days ago...I issued an edict... an edict declaring an end...to the harbouring of prisoners-of-war. I promised them freedom. But they shall have to *earn* that freedom!"

A ragged swell of cheering and jeering greeted that statement. Again, Calidius had to hold up both hands, palms facing outwards, for silence... which eventually arrived.

"Their choice was simple. To die immediately. Or to fight in these games...with a chance of survival...and the certainty of honour."

More cheers. Calidius raised his hands again after several seconds, a vague and patient smile playing about his normally-cold features. "I am delighted to say...that none of them...chose to die immediately."

This time a big roar of approval greeted his words. Again, he patiently waited for the hubbub to die down before raising his hands again. "If they do die today...they will undoubtedly die...with their honour intact!"

More cheers.

"And so...first of all...they will be pitted against...each other!"

That announcement brought some discontented noises, and even a couple of boos. Calidius allowed a cold smile to spread across his face so that the crowd knew he was only playing with them, that he forgave them for their bad manners...and that there was clearly better fayre to come.

The noise eventually fell to a hush.

"That contest...will take the form...of a melee. And when they have halved their number...to around one hundred...we will then bring on... your local favourites."

That got a much better reaction.

"They will fight Thera's best – The Twenty – twenty men at a time!"

That got a good reaction, too, albeit a little delayed as the ramifications sunk in.

"And for those who survive...they shall have...the greatest honour of all. Because naturally...as this is the capital of the world...they shall also face...the very *best* in the world!"

This time, the crowd noise went up several levels and took some time to fall silent.

"The handful of survivors shall fight...Imnal the Invincible!"

Raucous cheering greeted the naming of one of the world's most famous gladiators, from Imnal, around seventy leagues west of Thera.

"They shall fight...the Dimunian!"

More wild cheering.

"And they shall also fight…the Demon of Dadmir."

Absolute bedlam broke loose within the Mesocluso. This was clearly going to be a blood-fest to end all blood-fests, and the prisoners-of-war were facing almost impossible odds.

When they eventually fell silent again, Calidius knew that it was time to wind up the introductions and get on with the contest.

"So, fellow Therans. *Are you ready?*"

The crowd went crazy. Over the raucous din, Calidius turned towards the gates at the end of the arena to his left-hand side, raised his left arm, and then let it fall to indicate that the gates should be opened at that end. He then turned to his right, raised his right arm and let that fall, too.

Moving cautiously out of the wings at both ends, came a ragged hotchpotch of men, dressed in everything from splendid military uniforms to gladiatorial garb, to heavy armour, to just loin cloths, while some poor fellows were dressed in out-and-out rags. In all, around a hundred men advanced from each side. All formerly prisoners-of-war, they had each been armed the same way, with a simple sword and small circular shield.

The men from both halves advanced, nervously, until they were a few yards short of the centre-line on each side where two officials held up their hands to halt their advances. Most of the prisoners-of-war would be expecting only a handful of their number to survive today. As it turned out, mused Calidius, maliciously, they were being overly optimistic!

A cruel half-smile crossed his face at that thought as he searched for Raul Kezidia and Carlos Belastona. He soon spotted them – together, as ever, yet profoundly chalk and cheese. Both heralded from Obbila in northern Pinashia, and had been captured three years ago when their province of Ebquas had declared its independence, not just from Pinashia, but also from the Theran Empire. It had been a ludicrous move for such a tiny province, although they had managed to expel all ruling Theran and Pinashian officials from their capital at Obbila and even ran their own Parliament for a month – until the Theran war machine had descended upon them and crushed their little rebellion. Both Kezidia and Belastona had been prisoners-of-war at Thera, ever since.

Of the two, Belastona had been president of the briefly free Ebquas province, and Kezidia had been his bodyguard. Belastona was now in his late fifties, stooped, thinning grey hair and of average build and size, looking totally lost holding a sword and shield – which looked all-the-more bizarre as he was still clad in his Ebquas garb of white shirt, white breeches and a black waistcoat along with a scarlet beret and scarlet sash around his middle. Kezidia, meanwhile, was the total opposite: long, flowing dark hair and a man mountain, six foot five inches tall, arms as thick as some men's thighs and both sword and shield looking like toys in his massive paws. Kezidia had already distinguished himself in the Mesocluso, where he had willingly offered himself as a gladiator in the hope of eventually earning himself a pardon. He had soon earned the nickname amongst the Theran public of the Pinashian, and despite his prisoner-of-war status, he had become a fan favourite. Naturally, he was clad as a gladiator, with bared arms apart from two manicae, and his shoulders protected by a thick leather jerkin which was matched by a gladiatorial leather skirt and sandals.

Looking to his left, Calidius now sought out two other prisoners-of-war from closer to home. Amongst the plethora of olive-skinned Eastern Alliance POWs, the copper-skinned Rysians and the dark-skinned Dimunians and Craafians – many of whom looked more than capable of handling themselves against trained gladiators – Calidius spotted the light brown-skinned northern Liatians, Paulo Neiroa and Fabio Nabaio. They had been confined to Thera ever since their failed plot to reintroduce the independent republic of Morsannia, five years ago. According to Theran law, they should have been executed for treason, but Calidius – ruling in the absence of his hedonistic father – had refused to make martyrs of them, and had treated them as prisoners-of-war. *Expurgatio* offered a potential honourable pardon for them. Calidius' lips twitched in anticipation.

Both former captains in the Theran army and both in their late thirties, Calidius noted that Neiroa and Nabaio had also dressed sensibly as gladiators. Elsewhere, Calidius saw more men he wanted to be rid of.

Turning to the horn-master, he nodded once – after which the horn-master gave a three-second blast to signify the start of the contest, prompting the two officials in the centre of the arena to quickly withdraw to the sides.

Initially, nothing happened, apart from a lot of eyeballing and fidgeting and so the crowd soon became hostile, baying at the two sides to get stuck into each other. The first move came from *within* the ranks on the right. A man dressed in the tunic of an Adcian soldier stepped up behind Carlos Belastona and buried his sword in his back. Calidius smirked as half of the sword emerged from the former Ebquas president's chest. He had promised the Adcian a pardon if he did the deed. The fool clearly hadn't done his homework on whom his victim was or how efficient his bodyguard was. He received his 'pardon' a second after he withdrew his sword – at which point, he was already missing a head.

That not only brought the crowd to their feet in an explosion of noise, but at a stroke, it negated the concept of one half against the other, and prisoners-of-war began slaying those stood nearest to them.

On both sides.

It soon became every man for himself as the arena descended into carnage.

After ten minutes of slaughter, Calidius noted that the sand in the centre of the arena was actually redder than it was yellow. He also noted that not only was Raul Kezidia still standing – and without a scratch on him – but so were the two Liatians, Paulo Neiroa and Fabio Nabaio. The contest had now moved into a cagier stage, though. The weak were all dead – perhaps around eighty of them – and the competition was down to the true fighters. Calidius watched, as alliances were formed to turn two onto one or three onto two, but all the time, Raul Kezidia – the Pinashian – trusted only himself.

When the numbers had finally reduced to around one hundred, Calidius called an end to the bout and the horn was sounded again. The survivors were then shepherded away to the left by guards armed with pistols or crossbows; any wrong move by a surviving prisoner-of-war, and they would die instantly. Calidius then sent another detachment of legionaries into the arena to finish the grievously or mortally injured, each by a single sword-thrust to the heart. *Let it not be said that Calidius Antoninus Dominicus was not a merciful man.*

Their grisly task complete, the arena was flooded by dozens of stretcher-bearing servants in black robes, who began systematically clearing the battleground of corpses and filling the mortuaries at each end of the arena. Other servants followed, pouring sand onto the copious amounts of spilled blood and raking the surface level again, while throughout this activity, the noise amongst the crowd remained electric; the melee had been a spectacular sight and the crowd's bloodlust had been ramped up by several degrees.

With the arena cleared, Calidius stood again. A gradual hush fell over the arena. The Emperor surveyed his people, a light smile playing about his lips. He then took a deep breath. "Was that good?" he shouted.

A thousand "Ayes" greeted his question, many waving their hands or hats or punching the air.

Calidius waited for the hubbub to die down. "Very well," he said. "Your entertainment is now about to become…more professional. Without further ado…please welcome to the arena…your very own Theran champions. Bring out The Twenty of 1789."

A group of ten trumpeters belted out an introductory salvo, at which point, twenty magnificently-clad gladiators, armed with sword and slightly larger shields than their predecessors, swaggered into the arena from the right-hand side, fanning out to each side of the entrance. They then began to walk around the perimeter of the arena, milking the crowd and immersing themselves in their adoration.

After five minutes of theatre, Calidius stood again, and the noise levels fell away. At the same time, The Twenty strolled towards the centre of the arena, where they formed a perfect circle, each of them facing out towards the crowd. "It is now time for our surviving one hundred prisoners-of-war, to pit themselves against The Twenty!"

A great cheer went around the arena again.

"They will fight them...twenty at a time. Any prisoner-of-war still standing...at the end of this bout...will have earned their place in The Twenty themselves. Particularly if there are any vacancies!"

Another cheer went up at those words. The crowd were now in little doubt as to how high the stakes were for every single combatant, although the cleverer amongst the watchers had already worked out the brutal logistics for the challengers.

"So, without further ado...bring out the first twenty challengers."

Those twenty challengers emerged from the left-hand side of the arena, each walking cautiously, but each with a look of determination about them, too. The odds were very long, for sure – but not impossible. At the same time, The Twenty arrayed themselves in two rows of ten, staggered such that those in the back row stood in the gap between those in the front row.

The twenty challengers stopped forty feet from their foes. Calidius had the vaguest of smirks on his face. As planned, he was looking at the weakest twenty challengers. He then nodded at the horn-master, who let rip with another three-second blast. The Twenty immediately took the initiative, and five challengers were dead within seconds. Within two minutes, all twenty prisoners-of-war were dead, and each of The Twenty were still standing, with only a couple receiving minor injuries. The dead were rapidly cleared away, the blood left where it had been spilled, before the next twenty were led out. They fared about as well as the previous batch, although one of The Twenty had been forced to retire due to a nasty gash in his right side, and so The Twenty had now become The Nineteen. The third batch were then led in – and Calidius was furious to see the Pinashian in this group; Kezidia should have been held back to the *last* twenty. Calidius briefly considered intervening, but that would ruin the flow of the competition, and the crowd was already beyond excited to see how the Pinashian would fare against the best fighters in Thera.

What happened next went against the plan...but Calidius had to admit it was a fine spectacle, and so he allowed the bout to run its course. It certainly didn't surprise him that the Pinashian had helped reduce The Twenty to sixteen, but those surviving professionals had gradually cut down the prisoners-of-war to a desperate group of seven: it was now more than two onto one. At this point, Calidius called an end to the bout: he couldn't afford to lose the Pinashian, yet, so he instructed the officials to take the seven survivors back to the preparation rooms and ready them for a later return – despite a few brave boos from the crowd. The next twenty prisoners-of-war were then led out and managed to reduce The Twenty to fourteen before their own losses tipped the scales in the professionals' favour and all challengers were slain. Again, being reduced to fourteen at this stage, wasn't going to plan, but Calidius had no choice but to go with fate and take solace in the fact that the crowd were in bloodlust ecstasy.

This left the final twenty prisoners-of-war, which included Neiroa and Nabaio, plus the seven who had survived the third bout, including the Pinashian. It was at this stage that Calidius slightly adjusted his plans; twenty-seven versus fourteen battle-weary gladiators could not be allowed. First, though, he gave the order to clear the arena in readiness for the final bout – and out came the black-robed servants again to remove the dead and to throw sand over the many new pools of blood.

Once the fighting area was ready, Calidius stood again. A hush of expectancy fell over the arena. "Bring forth the surviving challengers," shouted Calidius. To the left, the twenty-seven prisoners-of-war emerged, presumably fancying their chances against just fourteen professionals and with the presence in their own ranks of the Pinashian – although Calidius noted that six or seven had inhibiting injuries. Perhaps that was why their advance was tentative, despite the fanfare played for them by the dozen trumpeters. Calidius then turned to his right. "Bring forth The Twenty."

This time, the crowd went wild, as their fourteen surviving heroes emerged – albeit with not quite as much swagger as they had entered the arena an hour before. They stopped their advance around forty feet from the much larger number of challengers, with two brave officials in the middle dividing the two sides. This time, The Twenty stood side-by-side in one row of fourteen. The grand finale was about to begin – but the silent crowd were sensing a twist to proceedings. Calidius did not let them down. He took a deep breath. "Clearly, we have weighted odds," began Calidius, again projecting his voice expertly. "To even things up," Calidius paused, milking the moment, "please welcome into the arena...on the side of The

Twenty." Calidius paused again, before his face twisted with vicious anticipation. "Imnal the Invincible!"

And in from the right, strolled a man clad only in a loin-cloth – but which ensured that every magnificent muscle on his insanely abnormal six-foot five-inch frame was on view. Although the same height as the Pinashian, his bulk was even greater. He didn't have a sword or a shield, though – merely a net and a long, wickedly pointed, three-pronged trident. As ever, Calidius considered him a monstrous sight – a freak – but the crowd went berserk, recognising one of the greatest gladiators of all time. Imnal went and stood in front of the surviving fourteen of The Twenty, dead-centre.

It took the crowd another two minutes to quieten down before Calidius' next announcement. "I now give you," he bayed. "The Dimunian!"

This time, the gladiator swaggering into the arena was of the darkest skin-tone on Thera. He was also supremely muscled, although much sleeker than Imnal. Again, he was clad only in a loin-cloth...but most freakily of all, he stood at a towering six feet ten inches tall. The Dimunian, however, carried two swords and, as he approached his team, he began twirling both swords around his body in a phenomenal demonstration of dexterity. The crowd's reaction went up yet another notch. Like Imnal the Invincible, the Dimunian was undefeated. The Dimunian moved to the right and stood around half way between Imnal and the right-hand flank of the fourteen survivors of The Twenty.

Again, it took another two minutes for silence to fall – even though the crowd knew pretty much what to expect next. Sure enough, Calidius delivered. "And finally," he announced, his eyes burning with fervour," I give you...the Demon of Dadmir."

Absolute pandemonium greeted the final announcement, and the noise remained at insane levels as their latest hero strode out. The Demon wore a helmet – which was naturally fashioned into the image of the vilest of demons. The story went, that the Demon's real face was so hideously disfigured, that his mask was preferable. Interestingly, though, the Demon of Dadmir wasn't as toned as his two fellow celebrity gladiators, but he did nothing to hide his massive frame, particularly his enormous belly which overhung his loin-cloth. That solid belly did not wobble an inch, though, while in his right fist, he held the largest war hammer in the empire; indeed, it was more than half as tall as he was, but the Demon's enormous strength meant he wielded it effortlessly. The Demon of Dadmir then went and stood half-way between Imnal the Invincible and the left-hand flank of the surviving Twenty. It was now twenty-seven versus seventeen – but there was little doubt in the crowd's collective mind as to where the advantage now lay.

When the crowd finally settled down again, Calidius announced that he was honouring his promise that the prisoners would stand a chance of surviving this day, and earning their freedom, by offering them these extremely favourable odds of twenty-seven versus seventeen. He fooled no one in the crowd, though. They knew very well that each of the three man-mountains was perfectly capable of taking on three or four opponents simultaneously – and winning with ease. Perhaps the prisoners-of-war knew this, too.

The crowd then waited with baited breath, as Calidius turned to the horn-master and nodded once. What happened next took everyone by surprise, except the Pinashian and four of his fellow-challengers. They didn't wait for the three-second horn blast to finish. They charged the Demon of Dadmir, and although the Demon managed to swing his warhammer twice to take out two of the challengers, the Pinashian thrusted once with his sword to the Demon's exposed left-hand side, and The Twenty were instantly one man-mountain down.

Elsewhere, it was chaos. Four challengers had attempted to pull a similar move on Imnal the Invincible, but Imnal had used his net and lethal trident to great effect, disabling two with his net, a third right through his abdomen with the trident and the fourth through his face. Further over, the Dimunian's whirling swords were dismembering challengers' heads and limbs with ease. However, on Calidius' nearside, the Pinashian and his team had already killed or severely wounded three more of The Twenty such that the challengers were in the process of wiping out The Twenty's left flank – until Imnal the Invincible saw what was happening. By this stage, he was missing his net, but with a great roar, he launched himself at The Pinashian with his trident. Kezidia was an experienced gladiator by now, though, and had eyes in the back of his head. Belying his own great size, Kezidia flung himself to his right and rolled clear of Imnal's thrust. Off-balanced, Imnal had all on to defend against two challengers, but Raul Kezidia, the Pinashian, was back on his feet in an instant and sacrificed all of his honour by burying his sword into the back of Imnal the Invincible before rapidly withdrawing to avoid the slash of another opponent – at which point one of his own team performed similar honours into his attacker's unprotected back.

Against all the odds, the challengers were winning. With the Demon dead and Imnal appearing to be fatally wounded, Kezidia hollered at his team to fall back so they could assess their advantage. The Dimunian briefly considered continuing his drive forward, but when he realised his team weren't following him, he also fell back. All this time, the noise from the crowd was off the scale, as they witnessed the tide turn. With the two sides now separated by around sixty feet, it was easier for the crowd to count: and the result was now fifteen challengers against a mere eight survivors of The Twenty, including the Dimunian.

Calidius' eyes then fell on the fairer-skinned pairing of Paulo Neiroa and Fabio Nabaio. Both were covered in blood, but Calidius' eyes had followed their fights enough to know that most of it was not their own. The two former legionary captains had proven to be expert fighters. And, with the best challengers having been saved until last, they were a lethal team, led by the Pinashian who wasn't far short of the three man-mountains in terms of presence and reputation.

Knowing they had to press home their advantage, Kezidia moved over to his team's left-hand side so that he was facing the Dimunian. Neiroa and Nabaio did the same and were joined by two other formidable challengers. The five of them were clearly going to target the Dimunian, leaving their ten fellows to take on the surviving seven members of The Twenty. It was a sensible move, and gave the challengers a genuine chance of success. It was also a moment of such gravitas, that a hush fell over the arena – and then Kezidia gave the order to charge. For perhaps the first time ever, The Twenty fell back – except for the Dimunian, who feared no one. He fought like a man possessed, but soon found himself overwhelmed by the sheer number of his attackers. Very gradually, he began to pick up injuries which reduced the power and effectiveness of his whirling swords. Seeing the way this final battle was going, and fearing a backlash from losing all three fan-favourites in one Games – not to mention *all* of The Twenty – Calidius quickly nodded to his hornsmen, who unleashed a tumultuous combined blast to signify an end to the contest. However, the Pinashian and his men initially ignored the horn-blast, and hence one of them sprouted a dozen quarrels from Theran soldiers standing on a raised platform on the opposite side of the arena to Calidius. Another two followed on Calidius' side. The survivors immediately ceased their assault and fell back, their hands raised.

Calidius quickly assessed the casualties. The Dimunian had already killed one of the five who had attacked him and another had died of crossbow bolts, leaving just the Pinashian, Neiroa and Nabaio from that quintet. Of the other ten prisoners-of-war, only four had survived, while five of The Twenty were still standing. Thankfully, Thera had a wealth of suitable gladiators to replenish them. Not so the Demon of Dadmir and Imnal the Invincible – although Calidius did note that Imnal was still alive, but surely mortally wounded?

Amidst the tumult, the seven surviving ragged, blood-stained and exhausted prisoners-of-war, two of whom had hideous injuries, were eyeing Calidius for his next move. Despite their incredible feat, secured against the most brutal of odds, there was no triumph or back-slapping. Similarly, the Dimunian and the five surviving Twenty had backed off towards the right-hand side of the arena, shell-shocked at the way the fighting had unfolded, at the losses they had incurred and the incredible bravery and skill of their opponents. The retreat of both sides had also revealed the extent of the carnage. The arena was littered with bloodied corpses and a handful of dying combatants – including the prostrate Imnal who was still somehow hanging on to life.

It took a good ten minutes for the crowd's bloodlust and fervour to abate, wholly unsurprising given they had just witnessed possibly the bloodiest gladiatorial contest of all time, not to mention the death of one and probably two of the greatest fighters of the modern gladiatorial era. By this stage the Dimunian and the five surviving members of The Twenty had vacated the arena, and the seven victors had congregated in the centre, facing their emperor, waiting to be granted their insanely hard-earned pardon – or, perhaps, a transfer to The Twenty.

Eventually, the crowd fell silent again.

Calidius stood, and expectation hung heavy throughout the arena. Clearly, it had not worked out the way he had expected, and he had mixed feelings at the death of the Demon of Dadmir and fifteen members of The Twenty, as well as the likely fatal injuries to Imnal. He had, however, provided Therans with the kind of spectacle he had promised them. He had also prepared for this eventuality.

"Therans," he began. "I give you your seven extraordinary champions."

The crowd noisily hailed those exhausted champions, and both Neiroa, Nabaio and one of the other survivors actually raised their hands in acknowledgement. Of the other four, two were barely able to stand, while the Pinashian, just stared balefully at Calidius.

Calidius waited for the crowd to fall silent again. "However," he said. "These men are still prisoners-of-war…each guilty of treasonous activity… against the Theran Empire. And we must remain strong. Because," he paused. "In unity there is strength!"

This time, the crowd responded more to Calidius' liking.

"That is why," said Calidius, nodding at liveried soldiers at both ends of the arena to walk forwards, "we must give you one final offering…for your delectation."

The mood amongst the seven survivors suddenly changed to one of wariness. They were still armed with bloodied weapons, but massively outnumbered by legionaries. Twenty of the latter – ten on each side – had stopped short of them. They then each fell to their knees, and between them, they opened previously unseen sand-covered flaps and dragged a series of chains backwards, pulling open enormous trap-doors on both sides, revealing descending flights of stone steps. The soldiers then quickly retired to their respective ends of the arena.

Several seconds passed.

And then up from the right-hand flight of steps, came an enormous slavering tiger, shortly followed by another. Three more then appeared from the left-hand steps. Each tiger was growling and salivating, their drool spilling to the floor to mingle with the sand and blood. And the smell of the latter was already driving the tigers into a frenzy.

Fabio Nabaio's sword dropped to the floor as he understood the reward they were about to receive for their unprecedented bravery. But Raul Kezidia decided to face his final challenge with the courage he had shown all of his life. He knew very well that these tigers would have been starved for days, and that he stood little chance of killing one, never mind all five. Nevertheless, he advanced, sword raised.

The finale was brutal. One of the surviving challengers turned his sword on himself, seconds before Paulo Neiroa's head was violently torn off by one of the tigers. The Pinashian actually managed to fatally wound one of the tigers – to great acclaim from the crowd – before he was hideously mauled to death, great gashes appearing across his magnificent physique before he was eventually taken down and then gorged upon.

Thereafter, the mood of the crowd became mixed. Some had enjoyed the thrill and spectacle of a lifetime, with a most unexpected and brutal but fulfilling finale. Others were clearly unhappy with the 'reward' meted out to the victors, prisoners-of-war or not; especially to the Pinashian, who was a great crowd favourite. And a significant portion of the crowd actually turned their backs on the carnage, finding such deaths unpalatable; a bridge too far, even for the Mesocluso in Thera.

Sensing this disquiet, for the first time in both his short official and previously long unofficial reign, Calidius Antoninus Dominius experienced a niggle of doubt. Indeed as he disappeared down the steps behind the imperial enclosure to the waiting banquet, he found that he didn't quite have the appetite he had been expecting.

CHAPTER 121   MAGNUS

43rd Tertiar, 1789   Day 134, 14:25

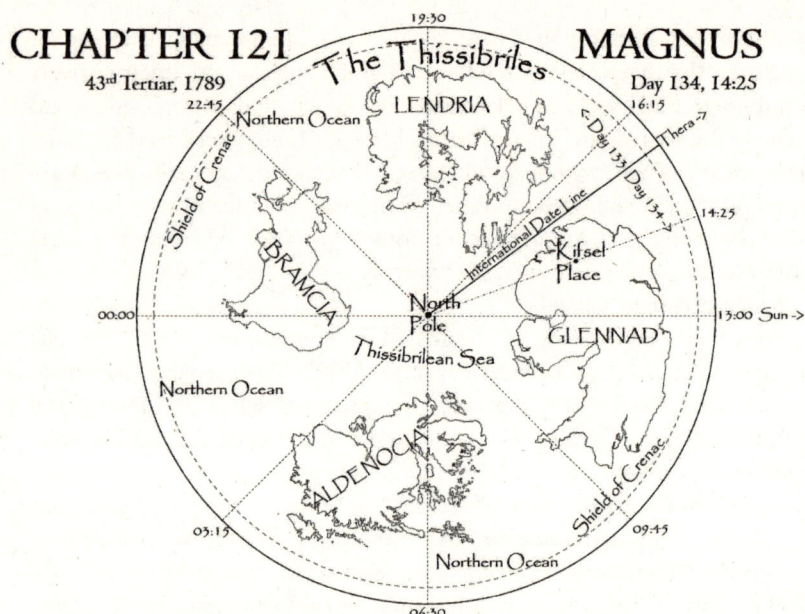

"You see where the path goes over the lip, just ahead?" said Yarhill.

"Yes, Corporal."

"The path climbs to the right and through a steep gorge. When we get to the other side of there, you'll see the plateau on which Kifsel Place was built. The monastery is tucked away in the side of the mountain."

"How long?" asked Magnus.

"Just another half an hour at the most, Sir."

"Finally!" exclaimed Magnus, rolling his eyes. It had been nearly twenty-six hours since they'd actually seen anybody else. They had been hiking up a steep valley, with the mountains rising another three or four thousand feet above them on both sides, and had seen a group of climbers clustered around the top of Dawkids, so far away they had looked like ants crawling around the top of their sky-nest.

It was now the eighth and final day of Magnus' gruelling haul from Ghantiss to Kifsel Place: four days on a boat and four slogging their way through foothills and then the highest range of mountains on Glennad. They'd actually made faster time on foot than expected, largely thanks to the guidance of Corporal Yarhill and Private Ginsten from the Les Antonocca militia. On Day 131, they'd arrived in the foothills and stabled their horses, as Yarhill had assured them there was no way you could get a horse up some of the steeper paths. That stable had been the last before Kifsel Place, some twenty leagues distant and at a considerably lower altitude. The next four days had been spent largely climbing and Magnus' calves had gone way beyond protestation. The only saving grace was that the weather was as glorious today as it had been yesterday; azure skies, troubled only by the occasional wispy cirrus clouds.

Magnus turned to his captain, a tall and lean man of around six feet, who sported a rather fine handlebar moustache. "Well, the men still seem in good shape, Potts."

"Aye, Sir. Thank you, Sir."

Just as Yarhill had described, the path began to bend to the right, still heading upwards. They found themselves walking through a narrow gorge, with nigh-on sheer walls climbing to their left and right, but up ahead, Magnus could see the terrain begin to widen out. Shortly afterwards, the tiny wood-built village of Kifsel Place came into view. Then, to his left, the five famed stacks were slowly revealed. Of course, Magnus had read about the spectacular monastery at Kifsel Place, he had seen a number of drawings in books, and he had also listened to first-hand accounts of people who had visited – but even he was completely floored by how impossible it all looked. Immediately, he could see the four bridges crossing from one stack and it's set of buildings to the next, with each stack rising higher than its neighbour and ascended via steps cut into the rock-face of the next stack.

A few paces further on, they stopped at a T-junction, with the main path through the Umbricans continuing straight ahead, and the village on its right-hand side. To their left, a path snaked away to the south and to the gates of the monastery and its gravity-defying architecture, whilst all around, dozens of jagged peaks reared above them into the blue sky.

Magnus eyed the path to the monastery warily. It didn't look wide enough to accommodate a side-by-side approach and there was no barrier on the outer edge of the path to the right; it appeared to just drop away, and from where he was standing, Magnus couldn't see the bottom. Worse still, the path appeared to slope gently from left to right, from rock wall to precipice. "Well," he said, to Potts and Yarhill. "There won't ever be an army approach this place with any success!"

"You're not wrong there, Your Royal Highness," said Yarhill. "Although it has been attempted."

"Really?" said Magnus. "When was this?"

"The time of Eric II, in the late 13th century. The abbot stopped paying his taxes, so Eric sent a regiment to take the money owed, or the same amount in gold. There's always lots of gold in churches, and St Affo's there," he said, nodding up at the church tower on the fourth stack, "has always been particularly laden."

"Yes," agreed Magnus. "For an institution that's supposed to give so much, they also appear to *have* plenty, too. They also have a number of precious artefacts, too – including this ancient Wrothswirk Stone that I would quite like to see whilst we're here. But above all, let's hope they have two much-wanted fugitives as well."

"Indeed, Sir. Shall we go?"

Magnus took a deep breath. He didn't want to show any fear in front of his men. "Quite right, Yarhill. Do lead on."

"Sir," said Yarhill, and with that, he turned and began to stride confidently along the narrow path. Magnus followed, with Captain Potts behind him and the rest of his soldiers spread out in single file behind Potts, with Private Ginsten bringing up the rear. Once in transit, Magnus was able to confirm that the edge did indeed drop away for around a thousand feet or more to their right. He only looked once.

They had only gone a dozen strides further when the bell began to ring out from the top-most stack. Magnus nearly jumped out of his skin, and let loose a stray curse. Potts, behind him, issued a nervous laugh. "Aye, me too, Sir," he said, patting his own heart several times.

Magnus just nodded, and continued to walk southwards with the clanging of the bell resounding around the valley. There was little chance of conversation until the bell had run its course, so Magnus kept his hand on the rock-face to his left and alternated his eyes between the path before him and the monastery ahead. On one glance up, his attention was briefly attracted to a mountain stream cascading down the rocks on the other side of the gorge. The distraction forced him to stumble slightly and his heart leaped into his mouth. *Keep your eyes on the floor, you fool.*

The next shock came when the echo of the 15th bell-ring was slowly dying away – as a large bird darted out of the rock face to his left. "What the -." Magnus stopped himself, remembering his upbringing. The thing was as ugly as sin, largely black, but with a bald pink head. "What the blazes was that?"

"It's a vulture eagle," threw Yarhill back over his shoulder. "They don't attack men. They've been known to attack sheep and goats, though."

"Ye Gods!" exclaimed Magnus, grimacing, half imagining one of the ghoulish things trying to peck his eyes out. "Can we just get to the darn monastery, please."

As they approached the entrance to the monastery, the path finally widened a little. Magnus also noticed that the vulture eagles were more prevalent, the closer they got. "Are the monks feeding these brutes?"

"Rumour is they do, Sir. Monastery rats, apparently."

As Yarhill was replying, the wicket gate opened in the huge double monastery doors, and two brown-robed monks stepped out. One was a good half a foot taller than the other, and the smaller man had the misfortune to be extremely wide, whilst also having the darkest and thickest eyebrows Magnus had ever seen. As Magnus approached, they both bowed their heads. *No tonsures.* Magnus was surprised. "Your Royal Highness," said the tall monk. "This is a most unexpected honour. Had we known, then we would have prepared properly."

"That's perfectly all right, Brother, erm…"

"Brother Stephen, Your Royal Highness. This is Brother Clarence."

"Brother Stephen, Brother Clarence," he said, nodding his head in greeting. "No special treatment is required. We will only be stopping for one night, and our business is, well, political, shall we say."

"I fear you seek the kidnappers of your beloved sister, Your Royal Highness. If so, I regret to inform you that no such brigands are being harboured here."

Magnus' heart hit the floor. They were being told they'd had a wasted journey before they had even stepped over the threshold.

"You have had no recent visitors?"

Intriguingly, Magnus spotted a flicker of uncertainty in Brother Stephen's eye. Perhaps their journey wouldn't be wasted after all. "We have had a number of visitors – mainly on Day's 129 and 130 – for our annual Cleanse the Spirt expedition to Dawkids and Keplif Scale. People come from all over the kingdom, and this year, as you can see," he said, raising his right hand, "we have been blessed with stunning weather."

Magnus' mind flicked back briefly to yesterday. "I do believe we saw them on top of Dawkids at around about 14:00 yesterday."

"That would have been they, yes."

"Tell me, Brother Stephen. Did this group, perchance, include a forty-year-old woman – very attractive – and a fifteen-year-old girl?"

Brother Stephen creased his brow as if trying to remember. "There were females in the group, Your Royal Highness. Around a dozen of them. But they were people known to us – wives and daughters, who come here most years. Did you have anyone specific in mind?"

"The girl would have been from Ghantiss."

"One of the families comes from Ghantiss, Your Royal Highness, but the mother is, how can I say?" Brother Stephen paused, apparently considering his words. "Her appearance doesn't meet your assessment – and she has two boys; no girls. And then there is a woman and her husband who are pushing fifty, with two girls clearly older than fifteen. May I ask: who are these people that you seek?"

Magnus looked at Brother Stephen very hard. The monk just stared back, innocently, holding his gaze with a gentle smile on his face. *If you're lying to me, I shall wipe that saintly look off your face, monk or no.* Nevertheless, Magnus maintained his civility. "It is of no matter," he said, eventually. "Perhaps you could arrange somewhere for my men and I to rest and refresh ourselves. And then a tour of this magnificent place would be very welcome. We have come a long way."

"Of course, Your Royal Highness."

"I'm particularly keen to see if this famous Wrothswirk Stone of yours possesses the, erm, interesting properties that many have written about over the years."

"I'm afraid you will be disappointed then, Your Royal Highness. I have touched it many times, and I'm afraid it is as inanimate as every other stone in the Umbricans."

"Oh, how disappointing," responded Magnus, genuinely crestfallen. He'd had half an instinct that there was some truth in the writings and that he, as royalty, might be able to tap into its supposed 'powers'. "Will the abbot be available to conduct the tour?" he asked, changing tack.

"Abbot Geoffrey is away with the Cleanse the Spirit expedition, Sir. It is he who leads the prayers on the mountain summits."

"Isn't he a little old for that? I'd heard he was pushing seventy."

"He is seventy-one – and as fit as a fiddle, Prince Magnus. May I ask," began Brother Stephen, neatly changing the subject. "Are you and your men in need of a meal now? Only the refectory is still serving lunch."

"That would be most welcome, Brother Stephen," said Magnus, forcing himself to smile. Inside, though, he was roiling with frustration – but as the two monks ducked through the wicket gate to lead them into the monastery, Captain Potts leaned in towards him. "Don't despair, Sir. I'm not convinced he's just told us the entire truth."

Magnus looked at Potts, and nodded. "You too, then. I hope you are right. If you are…things are about to get very interesting."

Two hours and a delicious roast pork dinner later, they were about to be given a tour of the four stacks that rose spectacularly above them, when

Captain Potts leaned in towards Magnus again, his voice an urgent whisper. "Emilya Luca and Elyse Dolmen have been here, Sir."

Magnus went taut with anticipation but quickly recovered his composure. "Brother Stephen," he said, with a quick smile. "Would you mind pointing us in the direction of the lavatories, please. Captain Potts and I have drunk too much of your excellent tea!"

"Of course. It's the square building over there," he said, pointing to a functional-looking block in front of the bridge over to Bloomer.

Magnus and Potts did indeed use the lavatory to relieve themselves, nodding at two portly-looking monks who were on their way out as they went in. However, on the way out, Magnus steered Potts onto the blind side of the lavatory building. "What have you found out?"

"They've been here for several weeks, Sir – since shortly after you got ambushed outside Earl's Leet."

"And the monks are happy with that are they? What I mean is, I don't see any other women here."

"Well, that's rather on-point, Sir. The three brothers we spoke to are very unhappy about their presence. From what I could tell, it was deeply challenging the faith of all three, particularly a strange fellow called Brother Obadiah. I think that these three would gladly hand the pair over to us and be rid of them for good."

"How interesting. And are the women here now?"

"No, Sir. They've gone on this Cleanse the Spirit expedition to Dawkids and Keplif Scale, along with the abbot and about forty others. They're not due back for another two days."

A cold smile began to spread across Magnus' face. "So, we won't have had a wasted trip after all." The smile vanished. "And what about Oscom and Black?"

"No one matching their description, I'm afraid."

"Any chance these monks have been lying?"

"I'd say not, Sir. What could the monastery possibly gain from harbouring criminals who are wanted for the kidnap of Princess Alicya, or possibly worse? And these three monks that we have an understanding with: they're not regular monks, Sir. Not like Brother Stephen and Brother Clarence – and pretty much all of the other monks we've chatted to."

"What do you mean by 'not regular monks', Captain?"

"They seem like wrong 'uns, sir. They're not warm-hearted. I'm pretty sure they would have told me if Oscom and Black were here; they don't strike me as the sort to cover up or do anyone else a favour."

"Unless they're in league with them, of course?"

"That's not the kind of 'unpleasant' I meant, Sir. It's a strange unpleasant; misfits. It's difficult to explain."

"Well, they sound like potential allies to me. Right," said Magnus, clapping his hands together once. "We've had an exceedingly tough eight days getting here. I suggest we take it easy for the next two days, have a good look around this amazing place and enjoy ourselves. If nothing else, let's just enjoy the food, as that was rather delicious in there," he said, indicating the refectory. "And all the time, we can keep chipping away at your three monks – and others – on the off-chance anyone does know something about Oscom and Black."

"Sounds like a good plan, Sir."

"And obviously, we shall intercept that expedition in two days' time. We'll arrest Luca and Dolmen the second we spot them – for aiding and abetting Oscom and Black. Chances are that their arrest will flush out our real targets. Well, Oscom at the very least." *And he's the only one that I really want.* "Clearly, we won't be saying any more on the matter to any monks. We don't want anyone to run on ahead and tip them off."

"Absolutely not, Sir."

"Right, then, Captain. Let's go and have this tour then – safe in the knowledge that we are *finally* making some progress.

CHAPTER 122 — EMILYA

44th Tertiar, 1789   Day 135, 21:00

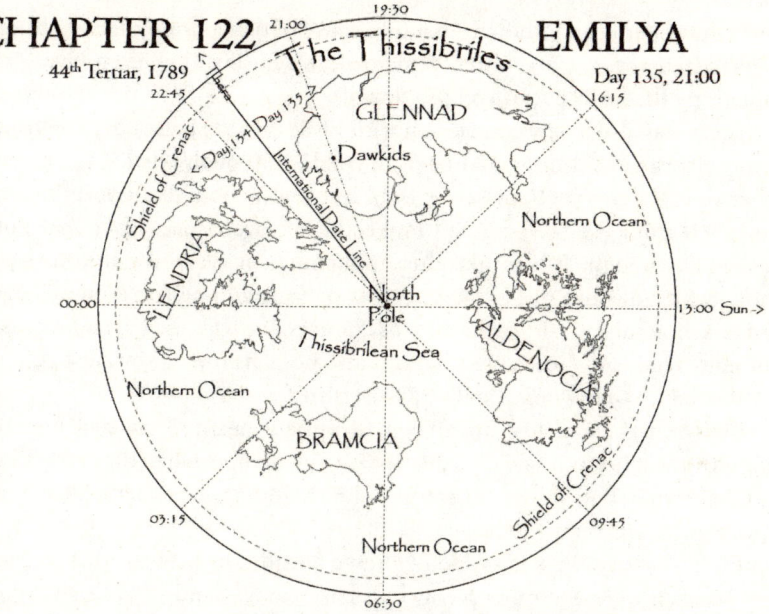

"At last!" exclaimed Emilya, as the wooden base-camp hut at the foot of Dawkids came into view, just as the bright star they had been following in the late evening sky disappeared behind a peak to the east. It had been an exhausting but exhilarating day – although not quite as exhilarating as yesterday. Reaching the top of Keplif Scale had even eclipsed the Dawkids experience – simply because it was higher, more difficult to summit and you could see even further from the top – including the stunning view to the east of the deep blue Lendrian Channel. In fact, the air had been so pure and clear that they could even see the fuzzy western coast of Lendria itself on the eastern horizon. Much closer to home, a large section of the east coast of Glennad had been laid out below them, looking just like it did on Glennadian maps! It had felt like the roof of the world and Emilya still caught her breath whenever she recalled it.

Abbot Geoffrey had then led them in prayer again. The peace and stillness this had brought had matched that experienced on Dawkids. She still didn't know whether this was the abbot's holy spirit, the influence of energy lines, or just from being at one with nature. Or from Elyse's Goddess. *Welcome to our world, Emilya. She feels you too.* Whatever it was, it was like nothing else she had experienced before this trip, but Emilya somehow knew that this peace was with her right now, and would remain so throughout her life – although that odd sense of being unfulfilled as either a receptacle or a transmitter remained, albeit fleeting, even evasive; something that she couldn't yet pin down.

There was also a new connection with Elyse that she hadn't experienced before. It was like a door had been opened – although what was on the other side, she was yet to discover. But Elyse knew about that door; Emilya could tell from the way she had looked at her ever since. Elyse had not pushed it, though. It was like this awakening, or whatever it was, was enough for now. But Emilya sensed that there would be some interesting conversations ahead, although she was comfortable with the current hiatus, not quite ready for those conversations and perhaps revelations, just yet.

Welcome to our world, Emilya. She feels you too.

Emilya had asked just once what Elyse had meant. Elyse had merely smiled back at her and said that she would explain more when they returned to Ghenetenos but, in the meantime, she should *keep looking within*. For now, Emilya was happy to leave it at that.

Emilya's attention was suddenly drawn ahead, to where Brothers Edric and Mervyn were opening up Dawkids base-camp – and where they were apparently greeted with a surprise. Emilya could see the two monks conversing with what appeared to be an occupant inside the hut. They then looked over at her and Elyse, and then back to the interior.

"Come on, chaps," called a man in their group. "We need to put our tired legs up!"

"Of course," responded Brother Mervyn. "Come in, all of you. Make yourselves at home. Feel free to grab the same camp beds you did on our outbound journey."

As they began to shuffle towards the entrance, Elyse took Emilya's hand – just before the diminutive form of Brother Clarence was revealed, standing inside the hut. "Hello, you two," he said, with a placating smile.

"What's the problem?" asked Elyse, as they were joined by Abbot Geoffrey, who was also intrigued by Brother Clarence's presence. Emilya also spotted Clyve and Jared looking back with concern as well.

Brother Clarence sighed, raised his caterpillar eyebrows and then looked directly at both girls. "We had visitors whilst you were away".

"But you have visitors all the time," said Elyse, likely knowing the answer to her question before she actually posed it. "What was so special about these visitors?"

"It was Prince Magnus. With around twenty soldiers."

"Good Lord!" said the abbot, thereafter lost for words. At the same time,

Emilya's legs almost gave way and she began to visibly shake. Elyse put a protective arm around her to provide both comfort and to hold her up, while Clyve and Jared approached, having spotted Emilya's distress. Brother Clarence, meanwhile, was also looking concerned, and his face had gone a shade redder than normal. He didn't seem entirely surprised at Emilya's reaction, and raised the palm of his hand towards the abbot as if to say, *I'll deal with this*.

"Did you say that Prince Magnus was at the monastery?" asked Jared.

"Yes, he was," confirmed Brother Clarence. "And I'm sorry, ladies, but he specifically asked if we had two women staying with us. His exact description was: 'a forty-year-old woman – very attractive – and a fifteen-year-old girl.' He said that the girl would be from Ghantiss and the woman from Ghenetenos. He was quite clearly describing you two."

Tears began to roll down Emilya's face.

"What did you tell him, Brother Clarence?" asked Elyse, her arm still supporting Emilya.

"It was Brother Stephen who spoke to them. It was also he who sent me here. He told Prince Magnus that there were women visiting right now for the expedition, but that none matched your descriptions. Of course, asking after you two was only a side-issue. Magnus was primarily looking for Harry Black and Jake Oscom."

"He was searching for Black and Oscom?" asked the abbot, aghast. "At Kifsel Place monastery?"

"He was, my abbot. He and his men will be staying for two nights – and we strongly suspect that they are hoping to intercept Miss Elyse and Miss Emilya when you're due to return tomorrow."

Emilya's heart was still racing, but she also recognised how extremely fortunate they had been. Not only in being away when Magnus had arrived, but for also missing them in the mountains, too; chances were, they had both walked in and out of this valley via the same route, barely a day apart. She recalled the 'ants' she had seen on the valley path from the top of Dawkids, and realised that, timing-wise, those ants may well have been Prince Magnus and his men.

"And what did Brother Stephen tell him?"

"He explained that we would never harbour criminals. His Royal Highness was most put out at what appeared to have been a wasted journey – until he started asking us about Miss Elyse and Miss Emilya."

"But you say that Brother Stephen denied having seen anyone of the description of these two ladies?"

"He did. As would I. Alas, Magnus' men were questioning other monks, so it is likely someone told them that Miss Elyse and Miss Emilya have spent several weeks at the monastery and that they were on this expedition. Hence why Brother Stephen sent me on ahead to warn you. I have brought plenty of supplies. We thought it wise for Miss Elyse and Miss Emilya to remain here with me, whilst the rest of the party return as planned – and then Prince Magnus will leave Kifsel Place empty-handed."

"And very angry, too," finished Elyse, quietly.

"I have to ask you, Miss Elyse," began the abbot. "I cannot believe that you would know such a person as Harry Black, but do you, perchance, know this Jake Oscom?"

Elyse saw little point in sustaining their deception. "I do. We both do. And he's a good man. He certainly didn't kidnap or murder Princess Alicya, as he was with Emilya and I when she disappeared."

"Ah," said Brother Clarence, simply. He paused for a few seconds. "I pride myself on being a good judge of character. Throughout your stay, you have been charming, hard-working, kind and, above all, honest. I did *not* see any of those qualities in the short time I spent with the prince."

Brother Clarence's words caused even Elyse to fill up, and the intense reactions from the two girls had started to attract the attention of some of the others in the group. Several people asked if they were all right. Abbot Geoffrey nipped it in the bud, shooing them away and stating that he would explain all after they had eaten.

As some of the team began preparing a vegetable broth, Emilya and Elyse kept themselves apart, allowing only Abbot Geoffrey, Brother Clarence, Clyve and Jared to share their conversation. Between them, they poured out their whole story and, once told, Clyve added in what he knew of Jake Oscom, talking of the years he served under him in the Bramcian Navy, an exemplary man of honour with an impeccable service history who put his crew before himself – although he omitted the tragedy in Byastwerthy that had ended Jake's naval career.

"So," said Brother Clarence. "It would appear that the general rumours about the prince are true, then."

"He and his friend had their dogs tearing poor Theo apart, and they were *enjoying* it," said Emilya, tears welling up again at the horrible memory. "How do you fight a man like that? A man, also, who's every action is protected by the state and the royal family? We've said on many occasions since we heard the news about the Princess Alicya, and the total lies being put about regarding Jake and Harry Black, that Prince Magnus *himself* is probably behind the Princess' disappearance."

"Oh, now hold on there, my dear," interceded the abbot. "You can't go around making statements like that. Everyone should be innocent until proven guilty."

"What, you mean like Jake and Harry?"

"Come on Emilya," said Elyse, putting her arm around her. "The abbot is only trying to help."

"Well, forgive me, my abbot, for being pre-judgemental," began Brother Clarence. "But blaming Jake Oscom for the disappearance of his sister, would rather neatly clear up all of his loose ends in one fell swoop, if he is *indeed* behind Alicya's disappearance. And as our ladies here swear: Jake Oscom was with them in Ghenetenos at the time she vanished. This, sadly, would make Miss Elyse and Miss Emilya witnesses that he can ill-afford to speak out. So, under *no* circumstances should we allow Prince Magnus to take them."

The abbot pondered on Brother Clarence's words for a few seconds. "Brother Clarence," he said. "You put me to shame. Of course, we shall do everything in our power to keep you safe and undetected."

"Brother Stephen suggested that when you return tomorrow, I should stay here with Miss Elyse and Miss Emilya. We have enough supplies for a week, but we estimate that once Prince Magnus realises that the ladies aren't in your party, he will depart – as his priority remains capturing Mr Oscom and Mr Black. Once they're gone, Brother Stephen suggested sending a messenger here to inform us that we are clear to return."

"That sounds like a sensible approach," agreed the abbot. "I need to make sure that everyone on this little expedition sings the same story. Fortunately, we have in our group some of the best examples of humanity I have ever known. These people will support you to the hilt, Miss Emilya. That man shall not have you."

CHAPTER 123   DAVY

44th Tertiar, 1789   Day 135, 06:00

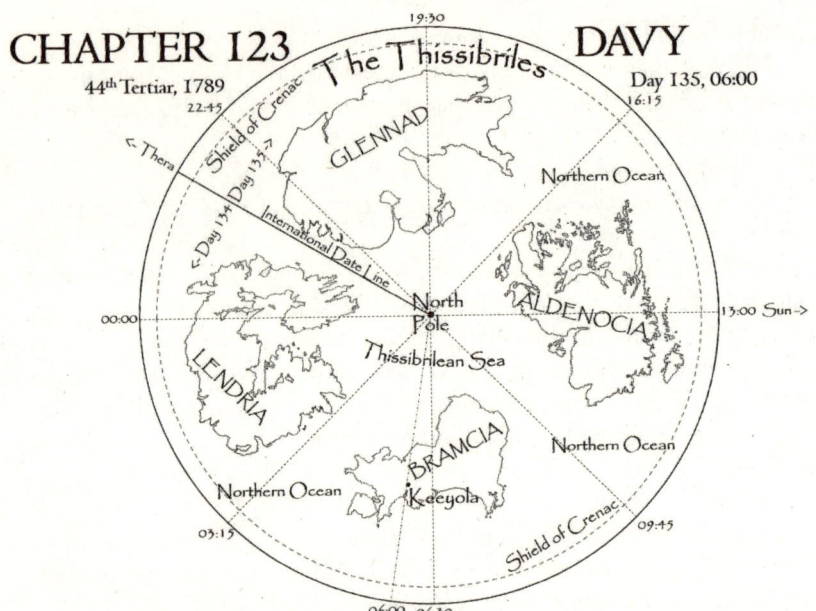

Davy had just finished a night shift, which had run from 23:20 the previous night to 06:00 this morning. The Keeyola mine ran for 26 hours, 365 days a year – and hence it had been easy to keep Davy and Wickham apart, with Wickham and his cronies having worked the previous late shift (14:40 to 23:20). However, Keeyola also did widescale surface mining as well, and Davy had agreed to stop behind for an hour with Rhys Connor and watch the surface miners at work, who worked two daytime shifts from spring to autumn, and one daytime shift in winter.

Rhys was currently regaling him with the site's history. "The mine was set up by the Oakeley family who owned this land a century ago," he was saying, as they headed towards a viewing platform over the quarry. "Originally, they allowed miners to work the open-cast site who paid an annual fee of twenty shillings to the Oakeley's for the privilege – and then had to make more than twenty shillings a year to stay solvent! Of course, the Oakeley's soon worked out the value of the product they were sitting on and set up the Keeyola Slate Mine Company in 1707. Incidentally," said Rhys," Keeyola is an anagram of Oakeley."

"Anagram?" asked Davy.

"Aye, it's a word made up from the letters of another word, but all jumbled up. I'll have to take their word for it, given I can't read nor write.

Can you, by the way?"

"Aye, not bad. The Cabrenar Colliery ran a Sunday School for the children of the miners – and as my Da worked Cabrenar, me and my sister got a sort of education."

"Lucky you, Davy. You should make use of those skills, man. Anyway," said Rhys, switching back to education mode. "Here at Keeyola, they started mining underground in the mid-1730s and now over one and a half thousand miners, quarrymen and others work here. That means our settlement here is as large as some Bramcian towns."

By this stage they had reached the viewing platform, and Davy shook his head in bewilderment as he watched the quarrymen, as they were also known, traversing the rockface by swinging to the left and the right whilst secured only by a single rope. Davy spied one quarryman away to the right of the rockface with his enormous iron crowbar wedged into a crevice in the slate. He was leaning right out from the rockface, suspended by his single piece of rope, and Davy could see the bloke's biceps bulging from two hundred yards away as he heaved the crowbar back and forth. He then watched as a whole section was prized loose and tumbled dozens of feet below where it hit the quarry floor resulting in a huge cloud of dust.

"A lot of men have died over the last century doing that, Davy. Above and below. Very dangerous."

"There are men on the ground?" asked Davy, aghast.

"Watch," said Rhys.

Once the dust had settled in each of several locations, Davy heard a shout and then spotted boys running forward with carts. Rhys was now explaining that sometimes it took two or three of them to lift some of the heavier blocks and hoist them onto the back of the carts. Davy imagined their little hands must be slick with blood as they didn't appear to be wearing any gloves. The boys then set off, dragging the creaking carts behind them in the direction of the cutting sheds – which was to be their next destination, if Rhys could get them in.

The nearest cutting shed entrance was being guarded by a burly bloke in his thirties with jet black hair that fell to his shoulders. "You mind if we pop in and watch the boys dressing, Bryn?" asked Rhys.

Bryn looked hard at him, and then stepped aside. "Don't bloody touch anything," he commanded.

"We won't," promised Rhys. "Come on Davy."

The cutting shed was vast, and very noisy, mainly due to the multitude of chiselling and hammering that was going on. There must have been a hundred cutters and dressers working in there. And everywhere, there were thousands of completed slates, stacked in neat piles – from just a few hours work. The air in the cutting shed was also thick with dust from the multitude of sawing, cutting and splitting, and Davy realised there was a thin layer of dust underneath his boots, too.

The nearest cutter was working on a large slate block around six inches thick, and was busy making it roughly rectangular by cutting off the angles with his hammer and chisel. The cutter then balanced the rectangle against his foot and, began making an incision with his chisel about an inch from the top edge. He repeated that to the left and the right and then, as if by magic, an inch-thick rectangle of slate slid off the top end, super-smooth on both sides. He then repeated that five times more. Satisfied, he gathered the six one-inch-thick pieces of slate and sat down, balancing the block against his knee. Striking across the block to his left, he then split each of the six pieces into two until he had twelve thin pieces of slate, all perfectly smooth. He then cut the twelve down the middle by chiselling the top of each and then both sides, and then using a thin wedge along the top which he prised into the gap, gently working it back and forth until the slate split and two perfect rectangles were produced.

"It's not as easy as it looks," shouted Rhys.

Davy watched as the worker cut each remaining block until he had twenty-four thin slate rectangles. The block of twenty-four was then stacked alongside hundreds of others, where another worker was taking them to punch holes in the top and bottom.

"They'll be used for roofing," shouted Rhys into Davy's ear.

Davy watched the second worker place the first slate underneath a machine, and then pull hard on a metal bar. This activated a thin metal spike which slammed down to punch a hole in the slate. He then turned it around and put a hole in the other long edge.

"The tilers will secure those slates to thousands of roofs in the Thissibriles by hammering nails through those holes – which then fix the slate to the wooden joists beneath the laid tile."

By the time they exited the cutting shed, Davy was certain he preferred underground mining to being a quarryman or working in the cutting shed – as the cutting and dressing processes seemed fairly monotonous. He was even more certain he needed his bed. "Listen, Rhys. I appreciate the tour, but I need to get back home and hit the sack, mate."

Rhys nodded. "Me too, mate."

It took five or six minutes to walk down the hillside to Keeyola village.

By the time they separated, Davy was nearly dead on his feet, although he was happy that he'd made the right choice to uproot himself and Daisy to come to Keeyola. Of course, he hadn't had the best of starts with the incident four days ago, but thankfully, Wickham had also heeded the warning from Mr Masters and their paths hadn't crossed since. Maybe with a bit of time, the rift with Wickham and his cronies might heal.

Tired, but upbeat, Davy turned into the walkway that linked the main street through Keeyola Village to the row of cottages where he and Daisy now lived. When he was half way down, though, part of the light at the end disappeared, blocked by two figures who had appeared. Two stationary figures. Davy's instinct for danger kicked in and he turned around to look back the way he had just come. Two more figures were blocking the exit that way, too. One of them was Wickham.

So much for healing the rift.

There was nothing Davy could do other than stand still and wait for the four men to close in on him, determined to try and talk his way out of this one. Then he saw the club that Wickham was holding. "Hey, Ceri, come on, man. There's no need for this." He turned to the two men approaching from the direction of his house. "Pat, Marty, come on."

"You're not wanted around here, Sheerin," said Wickham. "You had your chance to piss off and avoid this, but you chose not to. Now we're here to teach you a proper lesson."

Davy realised he was going to get beaten, no matter what he said or did, so he decided to say what was on his mind. "And this is how slate miners settle their differences is it? Armed, and with four against one unarmed man? I think that makes you a prize-winning coward, Wickham."

Any thoughts Davy had that calling Wickham a coward might result in a one-on-one challenge were soon dispelled. Wickham raised his club and tried to bring it down savagely on Davy's head – but Davy dodged to one side and tried to sprint past him, intending to use speed to bowl past the other man who was now behind Wickham. The man pre-empted the move and tried to block Davy. He half succeeded, and that was enough to slow him down, giving the other two – Pat Roach and Marty Smyth – time to jump on his back and wrestle him to the floor through sheer weight.

A struggling melee ensued, with the three men eventually pinning Davy to the floor. "Now, Ceri," said Marty Smyth. "Do him now."

Wickham hadn't needed prompting. As the three other men moved clear, his club was already falling – straight towards Davy's head. Davy whipped his head to the left, and took the full brunt of the blow on the top of his right shoulder. He cried out in pain, but knew he now had only one chance to save himself. Like lightning, Davy lashed out with his right foot, snapping the steel toecaps of his boot on the outside of Wickham's right knee, just as Wickham placed all of his forward weight onto his right foot, club raised for a second blow. Davy actually *felt* Wickham's right knee dislocate…and then the man was screaming in agony.

Davy was on his feet in a flash, blocking a punch from the man he didn't know and landing a haymaker back to his cheek. Spinning around, Davy largely avoided the attempted grabs of Pat Roach and Marty Smyth, who only succeeded in pulling Davy's coat off, and suddenly, there was daylight between himself and the end of the walkway. By the time he'd reached his own street, people were coming out of their houses to see what the commotion was all about. "What's the matter, lad?" asked his neighbour, Tyler Roberts.

"Attacked me with a club, Ty," he said. "Wickham and his cronies."

The audience crowded into the mouth of the walkway. Through his agonised cries, Wickham managed to shout out: "I'm going to fucking kill you, Sheerin."

"Oh, you are, are you?" shouted back Tyler Roberts. "We'll see what Magistrate Brooks has to say about that, shall we? That's a very serious threat, Wickham. And as for you men," he said, berating the other three. "Four on to one? And armed? Shameful. Absolutely shameful."

"Why don't you come down here and say that, Roberts," sneered Pat Roach.

By this stage, though, Tyler Roberts had been joined by two older miners, so Tyler ignored the challenge. "I'll also be telling Mr Masters about all three of you before I start my next shift. In the meantime," he said, eyeing the grotesque angle of Wickham's right leg, "I suggest you get your stupid mate down the infirmary. Although it looks like his running days are over!"

Before Davy could hear Roach's response, he saw Daisy come running out of their cottage, appalled at the escalating scene and recognising that her Davy was at the heart of it – again. "What's happening, Davy?"

Davy's shoulder was beginning to hurt like hell. "Wickham," was all he managed to gasp.

"You're hurt!" she said. "Let me look."

Davy sat down in the middle of the street, and unbuttoned his shirt, allowing Daisy to pull it to one side. There was already a huge bruise visible, and the shoulder appeared sunken. "Oh God, Davy. I think he's broken your shoulder. How are you going to work with that?"

"At least he's still alive, love," said the returning Roberts.

"Thanks mate," said Davy. "For that," he said, nodding down the walkway where he could see the back of Wickham, hopping along on one leg, with his arms around a mate to either side.

"How the bloody hell did you come out of that with just one big bruise?"

"Luck, Ty. Pure luck. Do you mean what you say – about reporting the incident to Mr Masters?"

"We need to do more than that, lad. This has to go to the magistrates. You can't give him another chance. And I heard him threaten to kill you. He needs to get sent down for this. And yes, Mr Masters needs to know."

"But he said he'd sack me if I was back in his office in the next five years."

"Did the incident take place at the mine?"

"Well, no, but -."

"There you go then. You can't be held responsible for this, it's happened off-shift, off-site, and it was Wickham who attacked you, four onto one. Masters needs to know. I'll stick up for you."

"Me too," said Mrs Gemmill, who lived opposite the walkway. "I saw all four of 'em attacking you." Several others also added their support. Wickham had obviously not made too many friends in Keeyola.

"You need to press this one home, Davy," Tyler Roberts was repeating. "Wickham isn't going to let this go, so he has to go himself."

"I didn't want any of this," said Davy, down-heartedly.

"Let's get you back into the cottage, love, and let me treat that shoulder." Daisy smiled encouragement at him. "And Mr Roberts is right. None of this is your fault."

Half an hour later, Davy was lying on their bed, a cold compress over his shoulder. Daisy was stroking his arm, trying to hold back the tears. "We've had nothing but trouble since we came here, Davy. I wish we'd never left Cabrenar."

"Well, I don't," said Davy, stubbornly. "The work's OK, the money's decent and I've started to make friends. Tyler's right about Wickham. He isn't going to let this grudge go, and certainly not after what I've just done to his knee."

"It's not just that, though, Davy. It's…"

"What?" asked Davy, now sitting up, concerned. "What else is wrong? You've made friends yourself in this street. Everyone here is fine."

"I don't know. It's just that…it's just…"

"What are you trying to say, love?"

"You'll think I'm being neurotic."

"Just tell me what's wrong."

"Last night," she said. "Last night, I could swear someone was in our house – downstairs. Being on my own, well, I was terrified."

Davy looked hard at Daisy. "Did you hear anything?"

"Yes, just subtle noises, a few creaks."

"That's just the house settling, love."

"I felt a presence in the house, Davy."

"Well, is there any evidence of a break-in? Has anything been taken?"

"No. I've checked everywhere, and I can't see anything missing. Apart from your medal, that is, but you took it in to work, didn't you, as Mr Masters had suggested?"

"No, I didn't, Daisy. I decided it would only wind up some of the slate miners so I left it in the drawer."

"You left your medal in the drawer?"

Davy looked at her, and then swung his legs off the bed, grimacing at the pain in his shoulder. He hurried downstairs, went into the living room, straight over to the sideboard, and pulled the top drawer open.

He turned around, just as Daisy was entering the living room. "It's gone, Daisy! My medal's gone!"

CHAPTER 124   ALICYA

44th Tertiar, 1789   Day 135, 21:00

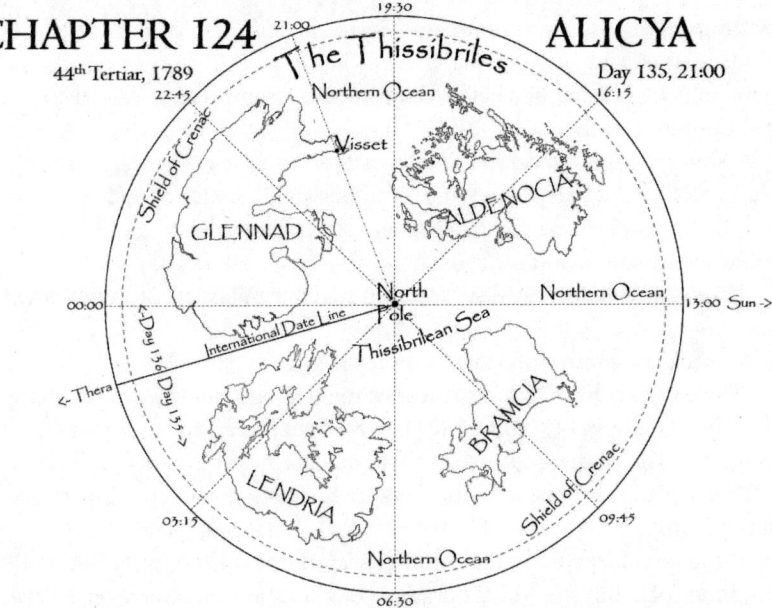

Alicya hadn't ventured out in eleven days, since the faeces-throwing incident, in case she suffered further abuse from the small-minded of Visset, or in case anyone recognised her as the Princess Alicya, and not Alyona from Ghantiss, second-cousin of Gawain Piran. During that time, Gawain had been wonderful: loving, caring, attentive. And very passionate too. That last thought made her smile and feel warm inside.

Soon, they would be married, too. They would move to Sattellus where Gawain would join Charles Green at his old friend and mentor's practice and they would be free of persecution. Of course, Princess Alicya would never be found...*and Magnus would have his wish*. But she would have hers, too. The real loser in all of this was the ex-naval captain, Jake Oscom. If he was captured, Alicya would face a dreadful moral dilemma, as Oscom would likely be sentenced to death for her 'murder' – albeit an unproven crime. But the ramifications for stepping forward and revealing the truth would be devastating for so many, not least herself as she would likely lose Gawain – *and* lay him open to some dangerous repercussions. Alicya therefore prayed each night that Jake Oscom would remain uncaptured and find happiness, perhaps elsewhere in the Thissibriles.

Her thoughts were interrupted by a knock at the front door. As she was on her own, her immediate response was to ignore it; it surely wouldn't be anything good. But as Gawain was away on one of his corpse-moving exercises, there was an outside chance that something could have gone wrong and he needed her help. Alicya took a deep breath, walked to the front door and opened it.

A smirking face stood on the doorstep. "You'll not be marrying him now," said Ashlyn. She pouted once, emphasising her cherry-red lip-paint. "Not unless you get married in a prison chapel, that is."

"What do you mean?"

"Inside knowledge, my dear. He used to tell me all sorts of things when he was in my bed."

Alicya went white with fear. "But they'll -."

"They already have. But don't worry, my dear. It's not the death penalty for body-snatching. My father estimates he'll get fifteen-to-twenty years for it, though." The cherry-red gash on Ashlyn's face now reached almost from ear-to-ear. "Why, he'll be over forty before he's even considered for release. An old man."

Alicya could feel her fight draining away and was close to sliding to the floor in despair, but she willed herself to remain standing. *Come on, Alicya. She might be lying to you.*

With fresh determination, she ducked back inside and grabbed her black sable cloak, making sure she had her key, and then stepped outside and shut the door.

"You'll not find him down the docks tonight," said Ashlyn, her voice dripping with scorn. "He'll most likely be in a Visset magistrate's cell, awaiting trial tomorrow. Then he'll be sent off to Pannezec jail," she shouted at Alicya's retreating back.

Alicya forced herself to ignore Ashlyn. *Do not turn around.* Instead, she hurried across the road in the gathering darkness and began making her way down to the harbour, thankful for the full moon and a clear starry night. One particular star high in the night sky was burning brighter than most, Alicya noticed. As she hurried along, though, she found herself wondering whether this might just be another plot by Ashlyn to have her mugged as night fell around the port town. But there had also been plenty in Ashlyn's eyes that suggested the woman wasn't lying; a mugging was small-fry revenge compared to consigning her ex-fiancé to years in jail, and the triumph in Ashlyn's eyes had not spoken of small-fry.

With some relief, Alicya made it to the sea-front without incident, but it was with an increasing amount of foreboding that she hurried around the harbour towards Gawain's cutter, *Morwenna*. Visset tavern life along the frontage was in full swing to her right as she approached *Morwenna*, but she didn't pay any attention to the cat-calls and whistles being directed her way by groups of inebriated men of all ages.

Morwenna was silent. Gawain wasn't here. With a sinking feeling, Alicya realised the likelihood of Ashlyn telling the truth had just increased significantly. Her only hope was that Gawain would normally have moved his cadavers by this stage, so there was a chance she had missed him by heading down a different street to the one he was heading back up.

"You missed all the fun, Princess."

The phrase shocked Alicya on a number of levels – until she saw the speaker – a man perhaps in his early sixties and possessing less teeth than gaps, tankard in hand, leaning back in his chair at the tavern opposite. And he likely called all young ladies 'Princess', too.

"What do you mean?" she asked, walking across the road.

"His nibs, the doctor. Been taken down a few pegs, he has."

Alicya's fear and despair was suddenly overcome by anger. "Bitch!" she snapped.

"Whoa, that's a bit strong, isn't it? He was only collecting corpses."

"I wasn't referring to Doctor Piran. I was referring to the creature who sold him out."

"Oh, I get it, Princess. You're his, erm, his, erm..."

"'Cousin', I believe is the word that you're looking for, sir."

"Aye," said Gap-Tooth, with a broad, gappy grin. "Happen I was at that."

"I take it he was arrested by the local magistrates?"

"Aye, he was. They caught him red-handed, him and his two lackeys, hauling what looked like a heavy sack off the Sea Bus."

If the situation hadn't been so desperate, Alicya might have laughed at that. Gawain's little play on words. "The locals call it the Sea Bus," he had told her. "My name for it, too – but C-Bus, with a letter 'C' at the front. It's short for *cadaveribus*, which is Old Theran for 'corpse'."

Oh, Gawain! The joke is no longer on the simple folk of Visset.

"Do you know where he is now, please?"

"He's being held in the cells beneath the town hall, Princess."

"Feel free to come and keep my bed warm tonight, love!" shouted out a brash man in his forties, with an enormous beer-gut.

"Oi, you leave it out, Trowell," said Gap-Tooth. "How would you feel if the magistrates had arrested your Minnie?"

"Fuckin' blessed, mate," he shouted back, to great roars of laughter from his mates.

Alicya had heard enough. She began to stride back along the harbour frontage towards the centre of town which was set two streets back from the seafront, gales of laughter, catcalls and lewd suggestions echoing in her wake.

The town hall was a fairly unremarkable building, resembling so many of the others in Visset's market square. That wasn't to say it was unattractive; most houses in Visset were attractive, having been built in honey-coloured brick with their three tiers, arched doorways and terracotta tiles. The only thing that differentiated the town hall from its neighbours was the balcony on the first floor immediately above the arched doorway, where either the mayor or the town crier would make announcements and proclamations. Even at this hour, the town hall was open, so Alicya pushed open the doorway, and found herself in a reception area with a nice dark red carpet. There was a bored-looking sergeant from the local militia sitting behind the desk, and even Alicya's appearance didn't seem to have interested him very much.

"It's a bit late for visiting, madam," he said, barely stifling a yawn.

"I'm the cousin of Gawain Piran."

"Are you now?" he responded with a little more interest. "And you'll be wanting to see him, no doubt."

"If it's not too much trouble."

"Trouble is exactly what it'll be too much of, madam. Visiting is tomorrow morning between 10:00 and 12:00, and tomorrow afternoon between 15:00 and 17:00."

"But I'm assuming he'll be on trial tomorrow morning?"

"Aye, that he will be."

"Well, I won't be able to see him then, will I?"

"You will if you attend the town court in the stalls."

"That's not what I meant and you know it. I demand to see him before the trial."

"Demand, do you? On what authority?"

Alicya did her best to control her anger, and somehow managed a sweet smile. "Please will you let me see him, Sergeant?"

"And what's in it for me?"

"I beg your pardon? What do you mean?"

"Well, it seems as if you're asking me to break the house rules, madam. If you're expecting old Sergeant Locke to do that," he paused, looking her up and down, "there needs to be a price."

"What sort of a price?" asked Alicya, unbuttoning her purse.

"Not that kind of a price, madam."

"For a second, Alicya was confused as to what he meant. Then the penny dropped. "You surely don't mean…"

"I have no idea what you think I might not mean," responded Locke, innocently.

Alicya pulled a shilling out of her purse and put it on the reception desk. "You won't be getting anything other than money out of me, Sergeant Locke. And if you make any further lewd suggestions, I shall report you to your superior officer."

"You can go and tell him now if you like. He's otherwise engaged at Ma Winters', but I'm sure he'll speak to you when he's finished his business there."

Alicya rolled her eyes in despair, getting the message loud and clear that the Sergeant's captain was visiting a den of iniquity and was therefore scarce likely to reprimand his sergeant for an unsubstantiated pass. She therefore drew out another shilling and placed it on the reception desk.

This time, Sergeant Locke rolled his eyes. "You aint going to go away, are you?"

"Certainly not."

Locke sighed and then hauled himself to his feet. Alicya was startled to see that Locke must be at least six foot four inches tall. He then grabbed a large ring of iron keys from a hook on the wall behind his desk and then stumbled over towards a locked door at the far end of the reception area. Alicya instantly smelt alcohol on his breath. No doubt his captain didn't disapprove of that practise, either. It took the Sergeant three attempts to actually get the key in the lock, and then it was the wrong one. After another thirty seconds of faffing, he finally opened the door to the inner cells of the town hall. "Down the steps and he should be third on the right."

"Thank you, Sergeant."

Locke just looked at her and said nothing – so Alicya stepped tentatively through the door. The Sergeant then locked it, as befitted his name and looked at her through the grille. "Just give me a shout when you're done and I'll let you out. And don't be longer than half an hour."

"In that case, Sergeant, please don't fall asleep," she said, not un-humorously.

"Me!" said Locke, feigning innocence. "Fall asleep on duty! Perish the thought, madam!"

Alicya smiled at him, and this time Locke winked back, before walking back towards his desk. Alicya then followed the spiral staircase downwards. At the bottom, there was a long row of cages on both the left and the right.

It seemed remarkably quiet given the number of folks drinking on the harbour frontage, but then again, perhaps it was a little too early for candidates to start filling up the cells.

The first cell on the right had just a single bed and a single slop bucket. Whoever was populating the cell was hidden under the single blanket on his bed. The second cell on the right contained an old man, painfully thin and stooped. He was talking to himself in a cracked old voice and seemed to be berating someone. He didn't even notice her – unlike second on the left, who made a grab for Alicya through the bars of his cage. Just in time, she pulled back. "Do not touch me, you, you…" She had no words as she looked at the wild figure in cell two on the left. Unshaven, hair sticking up on top, and sticking out both sides, soiled clothing, and the smell…

"Alyona. Alyona, is that you?"

Alicya hurried along to the next cell on the right. Gawain was already at the bars and they grasped hands immediately. "Oh, Gawain. What are we going to do?"

"Don't get dispirited, my love. I might get off."

"It was Ashlyn, of course. She's already called to gloat."

"Well," said Gawain, quietly. "I didn't think she would stoop so low."

"Why might you get off?" asked Alicya, Gawain's previous sentence now registering.

"First offence. Pillar of the community. I am clutching at straws, though."

Alicya's expression changed several times during Gawain's last sentence. "And what's the worst-case?"

"I'll be honest with you, Alyona. Five years. But I'd lay odds on six months to a year."

"She told me fifteen-to-twenty years, the…" Alicya just stopped short of saying it.

"I'll bet she did."

"Six months to a year, though!"

"Well, it's better than five years. And a veritable heaven compared to twenty."

"I suppose, but…"

"You can carry on living in my house, darling," he said, cupping her face through the bars. Alicya melted again. This was so unfair. "I still have enough money to pay the rent," Gawain was saying. "I may have to let Mrs Baker go, though. So, you'll need to look after both apartments – and cook for yourself. And if it is a year, we just sit it out and wait. Once I'm released, we get married and move to Sattellus or somewhere else, and I either join an existing practice or set one up myself. Ashlyn can just eat herself up from the inside. All she will have achieved is a delay of the inevitable, and in a year's time, we'll be happy and she will still be bitter, twisted and lonely."

Alicya took Gawain's hand in hers and kissed it. "I will wait for you, Gawain. Forever, if necessary. I will keep your apartments and garden tidy and count off the days. In fact, I shall count off the hours. And yes, you're right about Ashlyn. She had already lost before she did this. If I ever see her again, I shall be perfectly civil to her. That will likely annoy her more than if I attacked her."

"Good girl, that's the spirit! We'll have a release date after tomorrow's trial. We just fix that date in our minds and count down every day until then."

Gawain then gave Alicya a warm and loving smile. "I mean, it's not like the world's going to end before then, is it, love?"

CHAPTER 125   CALIDIUS

45th Tertiar, 1789   Day 136, 02:00

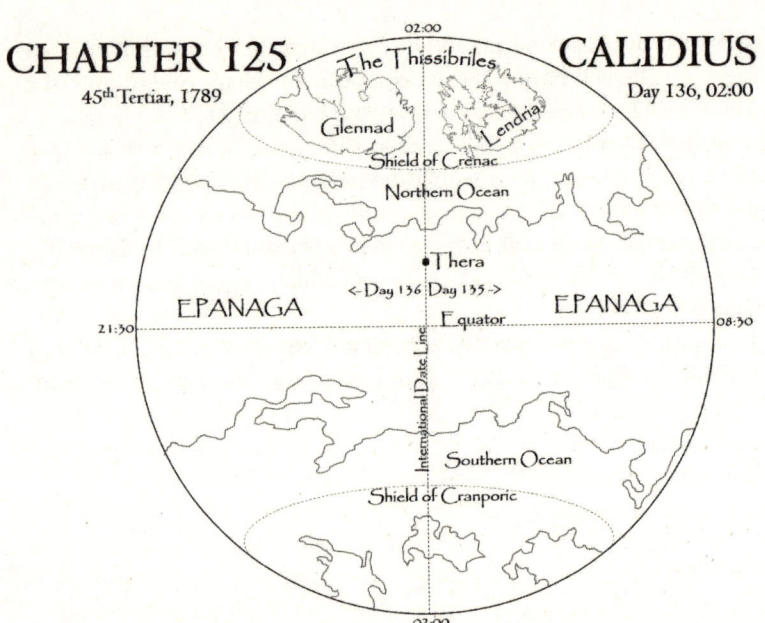

Crouching behind some laurel bushes, the sound of crickets and cicadas all around them, Calidius was dressed the same as General Macrinus and their five legionaries: lightweight burgundy tunic with over-armour, helmet and greaves, complimented by sword, dagger and a holstered pistol. Although Calidius favoured steel to take down an enemy – as it was much more personal – pistols were a necessary precaution in case their enemies were similarly armed. And although they were unlikely to experience resistance, the apparel was also a necessary precaution – despite it making him sweat profusely in the night-time humidity. Indeed, there was likely to be little resistance all over the city, as two thousand legionaries descended on addresses painstakingly researched by General Macrinus and his aides over the last twenty days or so. The occupants of those addresses would mostly be asleep, and even those who were not would not be expecting raids of this level of swiftness and brutality.

"How certain are you that all of these people are thieves?" Calidius had asked Macrinus earlier that day, as they had pored over the lists together.

"Ninety per cent, Your Imperial Majesty."

He had looked hard at Macrinus. "So, we will potentially be slaying around ten per cent of innocents?"

"They aren't innocent, Emperor. Those we aren't certain of have all committed other crimes. Deception, dishonesty, embezzlement, acts of violence, acts of deviancy, plus numerous other transgressions.

"Excellent. And our own target for tonight?"

"A special kind of thief, Emperor. You actually know him."

"I do?"

"Yes. He is Afinius Aemilianus."

"The censor?"

"The very same."

"And what is the nature of his thievery? Although I can probably guess."

"Indeed, Emperor. Clearly, he is responsible for maintaining the census and, ironically, for supervising public morality. However, it is his other duties that were brought to my attention some months ago now."

"Do tell more."

"As you know, he is also responsible for the superintendence of our public buildings and the erection of all new public works. Unbeknown to most, he introduced a new building tax, three years ago."

"But I do know of this tax, General. It was a tax on windows, known as the Glass Tax. What of it?"

"It's a very simple deception, Emperor. Only half of the payments of Glass Tax goes to the Imperial Bank. The other half goes to an institution known as the Imperial Buildings Fund, or IBF."

"Yes, that's right. And the IBF funds are put towards the building and maintenance of public buildings, as befits Afinius' role."

"Incorrect, Emperor."

"Incorrect?"

"It is the small matter of a plural, Your Imperial Majesty. The IBF that you are familiar with is the Imperial *Building* Fund. The Imperial *Buildings* Fund – note the plural – is a wholly different institution.

Calidius had looked hard at General Macrinus at that point, already quite clear where this was going. "And no doubt this imposter IBF organisation is owned by Afinius himself?"

"Not quite, Emperor. It is owned by his brother, Saloninus Aemilianus."

"Who shares these copious funds with Afinius, no doubt?"

"Indeed. You will be in little doubt when you see the size of his villa."

"And Saloninus?"

"I have allocated Romulus and his squad to deal with him."

"Excellent work, General. As ever. Out of interest, how were you planning to deal with Afinius and Saloninus before *Expurgatio*?"

"My spies were still building the evidence, Emperor. He would have been outed in due course. *Expurgatio* has merely hastened his demise."

Calidius had felt a brief inner rage at that point. Afinius and Saloninus Aemilianus had taken his father, his empire and now himself for fools. A quick knife drawn across the throat was too lenient for them. Now, hiding in the shadows outside Afinius' villa, Calidius was ready to mete out that justice, personally. "Your men are briefed?" he whispered to Macrinus.

"Absolutely, Emperor. As are Romulus' men. If at all possible, we take Afinius and Saloninus alive, and then we butcher their families in front of them."

"Good. How much longer?"

"Another five minutes, Emperor. The dogs have taken the meat."

Calidius was impatient to deliver justice. All over the city of Thera, between the appointed time of 02:00 and 02:30, thousands of thieves were about to encounter pragmatic Theran justice. But it made no sense rushing in when they knew that the grounds of Afinius' villa were being patrolled by vicious dogs.

Five minutes later, one of Macrinus' soldiers returned from the main gate where he had been observing the dogs. "They're all down, sir."

"Right, we're going in. Alcius. The mattress."

Calidius watched as an old mattress they had brought with them was flung over the wall above them – where it neatly caught against and straddled hundreds of lethal shards of glass.

"Alcius," whispered Macrinus. "Guard duty for you, as agreed."

"Yes sir," agreed the young legionary, standing to attention.

"I'll go first," said Macrinus, pulling on his thick leather gauntlets and handing over his sword and dagger. Give me a leg up."

Alcius cupped his hands whilst Macrinus put his left sandal into them before launching himself up onto the apex, stomach first, taking great care not to make contact with any of the adjacent shards. Macrinus froze, his eyes darting left and right, but he spotted no activity in the complex beyond the wall. "All clear," he said, eventually, raising himself onto his knees, still atop the mattress. He then took his proffered sword and dagger and dropped them silently down the other side into a flower bed before turning, hanging from the top of the wall and dropping into the villa's grounds. The mattress remained pinned in place.

All remained quiet, so Calidius and four soldiers followed. Once down the other side, all six men remained still, swords now sheathed and pistols out and cocked, ready for any challenge in what was slightly better light thanks to two flickering lanterns on the driveway, nearby. The sound from the insects remained a constant. Then something rodent-like announced itself, foraging in the impeccably-cultivated foliage in front of them before disappearing down its bolt-hole. Another twenty seconds passed. Satisfied they were undetected, Macrinus gave the nod to proceed.

As they approached the villa, Calidius could make out a few features thanks to more flickering lanterns and the bright moonlight. He also noted that Nessemi was shining particularly brightly tonight, high in the night sky to the east. It served to remind him why this was necessary.

Alongside the paved approach to the front entrance was low-cut foliage and a couple of pruned trees which looked like giant sentinels on either side. Calidius could also see several dark, prone shapes on the ground – Afinius' dogs. As they silently passed the first, Calidius could see that it wasn't breathing, and inwardly congratulated Macrinus for using a lethal dosage on the poisoned steaks he had thrown over the walls, thirty minutes earlier. His most-trusted general rarely left anything to chance.

They eventually arrived at the large double doors without event. Macrinus checked them. Locked. "Wait here," he whispered, before moving across the villa to their right and disappearing down the side. After another minute, he returned. "One of the bedroom windows is open," he whispered. "I can't tell if it is Afinius' room, though. If it is, Emperor, we may have to silence him here and now."

Calidius considered for a few seconds. This was the reality. It was all very well planning a nasty public death for Afinius as an example to all Therans, but it wasn't worth risking his own or his men's lives by leaving someone alive to alert others. "Whatever is necessary, General."

Macrinus nodded back. "Thank you, Emperor. This is the plan. First, we swap armaments," he said, holstering his pistol and drawing his dagger. "As agreed, we're going for quiet deaths. Second, I go in on my own and make an assessment. If there are two occupants of the bedroom, I hold up one finger and one of you soldiers joins me inside. Silently. Dagger at the ready. If, perchance, there are three, I hold up two fingers and two soldiers join me."

Perchance indeed, thought Calidius, briefly reminded of his father's final seconds and his two bed-fellows.

"We kill the occupants of the first bedroom without a sound," continued Macrinus in a whisper, "and then move systematically through the villa, taking the rest. If we are fortunate enough to have left Afinius till last, we take him alive."

With the plan agreed, the six of them set off around the right-hand side of the villa and soon arrived at the window in question, which sported two wooden shutters wide open and sitting flush against the wall to each side of the window. The window ledge was only a couple of feet off the ground, so Macrinus easily clambered up and over without a sound. Looking through the window into the shadowy bedroom, they all saw Macrinus hold up one finger. The soldiers quickly nominated one of their number to join Macrinus, and twenty seconds later, the two occupants of the bedroom had had their throats cut in near-total silence – save for a vague gargling sound as the occupants clutched at their opened throats.

Once inside, Calidius went straight to the bed, found a candle and lit it. Holding it up, it was clear that neither of the two dead occupants was Afinius. In fact, they weren't even adults. They were two boys – likely sons who had had the misfortune to have been sired by a corrupt, high-ranking thief. Calidius didn't spare them another glance. These were unprecedented times, and he'd done them a service compared to what might happen on Day 183.

They quickly moved out into the corridors of the villa. There were four more doors on this corridor, and Afinius' grandiosity and self-importance had given away which room belonged to him. They therefore went through the three lesser rooms first, executing two more youngsters and several servants, as well as a woman sleeping on her own who Calidius assumed to be Afinius' wife – leaving the largest double doors until last.

Happy there was no one left alive in the villa other than Afinius, Macrinus made no attempt to hide his presence. He pushed open the doors. The light was better in this room, as Afinius had left his candles burning. A middle-aged, overweight and balding man, he was lying naked on top of his bed, and was still in a deep sleep, despite the intrusion. His companion, though, was wide awake, and clearly not Afinius' wife. Probably in her late teens, and blessed in every place a woman could be, the girl snatched at the bedsheet to cover her modesty – an action which finally brought Afinius around. Through sleepy eyes, he struggled to take in the tableau that greeted him: six soldiers armed with daggers, one of whom was General Macrinus, and another, surely not…

"Afinius Aemilianus," said Macrinus. "We are here to detain you for embezzlement against the Empire. You will stand trial and will be executed, later today."

"Wh, wh, what embezzlement? General, Emperor, I beseech you." He fell out of bed and knelt, naked, at the feet of the Emperor he now recognised. "Your Imperial Majesty, I beg of you, I have done nothing. Please, I beg mercy. I have served your father for twenty years."

"You likely defrauded my father for twenty years," said Calidius, dispassionately. "You'll make no inroads on me. You'd do better begging for the souls of your slaughtered wife and children."

At that, Calidius nodded at the soldiers to apprehend Afinius – for whom Calidius' last words were just sinking in. "My wife and children? You haven't -. Oh, please, God, no. You haven't -.

"Get this whimpering wretch out of my sight," ordered Calidius. As Afinius was dragged wailing from the room, Calidius turned to Macrinus and nodded at the terrified naked teenager. "Yours or mine?"

Macrinus issued a rare smile. "Mine, if you don't mind, Your Imperial Majesty."

"Fair enough," conceded Calidius. "I'll let you, erm, finish off here. No loose ends. Then you'll make your own way back to the palace, yes?"

"Don't worry, Emperor. I'll be there for the debrief at six."

Calidius nodded once, then issued a cold smile. "Enjoy," he said, before exiting.

As he shut the door behind him, Calidius heard the trapped girl's whimpering go up an octave, before screeching could be heard. He then increased his pace to catch up with his soldiers and their prisoner. A plan was already forming in his mind. Today's schedule involved the retrospective announcement of Edict No 4. So, to keep the masses more engaged, he would be executing Afinius immediately after the proclamation. His crimes would be read out, and then he would be publicly hung, drawn and quartered. All being well, that would be alongside the three most prolific thieves in the city. Common thieves, those three, though – whereas Afinius' execution would show the masses that no one was immune from *Expurgatio*.

CHAPTER 126   MAGNUS

45th Tertiar, 1789   Day 136, 13:30

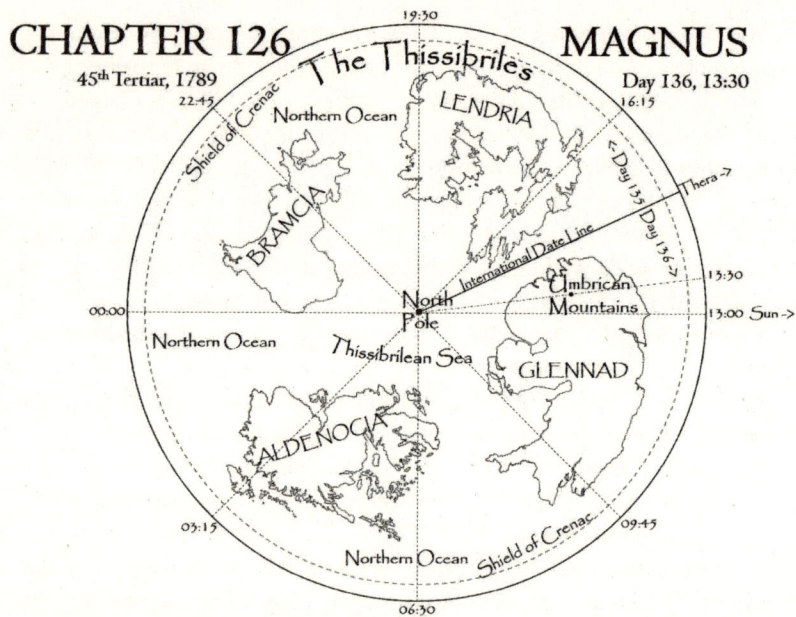

"There they are, sir," said Captain Potts, pointing to a bend in the valley, far below, where around forty people with back-packs were walking slowly up the gorge towards them. The path separated in a V-shape halfway between them; their own path which headed back towards Les Antonocca, heading initially in a north-westerly direction, while the other party's path was incoming from the north.

"Oh, happy days!" said Magnus, quite unable to keep the smirk off his face. It had been forty-four days since he had last seen Emilya Luca in that courtyard, although it felt more like a year. "I am so looking forward to seeing the expression on that urchin's face."

It took another twenty minutes before the two parties converged, and Magnus had spent all of that time straining his eyes to see if he could pick out a woman accompanied by a fifteen-year-old girl. There had been two or three possibilities, but none had looked exactly right. Abbot Geoffrey was leading the monks, and Magnus moved forward to greet him.

"Pon my soul!" exclaimed the abbot. "You're not…"

"I most certainly am," said Magnus, although his attention was elsewhere, his eyes darting up and down the column of people before him. "I was rather hoping you were going to be able to help me, Abbot."

"Help? Are you lost, my son?"

Prince Magnus looked hard at the abbot. Was he trying to be funny? "I'm looking for someone, Abbot. For two people, actually. I am reliably informed by a number of your monks back at the monastery that those two people are in your party."

"To whom do you speak of?"

"Elyse Dolmen and Emilya Luca. One is aged around forty, the other fifteen. I assume you know everyone in your expedition by name?"

"I do indeed, Your Royal Highness. But there is certainly no one of those names in this party. Nor back at the monastery as far as I know."

Magnus began to grind his teeth. *Was there nobody in this entire country who would tell him the truth? Not even a damn abbot?*

"Brother Martyn," the abbot was saying. "Have you heard of a Louise Dolmen, or – what was it," he asked, turning back to Magnus, "Emil someone?"

"Elyse Dolmen and Emilya Luca," said Magnus, through gritted teeth.

"No, Abbot Geoffrey," Brother Martyn was saying. "Those names mean nothing to me." Brother Martyn then asked the monk next to him, who had never heard of them either, and the charade then played out along the whole damn chain of Abbot Geoffrey's expedition team.

Magnus rolled his eyes and took a deep breath. There was nowhere to go with this situation. He could clearly see that neither fugitive was in this line of people, although he was tempted to take two of this lot as hostages to force them to turn up his quarries. However, he couldn't really afford to alienate the church and, at the end of the day, the two women weren't the real prize they were searching for. And in any case, he had one more play to make. "Very well," he said, eventually. "Nice to meet you, Abbot Geoffrey. You have a remarkable monastery. And please thank Brother Stephen for his hospitality over the last two days."

"I will, Your Royal Highness. Before we go our separate ways, though, I take it you're looking for these men who have taken your sister, right?"

"I am indeed. Last seen running from New Hivetha into these mountains, as it happens, albeit a good thirty leagues east of here. Hence why I had hoped that they might have sought sanctuary at your monastery, but it seems my hopes have been dashed."

"We would never take in such men, Your Royal Highness. And these two women you seek. Who are they?"

Magnus looked hard at Abbot Geoffrey, but could do no more than play his game in plain sight of so many monks and civilians. "They know the two fugitives. They may even have helped them evade capture several weeks ago. I had hoped they might therefore know where Oscom and Black might be hiding out."

"Well, I'm sorry your sortie into the Umbricans has failed to bear fruit. I hope that you find your sister alive and well. She is in all of our prayers. But if we are too late," added the abbot, his eyes boring into Magnus', "I believe that divine justice will prevail. Either in this life or the next." He then patted Magnus on the shoulder. "Now, if you would excuse me, my son, I have an expedition to lead home. Good luck, Prince Magnus."

And with that, Abbot Geoffrey strode piously on up the hill, his head held high, leading his party of monks and civilians in single file past Magnus' soldiers.

When they had gone, Magnus was still grinding his teeth. "Divine justice will prevail!"

"I beg your pardon, sir?" said Captain Potts.

"Nothing, Potts. This isn't over yet. We're fairly certain that Brother Cyrus was telling the truth, so I'll bet the crown jewels that Emilya Luca and Elyse Dolmen are still holed up where they spent last night. Other than Yarhill and Ginsten, do we have anyone else in our troupe who knows these mountains well?"

"Private Furness, Sir. He was brought up in Worrab, and climbed these mountains regularly as a boy."

"Bring him up."

"Potts called up a stocky, brown-haired soldier, from half-way down the chain of Magnus' men. "Furness! Over here, please."

Furness snapped to attention, and marched up the line towards them. "Yes, Sir?"

"At ease, Furness," said Magnus. "I hear you know these mountains well?"

"That's right, Sir."

"Do you know how to get from here to Dawkids basecamp?"

Furness hesitated slightly in his response. "I know how to reach it from the east, Sir."

Magnus rolled his eyes. "Now that's not what I asked, is it?"

"Sorry, Sir. I should be able to find it from here, Sir."

"Excellent, Furness. Captain Potts," said Magnus, turning to his captain. "I want you to take Private Furness here, and one other soldier, and arrest Emilya Luca and Elyse Dolmen for me, please. I am fairly certain you shall find them at Dawkids basecamp, or somewhere between here and there. Make sure you are alert at all times in case they see you first and try to give you the slip."

"Yes, Sir. We won't fail you, Sir."

"I sincerely hope not. It's now just after midday. If they remained at Dawkids basecamp this morning, it wouldn't make any sense to leave there until tomorrow morning, at the earliest, as it is a good fifteen-hour trek from there to the monastery."

"That does make sense, Sir. Unless they are an hour or so behind the others."

"If they are, Potts, you must give a long blow on your horn. The noise may well carry to us in these mountains, and it would gratify me greatly to know that we have *finally* made some progress."

"Yes, Sir. Of course, Sir."

"Once you have them, you will take them back to Ghantiss over land. I suggest you take the mountain path and beyond down to Earl's Leet, commandeer some horses, and return via the Earl's Leet, Ghenetenos and Ghantiss route. We did that leg in four days at the beginning of the month. When you get to Ghantiss, please deliver them to the palace and ask for me, assuming I get back there first. If you beat us to it, please ask for a man called Marler, and tell him to keep our guests comfortable until I return."

"Yes, Sir. Marler, Sir. Very good, Sir."

"And you never know. The rest of us might just have some long-overdue luck, and come across Oscom and Black in the north-western Umbricans. Either way, I very much look forward to renewing my acquaintance with Emilya Luca." Magnus then sighed before continuing. "I'll tell you this, though, Potts. If you don't find those two women between here and Dawkids basecamp, I believe I may return to Kifsel Place monastery one day, to personally gut Brother Cyrus."

CHAPTER 127   JAKE
45th Tertiar, 1789   Day 136, 14:00

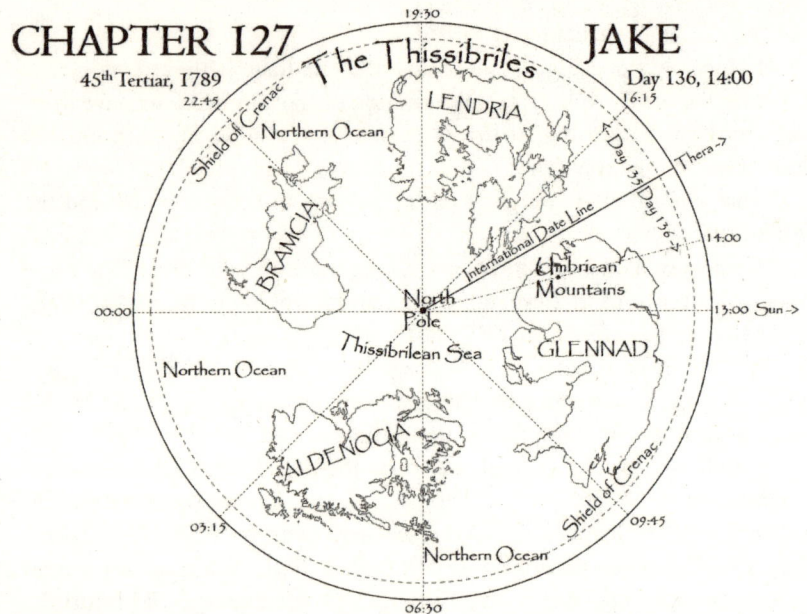

Jake was never one to complain, but he longed to be warm again. Ever since he and Swede had dropped into the water in the harbour at New Hivetha, he had been permanently chilled to the bone. Once immersed, both he and Swede had used the diversion created by the shooting of Turnip and the chase after Harry Black, to move from the shelter of one boat in the harbour to another, always moving up the coast in a northerly direction. Their luck had lasted for an hour, until soldiers had boarded the boat they had vacated and presumably been alerted to two missing male passengers matching their description. Jake and Swede had observed proceedings from behind a tug at the opposite end of the harbour, tantalisingly close to the northern arm of the bay and disappearing out of sight of New Hivetha's promenade. Meanwhile, back on land, half the soldiers had been despatched after Harry Black, and Jake had later spotted them heading up the path towards the mountains. They hadn't had dogs with them, though, so Jake hadn't fancied their chances. Not that this had helped himself and Swede, bobbing around in the harbour on the blind side of a tug.

One hour had passed, then three, and all the time, the soldiers who hadn't gone after Harry were sweeping the bay in small boats looking for their two other fugitives. The tide had come right in, and by mid-afternoon, it had started to go back out again – which was when two soldiers actually boarded their tug, forcing them to duck underneath the boat and hold their breath for bouts of thirty seconds, praying that when they came up for air, the soldiers weren't looking over the sides. Incredibly, they had remained undiscovered – although the chill in their bones had properly set in by that stage.

By evening, the two of them were borderline hyperthermia, but still the soldiers had not dispersed on the seafront and still they were scouring the bay. And why wouldn't they? This was the best lead the Glennadian Army had had for several weeks in their search for the fugitives.

In the end, they had stayed in that cold water until darkness had fallen. They had then managed to swim towards a small rowing boat which was resting in deep shadow below the harbour walls. Despite guards still patrolling the distant promenade, they had managed to clamber in, cold water sluicing off them and an even colder wind biting through their soaked clothing. They had then silently cast off and hugged the shadowy contour of the harbour wall, making only the slightest splashing noises with their paddles which would not carry to the promenade. Jake hadn't thought for one minute they would get away without being spotted. It had even got to the point where they were both shivering so violently that they barely cared about being caught, as at least if they were intercepted, they would have got a night or two in a warmer cell before they were executed for the false crime they had been accused of.

Despite the hyperthermia, Jake recalled the moment of disbelief as they had steered the rowing boat around the northern arm of New Hivetha's harbour and moved out of sight of the port. They had then rowed ashore, three hours later, three leagues further up the coast, just before the prominent headland that marked the eastern-most point of Glennad. Their options, though, had been limited. Getting a boat to Lendria was now a non-starter, while the coastal road was overrun with soldiers. That left only one option; the option already taken by Harry – even though reinforcements would soon be heading that way to try and take him. More importantly, Emilya and Elyse were taking refuge in the middle of the Umbrican Mountains, and Jake feared that Magnus would now be sending troops there just to rule out Harry, himself or Swede seeking sanctuary at the monastery. One way or another, they had made a right old mess of things, and the constant worry that troops would descend on the monastery, and both find and arrest Elyse and Emilya, was forever eating away at him. Jake was fully reconciled to the fact that, should he get wind of such an arrest, he would be handing himself in and absolving Elyse and Emilya of all responsibility.

It had been four days after seeking refuge in the mountains that Harry Black had found them. Jake and Swede had been forced to take shelter in a cave high above a mountain pass some twelve leagues north-west of New Hivetha, as Swede had taken ill. The symptoms had started the day after their escape from the bay, with uncontrolled shaking. By the second day, he had developed a rattle in his chest, and by the third day, he was coughing uncontrollably. Jake had found the cave, and had even risked starting a fire to try and keep Swede warm, but when Harry found them, Swede was too weak to even sit up. Harry had guided Jake out of the cave. "You know he's done for, don't you?"

"Aye," Jake had replied. "Chronic pneumonia. I'm just trying to do my best for him."

"The best for him and, more particularly, for us, is to put him out of his misery," Harry had said, tapping his holstered pistol.

"I can't do that Harry," Jake had said.

"I've known him a lot longer than you," Harry had come back with.

"I'll not do it, Harry. In any case, we can't afford to discharge a bullet. There may be troops in the vicinity."

"That's true," Black had agreed. "But we have knives, too."

They were saved having to make that decision during the following night, when Swede began to drown on the fluid in his own lungs. At 02:40 in the morning, they had been holding a hand apiece when he had passed away. With nowhere fit for a burial, they had left him in that cave – either for Magnus' troops to find or a pack of mountain wolves. Having remained awake until first light, they had then begun to put distance between themselves and the cave, heading in a north-westerly direction, determined to traverse the entire mountain range a good fifteen leagues to the north of Kifsel Place, their logic being that if they were spotted, it would at least draw the pursuit away from the monastery.

After twelve long days in the mountains, they had finally begun to descend towards the plains of north-eastern Glennad, with a plan to cross them disguised as cattle-herders. This would enable them to avoid the main inland settlements as well as the big coastal settlements of Merroc and Kinnslyng, instead targeting the treacherous marshlands between the two. Assuming there was no news of Elyse or Emilya's capture, Jake's plan was to cross the Giant's Channel and then lose themselves in the Forest of Viperollo. It was a route and destination that would be way down on Prince Magnus' guess list, and it also gave them half a chance of being able to slip away from Glennad via the country's third-largest port at Viperollo, or perhaps from nearby Hedenbrika.

"Exactly fifty hours, Harry," said Jake.

"Since we last saw troops?"

"Aye."

"It was a good plan, Jake. Hugging the north-eastern fringe."

"Aye, but I still fear the reason for the low number of troops here, lies at Kifsel Place."

Harry Black patted Jake on the back. "There's nothing you can do about it, my friend. And in any case, if Prince Magnus and his men raid the monastery, they will only be looking for you and I."

"I hope so," said Jake, wearily.

"And even if they *do* find them there, what are they going to charge them with? The only thing either of them has done, is that Emilya injured a dog – in self-defence. Take it from me, Jake. If the Princess Alicya is genuinely missing, or even dead, Prince Magnus will have a lot more to worry about than hunting down a fifteen-year-old baker's daughter and a middle-aged lady healer. And if he is stupid enough to accuse said fifteen year-old baker's daughter of abducting a princess of Glennad, he'll get laughed out of his own court! So, let's face the facts, Jake: if Alicya really is dead, and he did it himself, the only result he needs is arresting you and I and executing us for his own heinous crime."

"Exactly," said Jake. "Which is why if he finds Emilya and Elyse at Kifsel Place, he will use them to smoke us out."

"Well, if he does, we'll have to reassess."

"I will never put myself before either of them."

Harry Black stopped in his tracks, forcing Jake to stop, too. He looked Jake in the eye – a man who had told a thousand lies in his disreputable career. "And neither will I, my friend. Neither will I."

Jake looked back at Harry Black, almost convinced the man meant what he said. Maybe even Harry, himself, was convinced. The truth was, Harry Black didn't need to give himself up as well. Magnus only needed one man to confess to murdering his sister. In the end, Jake just nodded once, and they carried on heading downhill.

"Of course," continued Harry. "Given our proposed route, our problem is going to be finding out what's going on – as we'll not hit civilisation again until Viperollo."

"I do a passable accent of a north-eastern farm-worker," drawled Jake. Harry laughed at that. "But seriously," continued Jake. "With this being a national incident, even folks out here should be relatively up-to-date." He then stopped and pointed at a farmstead nestling in the valley they were descending towards. Both sheep and cows were visible in the fields around it. "I think we've found our livestock, Harry."

"Aye, there they are," he agreed. "Are you still insisting on reimbursing them?" he asked, with distaste.

"I am."

"Won't you reconsider? Or at least consider reimbursing them several years down the line?"

"Nope."

Harry Black stopped walking. "Listen, mate," he began. Jake stopped and turned around to see Harry giving him his most earnest of looks. "I get that you're an honest bloke and all that, and I've forced myself to compromise, so far. But pushing large sums of money under the front door the same night that a number of their cattle goes missing, is just going to get noticed, matey. At a high level."

Jake sighed. He knew Harry was right.

"They'll know we've been here; they'll draw a line from New Hivetha to the plains, and will likely work out what our plan is. It's much better that this appears like a standard case of cattle rustling. You know that, very well, don't you?"

Jake looked at Black for a long time, then shook his head. "This is why you've never been caught, isn't it?"

Harry Black gave him his widest smile. "Good man, Jake. You know it makes sense!"

Alas, twenty minutes later, as they wound their way down a remote path, their plan was rendered redundant. They could see three small villages on the plains below – one to the south, one to the north and another dead ahead to the west – and all three were completely overrun with red and white-liveried soldiers.

CHAPTER 128 EMILYA

45th Tertiar, 1789   Day 136, 20:00

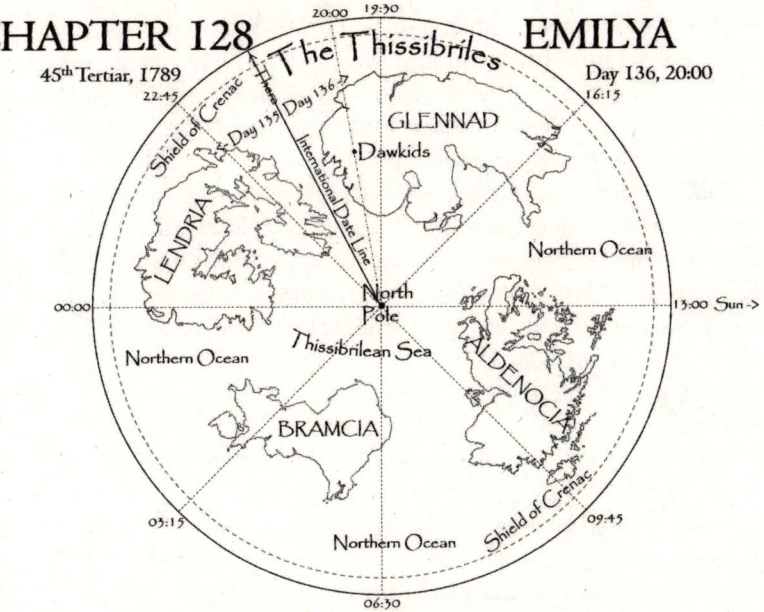

Emilya and Elyse were playing their seventh game of Shield, under the watchful tutelage of Brother Clarence. A strategy board game, the aim was to defend the Thissibriles against the Theran aggressors, one player assuming the role of the defenders and the other that of the attackers. So far, Emilya had won five out of the six games, three as the defender and two as the aggressor. Now, playing the role of the Theran aggressor for the third time, she was closing in on victory number six.

The board was circular, looking down on the top of the world, with the North Pole at its centre and the four islands of the Thissibriles ranged around it. A dotted line encircled the Thissibriles, representing the Shield of Crenac, whilst at the outer edges of the circular board, was the continuous northern coastline of Epanaga. The aim for the aggressor was to find weak points along the Shield, which changed location with each game according to pre-selected coordinates, and were found by a process of elimination. Ideally, the aggressor would have already manoeuvred their galleys into position to take advantage of the pending breaches, whilst the defender should have already aligned defensive forces.

Forces were represented by platoon or legionary counters and warship or galley counters, which moved across hundreds of small circles that made up the map, depending upon the throw of a dice. Alongside this, players carried out actions when landing on certain circles following the drawing of the next Action Card. Naturally, when landing on an opponent's circle, aggressor counters took defender counters and vice-versa. The game ended when the Grand Sovereign of the Thissibriles was taken, or the Therans were forced into retreat beyond the Shield.

Concentrating hard, Emilya watched Elyse make a fatal mistake, moving a counter for the final platoon of Glennadian soldiers to within striking distance of one of her legions who had already invaded southern Glennad. All she needed was to throw a six – and she duly did, feeling a tiny surge of savagery as she claimed Elyse's final platoon, leaving Elyse's Grand Sovereign wide open.

"Well played again, Miss Emilya," said Brother Clarence, clapping excitedly.

"Huh!" was all Elyse could manage. "I'm far too refined for the barbarity of war," she added.

Brother Clarence stood. "I'll go and warm some wine for a night-cap."

"Hmm, good idea," said Elyse.

Emilya also stood and began to stretch. "I'm exhausted," she said. "But at least tomorrow morning, we don't have to get up at five -."

She broke off as there was a knock at the door. Emilya and Elyse immediately froze, looking at each other in alarm. Brother Clarence was about to move over to the door, when it opened inwards. Three soldiers were framed in the doorway, each holding a musket.

"Don't be alarmed," said the tall man at the front, clearly their leader, and in the uniform of a captain. Despite her shock, Emilya noticed a rather fine handlebar moustache. The man raised his free hand in a placatory gesture. "We're not here to hurt anyone."

"Then why *are* you here?" asked Brother Clarence, the first of the three occupants to recover from shock.

"We have orders to search for two ladies – two ladies who match your descriptions," the captain said, nodding at Emilya and Elyse.

"On whose orders?"

The leader moved into the base-camp lodge and indicated his two fellow soldiers should follow. The last man closed the door behind him. "I suspect the ladies already know on whose orders, Brother, erm…"

"Brother Clarence."

"Ladies?" asked the captain, his eyebrows raised. Emilya noted that his moustache rose slightly, as well. Neither she nor Elyse responded, so the captain turned to Brother Clarence. "If you don't mind me asking, Brother

Clarence, why are you here, on your own, with two ladies who have been visiting your monastery?"

"Brother Clarence's shoulders drooped. "I suspect you know why. There's really no point in us trying to explain, is there?"

"Not really, Brother Clarence, no. Forgive me, ladies, but I have orders to escort you back to Ghantiss, starting first light tomorrow. You are free to circulate within this lodge, but please don't think of trying to escape. One of us will be on watch throughout the night, so I suggest you get a good night's sleep. We have a long journey ahead of us."

"I don't suppose you'd care to hear our side of the story?" asked Elyse.

"I am a soldier, madam, not a judge or member of a jury. I undertake orders. And my orders are to take you to the palace at Ghantiss."

"Why?" asked Elyse, simply.

"It wasn't for me to ask Prince Magnus why?"

"Well, why were you in these mountains then?"

"We are searching for the kidnappers of the Princess Alicya."

"Well, congratulations!" said Emilya, sarcastically. "You've been walking around these mountains *with* the kidnapper of Princess Alicya for the last three or four days. Why didn't you ask *him* where she is?"

The captain looked confused. "But we haven't seen either Jake Oscom or Harry Black."

"Jake Oscom was with us when the Princess Alicya disappeared," said Elyse.

The captain frowned. "Are you saying that *you* were involved in the kidnapping?"

"No -." Elyse rolled her eyes. "Sorry, what is your name, Captain?"

"Captain Potts, madam. This is Private Furness," he said, indicating a stocky young man in his early twenties with brown hair, "and this is Private Rydal," he added, indicating another young soldier, this one ginger with a friendly face full of freckles.

"Well, no, Captain Potts. We were no more involved in the kidnapping – if such an event has even happened – than either Jake Oscom or Harry Black – or you or Private Furness, here, for that matter. Jake Oscom was with us on the road to Ghenetenos on the 5th Tertiar."

Potts initially looked even more confused, but then the fog lifted from his eyes. "But if you two had no involvement in the kidnapping, why are you hiding up here in the mountains?"

"We're not hiding," said Emilya. "We're just returning from the expedition of a lifetime."

"Then why were you not with the rest of the expedition party?"

"I was sick, earlier today," said Elyse. "And Brother Clarence here agreed to keep an eye on me."

"Ladies, please," said Captain Potts. "I may only follow orders, but it is quite clear to me that you have been taking evasive action. And Brother Clarence here, was at the monastery two days ago, so he *certainly* didn't come down from Dawkids with you. Your best course of action is to comply with Prince Magnus' instructions and, if you are innocent of any crimes, the magistrates in Ghantiss will ensure that justice is served."

Emilya and Elyse began simultaneously scoffing at that statement, but Potts cut through their objections. "All right, that's quite enough. There will be plenty of opportunity for you to talk to me on our long journey back. Not that anything you say will detract me from my duty. Now, Brother Clarence, we have walked a long way and we were rather hoping you might be able to provide us with some food and drink."

Brother Clarence shook his head, sadly. "Captain Potts, you seem like a nice fellow, and I will gladly serve you food and drink. But I fear you are aligning yourself to the wrong cause."

"I take orders from the army and from a royal family that has the best interests of our country at heart."

"Or the best interests of themselves in Prince Magnus' case," said Emilya, huffily.

"All right, that's quite enough, young lady," said Potts. "Prince Magnus is distraught at the disappearance of his sister. Why would you ever suggest such a thing?"

Emilya opened her mouth to fire off another insult, but was stopped by a warning glance from Elyse. "Oh, I'm going to bed," she said, before walking away huffily, and throwing herself down onto a random mattress in the dormitory. But as she lay there, listening to the murmured conversations between the soldiers, Elyse and Brother Clarence, her mind was in overdrive. For starters, there was around one hundred leagues between here and Ghantiss with only a three-soldier escort. This certainly wasn't over yet.

CHAPTER 129 — ALICYA

1st Quarternar, 1789   Day 137, 12:00

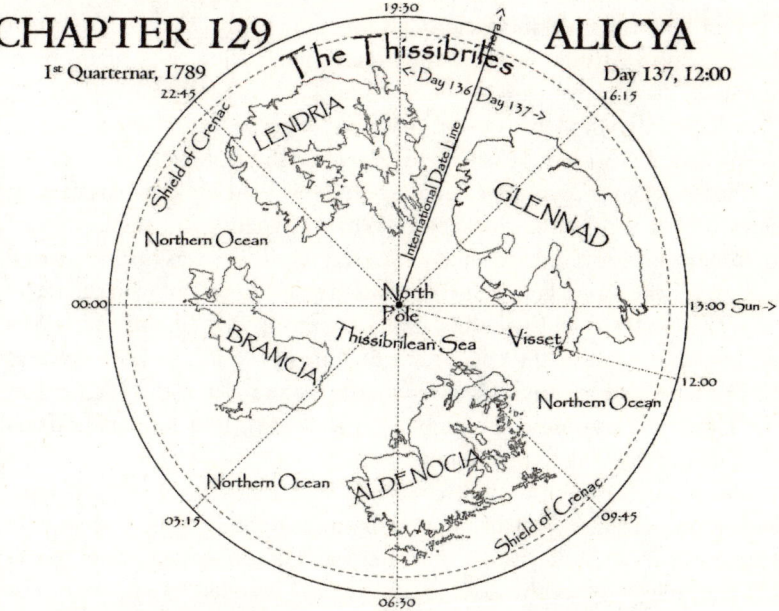

There was another dreaded knock at the door. Seconds earlier, Alicya had been sitting alone in Gawain's home and feeling miserable, knowing her lover was already residing in Pannezec Gaol, eight leagues west of here and beginning his two-year sentence for illegally exhuming corpses.

Alicya stood and wrung her hands – but the knocking came again – much louder and more impatient, this time. Fearing for Gawain's front door, Alicya moved warily out of the lounge and into the hallway. She immediately saw more than one shadow through the frosted glass semi-circle at the top of the front door. Her heart began pumping ever-faster.

Steeling herself, Alicya turned the key in the lock and opened the door. Facing her were several officers from the local militia along with a dour-faced magistrate called Raines whom she had met, briefly, at the ball at Visset Manor. A few paces back, she saw the wretched and smirking Ashlyn Douglas.

"Alyona Piran?" asked Magistrate Raines. The greying, thick-set magistrate also had a grim cast to his grey eyes.

"Yes?"

"Alyona Piran. You are under arrest for impersonating another, with the intention of disinheriting. Please get your coat and lock up the house."

"But I don't understand. Why would you think -."

She broke off as she saw Ashlyn step forward, two officials moving aside to reveal her still-smirking face. "Gawain Piran doesn't have a cousin in Ghantiss called Alyona. I went to the trouble of checking. So, you, my dear, are not who you say you are."

"Ask Gawain who I am. Go on. Ask him."

"Well, unfortunately, he isn't here," replied Ashlyn, sweetly.

"Please get your coat," repeated Raines. "Now." The look on his face sent Alicya on her way to the cloakroom. What alternative did she have? She would have time to think on what to do next whilst she was being escorted to wherever they were going. She still had the card to play of who she really was – that really would wipe that irritating smirk off Ashlyn's face. Alas, that would also mean the end of her dreams of a quiet life as a country doctor's wife, and goodness knows what for Gawain and the Glennadian royal family. All considered, thought Alicya, avoiding that combination was probably worth going to prison for.

Alicya put her thick sable cloak on, not knowing how cold their destination was going to be, but with unpleasant images of cells and dungeons and rats skittering through her mind. She also said a brief prayer for Vixey, relieved that the fox-cub had already reverted to nature and the woods behind Gawain's apartment, before pocketing the front door key. She then stepped outside and pulled the door shut. Two of the local militia went to grab an elbow each, but she shrugged them both off. "There's no need for that. I'm not going to run off."

"Very well, miss," said Magistrate Raines. "Please come with us." They were about to set off across the road, and had drawn level with Ashlyn on the path just inside Gawain's low front garden wall, when Raines turned to her. "Not you, miss," he said to Ashlyn, who had turned to walk with them. "You've played your part. The rest is now up to the authorities."

"Very well," agreed Ashlyn, rather truculently. "But make sure you lock this charlatan up," she sneered, looking Alicya up and down with disdain. "Who knows who she may target next, if you let her go free?"

It wasn't the words that made Alicya snap or their ludicrous insinuation. It was the reappearance of that hated smirk. Before she could stop herself, Alicya had brought the palm of her hand up and, with a savage whiplash, had landed the heftiest slap to Ashlyn's left cheek that her physique could deliver. The *crack* echoed audibly around the street, while Alicya had put so much hate and frustration into that one action that the blow actually knocked Ashlyn clean off her feet and into a set of rose bushes.

This time, the two militia did grab Alicya by an arm each to restrain her. Far from being ashamed, Alicya felt a moment of sheer elation. "Ha!" she vented, as she observed her hated tormentor with triumph. Conversely, Ashlyn had lost her cool and dignity, and was showing her true colours. As she staggered to her feet, her expensive woollen coat snagged on some rose thorns and tore open when Ashlyn tried to forcefully release it. It eventually ripped free. Now standing, Ashlyn's face was bright red with fury and her lip was cut on the left side, dripping with blood where the nail of Alicya's thumb had also raked her. *And if the Gods were good, she'd be sporting a purple cheek for the next couple of days.* "That was assault!" she spat at Raines, before her dark eyes bored into Alicya's. "I want her charged with assault as well."

"Fine," said Alicya. "Guilty as charged, and with plenty of witnesses. But I'll still be marrying Gawain, Ashlyn. One day in the future. And you'll still be a sad, empty and pathetic *husk*."

Ashlyn's eyes went wild for a second. Alicya had hit the right nerve.

"All right, that's quite enough of that," commanded Raines. "How very undignified. Miss Douglas, I suggest you run along home. We shall take care of the prisoner from herein. And rest assured, she will indeed be charged with assault, too," he said, giving Alicya his sternest frown.

"Make sure you send her to Quenway for at least ten years, Mr Raines. She's a dangerous woman," she finished, whilst tenderly holding the side of her face.

Alicya laughed aloud at that. She couldn't help herself. She was essentially a gentle soul and 'dangerous' was the most ludicrous of accusations to be levelled at her. Nevertheless, she could not rid herself of the sensation of just how *good* that slap had felt."

CHAPTER 130 — EMILYA

2nd Quarternar, 1789 — Day 138, 21:15

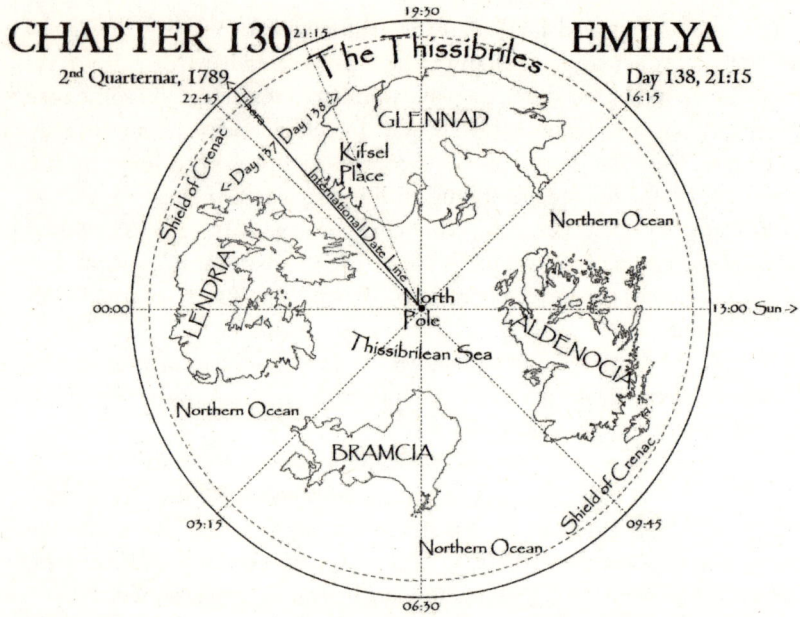

Emilya recognised the peak to her right, even though dusk was falling, while the bright star they had followed back to Dawkids basecamp two nights ago was now to the right of the peak in the north-east night sky. They were finally traversing the gorge which led up to Kifsel Place – and not an hour too soon. It had been a difficult journey due to the previous day's deluge of rain which had kept them pinned down in their Dawkids basecamp lodge for an extra twenty-six hours. With slippery rocks and grassy paths turned to sludge, Captain Potts had soon realised that his back-pack-clad prisoners would find it impossible to travel safely across the treacherous ground with their hands bound. Even with hands free, their passage had been slow. When the outskirts of Kifsel Place village finally came into view, Brother Clarence turned to Captain Potts. "Will you be staying at the monastery again, Captain?" he asked.

"I don't think that would be appropriate, Brother Clarence. I shall book myself, my two men and our two prisoners into the tavern in the village."

Prisoners! Emilya could still scarcely take that word in.

"Assuming they have rooms," Brother Clarence was saying.

"If they don't, then we shall use their stables," responded the Captain.

"You do realise that I shall report everything to the abbot, don't you?"

"You can report whatever you like, Brother Clarence. But I would advise against interference. These two ladies are prisoners of the Crown. Any attempt to interfere will result in repercussions. Indeed, Prince Magnus has the power to close your monastery down, if he so wishes."

"He'd do that? Dissolve our monastery."

"I didn't use the word 'dissolve', Brother Clarence. But theoretically, he could do that."

"Well, I suspect that you shall have at the very least, a protest in person from the abbot."

"In which case, he will be wasting his time and energy," said the po-faced captain.

Before he left for the monastery, Brother Clarence took Emilya's hands in his. "Be strong, Miss Emilya," he began, which made Emilya fill up. "And let God be your guide. You have done nothing wrong and no harm shall come to you. And Miss Elyse," he said, now taking Elyse's hands. "The same applies to you, my dear. These charges are preposterous, unfounded and based on lies," he added, darting a meaningful glance at Captain Potts. The look wasn't lost upon the Captain, and caused his handlebar moustache to twitch with discomfort.

"Goodbye Captain Potts, Private Furness, Private Rydal. I wish you a safe journey back to Ghantiss, and please take good care of your charges."

"On that, you can rely, Brother Clarence," responded Potts.

With his goodbyes said, Brother Clarence turned around and began to shuffle along the narrow path to the monastery. Emilya watched him go, wistfully, wondering if she would ever see the kindly monk again.

"Right, come along you two," said Potts, guiding them along the main path towards Kifsel Place's only tavern. As soon as they entered the place, Emilya recalled the sullen manner of the innkeeper and his wife. "Do you have lodgings for five persons, good innkeeper?" asked Potts – rather pompously, thought Emilya.

The middle-aged innkeeper approached them and Emilya noted that his grey, probably once-white apron had even more stains on it than before. He scratched his curly brown hair and then scratched his bushy beard. Emilya shuddered, wondering what creatures lived in there. "We have rooms, Captain," the innkeeper responded, having noticed Potts' insignia. "But no mixing, if you don't mind."

Potts looked momentarily confused, then the penny dropped. "There won't be any of that business, I can assure you. The two ladies are my prisoners, but I insist on one of my men being allowed to guard them."

The innkeeper regarded Potts through narrowed eyes. "All right," he agreed, slowly. "I suppose I can make an exception for the army."

"Good man," said Potts.

The innkeeper's wife approached them with two keys. Emilya noticed that her hair was still tucked into a grubby coif and the rest of her upper body still covered by a thick brown shawl. Without any hint of emotion, she asked the party to follow her across the common room and through a door at the back. "We've plenty of rooms, actually, Captain," she said, "as all of them doing that expedition have gone home now. So, you can have these two rooms on the ground floor," she said, putting the key into the first room and turning it.

An hour later, Emilya and Elyse had been allowed to change their clothing and the five of them were seated around a table with steaming bowls of leek and potato soup in front of them. Unsurprisingly, the conversation was sparse and stilted. However, when the innkeeper's wife came to collect their empty bowls, Elyse asked a question that had clearly been on her mind. "What happened to Big Bess, if you don't mind me asking?"

The innkeeper's wife stopped dead, and Emilya noticed her eyes dart before recovering her composure. "No one knows, miss," she replied. "One day she was here running the inn, the next day she'd vanished."

The innkeeper sauntered over to join them. "They reckon she'd got into debt," he added, scratching his beard again. "Tried to make us pay her last month of rent, they did."

"Who's 'they'?" asked Elyse.

"The authorities at Earl's Leet. It's them as owns this inn."

"So, you think she ran off to avoid paying her debts, then?"

"That's what the authorities reckon. There's still a warrant out for her arrest, but she's never been found. I reckon she did a runner to Lendria, as that's where she came from."

"That's what them monks reckoned as well, if you recall," the innkeeper's wife said to her husband.

The innkeeper shot her a look of pure venom, as if to say *'shut your mouth, woman'*.

Emilya and Elyse were immediately intrigued. "What monks?" they both asked, in unison.

"I don't know their names," said the innkeeper's wife, now trying to cover her tracks. "And they all look the same to me."

Mentally picturing Brother Cyrus and Brother Obadiah, Emilya acted on instinct. "They didn't include a middle-aged monk, did they? Receded dark hair, unusual goatee beard for a monk, and very dark eyes?"

"Or another with a large forehead and pockmarked cheeks?" added Elyse.

"None of 'em looked like that," said the innkeeper's wife, and abruptly turned away and headed back to the kitchens. Once the innkeeper followed her, Elyse leaned in to Emilya. "Pretty sure that was a lie."

"Why is this of significance to you, if you don't mind me asking?" questioned Captain Potts.

Elyse turned to regard the strait-laced Captain and paused before replying. "They were just very unpleasant, that's all," she said, eventually. "Not warm-hearted like most of the other monks. And Brother Obadiah had a serious problem with his right hand."

"I know the man," said Potts. "We spoke to him during our time at the monastery. I didn't notice anything wrong with his hand, miss."

"That's because you're a man, Captain," was Elyse's response – a comment that left the frowning captain none-the-wiser.

CHAPTER 131   WILL

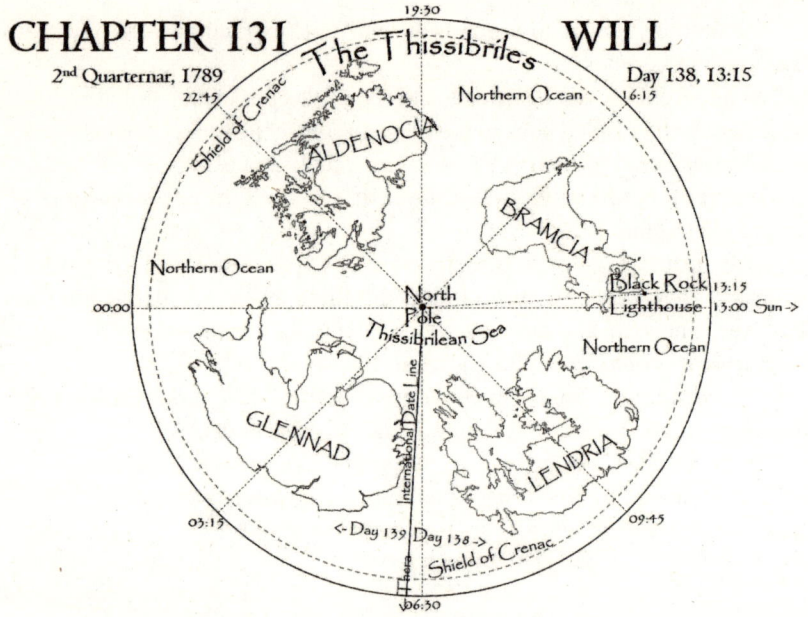

Even for Will, the novelty of living in a lighthouse was beginning to wear off after ten days of being holed up in one. Not that he could have enjoyed it much, anyway, given the terrible circumstances which had led to them taking up residence, and which had been followed by a permanent siege. They had been hopeful that, having lost access to the lighthouse, the smugglers would just give up and leave. But they hadn't. Their reasons weren't too difficult to work out. The four survivors in the lighthouse were witnesses to the cold-blooded murder of Matt and Tom's parents, for starters. Matt and Nate had also shot dead four of their colleagues, so no doubt they wanted revenge for that. But most of all, the smugglers still wanted the lighthouse for themselves so that they could put their delayed plan into action. No doubt they thought that all they had to do was wait until the four of them were either overrun after letting their guard down, or were starved into submission.

Worst of all was the distress of Matt and Tom at being unable to recover their Mam's body. They had been distraught at the thought that she would be taken out to sea, but the day after they had secured the lighthouse, the callous smugglers had dragged Kyra's body up the beach and used her as musket target practice – presumably in an attempt to goad the boys out of the lighthouse. It had very nearly worked, too. Will's eyes filled up as he recalled his desperate pleading with Matt to not exit the lighthouse, and the distress and wrath from the older brother that had followed. In the end, when Matt had somehow managed to reconcile what had happened, he had concluded that at least he and Tom would have two bodies to bury, if they ever got out of this nightmare.

Will didn't dare think what state poor Kyra's body would be in. And she was one of the kindest people he had ever met. *How could this happen?* Will felt emotions stirring inside that he had never felt before.

Today, Matt and Tom were fearing the worst for the Company man, who arrived once per month with post, supplies and a known shipping schedule for the following month – particularly if it was Old Jack whom they had known all their lives. Now in his seventies, the kindly Old Jack had more-or-less handed over to his son, Young Jack – although, as Matt had pointed out, Young Jack himself was now forty. Whoever showed up, though, the smugglers were scarce likely to let them live, once the visitor realised that the regular lighthouse family was no longer incumbent.

Will was looking out of the sea-facing window on the sixth floor, deep in thought. Choppy seas were just about all he could see, although he could just see the cliffs that marked the northern extreme of Black Rock Bay, and the white surf hurling itself against them. Will sighed. The events of ten days ago would remain etched in his memory as vividly as those at Cabrenar Colliery, last month; new and vivid memories of death, which he'd been spared at Cabrenar thanks to his temporary blindness.

They had found Eric, Matt and Tom's father, in the lantern room. He had been shot twice, but it was the bayonet through his heart that had killed him. "Dad," Matt had said, in a cracked voice. He had then fallen to the floor alongside his father. "Dad," he had repeated, over and over.

Will's eyes watered at the memory, and then he wondered if his Mam had done the same with Dylan's body? Had they even *found* Dylan's body? Oh, how Will yearned for the relative safety and routine of pulling a truck-load of coal through the mine.

Will's thoughts then moved on to Nate Turner. Nate had shown him nothing but parental care over these last few weeks – and yet the person he had known as his Da had died ten years ago, when Will was only two. He couldn't remember anything about him. But one day, he would return to his Mam. He hoped that would be with Nate, and that his Mam would tell him the truth.

Of course, that required they survive the current crisis. Nate had not been the healthiest of men before the running battle ten days ago, thanks to thirty years down a coal mine. But it wasn't his chest that was giving him the most discomfort. They had used the lighthouse medical kit to extract the musket balls from Matt's shoulder and Nate's bicep. That responsibility had fallen to himself and Tom. They had operated on Matt's shoulder first, with Nate providing instruction. First, they had given Matt a few healthy tots of rum from the lighthouse stores. They had then used a lit candle to heat up a surgical knife, while several other candles had provided flickering, but far-from-ideal light. Nate had then studied Matt's wound as best he could. "You don't want to cut any veins, boys."

"What do they look like?" Will had asked.

Nate hadn't answered the question. "I don't see any," he had replied. "But I do see the bullet. See, there," he had said, gently prying open Matt's wound and pointing to the dark head of the lead musket ball amongst the mess of Matt's deltoid. "Thankfully, it's in a fleshy part of his shoulder and doesn't appear to have reached the bone. You need to slowly insert the blade to the right-hand side, and then pry it out. Gently."

Tom had originally been given the knife as it was his brother. But his hand had shook so much, that Will had taken over. Will would never forget the moment his knife had first touched flesh. Matt had winced and shut his eyes, but he hadn't cried out. Once again, Will was in awe of the older brother's bravery. Will had then pushed the knife in further, and again recalled the sensation of that fleshy resistance, while the knife had caused further blood-gushing. He had also felt the ungiving resistance of the musket ball against the left-hand face of his knife. Matt had gasped, but still hadn't cried out. And then, the knife had sunk beneath the back of the musket ball and, as instructed, Will had eased it gently upwards and out. It had finally emerged with a wet *plop*.

Matt had slumped forwards in total relief, but had still managed to raise his head and smile at Will amid his tears of pain. "Thank you, Will."

Nate's bullet removal had been more complicated. It was embedded in muscle which was harder to dig out and there had been a lot more blood. The bullet was larger than the one he had just extracted from Matt, too. Poor Nate had even cried out as the knife kept sinking deeper, and the whole extraction process had taken all of thirty-five horrible minutes.

Since then, Matt's wound had healed nicely, but it had become apparent within three days that Nate's wasn't following suit. The whole area around the wound was an angry red, and getting redder by the day, whilst the hole made by the bullet and the subsequent extraction was crusting over with a yellowy-green hue. They had put wine in it, hoping the alcohol would help cleanse the wound, but nothing seemed to stop the redness and general gunk, and now it was oozing puss, too. Matt's fear was that Nate was suffering from lead poisoning and a severe infection. Will saw great concern in the older boy's eyes, and wondered if Matt feared that a worse operation might be called for.

Will shook his head to clear the memory, but immediately recalled their next grim task on that dreadful night: poor Matt and Tom's father. With Nate unable to move Eric on his own because of his wound, the four of them, including a catatonic Tom, had had to carry Eric's stiff body down six flights of winding stairs to the engine room on the ground floor of the lighthouse. Will had soon understood what was meant by a dead weight, while the constant twisting descent just added to the ordeal. Unfortunately, the engine room, with its two coal-burning engines that generated heat for the rest of the lighthouse, was the only practical place to put him – despite the heat being likely to accelerate decomposition. They had then conducted a bizarre service for Eric, with Nate attempting to perform the role of the priest, and Matt saying a few words about his Da. All Will could remember was both of them slurring their words, and some sentences being incomprehensible thanks to a cocktail of alcohol, grief and pain. They had then laid Eric to rest and covered his form with a blanket, with Matt swearing that they would soon perform proper burials for both his Da and his Mam – assuming the smugglers left poor Kyra's body be. Since then, they had remained on constant guard, with six and a half hour watches apiece rotating between the four of them.

The first raid had occurred the second night. There had been a couple of aborted attempts by the smugglers during the previous day to approach the lighthouse, but Matt had repelled them with the long-range musket that had belonged to his parents, sending at least one of their foes to their own appointment with a heated scalpel. The night-time attack had happened on Tom's watch, when the tide was out, but Will's new friend had not been found wanting. Tom's eagle eyes had picked out movement at the base of the structure, and before the group of five or six smugglers had had the opportunity to deploy their newly-constructed battering ram on the only entrance to the lighthouse, Tom had raised the alert. Seconds later, Matt and Nate had been lying face-down on the balcony outside the lamp room, pointing their muskets straight down. Despite their injuries and immense discomfort, it had been easy pickings. One of the dead bodies was still on Black Rock even now; the other two had been washed away.

The smugglers hadn't attempted the battering ram approach again. They had, however, shot most of the glass out of the lantern room when, a couple of nights later, they had stood on the shoreline eighty yards away and used it as target practice. That attack had also been met with brave return fire from Matt and Nate amidst the flying musket balls and glass. So far, the ability to return fire from a well-defended and elevated position had prevented the enormous candle and oil-based candelabra lantern itself from being disabled.

Today, Matt was certain the Company man was due, and so Matt was up in the lantern room, armed and on the lookout. Will decided to climb the wooden ladder to see if Matt had any news. As ever when emerging into the lantern room, Will looked in awe at the vast candelabra hanging from its sturdy iron hood, surrounded by now largely-shattered glass and the hood's metal framework. Given it was midday, none of the candles were lit, but it was still an impressive sight: an inner iron circle holding eight long candles, centre circle holding sixteen and an outer circle holding thirty-two smaller ones. And in the centre, was the great wick-and-oil-based flame that worked, in principle, similar to his old miner's lamp. At night, the combined light was so bright that you had to look away from it, particularly when re-lighting extinguished candles or replacing spent ones.

"Good afternoon, Will," said Matt, without looking backwards.

"How did you know it was me?"

"All three of you have very different approaches. Your Da wheezes, and now he moans at his bad arm, plus he has a much heavier tread on the stairs. Tom comes up the ladder faster than you."

"Tom's still fast asleep, by the way. As is my Da. I think I'd better relieve you later this afternoon, Matt. Da is getting weaker."

Matt turned to look at Will. "I know he is, Will. I can't say I'm not concerned."

"You still think it's the lead?"

"Lead's poisonous, Will. I'm worried it's got into his bloodstream. And as for his arm…"

"What will happen?" asked Will, fearfully.

"If he gets any worse, we'll need to get him to Aerasimbu Infirmary." Matt saw Will's look. "Aye, I know. How? Maybe today's the day the smugglers finally give up. Maybe the Company man will visit, realise something's wrong, and come back with the militia. I don't know, Will."

"What does he look like, the Company man?"

"It depends if it's Old Jack, Young Jack or someone else."

"Do they not wear a uniform, then?"

"No, they're just regular blokes, dressed in regular clothes – whatever's appropriate for the weather and time of year."

"What are the smugglers doing at the moment?" asked Will, going down on his knees and then lying flat besides Matt.

"The only one outside at the moment is Horse. Pig and Sheep were with him until around ten minutes ago, but they went inside our house. Horse is over there, look, hiding behind that cliff strut."

Will followed Matt's pointing finger to where a long stretch of cliff to the north of the cottage came down at an acute angle, meaning it was possible to hide on the south side of it and not be visible from the inbound path. There, in dark clothing against the dark rock, was a man in his late twenties, his dark-brown, shoulder-length mane blowing in the wind. Meanwhile, Pig had been so-named because he had a big, round, pink face and very little hair, whilst Sheep had acquired his name courtesy of the long woolly coat he sported. Other regulars included Donkey (because he had big ears), Camel (because he had a bit of a hunchback) and Hawk (because he was constantly looking everywhere when on duty).

Will watched Horse for a while, but he was doing nothing other than watching the inbound path, and so Will's attention was soon distracted by the great waves crashing against the rocks all around the little bay – until Matt suddenly went taut and grabbed his arm. A middle-aged man in a grey-blue greatcoat was striding purposefully down the north path, wearing a back-pack and carrying a battered carpet bag. "Young Jack!" exclaimed Matt. "Get back, Jack," he whispered. "Get back, man."

But still Young Jack kept on coming, oblivious to the danger. "We need to warn him!" cried Will. "Maybe shoot your musket, once."

"Just a moment," said Matt, holding up his hand, his eyes narrowed. "There's something odd here."

"What do you mean? Matt, Horse is going to kill Young Jack."

"If he is, then why has he not unslung his musket?"

Will looked closely. All Horse was doing was peering around the edge of the cliff. Matt was right. This was odd. And sure enough, when Young Jack drew level with Horse, all Horse did was to jump out on Young Jack, making the latter stumble with shock and end up flat on his backside. But instead of accosting Young Jack, all Horse did was issue a great long belly-laugh, which carried to them belatedly on the wind.

Will then watched Young Jack get to his feet and remonstrate with Horse, which made Horse laugh even louder. The two of them were soon joined by Pig, Camel and Hawk. Will braced himself to bear witness to yet another death…but inexplicably, Hawk went right up to Young Jack who put down his battered carpet bag and then took the proffered hand and shook it. Pig and Camel followed suit.

"What's happening, Matt?" asked Will, confused.

"It's bloody obvious, isn't it?" answered Matt, bitterly. "Young Jack's in on this."

"The man from the Company is siding with smugglers?"

"Aye, it's not as uncommon as you might think."

"But he knew your Mam and Da!"

"Aye, he got several drinks and a hot meal out of me Mam, every time he came," said Matt with disgust. "I can't believe Old Jack would be in on this, though. But I never liked Young Jack as much. There was always something about him…"

As they watched, they saw that Pig was talking animatedly. He then began gesticulating towards the lighthouse and miming the action of shooting a gun. It was abundantly clear that Young Jack wasn't impressed. He was now berating all of them in a very animated way.

Matt whistled. "He's their damn leader, isn't he?"

"It certainly looks that way," agreed Will. "What a beastly, nasty man."

Matt laughed at that.

"What?" asked Will.

"You have such a polite way with words, Will. I was thinking along the same lines, but my words were a bit stronger than yours."

"My Mam hated swearing. If either me or Dylan were ever caught swearing, she used to belt us on the backside with a slipper."

Young Jack was now staring at the lighthouse. "Can he see us, Matt?"

"He might be able make us out, aye. I must confess, I'm tempted to have a pop at him, too – but he's almost certainly out of range, and we need to save the ammunition for when they launch their next attack. I'm afraid we're running low, Will. And they probably suspect that."

"Hopefully, Young Jack will decide to call off the siege."

Matt turned to look at Will, initially with raised eyebrows. He then ruffled Will's hair when he saw the hope in his face. "I'll say this for you, Will. You are a first-rate optimist, lad."

CHAPTER 132 — DRAXAELEN

2nd Quarternar, 1789   Day 138, 13:00

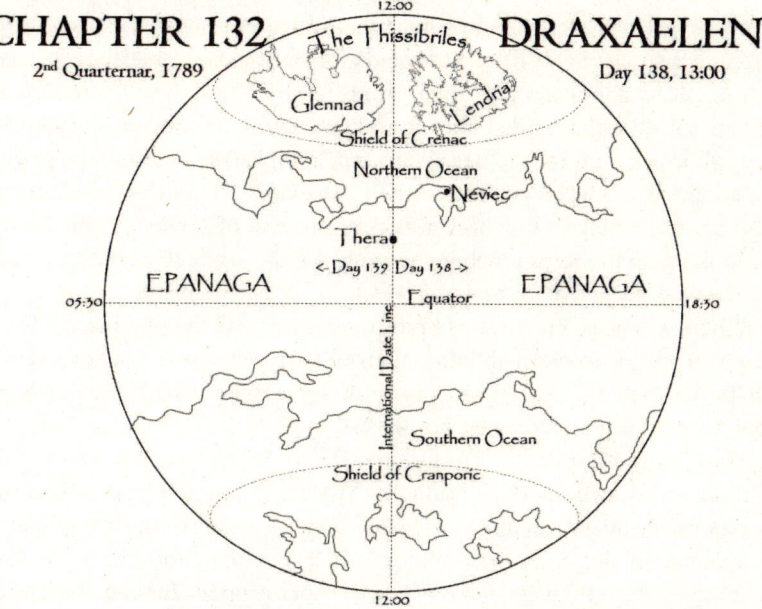

Neviec Arena was a very different place to the fighting pits. Whereas the pits were darker, close-up and personal, this was an open-air amphitheatre which invited in the blazing Liatian sun, and offered plenty of space for sizing up your opponent. Gravus had explained earlier, that today would be a breeze, as their opponents were to be untrained thieves, being given an alternative to the noose following their arrests off the back of Calidius' Edict No 4. The thieves had been told they would be fighting slaves and, apparently, some of them were showing open signs of cockiness.

Following the devastating cull in the pits, eight days ago, there were only fifty of them left, bringing the number who had died since they had arrived back from Rysia to around eight hundred and fifty. This made no sense. So many of those who had died were good fighters. Above all, they were good men, too.

"You are the best of the Neviec slaves," Gravus had announced the day after that hideous killing spree. "And the next time you step into a fighting arena, you will be classed as gladiators. You should be very proud."

Despite all of the carnage, Drax still respected Gravus. Drax's life had been as desperate as any man's could have been a month ago, but Gravus had given his days meaning and structure. Moreover, Gravus' daily training had given Drax a viable path to avenging his family; like his fifty fellow-slaves, he was now a lethal killing machine, both armed and unarmed. They were now also justifiably dressed as gladiators for the first time: bared arms with manicae, shoulders and torso protected by a thick leather jerkin, a gladiatorial skirt that ended above the knee, but which was protected by strips of brown studded leather all around, and gladiatorial sandals which also strapped and laced up around their calves. All fifty of them were now lined up in the preparation area at the eastern end of Neviec Arena. Drax was looking up the steps to where he could see the sandy floor of the arena and the blue sky above. In between was a wall of baying people.

"There will be no chains, this time," the muscular Gravus had said. "This time, you will be forearmed with one or two weapons of your choice. You will be let into the arena, ten gladiators at a time. "Yes," Gravus had emphasised. "As gladiators and not slaves."

Yes, but can we walk away as free men?

Drax was drawn out of his thoughts as Maxi Zoninus appeared, clad in his expensive aqua-shaded silks. He paused, half-way down the line of men. "You will soon climb into the arena, ten at a time" he announced. "At the same time, fifteen thieves will be released from the opposite side. They, too, will be armed. Your task is to prove beyond doubt, that you are worthy of being called gladiators. You *shall* vanquish your opponents, despite inferior numbers. Once you have fought – and won – you will each take a seat as guests of honour of the Governor of Neviec and cheer on your fellow gladiators when the next ten emerge.

"We expect the contest to be fairly evenly matched. But I am confident that by the end of today, we will still have at least forty-five of you with me. Prove me wrong, men, and come back fifty-strong."

As Maxi Zoninus finished his rallying call, a silence fell above in the arena. The Governor of Neviec was on his feet, introducing the games and explaining the format. Drax was scheduled to go into the arena with the second batch of ten gladiators. The first ten were limbering up, completing their stretching and making a few last-minute practice-swings with their weaponry. They had gone for a variety of arms: swords and shields were the most common – four of those – these being Drax's choice, too. But there were also three spear-carriers (also with shields), another carrying a formidable double-headed axe (no shield) and two carrying sword in one hand and dagger in the other.

A great cheer suddenly went up from above, and the guard at the top of the steps told the first ten to enter the arena. As the first of them emerged, the noise swelled to a crescendo. Drax felt the hairs on his arm stand up. God help him; *he was actually looking forward to this.*

Seconds later, a hail of catcalls and boos rained down from above. Clearly, the thieves had emerged from the opposite side of the arena. Then a horn blew and Drax saw his comrades rush forward towards the centre of the arena. He saw nothing for the first five minutes, as all of the action was clearly in the opposite half of the arena. During that time, he took the periodic raucous cheering to herald the death of a thief, although early on, there had also been a round of booing – which possibly meant that his comrades were down to nine. There were no further boos, though, and eventually, some of the action came down to the eastern end of the arena, which included Maurulen, one of his former *Demonata*, and survivor of the pit-fighting. Like himself and Garataelix, Maurulen was armed with sword and shield and was being set upon by two men in bright orange smocks. Other bright orange smocks were also visible, fighting other gladiators. Drax just managed to see Maurulen block a thrust from a spear with his shield before spinning around to his right and slashing the back of one of his opponents' calves before blocking a sword thrust from his other opponent. They then moved out of sight. The maimed thief tried desperately to regain his feet, but then Drax watched a spear explode through his chest to great cries of appreciation from the crowd.

Twenty minutes later, the bout was over. Unusually, the soldier at the top of the steps passed on the result: their status clearly *had* been elevated. "Your lot lost one man," he confirmed. "All fifteen thieves are dead. A fine effort. I wish you next ten the best of luck."

The butterflies in Drax's stomach were almost unbearable as he waited for the command to ascend the steps. When it came, both he and Garataelix ran up those steps and burst out into the arena with their eight colleagues to a cavalcade of appreciation. Again, the hairs on his arms were up. And then the thieves were released from the opposite end of the arena – again, all dressed in bright orange smocks, but again, dangerously armed and outnumbering them by fifty per cent.

With Garataelix to his left, and both shields central, they ran straight for the middle of the orange smocks, towards two similarly-armed foes. Just before they clashed, Drax was nearly distracted by a thief to his left who actually threw his spear at his onrushing opponent who was immediately impaled and thrown backwards. Their odds had instantly got worse. The next second, both his and Garataelix's shields blocked out their opponents' sword-thrusts while both men pivoted, Drax to the right and Garataelix to the left…and both jabbed their swords up into unprotected areas of flesh on their two opponents' sides. A great roar went up from the crowd. Now, their odds had improved.

Drax and Garataelix' momentum took them behind the line of the thieves, along with two more of their colleagues, while two other orange-clad bodies lay unmoving in the sand to their right. It was already eleven versus nine, but with the four of them having got beyond enemy lines, the remaining five of their colleagues were up against it – and so the four wheeled around and began attacking orange-clad fighters from the rear. Even before they had re-engaged, Drax saw another orange-clad form perish. It was the thief who had hurled his spear. He had been desperately trying to retrieve it from the body of the dead gladiator when one of Drax's fellow fighters pivoted away from his opponent, blocking a slash from a sword and at the same time plunged his dagger into the spear-thrower's side. It was now ten versus nine, which became a level playing field when Drax buried his sword into the gut of an unprotected orange smock. The thief alongside his slain colleague – a giant with a long, dark beard – suddenly realised what was happening and began screaming at his fellows to disengage and re-group. Drax and his gladiators allowed that; at nine versus nine, this was now a foregone conclusion.

Following the final bout, all seventy-five thieves were dead, while the newly-declared gladiator numbers had only been reduced by six to forty-four, with several others having received nasty injuries. Back in the preparation area, Maxi Zoninus was exulting as he moved amongst them, patting backs and shoulders. "Perfect," he was saying. "Absolutely perfect. You have all risen from nothing to subjects of public adoration in a matter of weeks. It is now time for you to move up to the next level. We will soon be leaving Neviec for Abri, where you will take on similarly-matched gladiators, and your first taste of what it means to be a professional. And some of you, one day soon, will grace the Mesocluso where you will obtain fame, adoration and fortune."

Maxi Zoninus' multi-colour-eyes then fell on Drax. He nodded in satisfaction, a vague smile playing about his swarthy features. "I am very proud of you all."

CHAPTER 133   ALICYA

3rd Quarternar, 1789   Day 139, 01:00

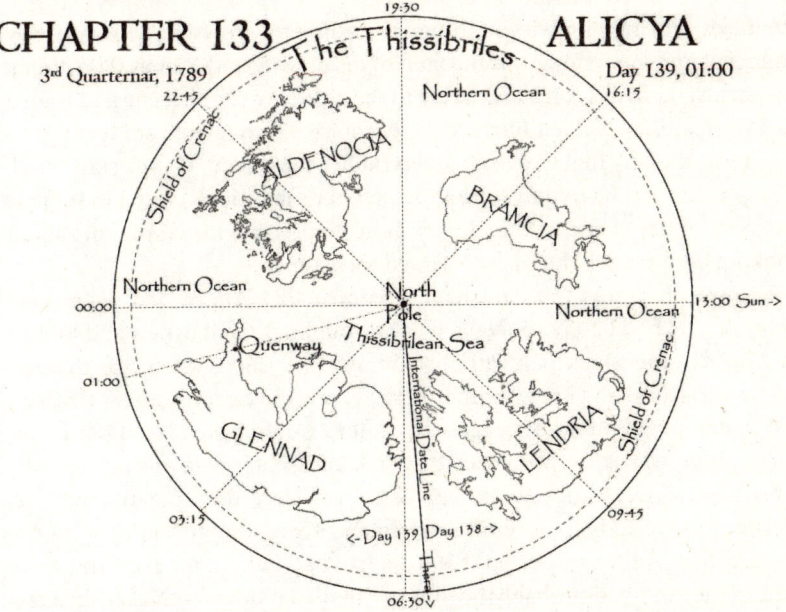

It had been nine hours since Alicya had been thrown into this stinking cell – this after being formally charged with 'Personation with intent to deceive'. That had followed a non-stop twenty-four-hour horse and trap ride up the coastal route from Visset to Quenway, along with three other prisoners from Visset. All three made Alicya's skin crawl, particularly one of the two men who was dressed in little more than rags which were probably crawling with fleas. He looked as if he was in his late fifties, but it turned out he was only thirty-eight. Ratcliffe, his name was, with the first syllable suiting his features perfectly. It turned out he had spent his entire life as a petty thief, in and out of prison – but this time, he was certain the noose was awaiting him. His eyes already looked dead.

The other man made Alicya's skin crawl for different reasons. The thirty-six-year-old Crowson was a former innkeeper who had "fallen on hard times". Although from what Alicya could make out, he had brought those on himself by conducting numerous affairs with other women and then assaulting his wife when she had finally confronted him about his infidelity. This had earned him a charge of grievous bodily harm passed by Magistrate Raines back in Visset last year – a person that Crowson hated with a passion – and a split with his wife. Even more outrageous in Crowson's eyes, was the Visset authorities granting his wife the inn and banning him from the premises, leaving him with nothing. According to Crowson, he was largely innocent and everything was the fault of his ex-wife and Raines – including his involvement in tax fraud relating to the alcoholic products he had traded in Visset, as they had left him with little choice but to turn to smuggling.

It was the way that Crowson looked at her that made Alicya's skin crawl, though. She was having to constantly pull her sable cloak closed to impede his view of her shape, and certainly didn't appreciate his comments about looking her up once they'd both served their time.

However, it was the dark-haired woman that Alicya had been most wary of. She had barely spoken a word throughout the journey, and looked at Alicya's expensive cloak with disdain. All that Alicya knew was that her name was Rosa. She knew neither her age, nor the circumstances that had led to her arrest – although, age-wise, Alicya would have placed her in her forties. She wasn't ugly, but her thin lips and sharp nose meant that she wasn't attractive, either, while her dark eyes were deep-set and intense. Those eyes were dismissive of Ratcliffe and Crowson, and openly hostile towards her. Alicya suspected that Rosa had had to fight for everything she had in life, and had probably been consistently let down – triggering a few pangs of guilt for Alicya's own privileged upbringing.

That cart journey had been a new low-point in Alicya's life, and took a turn for the worse when it had begun to rain around eight hours in. Alicya recalled her alarm that fleas and lice might get washed off Ratcliffe and swim towards her. She had pulled her sable cloak even tighter about her, but this hadn't stopped the water seeping through.

The rain had stopped and re-started another couple of times before they had finally arrived at the dour Quenway Magistrates Court at around 17:00, yesterday. All four bedraggled prisoners had been marched into the court where they each had a brief private hearing with Magistrate Godfrey who, unusually for a magistrate, did not wear the ubiquitous wig, choosing instead to expose his closely-shorn iron-grey pate. The effect made him look considerably more severe than his learned colleagues, and Alicya had been resigned to little leniency. Sure enough, Godfrey had described her as "a low-born, self-educated confidence trickster of unknown identity, who had wormed her way into the affections of a local GP with the intention of climbing into the realms of higher society, and no doubt disinheriting her unsuspecting prey in the process". Alicya had tried to object, but had been immediately closed down by Magistrate Godfrey, and aggressively so. "Silence woman! You will have the opportunity to defend yourself when this matter is referred to the County Court later this week, here at Quenway. Until then, you will be taken from this place to Quenway Prison Admissions, where you will be held until your trial."

That conversation had taken place at around 18:00, yesterday evening. The thought of spending up to a week in prison had terrified Alicya. First impressions hadn't helped, either. The prison, as one might have expected, was grim; a large rectangular single-story block made out of granite, and which extended over a wide area alongside the inhospitable seafront, a thousand yards-or-so north of the town of Quenway. Furthermore, there were only a few small windows, each fronted by iron bars. Worst of all, there appeared to be no segregation in the Admissions section; all sorts were housed here: men, women, children; from serious criminals to petty criminals; from people serving life sentences to those awaiting trial; from simple debtors to the insane.

It was almost comforting to be pushed into a communal cell along with Rosa and Crowson; thankfully, Ratcliffe and his fleas had been pushed into an adjoining cell. There were already eight incumbents, each seated on the wooden benches that ran around three sides of the cell, although one corner was not populated; the fourth side was floor-to-ceiling bars, with the central barred door securely locked and chained. Alicya had briefly wondered how the prisoners were expected to answer calls of nature. Then the smell hit her. At the same time, she saw why no one was sitting in the unpopulated corner. Worst of all, the slop-bucket was already brimming.

Alicya retched, then turned around to remonstrate with the prison guards, but they had already gone. Meanwhile, Crowson and Rosa had taken two of the three vacant pews, meaning her only seated option was to sit around five feet from the slop-bucket. Instead, she decided to sit down cross-legged on the floor of the cell with her back to the bars.

"You fancy a bit of fancy fanny, Cal?" asked one man to her left. He was in his thirties, dressed in filthy clothes and appeared to be addressing a man directly opposite him who looked like his twin brother – in appearance, dress and smell.

"Me and you at the same time, eh, Rab?" responded Cal. He then smiled to reveal a mouth full of rotting teeth.

"I don't see why not, Cal. I mean, this lot in here's perfectly happy to watch us have a dump. I reckon they'd enjoy watching a live shag as well."

It took Alicya a few more seconds to realise what they were proposing, and that she was the object of their proposal.

"I'm up for it, if you are," said Cal.

"Well, it's not like we've got anything else to look forward to, is it?" responded Rab.

Cal stood up at that and started undoing his filthy breeches. "I'm having first dibs then," he said, hurriedly pulling down his breeches. Rab was already tugging at his, but was a couple of seconds behind Cal.

Alicya sprung to her feet, gripped by an instant terror. The reaction of the other prisoners was perhaps even more terrifying – as they appeared totally indifferent to what was unfolding before them.

"Get those breeches pulled back up, now," commanded a voice from behind her. "Otherwise, I'll have both yer tabs off, sharpish, and pickled in the same jar of vinegar."

Alicya nearly collapsed with relief. It was one of the prison guards – a stout man called Trant. Whether he would have made good his threat, Alicya would never know, but Cal and Rab soon made themselves decent again, amidst much complaining to Trant. The prison guard just eyed them both, coolly. "You do realise that If you add rape to your long list of larceny, you'll both go to the gallows, don't you?"

"I've known plenty of blokes take a woman and only get a year inside for it," complained Cal.

"Or get away with it completely," added Rab. "And who's to say whether she wanted it, anyway?"

Trant ignored them both. "If I had my way, I'd hang both of you tomorrow. Thanks to twenty years of constant law-breaking."

"That's not very nice, Mr Trant."

"Shut up and sit down. And behave. If I hear any more out of you two before midnight, I might hang you both, personally. Without tabs."

Alicya turned around and faced Trant through the bars. "Thank you," she tried to say – but her mouth was so dry the words barely came out. Her heart fell, though, when Trant looked at her like something he might scrape off the underside of his big black prison-issue boots – before walking off without a word.

Half an hour later, Rab tried to strike up conversation with her. "You wouldn't have minded, would you gal?"

Alicya desperately wanted to give the man a tongue-lashing, but forced herself to keep quiet. She couldn't afford matters to escalate, and there were plenty of other occupants of the cell giving her looks ranging from open dislike to outright contempt. This wasn't a place for the faint-hearted, never mind a lady or a princess.

"What's the matter, gal?" asked Cal. "We not good enough to talk to?"

"You'll be sorry if you upset us, gal," said Rab. "Old Trant goes off shift soon. If he's replaced by Duggan, you might be getting three tabs instead of two."

"Leave her alone," came a guttural voice to her right. The speaker was a large, blonde-haired boy, probably aged seventeen or eighteen, who looked as though he may have learning difficulties.

"Or what, Molly?" sneered Rab.

"My name's Maurice, not Molly."

"You'll always be 'Molly' to me," taunted Rab. "Molly the baby girl."

Alicya saw Molly's face go red with anger. Rab had touched a nerve.

"Yeah, Molly the coward," added Cal.

"Molly who got beaten up by a twelve-year-old girl."

"Shut up, shut up!" shouted Molly, putting both hands to his ears.

The disturbance brought Trant back down again, so Rab and Cal immediately clammed up. Trant said nothing; he just stared at both Rab and Cal before walking back to his warm office again.

"I'll tell you what, Molly," said Rab, when Trant had gone. "How about me and Cal cut you in on fancy fanny here?"

Poor Molly looked confused at that, but Alicya found an unexpected ally in Crowson, who had evidently heard enough. He stood up and went to face Rab who remained seated. "What?" asked Rab, defensively.

"You look to me like a man who just talks the talk."

"What's that supposed to mean?"

"I'm sick of hearing your voice, your filthy language and your lurid suggestions. I was three-times boxing champion in the seventies at Visset. If I hear one more peep out of you tonight, reckon I'll be making you my personal punch-bag." With that said, Crowson continued to stare out Rab.

"All right, mate," said Rab, eventually backing down. "There's no need for that, is there?"

Crowson eyed him for five more seconds, and then turned around to confront Cal. "And if I see your tab appear one more time tonight, I will order Molly here to pull it off with one of his monster-hands."

Crowson then went and re-took his seat. He looked at her once and nodded. Alicya nodded back. It was funny how in a matter of hours, her understanding of scum had been revised down several times. She still didn't trust Crowson one inch, though, and knew very well that he would like nothing more than to add 'fancy fanny' to his own long list of female conquests. Alicya had also noticed that throughout the entire sequence of events in their communal cell, Rosa hadn't shown an ounce of interest.

The following two or three hours passed without further incident, and a number of the occupants of their cell had even fallen asleep, including Molly, whose snoring had stopped Alicya from nodding off herself. Alicya was grateful for it, too, as neither Rab nor Cal had fallen asleep, and both were continuously eyeing her. Despite the threats from first Trant and then Crowson, and some moral support from Molly, Alicya was still concerned that they might try and attack her – especially as she suspected that Trant had now gone off-duty.

Alicya found herself wondering how Gawain was doing in Pannezec Prison. It surely must be easier for a man? She tried to call to mind Gawain's smile and the sound of his voice, to help her through the night. If she could just make it through to daylight, she would hopefully have her trial and no doubt be sentenced – and would then be transferred to the main part of Quenway prison which, thankfully, was for women only.

She must have finally dozed off, despite Molly's snoring, as she was suddenly awakened by movement from behind as the cell bars gave outwards. Before she knew it, she was on her back outside the cell, and was being bundled forwards by both Rab and Cal and pulled backwards by a third man, who Alicya was shocked to see was wearing the uniform of a prison guard. Alicya then heard the guard gasp – before his arms and legs started thrashing wildly about. His grip on her was instantly released enabling Alicya to look up to see one of the brawniest forearms she had ever seen clamped around the prison guard's neck, slowly throttling him. The owner of the arm was in the cell opposite theirs, and had taken an unexpected opportunity to attack the guard that Alicya assumed must be this Duggan character whom Rab had referred to earlier. Unfortunately for Duggan, in his eagerness to inflict a sexual assault, he'd not engaged the eyes in the back of his head.

As people began to realise what was happening, human noise ramped up rapidly, in both her own cell and the adjoining cells, and the clamour soon became raucous. The picture then became even more chaotic when Cal's throat suddenly opened up above her and his blood began to pour onto her sable cloak. Behind him, the woman, Rosa pulled Cal backwards into the cell and then slashed her razor across Rab's startled face. As Rab fell howling to the floor, his hands holding his sliced-open face, Rosa took the keys from the belt of Duggan, whose bulging eyes now looked back at her lifelessly. Like a cat, Rosa then spun around and threatened those trying to exit their former cell with the razor blade. Their fellow prisoners immediately backed off, having seen first-hand how efficiently she engaged a razor, and Rosa then locked the rest of the prisoners, including the now wide-awake Crowson, back in their communal cell.

Rosa then turned upon Alicya who was still on the floor, absolutely petrified. "Get up!" she commanded.

Alicya's head was shaking in terror.

"I'm not going to kill you, woman. Get up!"

Alicya got shakily to her feet, at which point Rosa grabbed one of her arms and twisted it behind her back, making Alicya shout out in pain. Her other hand then held the razor blade to Alicya's throat. "Now, walk towards the door."

"What are you going to do?"

"Shut up and walk."

A minute later, Rosa used Duggan's keys to open the door into the prison foyer. Astonishingly, even though it was the dead of night, it was unmanned. As Rosa steered her across the foyer towards the prison entrance, Alicya tried to take stock. Given every development over the last two days had made her predicament progressively worse, it was with dread that she crossed the threshold and went out into the cold night air.

Perhaps she would soon be wishing she was sat in a cell with a disgusting slop bucket and eleven other people, at least one of whom was openly lusting after her and two who wanted to do much worse.

CHAPTER 134   EMILYA

3rd Quarternar, 1789   Day 139, 13:30

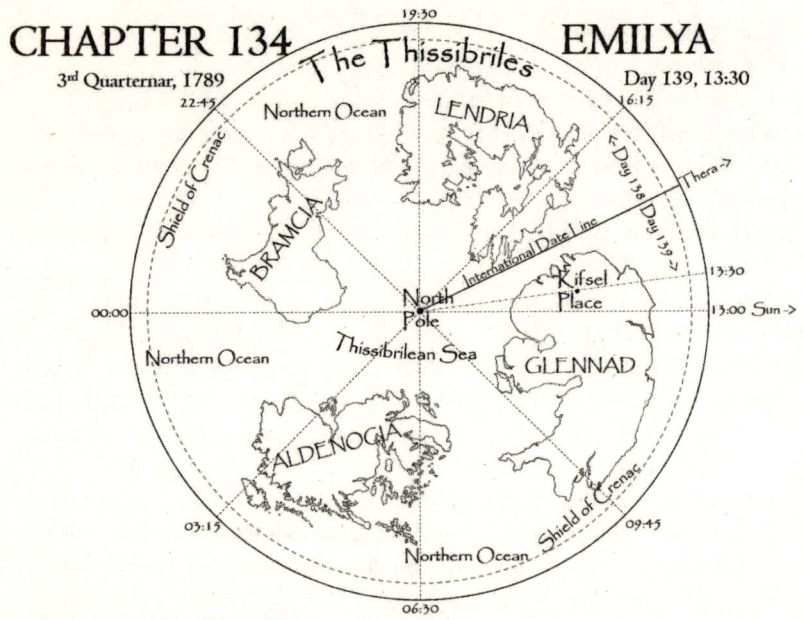

Emilya had been awoken in the early hours by rain drumming down on the roof of the tavern, and it hadn't stopped until twenty minutes ago. She had hoped the delay in leaving Kifsel Place might provide enough time for someone to come to their rescue: Jake and Harry, or Clyve and Jared, or even a platoon of armed monks! None of those things had happened, but at least Abbot Geoffrey had visited the inn late the previous evening to plead with Captain Potts on their behalf. True to form, the stubborn Potts had stood his ground.

Given they were now going back to Ghantiss, Emilya was half-annoyed they weren't already seven hours into their journey, and seven hours nearer to seeing her family again – as the more she and Elyse had talked about their predicament the previous night, the more they became reassured they had done nothing wrong. There was no evidence they had teamed up with Harry Black, as no one other than the Swans had seen them together – and even that brief encounter was only because Black had done a Stand and Deliver on them. Hardly their fault. Thereafter, they had soon gone their separate ways.

They had also ensured their discussions were audible when Captain Potts had been on guard duty, even drawing him into their conversations a couple of times, and Emilya could see that their alleged reputations as painted by Magnus, were not ringing true with the fair-minded Potts.

Neither had the glowing testimonies delivered by Abbot Geoffrey earlier that night. They might even have a future ally in the handlebar-moustached captain, and so Emilya was determined not to upset him.

"If you leave now," the grubby innkeeper, Farrell, was saying, "you'll get to the wood-cutters' cabin by dusk. You must have seen it on your way up?"

Emilya racked her brains, trying to visualise their final two days of ascent with Elyse and Jared. An image suddenly came to mind. "Yes!" she exclaimed. "It had a large horseshoe hanging from the door."

"That's the one, girl. The Forestry workers use it when they're felling trees high up in the mountains, but they rarely venture this far up, so you'll likely find it empty."

"Excellent," said Potts. "I don't want to waste another minute. The storm appears to have blown itself out so, ladies, men: we leave now."

All five of them hoisted their packs onto their backs, and Potts thanked the innkeeper for his hospitality. Then, with the skies clearing to the west, they headed in that direction and the beginning of a long descent.

The innkeeper had been spot-on with his timings. As it turned 21:00 and dusk was beginning to fall, the wood-cutters' cabin finally came into view – just as the first wolf began to howl. The hairs on the back of Emilya's neck were up in an instant. She had forgotten that primeval fear, as wolves didn't roam the upper reaches around Kifsel Place and so it had been a good five weeks since she'd last heard one.

"Don't worry, Miss," Potts was saying. "If they come anywhere near us, our muskets will make short work of them," he added, patting the barrel of the weapon that was slung over his right shoulder.

Slightly reassured for herself, but now concerned for the wolves, Emilya just nodded in response. Wolves needed to feed as much as any other creature; she'd just rather it wasn't on her.

Potts led the way to the cabin and pushed at the door with the large horseshoe hanging from the handle. It didn't move. "It's locked!" he said, disappointed. "Well," he said, turning around and dumping his backpack onto the floor. "I'd rather not damage Forestry Authority property, but needs must -."

Potts broke off in mid-sentence, a look of stupefaction on his face. His hands went to the object protruding from his chest. Foolishly, both Furness and Rydal turned around to see where the object had come from, and each immediately sprouted a quarrel apiece from their respective hearts. Both men sank to their knees, equally stunned. Both died seconds later. Potts, meanwhile, was trying to pull the quarrel out when another embedded itself in his right arm and another in his left leg…and then another in his heart.

It all happened in seconds. Throughout, Emilya and Elyse were paralysed with terror and disbelief. Then, it began to dawn on Emilya that neither she nor Elyse had been shot – sending her through a spectrum of split-second emotions: shock gave way to fear and then confusion…and then enlightenment – for surely Jake and Harry had come to rescue them. Nevertheless, she prepared to lambast them for killing the three soldiers who weren't bad men at all. Indeed, Captain Potts was a thoroughly decent man, and a father of two young children.

As Potts fell to floor, and then stopped moving, his eyes staring, Emilya felt an instant wash of grief and pity for those two children who were now fatherless. Then came anger and distress at the needless killing, and Emilya turned around, her eyes narrowed in fury. In the gathering gloom, she looked up the path, expecting to see the grinning faces of Harry Black and his two lackeys, along with Jake remonstrating at them for killing innocent men. What she saw, chilled her to the bone. In an instant, she knew what was happening, and worse, what was yet to come. For there, on the path above, now walking slowly down towards them with their crossbows lowered, were the robed and grim-faced figures of Brother Cyrus, Brother Gerald and Brother Obadiah.

Elyse understood their predicament, too. "Emilya," she said, quietly. "I want you to run down the path. Now! Run and hide."

"I can't," gasped Emilya. "I can't leave you. Not to them."

"Emilya, will you for once in your life just do as you're damn well told!"

"I will *not*," shouted Emilya, stamping her foot, and now beginning to cry. "I've already lost one mother. I will *not* lose another."

"Oh Emilya," said Elyse, briefly closing her eyes before putting her arms around her charge and holding her close. She kissed her on her forehead. "I love you so much, my darling."

Then it was too late. The three monks had surrounded them.

Elyse turned and looked at Brother Cyrus, her eyes flashing with fire. "What kind of ungodly monk kills innocent soldiers?"

Brother Cyrus looked back at her, and did the worst thing Emilya could have imagined. He smiled. Coldly. "Why, a loyal, dedicated and faithful monk," he answered, in his reed-thin voice.

"Is this where you brought Big Bess?" asked Brother Gerald of Brother Obadiah. That one statement told a thousand hideous truths.

Brother Obadiah just nodded his head, maintaining his vow of silence. Emilya then watched him lick his lips in anticipation before she noticed the repulsive bulge at the front of Brother Obadiah's habit. Meanwhile, Brother

Cyrus nodded towards a gap in the trees to the side of the cabin. "But we were godly enough to bury her."

By now, Emilya's mouth was bone-dry with fear, but Elyse was still looking at Brother Cyrus, her jaw jutting out defiantly. "I am under no illusions as to what is happening here, *faithful* Brother Cyrus. And you can do whatever you want with me. But leave Emilya out of this. Let her go. She's only fifteen."

"Old enough," was Brother Cyrus' economical response.

Elyse went to kick Brother Cyrus in the nether-regions, but he had anticipated the move. He stepped back, blocked the kick and then grabbed Elyse and threw her to the ground. Emilya turned to run, desperate to find help – some climbers, forestry workers, anyone – but Brother Gerald had grabbed one shoulder strap of her backpack and then forcefully hauled her back, before dragging her to the floor…where he roughly turned her over and then knelt on her, one knee digging painfully into her sternum, making it difficult for her to draw breath.

Alongside her, Elyse was fighting like a wildcat: scratching, raking, kicking, slapping – but Brother Cyrus was six feet tall and bulky with it. He soon had Elyse pinned down with his knees on her arms, so Elyse hacked up some phlegm and spat full in his face. Brother Cyrus' response was to slap Elyse hard across the face, which also caused the back of her head to crack against the hard ground as well. The next moment, Brother Obadiah managed to forget about his obsession for ten seconds, long enough to kneel down, force open Elyse's mouth and pour in a vial of liquid that he had just pulled out of one of his robe pockets.

Elyse hacked and coughed and tried her hardest to eject the liquid, but Brother Cyrus then brutally clamped her jaws together whilst Brother Obadiah rubbed her throat vigorously, forcing her to swallow the liquid. Then, pinned down under Brother Gerald's weight, it was Emilya's turn. Determined, Emilya clamped her jaws together as tight as she could, but Brother Obadiah just turned sideways, grabbed her upper jaw with his right hand and her lower jaw with his left hand. Terrified he was about to rip her jaws apart, Emilya immediately conceded, frantically opening her mouth, her eyes as wide as saucers.

The liquid tasted shockingly bitter, and Emilya could feel it travelling down her throat and into her alimentary system. It briefly occurred to her that she'd received a larger dose than Elyse, but her fears at that were soon overtaken as her world began to swim. By this stage, Elyse had gone quiet and Emilya could sense no further struggles to her left. Her last thought before she went under was for Edwyn…

As the veil fell, Emilya dreamed, seemingly for hours. Faces and places came at her, endlessly, thick and fast...she was travelling on land with her father, on the sea with Jake, on the Dominniul to Ghantiss highway with Harry Black, wearing a mask and holding up a wealthy carriage...and then she was standing in front of the Wrothswirk Stone with Brother Stephen, who was inviting her touch it...and she did...to be instantly transported to that unknown but terrifying place she had briefly experienced once before... causing a stab of fear to lance through her heart...and so she immediately retracted her hand...to find it being held by Abbot Geoffrey as they ran together up the narrow ridge to the top of Keplif Scale, stones skittering both left and right, before they launched themselves off the top...and then she was falling, falling, falling...now alone again...only to land gently, feet first, initially alone on a beautiful sandy and sunny beach... but then Edwyn was running towards her, a horse bizarrely cantering to each side of him...and so she smiled...except Edwyn was now screaming at her and pointing out to sea...and, as the sun disappeared and the whole world darkened, and the wind began to howl insanely, it seemed impossible, but the sea was blocking out the sky as far as she could see to the left and the right, and it was as high as the Umbricans...and the monstrous maelstrom came hurtling towards her at breakneck speed...and so she caught her breath, closed her eyes, tensed her shoulders, expecting to be snuffed out in the blink of an eye...except she wasn't...instead, as she opened her eyes, the water had become a much reduced torrent that was sweeping her down the narrow approach to Kifsel Place Monastery, washing her through the open monastery doors at an insane speed, before sending her and Brother Clarence hurtling towards the bridge over to Bloomer...where they would make the other side, they would make it...if only she could centre on the rope bridge...but the current was sweeping her to the right...off the edge...and she missed the bridge...but somehow grabbed one of the ropes hanging underneath and, although the rope burned her palms terribly, she managed to hang on...with nothing but fresh air between herself and the rocks a thousand feet below, whilst above her, Elyse was suddenly there, crying out aloud, holding her hands out to save her... before she inexplicably withdrew them and began to slap her own face, *slap, slap, slap...slap, slap, slap...*

Despite her drugged slumber, Emilya somehow knew that she must block out those *slaps*. They were anathema, poison. They were *wrong*. They did not exist. They *could* not exist.

Then things totally shifted.

With a start, Emilya realised that she was no longer hanging from a bridge by rope-burned hands, dangling a thousand feet above a chasm. Nor was she in motion. Nor were there any images. In fact, she was now sitting, cross-legged…but nowhere. Everywhere about her was black and featureless. All that existed…were those sounds.

Slap, slap, slap.

Those sounds that were *not happening!*

Emily closed her eyes tight and forced herself to think of her father's bakery, of Ghantiss' Market Square and the dancing figures around the Gothic Town Hall clock. She thought of Theo and his beautiful long lashes; of Edwyn and that wonderful kiss; of an azure-blue sky above the summit of Dawkids and an unbridled compunction to sing out loud. But it was no good. The hideous sounds remained, while now superimposed over each and every one of her safe images, came the hooded black eyes of Brother Cyrus, again and again, the same image forcing its way to the front. And now, his thin, cruel mouth was moving as well, and he was talking…in that reedy, soulless voice of his…

"Your companion is full of sin."

Those cold eyes burned even more intensely.

"She delights in leading men astray".

Brother Cyrus' eyes then began to penetrate right through to her subconscious, peeling it back, layer by layer, attempting to bring her back to the surface, back to full consciousness, back to a reality that she could not face.

"Tell me, girl. Have you flowered yet?"

Emilya shuddered in her sleep…and then shuddered again as alongside the image of Brother Cyrus and his black eyes, came the sweating monobrow of Brother Obadiah…and he was grunting…*grunt, grunt, grunt*…and oh, God help Elyse, his grunts were being released in time with the *slap, slap, slap*.

Then things shifted again.

The tide had turned.

Gradually, overpowering the reedy barbs of Brother Cyrus, came words spoken in the last few weeks by Elyse – except it was not Elyse's voice which rang clear and cultured inside her head. It was a calm, authoritative, female voice, that seemed both old and wise, yet youthful and vibrant at the same time.

"I recognised promise in you when I first saw you, Emilya."

"We are all connected, Emilya. We all contain the same energy."

An image formed – of sitting cross-legged at the top of Dawkids along with a calm and peaceful energy. And the voice…surely it couldn't be…

"The natural world – the earth beneath our feet – it has certain powers, Emilya. I just wish that we could have demonstrated that to you amongst the stones."

"It is all about how we can recognise those powers, Emilya, how we should respect those powers…and how we can harness them."

Brother Cyrus' voice was now barely discernible as Emilya focused upon the other voice; the other voice using Elyse's words.

"Mother Thera's power is everywhere, Emilya. But especially at Ghenetenos.

"You see, there are lines beneath the surface, Emilya. Energy lines.

"And where they cross, they create a vortex.

"It is still with us, beneath us. We can still feel that energy, we can absorb it…we can USE it."

And she *could* feel it. Right now, even here inside her drug-induced hallucinations. Right now, there was definitely power running through her slumbering form…as she lay upon Theran ground. Connected. A conductor. But could she use it? To rescue them both? More vindictively, could she use it to somehow bring *death* to these heinous, ungodly men?

Her anger and hate then spiked so intensely that she *knew* the death that she would choose for Brother Obadiah.

"The Wicker Man is a very old tradition, Emilya."

"I am disappointed in you, my child."

Slap, slap, slap. Those heinous sounds were returning.

So, Emilya thought harder. *"They sacrificed people to appease the gods, or to appeal to them."* Like she was appealing for help now…

"Grunt, grunt, grunt."

Emilya tried even harder to imagine Brother Obadiah incarcerated in the Wicker Man, his flesh being peeled away, layer by layer. But the more hate that she channelled the more the female voice faded away. In desperation, Emilya began speaking the words herself to drown out the horrible sound effects. *"They hold a big annual ceremony,"* she shouted inside her head. *"With the Wicker Man burned right in the centre of the stone circle at midnight. And YOU within."*

But no, it was no good. She had lost it. The 'power' was gone.

As consciousness began to return, Emilya scorned herself. The 'power' had never existed, had it? It had been just another product of her drug-infused imagination. *Sweet Thera!* Had she *really* thought that she could invoke the power of the planet? How pathetically naïve.

Anger and fear gripped Emilya as she began to awaken. She started to thrash in despair from side to side whilst also moaning out loud, knowing what those sounds were and trying desperately to block them out…until she felt a sudden pain and compression on her chest.

This time, Emilya's eyelids did flutter open – to find Brother Gerald kneeling on her again, while his hands had now acquired a vice-like grip on her head to stop the thrashing...and then Brother Cyrus was administering another dose of that bitter-tasting liquid.

Emilya choked and spluttered. Then, released from the vice-like grip, she began shaking her freed head from side to side again, thrashing about wildly, this time in bitter helplessness...aware that the wooziness was already beginning to take her back under again.

If she had even awakened in the first place?

"Keep the girl pinned down," she heard Brother Cyrus command, his voice sounding progressively more distant.

Mercifully, the grunting and slapping had now ceased.

"Brother Obadiah," she heard. "Are you now cured of your demon?"

As the question was asked, the strength was beginning to drain away from Emilya's limbs, and she soon lay still, albeit with her eyes and ears open – although her vision was now becoming increasingly blurry...but not blurry enough...for Brother Obadiah's ugly face had swum into view above her...surely real and no dream...his eyes wild, spittle dribbling down his stubbled chin.

"Are you cured?" repeated Brother Cyrus' far-away voice.

Brother Obadiah's wild eyes gradually found some focus. And Emilya saw him nod once.

"Then it is time to remove your temptation," said Brother Cyrus.

The instant she heard those words, Emilya knew that she couldn't allow herself to sink back into the arms of drug-induced oblivion. Not yet. She had to see Brother Cyrus' face again. Something in his tone and *what* he had just said had struck an even greater terror into Emilya. *She needed to see Brother Cyrus' face.*

But it was not Brother Cyrus' face which swam into view next. It was Elyse's. Her beloved guardian. Drawn and tear-stained and traumatised.

Then, with the very last of her consciousness, Emilya was horrified to see the glint of steel at Elyse's throat.

Surely, he wouldn't? He COULDN'T. He was a MONK!

And then, Brother Cyrus was there again...his face immediately to the right of Elyse's – or at least what she could see of his face, for his cowl was pulled forward, pitching the majority of his features into shadow. Only his cruel mouth and left eye was clearly visible, the latter blazing with whatever misaligned zeal drove the man. His thin lips then parted. "Permanently," came Brother Cyrus' reedy condemnation.

The knife flashed red from left to right.

As her consciousness gave up on her, Emilya's lips didn't move, but her soul screamed one anguished word as she descended into oblivion.

"Mother!"

The dreams eventually returned – but only after what seemed like many hours of nothing. Within each new dream-scene, Emilya searched with increasing desperation for Elyse, but hard as she tried, there was no sign of her beautiful guardian.

Was this significant?

Emilya railed against that thought, accusing her subconscious of ignorance; because she *knew* that she had *imagined* the knife. And in any case, since Dawkids, there had been that new link to Elyse…that open door…but with increasing despair, as hard as she searched for it, the new link evaded her, too…and the door remained closed…

When Emilya surfaced again, perhaps several hours later, she found herself cold, alone and lying on the hard floor of the log cabin. It was now pitch-black outside, and probably had been for several hours.

Her first thought through her wooziness, was one of surprise that she was still alive. Her next thoughts were for how long she had been unconscious, and for what had happened for the duration. And had she *really* been drugged twice or was the second episode simply part of the drug-induced hallucinations of the first? She had definitely been given a larger dose than Elyse the first time around, though.

Emilya swallowed to moisten her dry throat. Whether the red flash had been real or not, Emilya still felt numb at what she had seen…or what she thought she had seen…or what she hoped she had only seen in a drug-infused slumber. Common sense was telling her that these were monks and, unpleasant though they were, they wouldn't have killed in cold blood, they simply wouldn't.

But then Elyse's own words, spoken up in the refectory at Kifsel Place, came back to her. *"I'm afraid there are good and bad everywhere, Emilya. It's a fact of life that wherever you look, there are strains of malice."*

And what about the soldiers? Potts, Rydal and Furness? The monks had killed them in cold blood, without a second's hesitation. And by their own admission, they had killed Big Bess, too.

With her head gradually beginning to clear, Emilya knew that she had to discover the truth – even if that truth was devastating. At the same time, Emilyn tuned in to the sound of tools and voices coming from outside.

The light in the cabin was poor, lit by just two flickering candles, but Emilya could still make out the grubby window across the room, on the side facing the wooded slopes. There was further flickering out there, too. What were they doing?

Trying to sit up, Emilya realised that her hands were bound together, as were her ankles. Due to the lingering grogginess, it took her a while to sit up, but from there, she managed to manoeuvre herself into a kneeling position. That was when she saw the blood on the floor. Lots of it. Had it been there earlier?

With shaking, bound hands, she reached out with her fingers and tentatively touched the blood. It was still fresh and sticky.

A desolate moan built up slowly from within. It had not been a dream after all. This explained the broken link…and Elyse's absence from her dreams. Tears began to fall and sobs began to wrack. And yet, despite the towering grief and indescribable emptiness, Emilya still had to know what was happening outside.

Still sobbing and still on her knees, Emilya skirted around the blood and managed to shuffle over to the window before looking out. As her bleary eyes began to adjust to the gloom, those talons that were already tightly gripped around her heart began to squeeze, ever-harder. The three robed monks had their backs to the cabin. All three were busy shovelling piled-up dirt into four freshly-dug graves in the ground.

Four new graves!

Images of the three soldiers, peppered with crossbow belts flitted across Emilya's mind. Then came a series of cruel phrases and images from earlier, each one haunting her more than its predecessor and leading Elyse into her freshly-dug grave outside.

"Is this where you brought Big Bess?"

"Yes, but we were godly enough to bury her."

"I will not lose another mother."

"I love you so much, my darling."

"Brother Obadiah. Are you now cured of your demon?"

A nod.

"Then it is time to remove your temptation…"

"Permanently!"

Emilya Luca fell backwards and began to howl like a baby.

CHAPTER 135   ARRAN

3rd Quarternar, 1789   Day 139, 13:30

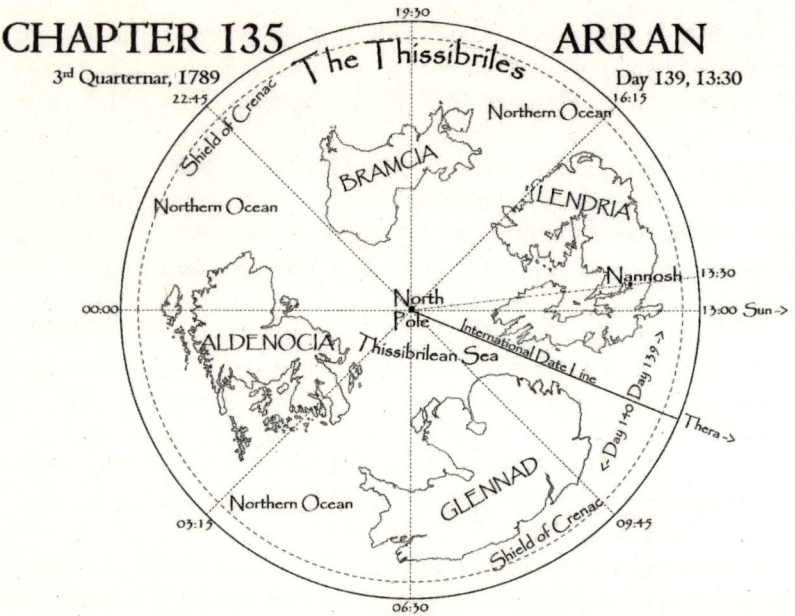

Arran Reed had been sick three times in the last hour. He was now sipping water in a desperate attempt to avoid a fourth rush for the lavatory. His condition wasn't down to an illness or anything he had eaten or drunk, though. It was because he was about to deliver world-shattering news to the Lendrian Coalition government.

Up until now, he had managed to cope with the enormity of his discovery. Perhaps this was because the pending event had seemed far enough away for him to still go about some semblance of a normal daily routine. But as that light in the sky had got progressively larger and brighter, and his daily trajectory charts had become more predictive and infallible, he could no longer kid himself. And last week, he and Professor Doran had predicted with confidence which hemisphere the asteroid would strike, but had held back announcing anything until their equivalents in Glennad, Aldenocia and Bramcia had been given the chance to corroborate. Their charts had crossed in the post with Daniel de Montfort's, the Astronomer Royal of Glennad – who was predicting a similar impact. Today, they had received corroboration from Thomas Danly of Bramcia and Charles Baxter of Aldenocia – although by this stage, Arran and Professor Doran were ahead of their contemporaries. They were now certain in which octant the asteroid would make planetfall. This was the news he would present in five minutes' time.

Of course, over and above the possible end of their world, Ella was also constantly on his mind. In Olindo, last week, he had remained true to his oath, and hadn't told her about George. But these latest predictions, well, maybe that would have to change. Yes, he had a duty to his country. But did he not also have a duty to the woman he loved? There may only be forty-four days left for all of them – including Mal, the luckiest man in the world. According to Ella, he did love her…in his own way…but he still made all the decisions…on where they went, who they saw, what clothes she wore, who her friends should be, what hobbies she should have -.

Arran was jerked out of his reverie by Professor Doran patting his leg. Looking up, he saw that the doors to the Ocateshia's office were opening. "Deep breath, m'boy," said the professor.

Arran did indeed take a deep breath, and then stood – although his legs still felt shaky. Nevertheless, he steeled himself and he and the professor made their way to the head of the vast table which dominated the office and which was again covered by an enormous green felt cloth. Behind them came Jim Geraghty, still the only other Lendrian astronomer they had taken into their confidence. Jim was carrying another of their enormous pre-prepared charts, which he draped over the easel behind Arran and Professor Doran at the top of the table. The first sheet had been left deliberately blank.

Arran watched as each member of the Coalition took their seats, grim-faced, each having far greater worry lines etched on their faces than they had at their first meeting, almost forty days ago. As was the norm, Lenahan Driscoll set the meeting in motion, but immediately made it known that they would be discussing the logistics of the preparations in the mountains later, once Arran Reed had imparted his latest findings on George.

"I have been told to prepare you all, myself included, for a moment of truth. I can only pray that our young and learned friend, is going to bring us a message of hope. Mr Reed," he said, turning to Arran, his eyes searching Arran's for some vestige of good news.

Arran's eyes dropped downwards. He then briefly closed his eyes and put both hands together over his mouth and nose, as if in prayer. His body language didn't go unnoticed and a gentle whisper of disquiet circulated around the room. This had not been his intention, so he quickly stood and issued a tight smile. He needed to clearly and concisely get to the point.

"Last week," he began, "Professor Doran, Jim Geraghty and I, concluded that George is destined for the northern hemisphere."

The impact of his words was like a body-blow to each man around the table. They had all been praying that a Southern Ocean existed, and that a

Southern Ocean would be the point of impact. Some of the Coalition politicians already had their heads in their hands.

"This has been confirmed by our colleagues in Bramcia, Glennad and Aldenocia." Arran nodded at Jim Geraghty, who turned over the first page on the easel. "We have prepared this representation of most of the northern hemisphere, looking down on the North Pole – since we are obviously most-concerned with our homelands. This will give us a visual foundation upon which to demonstrate the mechanics of strikes in various locations.

"We have covered all eventualities so many times that you are already familiar with the ramifications. What has changed, is that we now know that our best hope is a strike in the Northern Ocean…and everything that this implies. In other words, the total destruction of many, possibly all, of our coastal cities, towns and villages."

Several of the politicians around the table were looking quite ill, which briefly made Jake grateful that his own stomach appeared to have settled. "Our best hope," whispered an ashen-faced Aloysius Whyte, his words not directed at anyone in particular.

"Yes Mr Whyte," said Arran. "And if that happens, we can consider ourselves extremely lucky. Because given Epanaga circumnavigates the globe in the northern hemisphere at least all the way down to the equator, that is an *enormous* amount of land. We estimate that across the total surface area of the northern hemisphere, the balance is around sixty-two per-cent land and thirty-eight per-cent oceans. You don't need me to tell you that these are not favourable odds.

"However," began Arran, painfully conscious of the need to present a positive slant. "As you can see from our chart, we have divided Thera up into octants. Over the last seven days, the speed and trajectory of George has enabled us to estimate the likely time of impact, the likely octant of Thera into which George will enter…and also the likely latitude it will strike."

Murmurs of dread went around the table, until Lenahan Driscoll raised his hands for silence. Arran nodded at Jim to turn over the next sheet of paper. Every set of eyes in the room were riveted to the new contents on the giant easel – and one particular motif.

"Please note," continued Arran, "that our definition of latitude is very crude. We have essentially divided the northern hemisphere into three broad-brush definitions: Top, Middle and Bottom – where Bottom is from the equator up to Thera; Middle is from Thera to the Shield of Crenac; and Top is within the Shield of Crenac."

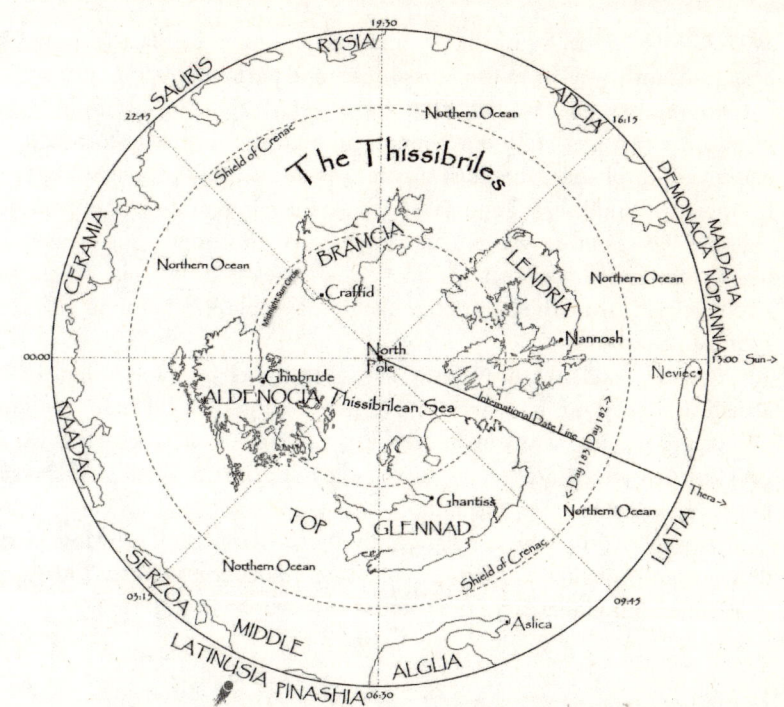

Arran paused again. This time, you could have heard a pin drop. "We now believe," he continued, pointing to the motif at the bottom of the map, "that the asteroid will hit our planet on 1st Quinar, between 04:00 and 05:00, local time, in the northern hemisphere, in the octant that includes far-eastern Aldenocia and far-western Glennad, somewhere in the top half of our Middle band or the bottom half of our Top band. Therefore, if the asteroid hits land south of the Thissibriles, it will be somewhere in the northern Epanagan countries of Serzoa, Latinusia or Pinashia."

Many pairs of eyes were boring into the lower left part of Arran's map, absorbing and calculating the likely ramifications.

"This means, gentlemen, that the best hope for our planet, and for our islands, is a strike in the Northern Ocean somewhere north of Serzoa, Latinusia or Pinashia. It goes without saying, that if that asteroid strays into the top latitude, and hits Aldenocia or Glennad, those islands will be largely destroyed – as, I'm afraid, will parts of Bramcia and Lendria due to the blast front that will radiate out from the point of impact. Several weeks later, any survivors on the surface would probably die of oxygen starvation, anyway – as may those sheltering underground. It will be a similar story if that asteroid hits Serzoa, Latinusia or Pinashia, although the blast-front would be significantly weaker in the Thissibriles, and particularly in Lendria.

"So, the best that we can hope for, is catastrophic devastation to our beautiful coastlines and our wonderful maritime cities. Most will be destroyed – probably even those on the opposite side of the pole in southern Bramcia and south-east Lendria – because the configuration of our islands will see the resulting waves channelled through our various straits, for which the funnelling effect will make the waves build higher. Waves will also propagate from the point of impact like a ripple effect around all of our southern coasts, too.

"For me," said Arran, walking across to the chart, "and being totally selfish, I suggest we all start praying that George will hit here," he said, pointing his stick at an area of ocean just north of where the words LATINUSIA were stamped on the outside of the circle. "That would result in the least damage to our islands.

"Irrespective of where it lands, though," Arran said, pausing in his delivery and turning to face his catatonic audience. "In forty-four days, gentlemen, our planet faces the greatest catastrophe in its history."

END OF BOOK TWO